A Shoot
in Cleveland

A Shoot
in Cleveland

❋ ❋ ❋ ❋ ❋ ❋ ❋ ❋ ❋

A Milan Jacovich Mystery

❋ ❋ ❋ ❋ ❋ ❋ ❋ ❋ ❋

LES ROBERTS

St. Martin's Press
New York

A THOMAS DUNNE BOOK.
An imprint of St. Martin's Press

Library of Congress Cataloging-in-Publication Data

Roberts, Les.
    A shoot in Cleveland : a Milan Jacovich mystery / Les
Roberts.—1st ed.
        p.   cm.
    "A Thomas Dunne book."
    ISBN 0-312-18663-0
    I. Title.
PS3568.023894S48   1998
813'.54—dc21   98-12135
                                                       CIP

First edition: June 1998

10   9   8   7   6   5   4   3   2   1

For Brud Turner
With love and gratitude

✿ ✿ ✿ ✿ ✿ ✿ ✿

ACKNOWLEDGMENTS

✿ ✿ ✿ ✿ ✿ ✿ ✿

The author wishes to thank, as usual, Dr. Milan Yakovich and Diana Yakovich Montagino.

Thanks too are due to my son, Darren Roberts, who lent his first name to one of the main players in this book. I am pleased to report that he shares nothing with the fictional Darren Anderson except, perhaps, the killer good looks.

The characters in this book are fictional, and any resemblance to persons living or dead is purely coincidental.

CHAPTER ONE

Everybody is addicted to something.

How about you? Tobacco, alcohol, cocaine, sex, gambling, food—what's your own particular jones?

Me? Except for the nose candy, I'm addicted to all of them, to a greater or lesser degree. I've smoked Winstons for more than twenty years, although periodically I try to cut down. I enjoy a beer, I'm inordinately fond of women, I like to bet on football games, and one quick glance tells you I haven't missed many meals.

But I suppose my big thing is coffee. I slug down a couple of pots a day. Not the fancy flavored kind, hazelnut or raspberry or vanilla fudge, but good old-fashioned coffee, strong as a linebacker, no cream, no sugar. And not decaf, either. Coffee without caffeine is like nonalcoholic wine—what's the point?

So I had two cups at home on this particular morning in August, filled a go-cup, which I drank on the drive down to my office in the Flats, on the banks of the Cuyahoga River in downtown Cleveland, and brewed up another pot there, all before nine thirty in the morning.

For the past four months I'd been drinking my office coffee out of a very special mug, big and heavy and substantial. It had belonged to my best friend, who'd had it made for himself after he'd gotten it into his head that drinking out of cardboard or foam cups could cause cancer.

The mug is white, and on each side is his name and a reproduction of a gold Cleveland Police Department lieutenant's badge, with his number on it in black. LIEUTENANT MARKO MEGLICH, 7787. My guts twisted every morning when I drank from it, knowing that he was gone now, that a thirty-five-year friendship begun when we were ten years old had been blasted away like a sapling in a tornado, in two terrible seconds, just across the river on a cold, wet night the past April.

His next in command in the department, Detective Bob Matusen, had given me the mug a few weeks after Marko had been buried with full honors, with cops in full-dress uniforms from almost every city in Ohio and quite a few from Pennsylvania, Indiana, and Illinois in attendance, as well as the mayor, the police chief, several members of the Cleveland city council, the lieutenant governor of Ohio, two U.S. congressmen, a couple of judges from the Common Pleas Court, and various other local politicos who had a free morning and were looking for a photo op.

I'm the first one to admit I hadn't been very good since then. I hadn't really worked. I hadn't been to a show or a ball game, hadn't seen much of my other friends. I'd been at the edge of a brand new romance, with an attractive woman whose dragon of a mother hardly scared me at all, but I'd let it go. I didn't have the heart for it.

I drank more than I normally do, too, far into the night, and then in the mornings I'd jog up Fairmount Boulevard, trying to work off the two or three extra beers.

I felt responsible for Marko's death. He'd gone above and beyond the line of duty to protect my back. To make sure that justice was done in a situation where justice seemed impossible. If not for me, he wouldn't have been where he was that night. He wouldn't have caught a bullet.

The shrink I'd gone to a few times had assured me that that

wasn't the case, and in my head I knew she was right. The demons that scratched and clawed deep down inside me were another thing.

Yes, a shrink. A psychologist. Slovenian men like me—like Marko—don't usually seek out the help of mental health professionals. We prefer solving our own problems in our own way. But I'd been sitting around since April without being able to let go of it, without seeming to get off the dime, and I'd figured it was time to talk to somebody.

It hadn't helped much, and after four sessions I'd stopped going.

My pal Ed Stahl had called and invited me to dinner at his big, spooky-looking old house in Cleveland Heights a few blocks north of the Coventry branch library. I usually see Ed every ten days or so but we hadn't gotten together for three months, and he wouldn't take no for an answer. So I'd bought a bottle of Jim Beam, one of Ed's addictions, and gone over there on a Thursday night.

As usual, the whole house was redolent with the smell of his ever-present pipe, to which he is also addicted. He'd ordered takeout from the Sun Luck Garden, a marvelous little Chinese restaurant on Taylor Road, one of my favorites and one of Cleveland's best kept secrets. I wasn't surprised; Ed isn't the domestic type, and I can't imagine him spending even an hour toiling over a hot stove, especially for another guy. I counted myself lucky not to have been served hot dogs and chips.

Ed is a newspaperman. Not a *journalist,* not even a *columnist,* although his bad photograph appears over a column in the *Plain Dealer* five days a week. He's a classic, stop-the-presses, two-finger-typist ink-stained wretch, and the Pulitzer Prize he won some eighteen years ago attests to his excellence. He's hardbitten, curmudgeonly, ulcer-ridden, nearsighted, relentlessly opinionated, and probably the only good friend I have left.

We ate the takeout at the big round table in his dining room where he has his Wednesday night poker sessions. I used to be a regular but hadn't attended since Marko died. The downstairs rooms aren't air-conditioned, and a large standing fan was blowing the hot air around. I washed the food down with Stroh's and he sipped his Jim Beam on the rocks steadily all evening in defiance of his ulcer.

When we'd finished eating, Ed switched on the Indians game and turned the volume down to practically zero. I hardly looked at it. I've been a big sports fan all my life, but lately baseball seemed beside the point.

Ed took the little white cartons into the kitchen to toss into the trash and emerged with fresh drinks for both of us. He handed me mine, standing over me silently for a moment. Then he told me about the job he'd heard about. The movie job.

I turned him down flat. "I'm not a baby-sitter," I said.

"No—you *need* a baby-sitter," he shot back. "Because you're acting like a kid. It's time for you to get out of the house, out of the office, back into the world of the living."

I shrugged. "Okay, so I don't play well with others."

"When are you going to go back to work? You've got to eat, don't you?"

"I'm okay for money. I have a little cushion."

"Lucky you," Ed said. "I've got enough in the bank to keep me going until about three o'clock next Tuesday afternoon."

"I don't want to get involved with any goddamn movie. I quit going to movies when Bogart died."

"And missed Sharon Stone? Madness!" He put his head down and looked at me over his horn-rimmed Clark Kent glasses. "How long are you going to keep on hiding under the covers, Milan?"

"Until it's not so scary to come out," I said.

"You're scared of getting hurt all of a sudden?"

"No. I'm scared somebody else will get hurt. Again."

Ed took a pipe from the rack on the dining room breakfront

and unzipped a worn leather tobacco pouch. "It's always going to be scary," he said. "It's a scary world. When has it not been?"

He was right, of course. After a hitch in Vietnam I'd patrolled the streets of Cleveland as a police officer, and I've served a long stretch as a private investigator. I've seen firsthand just how scary the world can be. It had never stopped me before; the fear is a thing you learn to live with, like chronic lower back pain. You never know when it will flare up or how bad it will be, you just go about the business of living, always knowing it's lurking there quietly, awaiting its opportunity.

And then Marko Meglich died trying to protect me, and the fear had blossomed rich and red like an obscene flower, eviscerating me. For the entire spring and into the summer I rarely turned on my TV set, hardly glanced at the morning paper. I found lots of things I could do alone, like revisiting the novels of F. Scott Fitzgerald, the mysteries of Lawrence Block, *Moby Dick, The Brothers Karamazov.* Interesting, I'd thought later, that I hadn't even wanted to read anything new, anything I'd never read before.

I'd been playing it safe.

"Look," Ed was saying as he stuffed flaky tobacco into the pipe bowl with his thumb, "the producers of this picture called me because they figured I knew everyone in town, and I gave them your name right away. From what they told me, this will be a no-brainer. They're going to be in Cleveland four weeks, shooting a movie, which is good for Cleveland, right? They'll spend a ton of money, and when it comes out in the theaters the city'll look good. They've got this young kid who's starring in the movie, though, Darren Anderson. Supposed to be Hollywood's young-stud flavor of the month, except he has a penchant for getting into trouble wherever he goes. They just want someone to make sure it isn't bad trouble. So you take the kid out to dinner after work every day, on them, you take him to some bars where he'll have a good time and won't get into a fight, and you tuck him in at night. You don't even have to think, Milan. And they'll pay you three hundred dollars a day."

"For baby-sitting." I pronounced it as if it entailed foul diapers, burping, and reading Dr. Seuss aloud.

"For security," Ed said, sitting down at the table with me. "Isn't that what you do? Isn't that why you call your company Milan Security? Look at it as a kind of bodyguard gig."

"Don't they usually have press agents for things like that?"

Ed nodded. "But his press agent just can't afford to spend a month away from her office. And they want somebody who knows the local ropes."

I picked up my beer. I usually drink it straight from the bottle or the can, but Ed always serves it to me in a pilsner glass. The cold against my fingers, the heft of it felt good. "I just don't think I'm up for it right now, Ed," I said.

He struck a wooden match and put it to the bowl of the pipe, sucking on it noisily. Smoke, an alarming amount of it, billowed out and up to the ceiling. "You're not up for much of anything these days, are you?" he said between puffs. "What's the matter? Have you completely lost your guts?"

I put the glass down on the table harder than I'd meant to. "That's kind of a bite in the ass, isn't it?"

"Only because I'm your friend, Milan." He bit down on the pipestem and jutted his jaw at me, a balding, bespectacled General MacArthur returning to Manila Bay. "Quit acting like the Lone Ranger. Every one of us is schlepping around a certain amount of emotional baggage. How well we carry it, how gracefully we go on with our lives, how we get over ourselves is a big measure of our success as human beings."

I fumbled in my shirt pocket for my crushed pack of Winstons. "So what you're saying is that I'm a failure."

"You never have been, Milan, not since I've known you. But right now, you could be failure's man of the year." He took the pipe out of his mouth and pointed the stem at me. "You think if it had been the other way around, if you were the one who died that night, that Marko Meglich would have just curled up into a ball and waited for the birds to come and cover him with leaves?"

I shook a cigarette out of the pack and lit it. The temperature was in the low eighties, but I hunched my shoulders against the cold, clammy chill of truth crawling up my back. No, Marko wouldn't have folded. If he'd been the survivor instead of me, maybe he'd think of me on an NFL Sunday and remember our days on the varsity squad at St. Clair High School and at Kent State. Maybe he'd remember how when we first met as ten-year-olds we'd bloodied each other's noses in the schoolyard, how he'd eased my way onto the police force after I came back from Vietnam and then turned sour when I walked away from the badge four years later.

But he'd go on. He'd make the hard choices.

I guessed I'd better start making them.

"All right, Ed," I said with a sigh that started down near my toes and forced its way up through my viscera. "I'll call your movie guy. I'll talk to him, at least."

So here I was in my office, in the venerable building I'd bought a few years before with the generous bequest of my late Auntie Branka, waiting for a representative of Monarch Pictures to come and give me my marching orders.

I'd never heard of Monarch. Ed had told me it was a fairly new independent, trying to muscle its way in with the big boys like TriStar and MGM and Warners. They couldn't have been doing too badly if they could afford to pay Anderson's salary. I don't know a damn thing about the movie business, but I knew enough to realize that he was a pretty hot box-office property these days—not quite in the Brad Pitt–Tom Cruise category, but getting there.

I'd hardly been in my office at all in four months—maybe twice a week to pick up the mail, and collect the rent and the list of complaints from my two tenants, the surgical supply company across the hall and the wrought-iron-monger downstairs. It was probably just as well. There had been a fire a few days before Marko died, and the repair and renovation work hadn't gone as swiftly as I might have liked. Thank God it was finally finished. I was depressed enough without having to spend my days sitting in a room that looked like a burned-out bunker in Bosnia.

I didn't like to think about that fire, because that's what had led to Marko's being with me that night, on the muddy incline on the east bank of the Flats where the bullet bearing his name had finally found him.

It was hot in the office, and smelled musty and sooty—I wondered how long it would take for the stink of smoke to go away—so I threw open the big windows and let the breeze from the river clean things out a little. The sun was shining, and across the water Terminal Tower was backlit by the summer sky. I hoped I'd be able to hear my client talk, because the gulls were in full throat, darting on graceful wings just above the edge of the water in search of breakfast and then wheeling upward in raucous conversation to shadow the brilliant blue of the morning.

Sidney Friedman's appointment was for nine thirty; he arrived at ten minutes past ten, validating the perception that people in the film business operated on what can best be termed their own sweet time.

He was a small, darting ferret of a man in his early thirties, with thinning sandy hair cut short and combed forward over his forehead, like Caligula's. His designer jeans were shrink-wrap tight, the T-shirt from whose neckband he'd hung his RayBans probably cost more than my best suit, and he was wearing Nike cross-trainers with no socks. In Cleveland the only people who don't wear socks live in cardboard packing crates under bridges.

"Milan Jacovich?" he said, pronouncing my first name like the city in Italy and my last with an incorrect hard *J* and a final *K* sound. "Hi, Sidney Friedman. Producer of *Street Games.*" He tucked his leather-covered clipboard under one arm and stuck out his hand for a moist, dead-fish handshake.

"Nice to meet you, Mr. Friedman. And it's *My*-lan *Yock*-o-vitch," I said. "What's *Street Games*?"

"You're kidding, right? That's the name of the picture we're shooting. Monarch Films. Thirty-four-million-dollar budget." He sniffed, whether from disdain or a coke habit I didn't know. "I guess you don't read *Variety*."

"I let my subscription lapse," I said. "Care for some coffee?"

He looked dubious. "What kind is it?"

No one ever asked me that before. "Maxwell House."

"Forget it," he said, and sat down in one of my client chairs, wrapping one leg tightly around the other like a first-grader who had to tinkle. "So you're the guy who's going to wrangle Anderson?"

"Wrangle?"

Heavy sigh. "In pictures we call the guy who handles the animals the wrangler," he explained.

"And Anderson is an animal?"

"No," he said. "Anderson is a world-class schmuck."

What, I wondered, could make a world-class schmuck worth eight million dollars for three months' work?

And then I remembered some of the grotesquely overpaid superstars of major league sports, and answered my own question.

Sidney Friedman flipped the cover of his clipboard open and began fishing through the papers in the pocket. "Darren Anderson is the classic Hollywood case of too much too soon," he said without looking at me. "He had a five-minute role in a Susan Sarandon movie three years ago and you could feel the shock waves all the way to Peoria. Next thing you know, he's on the cover of *Tiger Beat*, then *Rolling Stone*, then *Entertainment Weekly*. Geraldo had him on as one of the stars of tomorrow, and when he came out those little girls sitting in the studio audience actually *came*! I swear to God."

I wondered how he could tell.

"So then he plays Tom Hanks's kid brother, next he gets first billing under the title in a Sly Stallone picture, and with his fourth film all of a sudden he's numero uno. His price per picture goes from fifty thousand to eight million in eighteen months, which is in direct proportion to the growth of his ego. *People* magazine votes him the sexiest man alive, he buys himself a star on the Hollywood Walk of Fame, his press people are touting him as the new Brando, and the whole world is lining up around the block just for the chance to kiss his rosy pink ass. And since he's only twenty-four years old, the little dipshit actually thinks he deserves it!"

Friedman removed some papers and slammed the clipboard closed. "And that, Milan, is how you make a world-class schmuck!" He shoved the papers across the desk at me. "Here's your contract. Sign all four copies and keep one for your files."

I didn't look at it. "I'm not quite sure what you expect me to do, Mr. Friedman."

"Sidney. What's with the 'mister' shit? Mr. Friedman is my father, and he's dead. Hollywood's a first-name town."

"I know," I said. "But this is Cleveland."

Friedman leaned forward and frowned, to let me know he was now getting serious. "That's the point, Milan. Out in L.A. people look the other way when guys like Anderson come along, because it's the norm. But this is the heartland, and we don't want him getting into any trouble while he's here. Trouble that would engender any bum publicity for the picture. That's where you come in. Take care of him. Show him around. Make sure he goes to all the right places and none of the wrong ones. Make sure he doesn't take a poke at anybody—and if he does, that he doesn't get poked back."

"Does he like to take pokes at people?"

"It's happened. You know, a guy is in the movies, he's got a macho image, sometimes people want to try him. And the kid handles himself pretty well. We don't want any assault-and-battery charges or lawsuits, especially in a strange city. We're on a tight schedule."

"Is he into drugs? I'm not going to stand around while he makes drugs buys."

Friedman's eyebrows arched. "He doesn't have a drug *problem,* if that's what you mean."

"That's not what I mean. Look," I said, "this is a little out of my—"

"It's a piece of cake," Friedman interrupted.

"Playing nursemaid to an egomaniac punk isn't any kind of cake I want a bite of."

"Aw, Darren's not such a bad kid once you get him relaxed. He'll like you. You're a guy's kind of guy, I can tell. And so is he, for all his bullshit."

He leaned forward even more, frowning even more deeply. "One thing though, you gotta watch out for. Chicks."

"Chicks," I repeated dully.

"He can't keep his pants zipped. That's his Achilles tendon."

I tried not to laugh. "If you think I'm spending four weeks trying to keep a healthy twenty-four-year-old movie star from getting laid . . . "

Friedman shook his head. "I don't care how many times he gets laid, or how many women he does it with." He gave me a sly smile. "As a matter of fact, if you happen to know any hot numbers . . . "

"I'm not a pimp!"

His face lost a little of its Malibu tan. "Of course not. I didn't mean anything. I just thought—"

"You thought wrong, Mr. Friedman."

"Sidney." He sat back, relaxed, and waited for me to say it. His eyes *demanded* that I say it.

"Sidney," I finally said, grudgingly.

That seemed to make him feel better. A man of simple needs. "The thing is, see, he's not always discreet." He treated me to a just-between-us-guys smile. "You can't blame him, really. He gets twenty thousand pieces of fan mail a week. Women throw their underwear at him." He waved an airy hand. "Hell, he's not much older than a kid. All that testosterone—he's only human."

I pushed the contracts back across the desk at him. "Get yourself another boy," I said. "I wouldn't touch this with rubber gloves."

"Well, let's see about that," he said, turning the contracts around so they were facing him. He whipped out a pen—a Bic, to my disappointment—and made an alteration to one of the figures, then pushed the papers back at me. He'd scratched out the $300.00 per diem and written in $500.00.

"Now, that doesn't include any expenses you'll incur," he said. "That's all separate. Dinners, concerts. You can have a pretty good time on Monarch Films." His nose crinkled and he grimaced as if he were having a sudden attack of heartburn. "On me."

"I don't think you understand," I said. "I don't want the job."

"You haven't thought this out carefully, Milan." Friedman did a here's-the-church-here's-the-steeple with his fingers. "Remember Rob Lowe and his video-sex thing? After that he dropped out of sight like Amelia Earhart. We don't want that happening with Darren. He's got his whole life ahead of him. Hell, after he finishes this picture they're talking about him doing one with Gene Hackman. You know how much he could learn working with a giant like that?"

"Then get Gene Hackman to baby-sit him."

"Milan, I'm a proud man," Friedman said. "I don't like to beg. But I'm begging you now. You're just the kind of guy we're looking for. Because you can stop him from screwing up his entire career. You can make sure he behaves himself."

He looked at me with an admiration so phony that I almost gagged.

"And you're big and tough enough to see that he doesn't get into any fights. Come on, Milan, it's four lousy weeks here. After that we go down to Wilmington, North Carolina, to shoot interiors, then back to the coast." He extended the pen to me with the extreme confidence of a man who rarely hears the word *no*. "And you get to go on the set, meet all the actors and the director. Lots of pretty girls on this shoot. You never know, you might get lucky—big good-looking guy like you."

"Some of us can find our own women, Mr. Friedman."

"Sidney," he said. "Look, it's like going to a party. A big party, one that lasts four weeks, and the beauty part is, you're getting paid, too." The pen wavered in the air, like a rapier pointing at my heart. "And it'll just be evenings—during the day we can keep an eye on him ourselves. Come on, Milan, come on board with us. You'll have fun."

I doubted that.

He gave me a canny look that made me realize Ed had told him more about me than I would have liked. "What else have you got to do?"

The answer to that one was pretty clear—nothing. I had nothing else to do. I'd been turning down jobs all summer from past clients, and I hadn't tried to find any new ones.

I didn't for a moment imagine that getting involved with a Hollywood production would be any sort of "fun" at all. Phony, self-important people just got on my nerves, and I was pretty sure I would loathe Darren Anderson at first sight.

Still, maybe it was a no-brainer, as Ed had promised. Maybe I could just ride shotgun on this kid and not really have to think about it at all. For a guy suffering from serious brain overload, as I was, it might prove to be the perfect distraction.

"Make sure you change that per diem figure on all four contracts," I said, and reached out to take his damn pen.

＊　＊　＊　＊　＊　＊　＊

CHAPTER TWO

＊　＊　＊　＊　＊　＊　＊

A couple of years ago I saw Tony Randall having lunch at Piccolo Mondo in downtown Cleveland on a Saturday afternoon, and since I'd always liked *The Odd Couple* I kind of nodded to him as I passed by. He graciously nodded back. Other than that, the only movie stars I'd ever seen were when I had a bag of popcorn in my lap.

So I didn't know what to expect when I arrived at the location in Tremont on Monday afternoon, where an old, battered house was surrounded by several enormous equipment trucks, two generators, batteries of lights and silver foil reflectors, a microphone on the end of a twenty-foot-long pole, and a caravan of large double Winnebago trailers. A huge yellow crane with a movie camera and a video camera mounted on it was parked across the street. The only car parked in front of the house was a late-model Ford Taurus that looked as if it had been washed fifteen minutes ago.

Tremont is an old Cleveland neighborhood, just west of the river, across from downtown. Despite a late eighties effort at gentrification—there are a lot of old rehabbed Victorian houses there, and several trendy nighttime hangouts—it is still relentlessly blue-collar and ethnic, conforming to the image of Cleveland that most outsiders have. Seeing its slightly dusty streets aswarm with high-tech movie equipment and banks of kleig lights was like seeing the woman who slices salami in the corner deli wearing the Crown Jewels.

Three uniformed cops, security for the shoot, were hanging out talking to the truck drivers, who it turned out got paid a couple hundred dollars to do nothing but drive the trucks to the location and then wait around for ten hours until it was time to drive them back.

No wonder Hollywood movies, and by extension movie tickets, cost so damn much.

I asked one of the uniforms if he knew where Sidney Friedman was, but he'd never heard of him, a fact that would undoubtedly break the man's heart and crush his spirit.

So I wandered through a maze of cables and esoteric-looking equipment in search of him. There were at least seventy people standing around, most of them white, a few blacks and Hispanics; none of them Sidney. Half held clipboards, and only a tenth of them seemed to be doing anything. Most were dressed retro-hippie; if I'd seen them on Public Square I would have assumed they were homeless.

A shaggy-haired young man wearing a lightweight sports jacket over a denim shirt and blue jeans was sitting in a canvas chair under a red umbrella, a loose-leaf notebook with a green leather cover in his lap. On a little table beside him was an ice bucket, a bottle of Evian water, a glass with a slice of lime in it, and a big bowl of M&M's, from which he was carefully extracting and eating all the blue ones. He was the only one around who wasn't talking to somebody else.

"Excuse me," I said, "can you tell me where I can find Sidney Friedman?"

He looked up at me as if I were an alien life form just off the mother ship. He had a five-day growth of blond stubble on his chin and cheeks, his hair curled untidily around his collar, and his eyes were startlingly bluish purple, the color of spring irises.

"I couldn't hazard a guess. Sidney doesn't keep me informed about where he is every minute," he said dismissively, and went back to his quest for the perfect—blue—M&M.

I wondered whether he'd be willing to hazard a guess if I held him by his skinny ankles and bounced his head on the sidewalk.

I approached several other people, who either didn't know where Sidney Friedman was, or didn't care, or were too busy to vouchsafe even a one-word answer. Finally I asked a middle-aged man even bigger than I am, who stood about six foot four and must have tipped the scales at two-sixty. He wore his hair in a cute ponytail, like Debbie Reynolds in *Singin' in the Rain,* and sported yellow sunglasses and an Old Navy T-shirt. I tried to remember when we had become walking billboards for other people's products and why we had to pay for the privilege, at that.

He thought for a while and then suggested I try the farthest Winnebago.

Sidney was sitting at a table inside in air-conditioned cool with two other men and a woman, papers spread out all over. It looked like a schedule, but I couldn't be sure.

He jumped to his feet when I came in. "Ah, Milan. Good. Glad you're here." He introduced me around; I didn't really catch any names, and I was pretty sure they didn't get mine, either.

"Come on," Sidney said after the round of handshakes, gathering up his clipboard, "let's go meet Darren."

My few seconds in the air-conditioning had made me realize how hot it was outside. We made our way through the throng and the equipment and the cables coiled on the ground like sleeping pythons. When I saw where we were heading, I realized that Darren and I had already met—sort of. He was the young man with the iris-colored eyes.

"Sidney told me all about you," Darren Anderson said. "Why didn't you say who you were before?" His handshake was much firmer than Friedman's.

I didn't want to tell him that I hadn't recognized him, that I hadn't known what he looked like. He was, after all, a movie star, with the breed's overblown yet fragile ego. "I didn't want to be pushy," I said.

"Pushy is good sometimes," Anderson said.

"We've got one more setup," Sidney announced, studying his clipboard. "Then we'll wrap for the day. I thought you two could go out to dinner, get acquainted."

"Sidney . . . " Anderson said with a rising inflection. It came out a whine, like a teenage girl protesting, "*Mom . . .* "

"Cool it," Sidney said, all at once firm and parental. "You agreed to this. This was the deal breaker."

Darren sulked.

Sidney smacked me on the shoulder; he had to stand on tip-toe to do it. "I gotta go, Milan." He pointed to a rolling snack bar, its aluminum awning shielding the sandwiches and candy bars from the hot afternoon sun. "Grab a coke or a coffee or some-thing from the roach coach if you want. Find someplace where you can watch the scene. I think you'll get a kick out of it. Later."

He bustled away and was quickly swallowed up in the crush of people. Anderson closed the green notebook and rested it on his knee.

"Ever see them shoot a movie before?"

"No," I said.

"It's a drop-dead bore. Hurry up and wait. They'll shoot the same scene ten or twenty times over. You can get brain-dead just hanging around watching."

"I'm not planning on spending a lot of time on the set," I said. "Sidney just asked me to come down—"

"Next time bring a book," he suggested. And then his pretty-boy movie star mouth turned supercilious and cynical. "Or are you one of those people who don't like to read?"

"I read a lot. They don't give you a master's degree if you don't, Mr. Anderson," I said. "Even in Cleveland. You'll find we also have cable TV and flush toilets."

"There's a break," he said, and uncoiled himself from the chair. He wasn't much more than five feet ten. I wondered if they had him stand on an apple crate for love scenes, the way Alan Ladd used to.

He walked away, stopping to talk to a pale bearded man wearing a fringed buckskin vest over a T-shirt. After a few moments he nodded and went up the steps and into the house. A young woman carrying a large economy-size box of tissues and a small square black case stained with makeup scurried after him like his duenna.

I went over to the mobile cantina and bought a can of Diet Pepsi and took it out of the hot sun into the shade of a building. Someone yelled through a megaphone, "We're ready, people!" and everyone moved away from the front of the house, and fell silent.

Two men climbed onto the crane, one behind the movie camera and one beside it. The camera operator pulled his baseball cap low over his forehead and squinted into the eyepiece. The other, the bearded man in the fringed vest, was evidently the director, Boyce Cort, because all eyes were on him. He looked down and gave an imperial nod to the man with the megaphone, who raised it to his lips and intoned, "Let there be light!"

The banks of lights suddenly went on, making the glare almost unbearable and raising the temperature on the street at least ten degrees. In the bright afternoon of summer they seemed redundant.

"Camera!" said the megaphone man, and on the end of the boom the camera operator did something and set the camera whirring. Another man with a clapper board stepped in front of the lens, held the board out, and said tonelessly, "*Street Games*, scene 42, take one," clapped it, and stepped back.

The megaphone man said, "And . . . *action!*"

There was a moment's pause, and then Darren Anderson

came bursting out of the house and ran down the stairs, his face twisted into an agitated frown. From where I stood I couldn't hear him, but his mouth moved in a terse "*Shit!*"

They pay writers small fortunes to write dialogue like that.

Darren raced to the Ford Taurus, got in, started the motor, and drove off down the street and around the corner, leaving some rubber on the tarmac. The huge crane moved about thirty feet straight up in the air, swinging outward as the camera tracked the car's progress.

"Cut!" came the word from the megaphone man.

Everyone who had been standing still was all at once galvanized into action. They seemed to be rushing around for no particular reason, but I figured they knew what they were doing. The buzz of conversation grew loud, and Darren slowly backed the car around the corner and stopped in front of the house again. The camera and the men on the end of the crane came swooping back down to where they'd started out.

Darren Anderson got out of the car and went over to talk to the director. The woman with the makeup kit came running out of the house and started dabbing his forehead with a tissue. One of the other men got into the car, pulled it forward, then backed it up a few inches, his head hanging out the open window so he could see the chalk marks on the sidewalk.

The director talked to Darren for about five minutes; then Darren went back inside the house and they did it all again.

After the fifth or sixth take—frankly I lost track—I turned to a young woman standing beside me holding a script. She was wearing torn baggy jeans and was braless under a T-shirt with Shakespeare's likeness on it, along with the legend WILL POWER. Her hair looked as if she'd last washed it sometime in May.

"Who is Darren Anderson supposed to be in this picture?" I asked her.

Making a notation in the margin of her script, she replied without looking at me, "He's playing a tough cop."

I turned away so she wouldn't see me laugh. Any real cop I'd ever known could have eaten Darren Anderson for lunch.

They did at least fifteen takes of the scene; I didn't know what was the matter with the first fourteen. The crew got set up in a lot less time between the last four or five takes, as someone had shouted, "Come on, people, we're going to lose the light." With all the artificial illumination they had there, it seemed to me they could have kept shooting until midnight, but then what did I know.

It was arranged that I would drive Darren out to the house they'd rented for him in Bay Village, where he would freshen up and change. Then I was to take him to dinner.

"Kind of clue him in about Cleveland a little," Sidney Friedman had told me. "Mostly he never goes east of Beverly Hills."

When Darren saw my three-year-old Pontiac Sunbird he almost recoiled. To him it must have looked like a junker right out of *The Grapes of Wrath*.

It was after six o'clock, and the slight surge in traffic that passes for a rush hour in Cleveland was just about over. Neither of us said anything until we were well on our way to Bay Village.

"So," he finally said, "you're my nanny, huh?"

"I'm not sure I'd put it just that way."

"What would you call it, then?"

"Depends on how you look at it. I guess your producers wanted to make sure there'd be someone available who knew the city and could guide you around, so you'd be happy and comfortable when you weren't working."

"That's a load of crap and you know it," he said. "They're afraid I'll get into trouble, so they hired a big tough guy like you to hold my hand."

"I don't hold hands on the first date."

"I don't imagine you would. Well, you'll have your work cut

out for you, Milan, because that's what I do," he continued. "I get into trouble. I expect you not to get in my way."

There wasn't much of an answer to that, but it got me wondering. How was I supposed to stop him if he *did* want to get into trouble? I hardly thought Sidney Friedman would be happy if his star showed up on the set some morning with a fat lip or a black eye.

With some rue I realized that it was a question I should have asked before I signed the contract.

"What did Sidney mean when he said I was the 'deal breaker?' " I asked him.

"Just what it sounds like. If I hadn't agreed to let them hire a nursemaid for me, I wouldn't have gotten to do the picture."

"Are you that bad a boy, Darren?"

He turned and smiled at me, the iris blue eyes sparkling. "You have no idea," he said. "It's a curse."

He stared out the car window with interest as we headed west, commenting on the onion-domed Eastern Orthodox churches of the near west side, and seemed impressed when I told him that was where they'd shot part of the Oscar-winning film *The Deer Hunter.*

"Are you a native?" he asked.

"Born and raised. How about you? Where are you from?"

"My mother made a few pictures back in the seventies," he said. "Then she married my stepfather and gave it up—she never had much of a career anyway. I've always lived in Southern California."

"Well," I said, "welcome to the real world."

"I've been here for four days now. And if this is the real world, you can have it, with six points."

Bay Village is Cleveland's westernmost suburb, a little enclave of new money tucked along the lakefront into the corner where Cuyahoga County meets Lorain County, about twenty-five minutes from Public Square. It's now in the throes of new development. I would have figured the movie company would want their star to be a little bit closer to everything that was going on, but perhaps they thought that isolating him out here was a more prudent course of action.

The house was a sprawling single-level on Lake Avenue, big enough for a family of five. A lawn that could have accommodated a small herd of grazing cattle swept down to the shore of Lake Erie, and if you walked to the edge of the bluff you'd encounter a spectacular if distant view of the towers of downtown Cleveland.

Darren unlocked the front door and let us in. The rooms were big and spacious, impeccably furnished in a modern style I didn't much care for. Not a pin was out of place, and the air-conditioning was set high enough that I was glad I'd worn a jacket.

"You're very neat for a young bachelor," I said. "I kind of expected beer cans and empty pizza boxes."

"Be real," he said. "A woman comes in to clean every day." He pointed toward a wet bar. "Fix yourself a drink—I'll only be a few minutes." He started toward the rear of the house, then stopped and turned around. "This restaurant we're going to . . . You're wearing a tie. Does that mean I have to?"

"You're a movie star," I said. "You don't *have* to do anything."

He grinned at me and cocked his head, a quizzical expression playing around his eyes and mouth, as if it was a brand new concept. "I don't, do I?" he said, and disappeared down the hall.

I went behind the wet bar, ducked down, and opened the little refrigerator in search of a beer. It was well stocked, with an automatic ice maker, five different kinds of mixers, and two six-packs of Henry Weinhardt, a west coast brew that isn't readily available in Ohio.

I read somewhere that whenever the late Steve McQueen went on location for a film, part of his contract specified that the producers had to fly all twenty-eight of his motorcycles to the location so they'd be available for him. And I recalled that some rock group always demanded vast quantities of M&M's for their hotel suites, with all the brown ones removed. And that reminded me of Darren sitting alone amidst the confusion on the Tremont street, picking all the blue ones out for himself.

Where do people get such egos? Is it built in along with the talent, or do we, the public, who create and lionize celebrities and cheerfully pay high prices to see them, create the monsters ourselves?

A dimly remembered Shakespearean quote I'd come across in an English lit class at Kent State popped into my head: "Upon what meat does this our Caesar feed, that he is grown so great?"

Of course that was before most universities dumped the Bard and other so-called "dead European white men" from their curriculums in favor of "diversity"—obscure writers who were neither dead nor white men—and who probably wouldn't even have become writers if they hadn't read Shakespeare.

I found an opener and uncapped a Henry, swigging it right from the bottle. It was pretty good, I had to admit. Then I went and sat down on the long white sofa.

There was nothing personal about any of the furnishings in the house; it was obviously a short-term rental property. The only trace of its current, famous tenant was a pile of *Playboys* and *Penthouses* on the glass coffee table. And the little shit had the nerve to ask whether I was a reader.

After about twenty minutes Darren came out, dressed in a beige suit, a black silk T-shirt, and tooled leather cowboy boots. His blond hair glistened from the shower.

"Is this okay for where we're going?" he said, striking a *GQ* pose.

"It's fine. I hope you're hungry. This restaurant is supposed to be good."

He smirked.

"You think everybody in Cleveland eats at Burger King, huh?"

"No," he said. "I just figured you did."

"Why? Because I have an ethnic name?"

He shook his head. "Sly Stallone and Arnold Schwarzenegger have ethnic names too. You just strike me as kind of a—man of the people."

"That means anybody who doesn't make eight million dollars for twelve weeks' work?"

"Actually, it's sixteen weeks. And by the time my agents and managers and press people take their cut, and good old Uncle Sammy takes his, you'd be surprised at how little there is left."

"Enough to keep you in blue M&M's, though."

He laughed. "Come on, let's have a drink here before we go."

"I'm having one," I said, holding the Henry Weinhardt up.

"That means I'm one behind, then."

He stood there, looking at me for a moment.

"Am I supposed to run and make you a drink?" I said. "That wasn't in the job description."

"All righty, then." He went behind the bar, scooped up a handful of ice cubes and dumped them into an old-fashioned glass. Then he turned and took down a bottle of Jameson and filled the glass to the rim. "Nothing like a good Irish whiskey," he said.

"Are you Irish?"

"Does Anderson sound Irish to you?"

I shrugged. "I wasn't sure if that was your professional name."

"Oh, I was born Anderson," he said. "It's the Darren part my publicist made up. My first name is . . . " He smiled. "Naw, I'm not going to tell you."

"If I can live with Milan Jacovich, how bad can yours be?"

"Why didn't you change it if you didn't like it?"

"I like it fine. It's who I am. I suppose if I'd been born Scott Carson I'd be somebody else altogether."

"True enough," he said, nodding. "Well." He raised his glass. "Here's to Milan Jacovich, then."

I lifted my beer bottle. "I'd drink to you, but I don't know your first name."

He laughed. His teeth were very white, obviously capped, and his blue eyes twinkled. He had the boyish, fave-rave grin down pat. "If you tell anyone else, I'll have to kill you."

"Your secret is safe with me."

He looked serious all of a sudden. "I believe that, Milan. I believe you're the kind of guy that can be trusted all the way. That's what I meant when I said you were a man of the people." He stared into his drink. "Not too many folks in my business I'd trust with the family silver. Especially the knives."

"Doesn't seem like it'd be much fun living that way."

"That's why they pay us the big bucks," he said. Then he chuckled again. "It's Ralph. Can you believe that? Fucking Ralph."

"What's wrong with that?"

"Do I look like a Ralph to you?"

"I don't know," I said. "What does a Ralph look like?"

He thought it over. "Like not a movie star."

I had to agree with him. I raised my bottle of Henry again. "To Ralph Anderson."

"And *Street Games*," he said.

And we drank.

CHAPTER THREE

The restaurant I took him to was called the White Magnolia, a fairly new place on the west side, and as such, out of my territory. I'd heard good things about the food, though, and knew it was fairly expensive, catering to the upscale young business types who lived in Lakewood and Rocky River and spent conspicuously. It was, I thought, Darren Anderson's kind of restaurant.

"Two, gentlemen?" the host inquired. He had an iron gray crew cut and wore shirtsleeves and a tie. "Without a reservation it's going to be about twenty minutes."

"Okay," I said, "we'll have a drink."

I felt Darren stiffen beside me. "We have to wait twenty minutes?" he said. "On a Monday night? That's bogus, man."

I turned to him. "I'm sorry, I forgot to make a reservation."

"Bull shit!" he said, making it two distinct words. "I'm not going to stand here in the bar like some fucking peasant."

"Darren," I said, but it was too late. He'd reached out and taken hold of the host's arm just as the man turned to walk away from us.

"Just a minute, pal," Darren said, his affability dissolving into near ferocity. *"Do you know who I am?"*

"You're a guy who doesn't have a reservation." The host looked pointedly at Darren's hand on his arm. Darren removed it. "And that means," he said, a lot more politely than I would have, "I won't have a table for you for at least twenty minutes."

"No?" Darren reached into his pocket and started to pull out a roll of cash. I grabbed his arm and yanked him away, none too gently.

"Hey, what's the deal?" he said, shaking my hand off roughly. "I don't like standing around waiting in some out-of-the-way hash house."

The host had moved off, out of hearing. Thank goodness.

"This isn't the Polo Lounge, Darren. Nobody gives a shit if you're a movie star here. To them you're just another guy, and they don't have a reservation for you. So calm down and stop flashing your money around. What do you want to drink?"

He sulked in near silence through two Jameson's on the rocks, and as he started on a third a young couple walked in, gave their name to the host, and came and stood near us at the bar to wait for a table. When Darren saw them—or rather, her—he lit up again, with that celebrity incandescence like star-shine that cast its glow on all of us. I watched in fascinated horror as he filled with air, like a balloon in Macy's Thanksgiving Day parade.

The man was going prematurely bald on top and was tall enough to have played some college basketball. He wore the kind of wire-rimmed glasses I thought had gone out of style when John Lennon got killed, a gray pinstriped business suit, and a colorful tie that seemed to scream *young attorney on a partnership track*. The woman was probably in her twenties but looked younger, an attractive brunette wearing a modified miniskirt flattering to her slim, strong legs and a black silk blouse that exposed a little cleavage. Neither of them had a wedding ring. They both ordered merlot.

Darren gave the woman an iris blue twinkle. "Hi," he said, his voice low and throaty and insinuating, making it sound like an obscene phone call.

She stopped with her wineglass halfway to her lips, caught somewhere between uncertainty and attraction. Then she smiled at him over her glass and turned back to her date.

Darren took a little notebook from his inside pocket, scribbled something in it with a blue felt pen, and ripped out the page, wadding it up in his hand. Then he puffed up some more and moved a step closer to her.

"Tell me a little about this picture you're doing, Darren," I said earnestly.

It was like trying to distract a timber wolf from a rabbit. He'd sighted his prey now, and he was stalking.

"You wouldn't think this place would be so crowded on a Monday night," he said to the young woman. "It must be a pretty good restaurant."

She turned her head and looked over her shoulder at him. "It's a great restaurant." There was more than a little flirtation in the way she said it and in her smile.

He grinned back boyishly. "Oh. Well, I'm not from around here, so I didn't know that."

"I know you're not from around here," she said, her brown-eyed twinkles a match for his own. "You're Darren Anderson. I read you were in town making a movie."

At the mention of Darren's name, the woman's date began to glower, his own eyes narrowing to slits. An ordinary person in the presence of a celebrity usually either ignores the fact, fawns, or makes a surly attempt to chop the star down to size. This guy was opting for surly, you could almost see him sharpening his little hatchet.

"That's right," Darren said, ducking his head shyly. "But you have me at a disadvantage. You know my name, but I don't know yours."

"Dierdre," she said.

"Dierdre!" He closed his eyes as if transported. "That's a beautiful name!"

"And this is my friend Alan."

Darren gave him a dismissive glance. "Hello, friend Alan," he said, and turned his attention back to Dierdre.

Oh boy, I thought. I put down my drink and tried to move around between them, but Darren was too sharp for that. Shifting his upper body only slightly, he shut me out of the action. I guess he had some experience positioning himself for the best and most flattering camera angles. You used to read about Claudette Colbert and Joan Crawford doing things like that, but I didn't think actors cared about it anymore.

"I've only been here a few days," he said with a little toss of his curls. "So I really don't know Cleveland at all. I could sure use somebody to show me around. Somebody who knows good restaurants."

An angry flush suffused Alan's close-shaven cheeks. As for me, I was completely stunned. There's a Yiddish word, *chutzpah,* that loosely translated means one hell of a lot of nerve, and I was fairly sure Darren Anderson could qualify as the chutzpah poster boy.

"Say, my friend," the tall young man said, putting his wineglass down on the bar, "do you have a date this evening?"

Darren had to take a step backward to look up at him. "Why no, Alan. I don't."

"Well I do. So how about letting me talk to her?"

"Give it your best college try," Darren said. His expression remained guileless, open, choirboy innocent, but I could see the nervous bunching of his shoulders. He wanted it to happen, wanted to cause a fuss. It would draw even more attention to him, maybe even make the newspaper in the morning.

"Just who the fuck do you think you are?" Alan demanded, his fists balled up at his sides.

I went around Darren and stepped in front of him. "Let's not get excited," I said. "Just a little misunderstanding, that's all. Lack of communication. There's no problem here."

Alan took one look at my bulk and dropped his eyes and his fists at the same time. "There better not be," he mumbled.

From the aggressive, bemused expression on his face, Darren was getting ready to say something truculent, to stir things up again, but fortunately the host materialized like a guardian angel and told us he had a table. Timing is everything, I thought.

"It was nice talking to you," Darren told Dierdre, and extended his hand. When she took it, he brought it to his lips.

I could feel her eyes following us as we left the bar and trailed the host into the dining room.

"You've got the balls of a brass monkey," I said after we'd been seated.

He raised both hands. "There's no point in being a movie star if you don't take advantage of the perks. I figure I've only got a few years before some other young stud will come along and be the next me. I might as well enjoy the ride."

"You're the only actor I've ever heard refer to himself as a movie star."

"That's because that's what I am," he said easily. "I'm not an actor. There's a difference. Gene Hackman is a real actor. Morgan Freeman is an actor. Robert de Niro. They have real talent. A movie star is just a guy most women want to fuck."

"Oh. Sorry things didn't work out tonight, then."

"Don't be too sure." He winked. "I slipped her my phone number."

I shook my head. "You really *do* look for trouble, don't you?"

"Trouble is my middle name."

"Too bad," I said dryly. "It doesn't really go with Ralph."

"Besides, I wasn't worried."

"You should have been. He was a pretty big guy."

"I know. But that's why you're here." He raised his eyebrows and smiled ingenuously. "Isn't it, Milan?"

*　*　*

Our meal was quite good. It was also overpriced, but Monarch Pictures was paying for it. The tall young man in the power suit looked daggers at us as we were leaving, but other than that, the evening proceeded without further incident.

Feeling luxuriously stuffed, I drove the car onto Lake Road in Rocky River, the better to let my passenger get a look at some of the more scenic aspects of our city. Viewed from the western lakefront at night, the lighted towers of downtown Cleveland look like a jewel springing up out of the dark water.

"Good dinner," Darren Anderson said, gazing at the scenery. "I admit I'm surprised. And impressed."

"There's a whole world between New York and Beverly Hills," I told him. "You ought to get to know it."

"I have. I've never done a picture entirely in L.A. They shoot everything on location these days. Features, anyway. I've been to Texas, Florida. But I guess I'm just more—comfortable, I guess, with the west coast."

With the star treatment, I thought he meant. "You don't have much use for the 'little people,' do you,?"

"It isn't that so much. It's just that outside of L.A. they look at me like I'm some kind of freak."

"And you'd curl up and die if they didn't."

That raised an eyebrow. "I suppose you're right. I would. It's one of the problems that come with the territory." He adjusted the vent so the air conditioner was blowing directly into his face. "It's worth it, though."

"Because of the money?"

"That's only part of it. I've already got enough money to last me the rest of my life. It's all the other stuff that comes with it."

"The women, then?"

"Sure, that too. Mostly it's being treated like you're some-body special. Like you count."

"Everybody counts. Even the plumber and the pump jockey and the guy who installs your cable."

"Yeah, but the guy who installs your cable has to wait for tables in a restaurant, and when he finally gets one he's got to pay for the meal. He doesn't get to see every movie that comes out for free. He doesn't fly first-class and he doesn't get to get on the plane before everybody else. Designers don't give him free clothes and automobile companies don't give him free cars just so the world can see him using them. There aren't a hundred people just lining up to kiss his ass or light his cigarette or pour his drink or cop his joint. He doesn't get to pick and choose, and he sure as hell can't do just about anything he wants." He turned in the seat and smiled at me. "And he doesn't get big, kindly bodyguards to keep him from getting punched out when he fucks up."

I gritted my teeth, concentrating on the road.

"And if he did, this mythical cable guy of yours, he'd jump at the chance with both feet and never regret it for a single minute. Anybody would jump at it—even you, Milan. That's the fantasy, see. That's why movie stars are movie stars, why people look at us funny. We're living the fantasy."

When we got back to the house in Bay Village, he asked me to come in for a drink. It was cooler there, right on the lake, and he opened the sliding glass doors in the living room.

"Nice," he said, filling his lungs with air.

"It's not Malibu," I said, "but it's the best we can do."

He came back into the living room and sat down, resting his booted foot on his knee. "Listen, I didn't mean to be insulting about Cleveland."

"That's all right. I didn't take it personally. I'm not that crazy about Los Angeles either."

"No," he said, "Cleveland's really a nice city. Nice old buildings, nice lake. And the restaurant was great."

"I thought you'd like it."

"Actually, being out of L.A. is kind of a relief."

"Why?"

He took a slug of Jameson's. "At least here I don't feel like I always have to watch my back."

I frowned. "Maybe in my official capacity as bodyguard and troubleshooter I ought to know just what you mean by that."

"The bigger you get, the bigger a target you are," he said with a shrug. "A guy in my position makes enemies. Sometimes enemies he doesn't even know about."

"You mean people who just don't like you? Or people who'd actually do you harm?"

He waved his glass in the air as if there wasn't much difference. "Both, I guess. About six months ago someone tried to burn down my house."

I set my beer down on a coaster on the coffee table. "Tried?"

"It was in February. I live up in Coldwater Canyon, above Beverly Hills, and someone piled a bunch of brush and wood against the side of my house, doused it with gasoline, and set fire to it."

"Was anyone hurt?"

He shook his head. "I wasn't home that night. Lucky. December and January is the rainy season in L.A., and the brush was a little too wet to catch properly, so the fire just scorched the side of the house and then burnt itself out. The only casualty was the paint job, plus I had to have a little rehab work done on the sundeck."

"Any idea who did it?"

"Not really."

I pulled out my pack of cigarettes. "Mind if I smoke?"

"Makes no difference to me," he said.

I put a Winston between my lips and lit it. "What does that mean, not really?"

"It could have been a lot of people."

"Such as?"

A vertical crease appeared between his eyes. "What difference does it make?"

"Part of my job is seeing that nothing happens to you. Knowing who dislikes you enough to try to burn down your house might help."

He laughed. "Husbands or boyfriends whose women I got too friendly with. Some out-of-work actor who got overcome with jealousy. Maybe some loony movie fan who hated my last picture."

"Ever been stalked?"

"You mean by some woman?"

"Or man."

He laughed. "No, not really. Oh, there are a couple of skanky women who seem to show up a lot of the places I go—like at premieres and things. And I could paper a wall with the nude photographs and propositions and women's underwear I get in the mail. And there was this one woman—she lived in Boston, I think. She saw me on Jay Leno and decided that when I winked at the camera I was really winking at her, and she started sending me really hot love letters. At one point she said she was flying out to California to be with me. She even gave me her flight number and time of arrival."

"Did you meet her?"

His lip curled in scorn. "Get real," he said.

"Maybe you ought to have a full-time bodyguard, Darren. Look what happened to Gianni Versace."

He wrinkled his nose. "Different situation, wouldn't you say?"

"Maybe. How do all these people know your address?"

"They don't. They either write to my publicist or to whatever studio released my last picture."

"How do you get the letters, then?"

"I ask for them. I love getting fan mail. I get a charge out of it. I have four file cabinets full of it."

"Do fans ever write you at home?"

He went to the bar and refilled his drink. "Once in a while. It's not that hard to get a star's home address, especially out there. There are lots of little weird people who make a living selling celebrity addresses on the street corner. I imagine that's how the firebug did it."

"It must be scary being you sometimes."

He lifted his fresh drink in a toast. "It's *fantastic* being me, Milan."

The telephone chirped on the counter of the bar. He picked it up after the first ring and said hello.

"Oh, hi," he said, his voice dropping to a low, sexy purr. "How ya doin'? I was hoping you'd call." He turned his back to me, as if that would keep me from hearing him.

"Sure I want to see you. How about tonight?" He cocked his wrist to look at his watch. "It's not that late. Hell, out in California it's only eight o'clock in the evening." He listened for a minute. "Just for a drink or two, I promise."

Yeah, right, I thought.

"Great!" he enthused boyishly. "Got something to write with?" He recited the address of the house. "You know where that is? Oh, terrific. About fifteen minutes? I'll be here." His voice got even deeper. "I can't wait to see you."

He turned around, dropping the receiver back into its cradle, and gave me a satyr's grin.

I knew the answer, but I asked anyway. "Dierdre?"

The grin got even wider. "See you tomorrow, Milan," he said.

CHAPTER FOUR

Even though Darren Anderson's hedonism and absolute self-absorption irritated the hell out of me, the job wasn't really so bad, considering the perks.

I got to eat at some of Cleveland's finest restaurants, all courtesy of Monarch Pictures, which took a toll on my waistline while it tantalized my tastebuds. I met some interesting people who had been flown in from Los Angeles to work on the picture and while I don't think I'd want any of them as close personal friends, from a distance they were fascinating. They were citizens of an alternate universe.

I learned some things, not the least of which is that anyone in the motion picture industry can spot me as a rube from fifty yards away.

For one thing, I refer to their art and craft as "movies."

Film distributors, the ones who see to it that the cineplex in your local mall has something to put on all eight screens, call them "shows," I came to find out. People who work in the business say "pictures." Boring intellectuals who dress all in black, smoke brown cigarettes, and sprinkle their conversation with references to John Waters and Jean Luc Godard prefer "films."

Only the great untutored plebeians like me call them "movies."

I got to go places I'd never normally visit—like a sit-down dinner for fifty in a mansion in Shaker Heights "in honor" of

Darren Anderson, where bejeweled matrons turned to puddles of buttermilk as they sunned themselves in the young star's charismatic aura, while their pinstripe-clad husbands sulked in corners, swirling Glenmorangie in their cocktail glasses and muttering darkly about the city council.

Like discos in the Flats. My second night on the job found me in one of those clubs people go to because the music is so loud they can't even talk over the din and they know they have absolutely nothing to say. The revelers exhibited none of the reticence of the patrons of the White Magnolia; Darren was mobbed by hordes of young women all evening, only actually getting to dance twice, and both times everyone else stood back to watch. He finally cut one of the young women out of the herd, perhaps because her hair was a little less big than the others'. She told us that she was "in computers." She proved to be user-friendly—I was obliged to drive them both back to Bay Village and then beat a hasty retreat.

One night I decided to show him what was, for me, more familiar territory—Vuk's Tavern on St. Clair Avenue near East Fifty-fifth Street, the neighborhood bar only eight blocks from the house I grew up in. Vuk, the stoic, mustachioed barkeep who had served me my first legal drink on my twenty-first birthday, and who last saw a movie when Doris Day was still playing virgins, was singularly unimpressed by my illustrious visitor, and if any of his regulars even knew who Darren Anderson was, they didn't let on.

It wasn't that he didn't attract his share of attention. He was probably the only man who had ever walked into Vuk's Tavern wearing sunglasses after four o'clock in the afternoon. Certainly the long mahogany bar had never felt an Armani-clad elbow before. And when he ordered up a Jameson's, Vuk—né Louis Vukovich, but woe betide anyone besides his eighty-seven-year-old mother who calls him Louis—gave me a look that could have withered roses. Except for Heineken, there wasn't much behind the bar that was imported from anyplace more exotic than Canada.

There were three men in jeans and denim work shirts sitting at the end of the bar, and one of them was reciting a story about what was the high point of his life—I knew because I'd heard him tell it a dozen times, usually to the same two guys.

"Remember that night George Nozinich coldcocked me right here at the bar?" he was saying. "Just walked right up to me and coldcocked me."

"He coldcocked you righteously," one of the others said, nodding.

"I mean, I was just sitting' here havin' a beer. He was on the phone over there, and I went over and put some money in the jukebox. And afterwards he come over and he goes, 'Who put that fuckin' music on when I was tryin' to talk on the phone?' And I go, 'I didn't know you was talkin' on the fuckin' phone!' And he coldcocks me."

"That was, what, about nine, ten years ago? Man, I thought you was dead for a minute," the third one said.

"Right here," the storyteller went on, pointing to the stool he occupied. "Right here at the bar, George Nozinich comes up an' coldcocks me. Boom! I went flyin' all the way over there." He pointed toward the front door.

"Isn't George spose'ta get outta jail pretty soon?" said the second man.

The story and the responses had been played out so many times before, on those same three barstools, they were like an endless loop of film that kept running over and over again. But I knew why the victim kept reliving that long-ago night. Although it was hardly his finest hour, it was probably the one time in his life that he'd been the center of attention.

I looked over at Darren; he was listening to the story intently.

"You know George Nozinich?" I said.

He snapped out of his reverie. "I was studying."

"Studying what?"

He stirred the ice cubes in his drink with one long finger. "Him. Someday they might ask me to play a guy like that. A blue-collar guy. I was just studying him—how he uses his hands, the cadence of his voice. You never know when that might come in handy."

"You study everyone that way?"

"Sure. That's my craft." His smile was elfin. "I've been studying you, Milan. I'll bet I could do you pretty well."

"I'm not sure I want to see it," I said.

"You will," he said. "One of these days you'll ask me."

Despite his "studying," Darren Anderson quickly grew bored with Vuk's and suggested we go somewhere else after only one drink. We ended up in another disco, one on Detroit Avenue. I wasn't surprised when he scored again, this time with a redhead.

For all that, it was good having something to do again, even though it was a far cry from the industrial security work that makes up the bulk of my business. I had my days free, and I started spending more time in my office. I managed to return some of my phone calls, I made an appointment to consult with a small manufacturing firm in Willoughby, a picturesque suburb out in Lake County—I even cut down a little on my smoking.

Maybe Ed Stahl had been right, maybe playing keeper to Darren Anderson was good for me. It seemed to be easing me back into activity after months of inertia. At least it was something to do, and apart from the annoyance factor, it wasn't too demanding.

The demons that tormented my waking and sleeping hours were quieter now, more subdued, and didn't visit nearly as often.

Fairly early Friday morning at the end of the second week of the shoot, Sidney Friedman called my office.

"D'you have a tux, Milan?" he said when I answered. No good morning, no how's it going. Hollywood producers are often too busy to waste time on niceties.

I stifled a laugh. I had worn a rented tuxedo a few years earlier, when I'd been dating a neonatologist named Nicole Archer
and she'd dragged me to some tony fund-raiser for the Cleveland
Clinic. The time before that was to a college formal when I was
at Kent State. The only other black-tie occasion in my experience
was my high school senior prom.

"You're going to have to rent one, then," Sidney told me.
"You and Baby Jesus are invited to a formal party this evening at
the Renaissance Hotel."

"What kind of a party?"

"It's a benefit. Some big corporation bought a table, and the
CEO—guy by the name of Tom Maniscalco—thought he'd like
to have a celebrity sitting at it."

"Why do I have to go?"

"Because that's the job, Milan. You're Darren's date. I told
the guy you came along with the deal, and you're both expected."

"A benefit for what?"

"How should I know? What's the difference? You're not paying for it." I heard him rustling papers. "There's a tuxedo rental
place downtown. . . . You'll send me the bill."

"I'm a pretty big guy. They might not be able to fit me."

"They can fit a rhinoceros," he assured me. "That's their business."

In point of fact, I had to go to four places before I found
one, out in South Euclid, that could fit a rhinoceros—or at any
rate a fifty long. And feeling more than a little silly, I was wearing my rented finery when I picked up Darren on the set at the
end of the hot, humid summer afternoon. Most of the residents
of Tremont were sitting on their front porches in their undershirts, or less, drinking cold beer, probably none of which was
Henry Weinhardt.

Happy to escape the neighborhood, where my attire was
even more of a curiosity than the movie people were, I drove

Darren back to Bay Village so he could get dressed for the affair. He, of course, had brought his own formal wear from Los Angeles, just in case, and it didn't look anything like mine. His jacket didn't have any lapels, and his ruffled shirt was without a collar, and therefore instead of a tie he wore a big diamond stickpin at his throat. Somehow the outfit didn't look quite right on him.

I reflected that it was probably a good thing for Darren that they don't make many period movies in Hollywood anymore. Unlike vintage stars like Tyrone Power and Errol Flynn and Charlton Heston, who would have looked strange wearing anything but dashing period costumes, Darren Anderson, like William Holden and Bogart and Jack Lemmon before him, was every inch a modern-day man, the type who looked best in suits or casual wear. I was willing to bet that no one at the corporate table at the Renaissance Hotel was going to look anything like he did.

I would've won the bet, too.

The venerable Renaissance Hotel, formerly Stouffer's and before that the Cleveland Hotel, is right on Public Square and is connected to Terminal Tower and the Tower City shopping arcade. Darren and I had to walk a long way through the lobby area to get to the stairway to the grand ballroom, and of course he turned every head we passed—whether by virtue of his celebrity or his exotic Beverly Hills outfit, I didn't know.

At the ballroom entrance three very pretty young volunteers sat behind a long table handing out name tags and directing people to their seats. One of them, on whose left breast a large tag read *Hi, my name is KIM,* looked up at me, then over my shoulder at Darren, and squealed like a Sinatra fan at the New York Paramount in 1942.

"Omigod! Darren Anderson! Darren *Anderson!* Omigod!"

If there were one or two people in the foyer who hadn't yet noticed us, they were now most certainly alerted, and they started closing in on us like sharks.

"Oh," Kim burbled. "Oh. Omigod!"

Darren gracefully moved past me to bend low over the table and smile at her. "Hi there, Kim," he said.

She put her hand over her mouth, to stifle any further squealing, I assumed.

"Can you tell me where my friend and I are supposed to sit?" Darren asked her.

I thought she was about to go into convulsions. Instead she took her hand away from her mouth long enough to ask him for his autograph. She'd managed to smear her lipstick.

Darren whipped a blue felt pen out of his jacket pocket—I don't think he ever went anywhere without a pen—leaned over the table, and cocking one foot behind him the way June Allyson used to every time she was kissed by Van Johnson, signed the name tag on her breast.

Her blush was bright enough to light up the sky.

A self-possessed man in his sixties who looked as if he'd been born wearing his tuxedo made his way through the crowd toward us—or to be more exact, the crowd parted for him. With him was an attractive blonde about twenty-five years his junior wearing black satin several inches above the knee and looking very much like all the other women there dressed in black, and a pretty, awkwardly coltish teenage girl in a too fussy prom dress that seemed to exude organdy. Her large bust strained the fabric; the underwire bra she wore highlighted it.

"Mr. Anderson!" the man said, extending a hand. "Tom Maniscalco, Home Works Furniture. Welcome, it's good to meet you."

Darren shook his hand and thanked him for the invitation— but not before he'd slipped Kim a folded-up slip of paper from his handy little notebook.

Home Works is a prestigious manufacturer of modern furniture, with four show rooms scattered around Cuyahoga County and their plant and headquarters in Middleburgh Heights, a southwestern suburb. Tom Maniscalco, its CEO, is well known around town for his contributions to Catholic charities—and to hard-line conservative and mostly Catholic candidates for local offices, Congress, and the state legislature.

Introductions were made all around. The blonde in the black satin proved to be Mrs. Maniscalco—Alison, every ounce the classic second wife. The teenager was their daughter Bethany, who, finding herself at a party where the only people even close to her age were the busboys, seemed to waver between intense boredom and a kind of stupefied awe that she was in the presence of America's number-one hunk.

The Maniscalcos led us to the bar in one corner of the grand ballroom. While we were standing in line, I felt a tap on my shoulder.

I turned around, stunned to see Victor Gaimari.

"Milan!" he exclaimed in that peculiarly high-pitched, reedy voice of his. "What a pleasant surprise."

In his middle forties, tall and solidly built, dark-eyed and dark-haired, with a distinguished touch of gray at the temples and a Cesar Romero mustache that adds to his undeniable glamor, Victor still possesses the classic good looks of a golden-age matinee idol. A stockbroker with offices in Terminal Tower and a palatial home out in the small eastern suburb of Orange, a major player on the boards of several charitable and cultural organizations and one of the area's most eligible bachelors; he does the society circuit with a seemingly endless string of beautiful women on his arm.

He's also the underboss of the biggest organized crime family in Cleveland.

We have an interesting relationship. We've gone from being bitter enemies—shortly after I met him several years ago I broke his nose, and the next day he had some of his hired muscle boys beat me senseless—to a wary and sometimes convoluted mutual respect that has teetered on but never quite tipped over the brink of friendship.

His uncle, Don Giancarlo D'Allessandro, the octegenarian godfather of the Cleveland outfit, likes me so much that he kisses me whenever we meet.

I shouldn't have been surprised at the sight of Victor; this kind of glittering, glitzy orgy of self-aggrandizement is his element.

He took my arm, his face serious. "How are you doing, Milan?" he said. "Are you okay?"

He knew about Marko Meglich, knew about our lifelong friendship. Despite my dislike for what and who Victor Gaimari is, I couldn't help but be touched by his concern.

"I'm coming along, Victor," I said. "One day at a time."

He introduced me to the languidly gorgeous brunette at his side, whose name seemed to be Jimmy. One of Victor's former girlfriends was named Chickie. Maybe he had a thing for beautiful women with men's names.

Victor made a show of looking around. "Are you here with your illustrious charge from Hollywood?"

"Yeah. How did you hear about that?"

He simply cocked a satanic eyebrow and rewarded me with a wink that would have been arch had anyone else done it. There's very little that goes on in Cleveland and its environs that Victor doesn't hear about. "Sounds like very easy duty."

"Somewhere between wet nurse, chauffer, and pimp," I said.

"You'll have to make sure Jimmy meets him. She's a big fan."

I turned to the woman. "Is that right?"

She rolled her eyes toward the paneled ceiling of the ballroom. "Whatever," she said, making it two very distinct words.

Victor took her arm and guided her away, flashing me a small smile of apology. Victor's women tend to have more than men's names in common—most of the ones I meet are as decorative as ice sculpture, and fully as warm.

I snagged a drink and looked around for my client. He seemed to be in the middle of a large knot of people near the door. I shook my head. It was one thing when superannuated teenyboppers and high school girls slobbered all over him. To see him now, surrounded by staid-looking middle-aged tuxedo-clad executives and their satiny wives elbowing each other out of the way to stand next to him was truly a sight to behold.

I scanned the crowd, but I really didn't expect to see anyone else I knew. My closest buddies rarely pay two hundred bucks a plate for a dinner of hotel food and the chance to Be Seen.

I moped around the edges of Darren's throng of worshippers, never for a moment believing that I looked as if I fit in. I tried to catch his eye, thinking that if he looked desperate and in need of rescue I'd wade in there and tear him away. But he was in his element, positively beaming at being clucked at and fussed over, and I don't believe any woman's cleavage was escaping his attention and admiration.

Bethany Maniscalco was standing off to one side, looking completely miserable and almost as out of place as I felt. I went over to her and smiled.

"Tough night, huh?" I said.

"You know it," she said. "Usually I won't let them drag me to these things, but when I heard Darren Anderson was going to be here . . . "

"You like movie stars?" I said.

"I like *him*."

It wasn't my place to tell her that he was a womanizing, arrogant, self-absorbed little shit—I think it's cruel to destroy the illusions of the very young. Instead I said, "He's something, all right."

"He's gorgeous," she corrected me.

After I asked her how old she was—fifteen—and ascertained that she went to an exclusive Catholic girls' school down in Seven Hills, Bethany and I had to struggle to keep the conversation going. Nevertheless, her parents were making themselves very busy introducing everyone to their token celebrity, so we hung out for another five or ten minutes as though huddling together for warmth, both grateful that someone else was willing to talk to us. I told her I had a son a few years older than she, one who played football, and one a few years younger, but neither is a movie star and so she didn't seem very interested.

When it came time to find our seats, I was surprised that Victor Gaimari and Jimmy were at our table.

"How do you know Tom Maniscalco?" I asked him.

Victor gave me one of his patented Mona Lisa smiles. "I know everybody, Milan."

The guests were arranged in boy-girl-boy-girl fashion at the round twelve-person table. I was flanked by Alison Maniscalco and the wife of a thoracic surgeon; Victor was on the other side of Alison. Darren was between Bethany and Jimmy. I was uncomfortably aware of the fact that almost all of the five hundred other celebrants were watching our every move. Half of them were gawking at Darren Anderson, and the other half were looking at me as if wondering who in hell I was.

Nobody at our table said much to me during the first course; they were too fascinated by how movie stars chew. Darren handled it all with a certain tousled insousiance—I guess he was used to being stared at. I wondered if he was ever able to relax and be comfortable, or even if he wanted to.

As they were clearing the salad plates Alison Maniscalco finally tore her attention from Victor and discovered I was still alive.

"Milan, was it?" she said.

"That's right."

"You're not from the west coast, are you?"

"No, I'm from here."

"And how are you involved with this picture?"

"I'm sort of looking after Darren," I told her. "I'm a security specialist here in Cleveland. I have no dreams of becoming a movie star."

"Hmm," she said. "You like the job?"

"It's—interesting, I'll give it that."

"My husband usually prefers a little more enthusiasm from the people who work for him."

"Work for him?"

She ran a pink tongue over her lips to remove some errant dressing. She might have been licking off canary feathers. "Tom is one of the principal investors in this movie." She closed her eyes for a moment. "Today, furniture, tomorrow the world."

"I didn't know."

"Well now you do," she said, effectively putting me in my place, and turned away to talk to Victor, who turned on his considerable charm and gazed soulfully into her eyes. She was just his type, beautiful and brittle and too married to become a clinging liability, and I figured he would have her in bed within two weeks.

Across the table, Darren was expending considerable energy dazzling his two female companions, which had me worried. I tried to get his attention, and when our eyes finally locked for a moment, he gave me one of those mind-your-own-business looks.

My business, however, was keeping him out of trouble. I got him out of the banquet room as soon as he had dutifully danced with each of the six females at the table. He held them all close, his nose in their hair, smiling gently and whispering to them. He had all the good moves, I thought—but since one of the women he was flirting with was the consort of a mobster and the other was the daughter of one of his investors and fifteen years old to boot, I could smell trouble coming in triplicate.

At the time, I had no idea how much.

CHAPTER FIVE

The next night I took Darren to Johnny's Bar on Fulton Road on the near west side for dinner. Originally a blue-collar bar in a dirt-under-the-fingernails Italian neighborhood, in recent years it's turned into an elegant, upscale place where the dinners are so fantastic you skip breakfast and lunch just so you won't get too full to have the bananas Foster for dessert. It's probably my favorite restaurant in the world. A few years back they opened a downtown branch. Some of the area's most important people show up regularly, so I figured Darren, who considers himself important people, might feel especially comfortable there on a Saturday evening.

The evening was balmy and the air sticky with the usual Cleveland summer humidity as we pulled up to the curb, just across the street from Saint Rocco's Church—yes, there really is a Saint Rocco—and the valet absconded with my car. Darren glanced doubtfully at the restaurant's facade. It still looks like a neighborhood bar.

"What are we having, salami sandwiches?" Darren wanted to know.

"Trust me," I told him, and we went inside.

The small dining room and the bar area were packed, as usual. Couples, groups of three or four men in high-business drag, one table with three women—the usual crowd at Johnny's Bar. There was a momentary hush, a collective intake of breath, followed by an immediate buzz when we walked in. Almost everyone was looking at us, or rather, looking at Darren. I could hear his name being spoken in low whispers. Cleveland is funny about celebrities—I suppose we're as impressed by them as anyone else. But unless it's a local sports hero like Jim Brown or Bernie Kosar, someone everybody has seen get dirty and sweaty for the glory of the hometown, people usually don't bother them or ask for autographs; they just look and point—discreetly.

I glanced over at Darren. Obviously he heard the whispers too. But as usual, they seemed to galvanize him, to light him up from within. All at once he was taller and broader, and there was a confident set to his shoulders; he moved with an easy, lazy grace. A bemused smile played upon his lips as his iris eyes moved quickly over the room, acknowledging the recognition while in no way encouraging further intimacy. He was eating it up with a spoon; he was almost orgasmic with it. Charisma leaked out of him like water from a cracked bucket. Now I realized why he'd been so cool to me when I'd first approached him as he sat in his movie-star chair on the street in Tremont—I hadn't recognized him, hadn't given him the strokes, the hero worship, and awe he so desperately needed.

And it struck me then what Darren Anderson's personal little addiction was. Not drugs, not money, not even women. The name of the junkie monkey that rode his back was Fame.

I'd been smart enough to book a table in advance this time, and to my relief we were seated almost immediately. I don't think I could have borne it if Darren had made a scene in Johnny's Bar; I go there too often.

The waiter brought our drinks. In the low light, the kind that is especially flattering to men and women of a certain age, Darren's beard looked even scruffier than usual. I wondered how he managed to keep it at the same five-day length all the time. And why. He was playing a Cleveland policeman in the film, and certainly no watch commander worthy of the name would allow one of his officers out on the street looking like he'd just come off a week-long binge.

"What's good here?" he said, perusing the menu.

"Everything. I always like the long-bone veal chop, but you'd better wait to hear the specials before you make up your mind."

He played with the condensation on the side of his highball glass. "Milan," he said, "why don't you take tomorrow off?"

"How come?"

"We're not shooting tomorrow. It's Sunday." He looked up sardonically. "The Lord's day."

"I have Indians tickets," I said, "which are harder to get in this town than papal blessings. I have a connection on the newspaper—who's going to extract a pound of flesh from my ass for them. The Yankees are in town, too."

He held his hand out flat, palm down, and rocked it from side to side like a storm-tossed raft. "Baseball . . . " he said.

"It's not so much the game," I said, a baseball lover trying not to take it personally, "it's the going. Great ballpark—right downtown. You can see the skyscrapers looming over the outfield fence."

"Yeah, well, the fact is, I'm going to be busy."

"Darren, they hired me to stay with you."

"I know." He took a mouthful of Jameson's and gulped it down, wincing. "But I'm twenty-four years old. I can vote for the president, drink, enter into legal contracts. In short, I'm a grown man, and I'd like to spend a day on my own, thanks. Just one day."

"You're sick of my company?"

"I'm sick of being watched all the time."

I chose my words carefully. I didn't want to get him angry—it would just make things more difficult—but I had a bad feeling about his Sunday off. "I don't think Sidney is going to like this. He hired me to do a job."

"And you do it very well. You've showed me the sights, you've taken me to great restaurants like this one, you kept me from getting into a fight the other night. I think you've earned a rest."

"Sidney won't see it that way."

"Fuck Sidney."

"I can't. I have a contract with him. He signs my paycheck."

"He signs mine, too, Milan, but that doesn't mean he owns me, and it doesn't mean he's my mother. Neither are you."

The waiter came and recited the specials. Darren wanted poached salmon; I went for my favorite veal chop. We started talking about the meal—he was a big fan of Spago's in Los Angeles and considered himself a "foodie." Like me, he had recently gotten into cooking.

I didn't bring up the subject of his day off until we'd finished a shared bananas Foster and were drinking Armagnac.

"About tomorrow," I said. "I can't do it, Darren. It would be a violation of my contract."

He looked at me steadily, his iris eyes turning a darker violet. "I don't know what to say, Milan. I'm not used to people telling me no."

I shrugged. "I don't work for you, Darren. I work for Sidney Friedman."

He swirled his Armagnac around in its snifter. "When you come to the house tomorrow morning, then," he finally said, "I won't be there. You can come home with me after dinner, spend the night on the sofa, and then physically restrain me from leaving tomorrow. You're big enough to do it, but I've been in a fight or two in my day, and you're going to have to hurt me. I don't think Sidney would want that. Do you?"

Finishing my own drink in one too large swallow, I sighed. No matter how easy it might look at first, it never is. There's always a lump in the gravy.

"May I ask what you're going to do that's such a secret?"

"No. That's the whole point."

"I'm going to have to call Sidney and let him know about this," I said.

"Tattling to the teacher?"

"Doing my job. I don't make eight million bucks for a few weeks. I need my job, and if I don't show up tomorrow and you get into trouble, I'm going to lose it. So I'm covering my ass, if you don't mind."

"If I mind, will you do it anyway?"

"Afraid so."

He looked crestfallen. "I thought we were friends."

I almost laughed in his face. I'd talked to Sidney and some of the other people working on the film enough so that I knew what friendship was in Hollywood. If you can't make money off someone, if they can't introduce you to someone you can make money off, if they don't have any good drugs, if you're not going to have sex, what on earth is the point?

"What kind of a friend would let a friend get into trouble?" I finally said.

"I could make it worth your while, Milan," he said. "What would it take? Two hundred bucks? Three hundred? I know what they're paying you for this gig. Come on, what do you say?"

"Fuck you, Darren," I told him.

It wasn't terribly late when I got home. Darren had grown sulky after dinner and I took him back to his house, relieved at not having to go dance-club crawling again.

I called Sidney Friedman at his hotel, but there was no answer. I wasn't surprised—it was, after all, a Saturday night and the end of a long work week. I left a message, opened a Stroh's, and made myself comfortable in my easy chair in the den. I picked up a copy of *Sports Illustrated,* hedging my bets by switching on a futuristic movie on cable in which four enormous-breasted pleasure droids kept taking their tops off, and fell asleep in my chair.

Two weeks of eating rich food and drinking a lot was taking its toll.

In the middle of the night I got up and staggered off to the bedroom, somehow managing to set my alarm for nine thirty. When it jangled me awake, I brushed my teeth, made myself a pot of coffee, and called Sidney Friedman again.

He sounded sleepy and cranky. "You know what time it is, Milan? On a Sunday morning?"

"I wanted to catch you before you went off to church," I said.

"Very funny. What's up?"

I told him about Darren's day off.

"I don't like that," he said. "I don't like it one damn bit." I heard what must have been his beard stubble scratching against the mouthpiece on his end. "Your fault, Milan. You should have called me."

"I did call you, last night, and left a message. And I'm calling you this morning. My only other option was to knock him down and sit on him. Did you want him showing up on the set tomorrow with a black eye?"

He thought it over for a minute. "You could have hit him in the stomach."

"The point is, Sidney, what do you want me to do about it?"

"Sit tight," he said tersely, and hung up.

I made myself some toast, finished my coffee, and started on the Sunday *Plain Dealer*. Five minutes later Sidney was back on the phone.

"He's not home," he said, the words issuing like rapid-fire rounds from an Uzi. "At least he's not picking up. You'd better go look for him."

"Sidney, he could be anywhere. He could be in Columbus, or Pittsburgh. Or Chicago."

"Then maybe you should get out there to the house."

"And do what? If he's not home, he's not home."

"See if he shows up."

"He might not come back all day."

"Then wait for him," he said. He was practically hyperventilating, now, and his voice had risen into mezzo-soprano range. "You have a key, don't you? Go in, make yourself at home."

"I have tickets to the Indians game."

"You can watch it on TV," he said.

And that's what I wound up doing, looking hard to see if I could spot my sons, to whom I'd given the tickets, when the camera panned the crowd.

The movie company had rented Darren Anderson a Mercedes, although he had rarely used it, since a limo picked him up each morning and I drove him to wherever he wanted to go in the evenings. When I arrived at the Bay Village house at about eleven, however, the garage was empty.

The housekeeper hadn't come in, this being a Sunday, and Darren had either made the bed before he left or hadn't slept in it all night. I opted for the first, since the bath towel hanging over the shower door in his bathroom was still damp, and the half empty pot in the Mr. Coffee machine was still slightly warm to the touch.

In the bedroom hamper was the cerise sports shirt he'd worn the night before at Johnny's. He might have changed clothes and gone somewhere after I went home, but I somehow doubted it. I figured he'd slept here and left early in the morning.

But where had he gone? If I knew that, I'd go and get him, given the concern bordering on hysteria I'd heard in Sidney Friedman's voice.

Up to this point in our association, Darren was like any ordinary good-looking twenty-four-year-old man with money; I could pick out a hundred like him on any busy evening at the Nautica Entertainment Complex. Slightly more arrogant, I guess, because he was famous, and possibly a little more oversexed. But either Friedman knew something really worrisome about him that I didn't, or he'd been behaving fairly well when he was with me.

I looked all over the house for a pad of paper, a note he might have left, even tried that tired old black-and-white-movie trick of shading a pencil on a pad to bring out the impression of the number written on the sheet above, but came up empty. Then I remembered that little notebook Darren always carried with him—any phone numbers or addresses he might have written down would probably be there—tucked securely into his pocket.

I settled down in the living room and watched the ball game—the Tribe, still suffering from their mysterious, decades-long Yankee jinx, lost 4-1.

I read for a couple of hours—I'd been smart enough to bring along the novel I was halfway through.

There was a freezer full of frozen pizzas, and I heated myself one in the microwave and washed it down with a couple of Henry Weinharts. I watched *60 Minutes.* I sat through a movie on HBO—interestingly enough, one of Gene Hackman's.

I had another Henry.

I fell asleep on the sofa.

At about ten thirty I was awakened by the sound of a car door slamming outside. After a few minutes I heard a key in the lock. The prodigal had returned.

"Hey, Milan," he said. He was wearing a vacant grin that might almost be described as dreamy.

I, on the other hand, was what might be described as cranky. "Where the hell have you been?" I demanded.

"I've been having a good time," he said, his words a little fuzzy. "On my day off."

"Friedman was worried about you."

"Friedman's a producer. Worrying is his job." He moved to the kitchen as if he was on ball bearings. "Anything to eat here?" he said. I heard the refrigerator door opening and closing. He came back out with a fistful of Ritz crackers, half of which he shoved into his mouth, and went to the wet bar for a Henry. "You been here all day? I *told* you—"

"Worrying about what Friedman worries about is *my* job."

He twisted the cap off the bottle and drained half of it in one long, thirsty swallow. "And you do it so well, too," he said. His eyelids were at half-mast. He ate the rest of the crackers and finished the beer in another long draft.

"I've gotta crash, Milan," he said, drifting past me like a wispy cirrus cloud in a clear summer sky. "See you tomorrow night, okay?"

"Okay," I said.

He glided down the hall, still holding the beer bottle, and disappeared into his room, leaving me wondering what was slightly askew, what was different about him.

An unmistakable smell hung in his wake, overpowering the scents of beer, sweat, and sex. The tart-sweet odor of high-grade marijuana.

CHAPTER SIX

"Where the hell did he get the muggles?" Friedman sounded sharp and alert on the phone the next morning, even though it was not yet nine o'clock. But this was Monday—a workday—and the business of making movies starts early.

"I don't know, Sidney." I was at my kitchen table, wearing shorts and a T-shirt, my hair wet from the shower, drinking my second cup of coffee and eating a pastry from Lax and Mandel's kosher bakery on Taylor Road.

"You didn't tell him where to get it, did you?"

"I don't much like that suggestion."

"I don't like any of this, Milan. It makes me nervous. When I get nervous I can't eat, and when I don't eat I get nasty."

"Maybe he brought his own stash from California. But he didn't score it while he was with me."

"This is just the sort of thing I hired you to prevent," he said, every word dripping accusation.

"Then you shouldn't have rented a car for him." I said, although at eight million bucks per film, Darren Anderson could certainly afford to call a taxi. Or a sedan chair borne by eight Nubian slaves, if that's what floated his boat.

"I'm holding you responsible," Friedman said.

"For what?"

"For this picture. If he gets into trouble and can't finish this picture, I'm holding you responsible."

"Fine," I said. "Anything goes wrong, I'll just write you a check for thirty-four million dollars and we'll call it square."

Sidney started to laugh. "This is why producers get old before their time. Pay no attention to me."

"I don't," I said.

He let that one go. "And you have no idea where he was all day yesterday?"

"He didn't seem to want to share the experience with me. He was pretty stoned when he got in."

"Are you sure?"

"I smelled it all over him. Plus he had the munchies. The first thing he did when he got home was to grab a handful of crackers. My guess is he wasn't alone yesterday, if that's what you mean. He—connected—with several different women in the last two weeks."

"How could you let that happen?"

"I didn't know I was supposed to keep him celibate. If I remember correctly, you asked me if I could fix him up with any 'hot numbers.' "

"Sure I did," he snapped. "That way he'd have been happy and we could have controlled it."

"And I could have gotten myself a purple Cadillac and a beaver hat with a big long feather in it and listed myself in the yellow pages under 'procurers.' Look, he's just a young kid, his juices are flowing—I couldn't have stopped him if I'd wanted to."

"I just don't like not having control, Milan. Does he have any more dope?"

"How do I know? Want me to go into the house and search the pockets of his clothes? That'll make him happy."

I listened to the sound of his breathing for a while. "You'll be out at the location tonight?" he asked.

"If I still have a job, yes."

He took entirely too long to think it over. "You still have a job," he finally said.

I got to my office about ninety minutes later. I made a pot of coffee, checked my voice mail, and answered a few calls. Then I sorted through the mail. I couldn't seem to concentrate, though. I was too busy brooding about Darren Anderson.

While he was certainly capable of acting like a jerk and a boor and a spoiled brat, I couldn't see much difference between him and any other young man his age who drank a little too much and prowled after women.

Surely his womanizing must have been common knowledge, and anyway it seemed more likely to help his career than to hurt it, as had been the case with the young Warren Beatty. And if smoking marijuana was illegal, it wasn't likely to result in jail time, or anything other than a bemused publicity buzz. Sidney had assured me Darren didn't have a drug problem, and Saturday night was the first time I'd suspected him of using anything.

So what was the problem? What was the big deal about a twenty-four-year-old kid chasing women and smoking an occasional joint? Why had I really been hired? What was Sidney Friedman afraid of?

I got my answer just before noon. I was getting ready to go to lunch, but the chirping of the telephone caught me when I was halfway across the room.

"You'd better get out here right away," Friedman said, clipping off his words. "To the location. We've got big trouble."

"What kind of trouble?"

He sighed. "Darren Anderson trouble. What else?"

They were shooting that day in the Chagrin Reservation of the Cleveland Metroparks system, part of the "Emerald Necklace," the chain of parks and woodlands that rings the county. The location itself was Squire's Castle, a spot popular with picnickers, and recently with bikers.

Built from stone quarried on the property around 1890 by

F. B. Squire, a vice president of Standard Oil, it is indeed a castle. It resembles a German baronial hall, with bridges and stone walls, and flowing through the grounds a trout stream, but it was never finished, and it remains a ghostly shell standing on the side of a hill, overlooking a vast greensward that often serves as a playing field for pick-up touch football games. Visitors go inside the big vacant building and light fires in the enormous stone fireplaces to cook their hot dogs, and it's known to be popular among the teen set for make-out trysts on warm summer evenings.

It was a marvelously scenic place to shoot a movie.

When I got there at about one o'clock in the afternoon, it didn't look very scenic. All the movie equipment, the dressing-room trailers and prop and electrical trucks, and the full technical crew that had clogged the streets of Tremont for the past two weeks had been moved out to the Chagrin Reservation. The crew was trampling the grass and shouting at one another, making a riot of the tranquil pastoral setting.

There were so many vehicles in the parking area that it took me five minutes to walk from where I left my car to the front steps of the castle, where Sidney Friedman, in Calvin Klein jeans and a Ralph Lauren polo shirt, stood with a middle-aged, balding, self-important-looking man sweating in his gray pinstripes under the hot sun and a fortyish black woman in a white shirtwaist blouse, a straight blue skirt, and sensible shoes. Her eyes were camouflaged by blue sunglasses, but I recognized her as Florence McHargue of the Cleveland Police Department. She'd been a rookie when I was still in uniform, and everyone had agreed she was a young cop to watch. Now she was a full lieutenant—and the head of the sex crimes unit.

I felt my throat closing up.

Sidney introduced me to McHargue and the man in the gray suit, one Emmett Swindell. With a name like that he just had to be a lawyer, and he was.

"Milan, we have a real situation here," Friedman began, but Florence McHargue interrupted him.

"Mr. Jacovich, you were at Darren Anderson's home on Sunday, is that correct?" she said, flipping open the notebook she carried.

"From about eleven in the morning on, yes," I said.

"Why?"

I looked at Friedman. "I've been engaged by Mr. Friedman to show Mr. Anderson the town. Sort of a companion, I guess."

She rolled her eyes. "And why weren't you showing him the town on Sunday?"

"He said he wanted to be on his own for a day," I said. "You can't blame him—he's had hardly any time to himself since he got here."

"And you just let him?" Swindell said. "Knowing how he is?"

"How is he, Mr. Swindell?"

Florence McHargue silenced both of us with a look. "I'm asking the questions, Mr. Swindell," she said. "Did he tell you why he wanted to be by himself?"

"No."

"You didn't ask?"

"Not exactly."

She took off her sunglasses, holding them by one earpiece. Her eyes were dark brown and hard. "What does that mean, not exactly?"

"He pretty much told me it was none of my business."

"I see. And you were there when he came home Sunday night?"

"Yes."

"What time was that?"

"Ten thirty, quarter to eleven."

"Did he tell you where he'd been?"

"No. All he said was that he'd been having a good time."

Friedman was chewing on the end of a pencil. The lawyer shifted his briefcase from one hand to the other and drew himself up as if he were about to make his summation to the jury. "Under the circumstances," he said, and coughed discreetly.

"What circumstances?" I asked. Nobody answered me.

"Yesterday morning," Lieutenant McHargue said, "you told Mr. Friedman that Mr. Anderson had been smoking marijuana." It wasn't a question. Now my throat felt like I'd swallowed a golf ball.

"I didn't see him smoking it," I said. "And I didn't see any marijuana anywhere."

"But he appeared to be under the influence?"

I shrugged. "He might just have been tired."

"You can't tell the difference between tired and stoned?"

Emmett Swindell took a step forward. "Mr. Jacovich, we're looking at a pretty serious situation here."

"No, *you're* looking at it, Counselor. I don't know what the hell is going on. Does somebody want to tell me?"

Sidney scuffed his feet on the stone step and shoved his hands into the hip pockets of his jeans. Then he swung the wrecking ball. "Milan—we think that Darren spent all day yesterday with Bethany Maniscalco. That's what she told her parents, anyway."

I was too stunned to say anything.

"She's only fifteen years old," McHargue reminded me.

"Mr. and Mrs. Maniscalco are very upset, as you might imagine," Swindell said severely.

"You're Mr. Maniscalco's attorney?"

His nod was smug and self-satisfied. "You should never have left Anderson alone yesterday," he clucked.

"He was pretty insistent about it. After all, he's not a prisoner."

"Not yet," the lawyer put in.

"Counselor . . . " McHargue said, a warning lilt lifting the word high and dangling it.

I turned to the detective. "Are you going to arrest him, Lieutenant?"

"I don't know yet," she said. "But it's a distinct possibility."

"Where is he?"

Friedman jerked his head toward the dressing-room trailers. "I want to talk to him."

Swindell said, "I don't think that would be advisable."

"I'm not interested in what you think is advisable, Mr. Swindell. Right now he's not under arrest, and you can't stop me from seeing him."

"I can," Friedman said. "You're still working for me."

"Maybe. But you're a damn fool if you do. I'm trying to help you. Help both of you."

The producer's shoulders slumped. "All right," he said.

"Thanks. Which trailer?"

Darren Anderson was half reclining on a kind of bunk in the Winnebago, wrinkling up a loud plaid spread, engrossed in his script. He wore the sports jacket, denim shirt and blue jeans that I'd first seen him in, his "costume" for *Street Games*. Apparently the cop he was playing in the movie didn't change clothes very often.

"Don't you knock?" he demanded as I walked in.

"Get used to it," I said. "They never knock at Mansfield."

"What's Mansfield?"

"A state prison."

"That isn't funny," he said.

"It wasn't supposed to be. Did you spend yesterday with Bethany Maniscalco?"

He just looked at me, his iris eyes shining.

"She told her parents you did."

He shrugged.

"Do you know that the girl is only fifteen years old?"

"That's my big fan base, Milan." He closed his script.

"What the hell does that mean?"

"It means that the people who buy tickets to my pictures are usually teenagers. That's just how it is."

"What's that got to do with the Maniscalco girl?"

He shrugged again.

"Tell me what happened."

His frown was mild. "It's personal, Milan."

"Do you know that there's a cop from the sex crimes unit right outside, champing at the bit to get a piece of you?"

Under the heavy movie makeup his skin turned pasty white. He licked his suddenly dry lips. "There is?"

"Are you going to tell her it's personal?"

The script fell from his hands, dropping to the floor with a thud. He swung his legs off the bunk and stood up, casting glances into all four corners of the trailer, as if looking for an escape. But there wasn't one, and he knew it. The slightly arrogant air of insouciance was gone, the cocky grin and sexy pout, and the light in his iris-colored eyes had dimmed considerably. He didn't look like a movie star anymore, he looked like a badly frightened little boy.

"Did you have sex with her?"

His eyelids fluttered. "No. We just—you know, fooled around a little bit."

"Are you lying to me?"

He looked away.

Something dangerous was festering inside me like an evil-smelling flower. I took a step closer to him and he shrank back, pressing himself against the wall.

"You've done this before, haven't you?"

"What do you mean?"

"I mean underage girls. Your 'fan base.' You've been in trouble like this before. But the studios or your press agent always managed to get it fixed, right?"

I had him virtually pinned against the wall, and he squirmed away from me, or as far away as he could get in the confines of the Winnebago. "Jesus, lemme breathe!" he said.

"I'm not so sure you deserve to." I got right back in his face. "You know what cons call guys like you?" I said. "Guys who like young girls? Short eyes. You know what they do to short eyes in the joint?"

He was sweating now, sweating off his makeup, but he decided to play it tough, as though he believed he actually was the character he was portraying in *Street Games.* "Hey, don't get all moralistic on me, okay? I mean, it's not like she was a virgin or anything."

I was going to hit him. I knew if I didn't stop and get myself under control, I was going to knock him right on his ass. I took a deep breath, then another one, and turned away from him, heading for the door.

"Hey, you'd have done the same damn thing!" he said. "You see the body on that girl?"

"So long, Darren."

"Don't kid me. You wouldn't have thought twice about it."

I stopped, one hand on the doorknob, and turned back to him.

"Wrong, Darren. I wouldn't have thought about it at all."

When I got back out front, McHargue and Swindell were off at one end of the parking lot, their heads together. McHargue had put her blue glasses back on. Sidney Friedman was nowhere in sight.

I walked up the stone steps and into the castle, avoiding the cables snaking from the generator truck. Sidney was in the room off to the right, a large, gloomy one with a stone fireplace at one end, standing with the director, Boyce Cort, who was wearing his fringed vest, and a slim, gray-haired man with a light meter hanging around his neck. They were looking up at the ceiling.

"Sidney," I said.

He glanced up at me in annoyance. "In a minute, Milan, okay?" Then he turned back to the other two.

"Not in a minute, Sidney. Now."

Cort tilted his head back and looked down his aquiline nose at me. "Sidney—who is this rude person?"

"Someone who's bigger than you," I said.

He recoiled as if I'd slapped him. "Get off my set at once!" he ordered.

I made a move toward him. "Is that buckskin vest edible?"

"Milan, for Christ's sake," Sidney said, and took my arm, leading me off into the farthest room of the castle.

"Do you know who that was you just insulted?"

"Save the Hollywood shit for someone who'll be impressed," I said. "You weren't straight with me, Sidney. What's happened is your own goddamn fault."

"What are you talking—"

"You knew Darren had a problem with young girls, didn't you? Why didn't you tell me up front?"

"Would you have taken the job if I did?"

"You know damn well I wouldn't have."

"There you go, then," he said. "We talked to two other people first, but you came highly recommended by that newspaper guy, and you're big enough and tough enough to handle any trouble that might come along. I needed you. I still need you." He leaned closer to me, affecting a low whisper. "Maniscalco has four million dollars invested in this picture, and if he pulls it, there won't *be* a picture."

"I couldn't care less about the damn picture."

He waved his hand vaguely at the window, beyond which his crew were doing whatever it was they did. "Maybe you care about the ninety-four men and women from right here in Cleveland who'll be out of a good paying job if we shut down. Maybe you care about the other investors who're going to take a hosing."

"If I'm that important, you should have been paying me the eight million bucks. Sorry, Sidney, but you're SOL."

"SOL?"

"Shit outta luck. I quit."

"You can't quit," he said. "We have a contract."

"I didn't sign on to hold hands with baby-rapers. So I'm giving your contract back to you with detailed instructions."

"Hey, who the fuck do you think you're talking to?"

"A master manipulator," I said. "A guy who pays a pervert eight million bucks because it'll make him money. A guy who can't even remember how to deal off the top of the deck." I turned away. "A guy I used to work for," I said over my shoulder.

"Nobody talks to me that way," he sputtered. "I'll see to it that you never . . . " He trailed off ineffectually as I walked out.

I was pretty sure he'd been about to tell me that I'd never work in this town again, but "this town" was his town—Hollywood. Cleveland is my town.

Just before five I called the police department and asked for Lieutenant McHargue. I figured she'd talk to me because I'd once been on the job. I told her about my new nonstatus on *Street Games* and asked what was going to happen to Darren.

"I don't know," she said. "That Swindell guy was making lots of noise about Maniscalco pulling his investment out of the film, and that seems to have the producers in more of a panic than anything that might happen to Darren Anderson. We're going to go out to the house tonight and talk to the girl. Depending on what she says, we might be coming after Anderson in the morning."

I didn't know what Bethany Maniscalco would tell the police about her Sunday in the park with Darren. But as it turned out, it didn't really matter.

Because by the next morning Darren Anderson was dead.

CHAPTER SEVEN

Darren hadn't shown up on the set at seven A.M. as he'd been scheduled to. Boyce Cort had thrown a fit, proclaiming that he wouldn't have such wonderful light for the rest of the day, and stomped off to his trailer to sulk. Sidney Friedman figured Darren was scared of being arrested for statutory rape and had gone to ground, and Friedman was on the phone with his attorney in Beverly Hills, intently studying his contracts and insurance policies and completion bonds to ascertain whether or not he was covered. One of the local public relations people had volunteered to go out to Bay Village and check the house. She found the door open and Darren dead on the kitchen floor, shot three times with a nine-millimeter weapon. One bullet was lodged in his stomach and a second in his chest, very near the heart, and a third had taken away the front part of his head.

I didn't hear about it until I was home for the evening, eating a klobasa sausage sandwich with fried onions on about a third of a loaf of Orlando's Ciabatta bread sliced lengthwise, drinking a beer, and watching Vivian Truscott anchor the local six o'clock news on Channel 12. Naturally Darren Anderson's death was the lead story.

If it bleeds, it leads, they say in the TV news racket.

It's amazing how much bad news I've gotten from Vivian Truscott over the years. Almost enough to take it personally.

The story pretty much killed my appetite.

Darren Anderson had been a sexual predator who took advantage of teenage girls—and that turned my stomach. But the two weeks I'd spent as his nanny/keeper hadn't been that unpleasant, and when he let himself forget he was a movie star, he wasn't really such a bad kid. I don't know how well any of us would handle sudden wealth and fame and privilege at his age.

At any age.

And now the fame and privilege had bought him a nice cool drawer at the county morgue, and the show business future that had seemed so bright was snuffed out forever.

James Dean. Janis Joplin. River Phoenix. A thousand more. The fickle public isn't the only reason that celebrityhood has a short shelf life.

Any premature loss of life brings sorrow, but there was something eating away at my insides: the coroner had determined that Darren died between eight and ten o'clock the night before.

If I hadn't quit and stormed off in a huff that morning, I would probably have been with him then. I wasn't, and someone killed him.

For the second time in a year I'd been at least partly responsible for someone's death. It weighed heavy on my head and heart.

I knew, intellectually anyway, that if someone had wanted to kill Darren that badly, they would have found a time and a way of doing it. After all, I didn't sleep there. But what you intellectualize and what you know deep down in your viscera are two different things.

The ghost of Darren Anderson had become another one of my demons.

I wrapped up my half-eaten sandwich, put it in the fridge, and opened another beer. It wasn't going to help, but nevertheless I drank quietly but steadily into the evening, getting fuzzier with every bottle of Stroh's.

I couldn't remember getting into bed, but that's where I awoke just before nine o'clock in the morning with a dull roar behind my eyes and feeling parched, dessicated. Lying there on my back, my head throbbing, I studied the crack in the ceiling that looks roughly like the outline of Brazil, exploring the inside of my mouth with my tongue, fascinated by the feel of my slightly uneven teeth, the space between my two top front ones, and the silky flesh on the insides of my cheeks.

I got out of bed in stages, starting with my left leg—it took me about three minutes to complete the process. Then I lurched into the bathroom, gulped down one too many Aleves, and rinsed my mouth with Scope, wondering who the seventy-year-old man staring out at me from the mirror through raccoon's eyes was, and how in hell he'd gotten into my bathroom.

I put a pot of coffee on and showered and shaved while it dripped through. By the time I was ready to drink it, and to make myself a bowl of instant oatmeal in the microwave, I was feeling human again. Not terrific, but human, which was a major improvement. I switched on Lanigan and Malone on WMJI for a few badly needed chuckles.

The morning was slow going, however. The newspaper headlined Darren's death and I didn't want to read about it just then, so I read the sports page and put the rest aside for later.

When I pulled into the office lot just before noon I saw a Ford Taurus parked up front. At my approach, the driver's door opened and Bob Matusen got out holding a steaming cardboard cup.

About five foot nine, wiry, with kinky brown hair beginning to show flashes of silver, he'd been Marko Meglich's number-one guy in homicide, and now he was its de facto boss until the department could find a real lieutenant to move in and take over. He was wearing a nondescript brown suit with a red tie. However well Marko had trained him in the difficult and sensitive trade of a homicide detective, his late lieutenant's elegant fashion sense hadn't rubbed off on Matusen.

"Hey, Milan," he said.

"Bob."

We shook hands solemnly. I hadn't seen him since two weeks after Marko's funeral, when he'd stopped by to give me the coffee mug.

He looked at the dark circles around my eyes. "You look like you're fifteen minutes out of detox."

"It was a rough night."

He nodded. "Been there, done that," he said. "Got a minute?"

"Sure," I said, and led the way into the building.

On the second floor I unlocked my office door and stood aside so he could go in. It was uncomfortably warm inside, and the first thing I did was switch on the air conditioner.

"I'm going to make some coffee," I said.

He lifted the cardboard cup. "Great. I'll probably be finished with this by the time it's ready."

He wandered aimlessly around the big room while I filled the filter basket with grounds and poured water into the well of the coffeemaker. The last time he'd seen the office, it had been a disaster area, damaged by an arsonist's fire and the water and chemical retardants of Engine Company 21 not a hundred yards away.

"You got the place fixed up pretty good," he observed, tracing a pattern on the new hardwood floor with his toe.

"Thank God for insurance companies. It cost a fortune."

"Still smells like smoke a little, though."

"I know. That might not ever go away."

He sat in one of my client chairs, and we both lit cigarettes and chatted some more until the coffee was ready. I poured us each a cup.

He nodded at Marko's mug. "Still using that, I see."

"Every day."

"I miss the guy."

"Me too. That won't ever go away either."

He stared into his coffee. "This is kind of an official visit, Milan."

"Okay, I'll sit up straighter."

He did a good job of not smiling. "It's this Darren Anderson business."

"Oh."

"Yeah."

"I thought he bought it in Bay Village. How did it wind up on your desk?"

He leaned back and crossed his ankles, balancing his coffee mug on his lap. "The sex crimes thing. The alleged statutory rape happened in Edgewater Park. That's in Cleveland, so the department caught it. So we figured it'd make sense to work with the Bay Village cops on the homicide."

"What can I do for you?"

He looked vaguely uncomfortable. "I'm not happy asking this, Milan, but can you tell me where you were Monday night?"

I carefully stubbed out my cigarette in the ashtray on my desk, squashing just the glowing end as if I'd pick it up and relight it later, something I've never done in my life. "Are you saying I'm a suspect, Bob?"

He avoided my gaze. "You had an argument with Anderson Monday afternoon. You quit your job because you couldn't stand being around him. Monday night he's dead from gunshot wounds. You used to be a good, conscientious cop—if you were still on the job, what would you do?"

"I guess I'd come and talk to me," I said.

"Bingo," he said. "So?"

"So I was home. Brought in a pizza from Mama Santo's in Little Italy. Pepperoni and sausage."

"Good, the topping is important," he said dryly.

"There's still a couple of slices in the freezer. While I ate it, I watched the Tribe—they beat Baltimore. After the game I read a book. You want to know the name of it?"

"Nobody can alibi you, is that right?"

I shook my head.

He sipped at his coffee. "You make good coffee, Milan."

"It's French roast, from the Arabica at Coventry. I get ten percent off because I'm a member of public radio. WCPN."

"Yeah. So tell me about you and this movie kid."

"What about us?"

"What was your relationship? How did you get along? What did you do with him all those evenings, for God's sake?"

It took me about twenty minutes, but I pretty much laid out how it had been. He didn't take any notes while I was talking; I couldn't decide whether I liked that or not.

"The kid had trouble with his zipper, huh?"

"Lots of people do," I said. "I try not to be judgmental about it. But when it involves underage girls . . . "

"So you tell him to go piss up a rope, you walk out on the job, and he gets iced that night."

"Uh-huh."

"Maybe you shouldn't've quit."

"That occurred to me."

He sat there quietly until he finished his coffee. I lit a fresh Winston. Pretty soon the air got cooler. The clock ticked.

Finally he got up, put the mug down on my desk, and dusted a sprinkling of ash off his thighs. "Good coffee. I may come back for some more."

"Still think I might've done it?"

"I don't want to think so," he said. He looked at Marko's coffee mug on my desk.

"Thanks."

"Don't thank me. You're still on the list."

I picked up a pencil and started doodling on a yellow pad.

Ever since I was a kid in grade school, I've doodled the same thing—a gallows with an empty noose. I suppose a shrink could have a field day with that one, but it doesn't hurt anybody, and I kind of like it. "That sounds a little ominous."

"Procedure," he assured me.

"In that case, wouldn't it behoove me to look into this myself? I don't like being on the hook."

"That'd be a mistake, Milan. You'd just get in our way. We don't like that."

"I know."

He put one hand on the edge of my desk, leaning over me. "Marko let you get away with a lot of things—because he'd known you for thirty years or so. I haven't known you nearly that long."

"Message received, Bob."

"That's good. Don't let me trip over you in the dark."

"Uh-huh."

He straightened up. "Take it easy, all right?"

"All right, Bob."

He didn't offer to shake hands this time. I listened to his footsteps getting fainter on the carpeted steps. The downstairs door opened and closed, and then I heard the rumble of his car's motor.

Take it easy. I lose my temper and quit a job, and a guy dies because of it. And then I find out I'm a suspect in his murder. And Matusen says take it easy.

He's a riot, Matusen.

"I'm unsure as to exactly what you want from me, Milan," Victor Gaimari said. He was sitting at his big desk in his brokerage office on the eleventh floor of Terminal Tower, and through the window behind him I could see one of the many bends in the Cuyahoga River, and beyond, the smokestacks of the steel mills just south of downtown.

"I'd just like a read on Tom Maniscalco," I said. "You seem to know him pretty well."

He touched the impeccable knot of his Countess Mara tie. "I wouldn't say I know him well."

"Well enough for him to invite you to that benefit Friday evening."

"I get invitations like that every week—lots of them from people I hardly know."

"So you hardly know Maniscalco?"

"We're acquaintances, not much more than that." He smiled. "I know you better than I know him." He pushed his rolling chair back far enough so he could cross one leg over the other, taking care to preserve the crease in his elegantly tailored tan summer-weight suit. "Why even get involved with this, Milan? It isn't as though the Anderson boy was a good friend of yours."

"Maybe because the police are looking at me for it."

He laughed. "Be serious."

"I am."

His dark eyebrows formed two perfect arches. "Well, they have to look at everybody. You know that."

"I quarreled with Anderson the day he died and walked out on the job. I can't blame them for thinking about me."

"You don't really think they're going to make it stick?"

"No," I admitted. "I don't."

"Well, then?"

I shifted my butt around a little in my chair. The chairs in Victor's office are so soft and comfortable that they put the sitter at a distinct disadvantage. I kept sinking into the cushions of mine—it was like drowning in Jell-O. "I feel a certain responsibility."

"Admirable but misplaced," he said. "That's a little failing of yours. You think you're responsible for the whole world."

"I was hired to keep him out of trouble," I said.

"And then you quit."

"That's my point."

He considered that for a while, then nodded. Grudgingly. "That's why I want to find out about Tom Maniscalco." He frowned.

"No offense," I went on, "but I know how Italian fathers can be about their daughters. Anderson took advantage of his little girl, and Maniscalco found out about it. He was pissed off—enough to threaten to pull his investment out of that movie. Maybe he was pissed off enough to do something about it personally."

"It's possible."

"Or have it done."

"Tom Maniscalco isn't a Sicilian, Milan. His family is from near Rome. And he's as clean as a Sunday sermon in the First Baptist Church," he assured me. "Take it from someone who knows."

"Amerigo Bonasera wanted revenge on the men who dishonored his daughter in *The Godfather*," I reminded him.

"That was a movie, for Christ's sake!" Victor said with some heat, his usual facade of calmness and complete control cracking.

"Nevertheless . . . "

His big brown eyes narrowed, glittering. "Let me understand you, Milan. You're asking me if Tom Maniscalco came to our people and took out a contract on Darren Anderson? Just because he happens to be Italian? I find the very suggestion insulting."

"I mean no disrespect," I said quickly. Victor can be touchy about respect. So can his uncle. "And that thought never crossed my mind. But if the police are looking for motive, Maniscalco has a beaut."

"So do a lot of other people, I'd imagine."

I waited.

"Surely the little Maniscalco girl isn't the only one Anderson favored with his attentions in the last two weeks."

"No."

"Plus"—he raised a cautioning index finger—"you haven't been on the set every day while they were shooting this movie. You don't know who he might have rubbed the wrong way. The director, the producer, other actors . . . "

"The movie was getting made because Anderson was in it. Can you imagine anyone wanting the golden-egg-laying goose dead?"

"Yes," he said. "Yes, I can. For any number of reasons, many of which neither of us would think of."

"None of which are probably as compelling as Maniscalco's."

Victor shook his head. "He's not the type."

"Everyone is the type, Victor, if they're pushed far enough."

"Not Maniscalco. He comes with good references."

I tried not to smile. "You mean you?"

"I mean the bishop of Cleveland, among lots of others. Including me."

"I'd like to talk to him anyway."

He waved a hand at me. "Be my guest."

"Can you call him and set it up for me?"

He made a small, dismissive gesture with his hand, not much more than the slight lifting of his fingers from the surface of his desk. "Sure. I'll just say I know this guy who thinks you're a murderer and please show him every courtesy."

"You think it hasn't occurred to the police?"

"I think a little discretion is warranted here, Milan. Maniscalco is well known in the community. I don't think anyone would want the story spread around that his fifteen-year-old-daughter was putting out for movie stars. That's the kind of thing the newspapers and TV stations jump on like hyenas."

"It'll come out anyway, and it'll be his own fault. He filed an official complaint with the police."

He nodded. "But no action was taken on it, no arrest was

made. At the moment it's only a couple of squiggles in Lieutenant McHargue's notebook."

"You know the name of the sex-crimes officer assigned to the complaint," I said, impressed.

"I know a lot, Milan." He leaned forward, elbows on the desk, and spoke clearly and distinctly, as if he were talking to someone for whom English was a fairly new second language. "And that's the way we'd like it to stay."

Of course, I thought. The fix was already in.

I stood up. "You think you could make that phone call for me anyway, Victor? To Maniscalco?"

He looked up at me for a moment, then got to his feet. I don't fancy having people tower over me either.

"Can we count on your discretion?"

"Who's we, Victor?"

He put his well-manicured hand out across the desk. "Call me tomorrow, Milan. I'll see what I can do."

CHAPTER EIGHT

Unable to resume shooting their film without their star, the company of *Street Games* was sitting tight, waiting to see what would happen. People in the skill jobs who'd been imported from California by the producers still enjoyed their regular paychecks. For the contract workers picked up locally, the extras and the caterers and the cleanup people—tough luck.

Sidney Friedman was holed up in his suite at the Ritz-Carlton, a telephone growing out of his ear. He was trying to find a suitable replacement for Darren Anderson, he informed me irritably. The National Football League plays games less than forty-eight hours after a president is assassinated, Cincinnati Reds owner Marge Schott wants to start the baseball game again right after the umpire drops dead on the field in front of thousands of people, some of them children, and life goes on in the movie business.

But replacing Darren wasn't going to be easy.

The replacement had to be acceptable to the investors, i.e., someone who could reasonably be expected to bring audiences to the box office. "A guy who can open a movie" is the way the *Daily Variety* crowd puts it.

And of course Sidney was trying to find someone to work inexpensively, a dicey proposition now, because every agent in Hollywood knew that with an entire movie company twiddling their thumbs on salary in far-off Cleveland, he was up against the wall and desperate, and they had the opportunity to really stick it to him. Nothing personal, just business as usual.

So not only was Sidney Friedman, understandably, mad at me, he was too busy to talk to me anyway.

Boyce Cort was not busy. He had withdrawn to his three-room suite at the Renaissance Hotel on Public Square—his contract had specified he wouldn't have to stay at the same hotel as Sidney—and was working on what could not have been his first bloody Mary of the morning. He answered the door wearing a maroon Nike running suit, white tube socks, and no shoes. His long, thinning hair was uncombed, and the toast crumbs in his grizzled beard were evidently the remnants of an early breakfast. His head was slightly too large for his body, and he attempted to camouflage the fact by thrusting his chin forward, which gave him an air of bellicosity.

He peered up at me. "I saw you around a few times, didn't I? You were Darren's minder."

"That's right."

"You weren't very good at your job, were you? Or he'd still be alive."

That stung. A lot. "I quit my job," I said. "Before it happened."

The main room of the suite had a living-room area—sofas, armchairs, a giant TV set and a bar—and a conference area, with an enormous table and ten chairs. On the table was a tray bearing a crumpled napkin, a cup and saucer, a coffee carafe, and an egg-streaked plate. The air conditioner was turned up high, making the room feel like Duluth in January.

The television was tuned to *The Price is Right,* a show that has been around ever since I can remember. The host is grandfatherly, the models who point to the prizes are gorgeous, but the contestants are all dressed as if they've been pulled out of a line at a soup kitchen.

Cort picked up the remote and hit the mute button, so the fortyish woman who had just won something and was jumping up and down with excitement, her large breasts jiggling alarmingly under a yellow T-shirt, was doing so in dumb show.

"I don't think I have anything to tell you," he said. "And I don't think I'd want to if I did."

"Then why did you agree to see me?"

"Because I'm bored out of my skull, and even talking to you is better than watching this shit." He jerked his chin at the silent television set.

"There are movies on cable," I reminded him.

"Seen 'em. Seen 'em all."

"How about a book? There's a bookstore right downstairs in the Tower City shopping center."

"Movie people don't read," he said sternly. "We hire people to read books for us. We're visual." He sat down on the sofa, a man accustomed to having his orders obeyed and obviously unused to being questioned. "Come on, ask me whatever you want. I've never been grilled by a detective before; this should be fun."

Loads, I thought. "I wouldn't call it grilling. Weren't you questioned by the police?"

"Not yet. But they know I'm not going anywhere. We're going to stay here in town and finish this film. That's the way it works."

I sat down in one of the big brocade wing chairs, even though I hadn't been invited to do so. "Tell me a little bit about Darren Anderson."

"He was a movie star," Cort said, pronouncing the two words with all the exquisite care of Eliza Dolittle describing the rain in Spain.

"That's it?"

"That's it. It defined him, at least as far as I was concerned."

"Did you like him?"

"What's to like?" he shrugged. "Spoiled brat, not exactly a

giant talent. He had about as much concentration as a piece of bread—between takes he'd really lose focus, so it was always a job getting him back on track. He wasn't exactly a rocket scientist. And as good-looking as he was, I found him to be without charm and lacking a certain—grace, I suppose, for lack of a better word." He crossed an ankle over his knee; the bottom of his white sock was gray and stained, as if he only wore shoes when absolutely necessary. "Hitchcock was right, y'know—he said actors were like cattle."

"Anthony Hopkins? Daniel Day-Lewis?"

He looked up through the ceiling to heaven. "I should only have Daniel Day-Lewis in this picture."

"Then why did you cast Darren Anderson?"

"Because nobody'd believe Daniel Day-Lewis as a tough Cleveland cop. Not that I really thought they'd believe Doll Face, either." He pointed a finger at me. "Besides, I didn't cast him. This picture only got off the ground because he was in it. Don't ask me why, but his name puts the asses in the theater seats." He smiled. "He was cute."

"Cute?"

His eyes glittered a challenge at me. "That's right."

"So you got along with him pretty well?"

"I didn't kill him, if that's what you mean."

"That's not what I asked."

"Nobody really gets along on a shoot, Mr. . . . ?"

"Jacovich," I told him. "With a *J*."

"The hours are long, the work is hard, and there's a huge amount of money at stake. Tempers fray pretty easily. When an actor comes to the set poorly prepared, directors tend to get snarky."

"Darren wasn't prepared?"

"Oh, he knew his lines all right. But except for his pretty face, he didn't bring much to the party. It took all my considerable skill as a director even to make him adequate. It cost us a lot in terms of extra takes, it made things difficult for the other actors and the crew. And my personal opinion is that he was so lousy in the part that the movie was going to be a total disaster anyway."

He saw my look of befuddlement and laughed. "There's more to acting than standing there and saying what you're supposed to say, Mr. Jacovich. An actor has to have a visceral understanding of the role, has to literally inhabit it—by whatever 'method' he needs to use. Darren never bothered with niceties like that. He thought if he had enough close-ups, so everyone could see how gorgeous he was, and enough full-length shots of him wearing tight jeans, that was all that was required. That's a lazy actor."

Cute. Gorgeous. Doll Face. I could see a pattern forming here. "Did you think Darren was gorgeous, Mr. Cort?"

He sank back into the cushions of the sofa, wriggling with a kind of hedonistic luxury, finding the exact place where he was most comfortable, like a spoiled house cat. "My sexual orientation isn't the secret of the century, Mr. Jacovich. I've been out of the closet for years now."

"And was your relationship with Darren Anderson strictly professional?"

He was very still for a moment. Then he said, "You're not a policeman, are you?"

"Not anymore, no."

"And you're no longer working for this production, or for Sidney either?"

"No," I said. "I'm on my own."

"Then you can take your too personal questions and go fuck yourself. I don't have to talk to you. And I won't." He waved at the entrance to the suite. "I'm sure a big, capable detective like you can find the door," he said.

The White Magnolia wasn't open for lunch, so when I got there at two o'clock in the afternoon the chairs were still on top of the tables and the lights were on full. Apparently the cleanup workers and underchefs didn't care about the ambience or whether the lighting made them look romantically younger.

A bespectacled young woman was sitting on a stool at the end of the bar, totting up credit card slips with a calculator, her light blond hair in a youthful braid that reached the middle of her back and was secured with a large dark green bow, her legs pleasingly displayed beneath a black above-the-knee skirt. A cheerful young man wearing a Cleveland Browns T-shirt—for the last three years there have been no Cleveland Browns, but what would the world be like without hope?—called to me from behind the bar, where he was busily wiping down bottles.

"We don't open until five o'clock."

"I'd like to talk to the manager," I said.

"Sorry, he only sees vendors in the morning."

"I'm not a vendor. I'm a private investigator."

His smile lost most of its luster. People are usually either fascinated with PIs or scared to death of them.

"Is he in?" I asked.

He struggled over that one, as if it were a much more difficult question. "Second," he said, and came out from behind the bar and went into the back.

The woman stopped her calculating, took off her glasses, and smiled at me. "Private investigator? Really?"

"Really."

"What a neat job."

"It has its moments," I admitted.

"Are you investigating something now?"

I handed her one of my business cards. "No, I just like to hang out in restaurants when they're closed."

She grinned. "Silly question."

"No problem."

"I imagine there is a problem," she said, "or you wouldn't be here."

I held thumb and forefinger about half an inch apart. "Maybe a little tiny one. Nothing to worry about."

The host who'd made Darren and me wait for a table came out from the rear of the restaurant, a questioning look on his face. In the bright artificial light he looked older than I remembered him, perhaps late fifties. More solid. Tougher.

"Hi, I'm Leo Haley. I'm the owner," he said.

"It's a nice place."

We shook hands, I introduced myself and gave him a card, which he studied carefully. Then he favored me with the same scrutiny. "I've seen you before," he said.

"I was in here about two weeks ago for dinner."

I could see him flipping through the mental card file of customer's faces he carried around in his head. Then he frowned. "You were with a very rude young man."

"Guilty."

He squared his feet beneath him, his body language now a little less affable, warier. "I remember. So what can I do for you?"

"I'm trying to locate a customer who was in here the same night. I was hoping maybe you could help me out."

Haley didn't say anything.

"He was tall, about thirty, with a receding hairline and glasses," I went on. "His name was Alan something. His date's name was Dierdre—if that's any help."

"Uh-huh. What do you want with him?"

"I'd just like to talk to him."

His mouth smiled but forgot to tell his eyes. "Obviously we can't give out information like that, Mr. Jacovich. Our patrons wouldn't like it."

"The man I was with that evening, do you know who he was?"

"Mr. Rude?"

"It was Darren Anderson. The actor."

A look of concern crossed his face. "The movie star who got killed?"

"That's the one."

"Jesus," he muttered. "That's all I need."

"Mr. Anderson had a few words with Alan Whoever at the bar. He was paying a little too much attention to Dierdre, and Alan didn't like it."

The woman with the calculator was listening intently, making no pretense of working.

Haley said, "I have no idea who the guy was. I don't even remember him."

"If he paid with a credit card, you'd at least have his last name."

Haley shook his head resolutely. "I still can't give out that kind of information, even if I knew it. It'd be lousy for business."

I sighed. "Look, Mr. Haley, I'm conducting this investigation privately. Right now the police don't know anything about it. But I'm legally and morally obliged to tell them, and then they'd come in here and ask the same question. And that wouldn't be so good for business either. Maybe the newspapers would get wind of it—as you know, they're not writing about much of anything else. And that would *really* be lousy for business, wouldn't it?"

He chewed on the inside of his cheek.

"If you let me run it down and it comes to nothing, nobody needs to know about it," I said, a bit more gently. Since I work alone I have to be both good cop and bad cop. "You can count on my discretion."

Leo Haley wasn't happy. "I don't want this coming back on me."

"Of course not," I said. "But you don't want a killer walking around loose, either, do you?"

The color went out of his face like the instant fading of a photograph. "You think this Alan guy . . . ?"

"I don't think anything. I'm just running down every lead I can find." I gave him my warmest, fuzziest smile. "Will you help me, Mr. Haley?"

Five minutes later I was back in the postage-stamp office with the young woman, whom I'd begun to think of as Our Lady of the Calculator. She told me her name was Connie Haley. She was just over five feet tall, and at six foot three or thereabouts, I towered over her like the Colossus of Rhodes.

"You're Leo's wife?" I said.

"Daughter. It's a family business." She pulled open the top drawer of the file cabinet. "When did you say you were in here?" she asked, thumbing through the files.

"On Monday night, two weeks ago."

She pulled out a file and brought it to the desk. "This is kind of exciting," she said as she sat down.

"Just like on TV."

"I don't think so. On TV you'd have more hair, I'd have more boobs, we'd be trading scintillating put-downs, and we'd be in bed together before the second commercial."

I leaned over her shoulder to look at what she was doing. Her hair had a sort of strawberry fragrance. "It could happen."

"Sorry," she said. "I never sleep with anyone until the fourth commercial." She pulled out a packet of credit card slips, probably sixty of them, and began riffling through them with the quick, sure hand of a Vegas cardsharp. "These are all the credit card purchases for that evening. Who are we looking for, again?"

"Anyone named Alan. Or maybe Dierdre."

She looked up at me.

"It's a new world," I told her. "Sometimes the woman pays."

"Ain't it the truth." She flipped through them again and extracted one. "There's an Alan." After a minute she pulled out another. "Here's another one." When she'd finished she gathered the others up again, saying, "That's it. Two Alans, no Dierdre."

"Thanks," I said, and picked up the two slips.

"What if he didn't use a credit card? What if he paid cash?" she asked.

"Then I'm screwed," I said. "Before even the first commercial. But how many people pay cash for dinner these days?"

"One in a hundred, maybe. The dinosaur who still doesn't believe in plastic." Connie Haley took off her wire-rimmed glasses and looked at me. "Or if the guy is married and doesn't want his wife to know."

"He wasn't wearing a wedding ring."

"That doesn't mean he's not married." She smiled. "You're not wearing one, either."

"In my case, it means I'm not married."

"There is a God," she said, and winked broadly at me.

I examined the two slips. One bore the signature of an Alan Mitzenmacher, and the total was three hundred forty-six dollars.

I showed it to Connie. "You think two people could eat up three hundred forty-six dollars' worth at one meal here?"

"Not unless they were very hungry and had several bottles of our best wine."

"They were drinking merlot by the glass at the bar."

"Then it's doubtful," she said. "People who order expensive vintages usually don't drink house wine before dinner. Simply ruins the palate, don'tcha know," she explained with playful snobbishness.

"Tacky."

She flicked at the Mitzenmacher credit slip with her finger. "That was probably for a party of four to six. The usual dinner tab in here runs from fifty to sixty dollars a person, depending on what they drink."

I looked at the other slip. Alan Braxton. Nice WASP name. A hundred and thirty three dollars, including tip. A fifteen per cent tip.

"This looks good," I said, and jotted the name down in my notebook. "I appreciate your help, Connie."

"My pleasure. You should come back here for dinner again some time. The food is excellent."

"I know."

"So's the company, if you catch my drift."

I felt myself coloring. "Under Daddy's watchful eye?"

"Don't worry about Leo. Even he understands that every once in a while they let me out of the nunnery for good behavior."

"I like nuns on the loose."

She handed me a business card, bearing her name under the restaurant's logo. "Here," she said. "In case you ever get hungry."

CHAPTER NINE

Timing is everything.

I walked from the cool dimness of the White Magnolia out into the muggy afternoon, wondering why it is that whenever I'm attracted to a woman, or one finds me even remotely interesting, I'm always in the middle of a high-pressure investigation and don't have time to do anything about it.

I guess the answer is, if I'm *not* in the middle of an investigation I rarely get out of the house or office long enough to meet anyone, and in the months since Marko Meglich died I'd become downright reclusive. I'm not a regular churchgoer, so I can't count on running into attractive women at social events like mixers or bingo. I hate going into strange bars where I don't know anyone, and even if I didn't, most of the meet markets in Cleveland—like the upscale Spy Bar on West Sixth and the lower-end, crowded and smoky Blind Pig Speakeasy just across the street, the noisy little nightclubs in Tremont, the Flats, or on Detroit Avenue—are for the under-thirty set. Those are the ones Darren Anderson had returned to night after boring night, with me in reluctant tow.

I even tried answering classified ads a few apprehensive times, until I discovered that while those who take out personal ads are frank and open about whether they like candlelight dinners, long walks on the beach, and partners with a great sense of humor, they usually lie like hell about everything else, especially their looks, age, and weight.

And the one time I went to a "singles dance" I returned home not only alone but profoundly depressed. I'd rather stick pins in my eyes than go to another one.

So here was funny, pretty, dimpled Connie Haley flirting shamelessly with me, and I was running around trying to catch a murderer.

Maybe I'm in the wrong business. It's not the first time that thought had crossed my mind.

Back in the Flats half an hour later, bumping over the cracks and potholes on Scranton Road, I was still wondering what in the world I'd choose for a career if I quit doing what I do. With a bachelor's degree in business and a master's in psychology, I suppose I could find some other means of making a living, but it's been a long time since I put aside the cap and gown to go out and tilt at real-world windmills. Selling ties at Dillard's is an option, I guess, but it doesn't appeal. I've been my own boss for too long now to revert to clock-punching wage slavery.

My beeper went off, shattering my addled thoughts into tiny pieces. I've had a pager for several years now, but I always feel a little silly when it chirps in public; once it sounded off during a burial service, and in the shocked silence that followed every mourner turned to see who was crass enough to get a phone call at graveside.

I pulled the readout from my pocket; the number was Victor Gaimari's.

I called him right back. I have a speakerphone in my car, mainly because I'm too embarrassed to drive down the street with a receiver pressed to my ear. Now all I have to worry about is people wondering why I'm talking to myself.

"I spoke to Tom Maniscalco," Victor said when his overprotective secretary put me through to him. "He says he has nothing to say to you, and that any contact should be through his attorney."

"Emmett Swindell? I've talked to him already. The conversation won't go into the highlight film."

"I can't blame Tom, Milan, and being a father you shouldn't either. Tom certainly doesn't relish word of the incident with his daughter floating around town to fuel the gossip mills. And he doesn't see the point of talking about it anymore."

"He may not see the point, but there's been a murder."

"And the police are on the job. The man doesn't want people pointing their fingers at his little girl. Why don't you leave it at that?"

"I told you yesterday," I said. "I've got the guilts. I walked out on the kid and then someone killed him. If nothing else, I owe him a couple of days of my time."

He waited a beat and then said, "I don't think you do."

"Are you trying to tell me something?"

"I just don't think you have a responsibility here, that's all."

"And you'd prefer that I drop it?"

I passed by the Scranton Road Bridge and lost him for a moment to interference and static. Once I had a clear line again, I said, "What?"

"You're on a car phone?"

"Yes."

"Annoying damn things. I said that if you kept your distance from Tom Maniscalco it would make my life easier."

"Why?"

"Because he's a leading light in the Italian community, and because now he knows I know you. It would save everyone a lot of embarrassment if you just went away quietly on this one."

Various scenarios played out in my mind. After a moment I picked one and ran with it.

"Let me ramble for a bit, Victor, and see how I do. Maniscalco called you up after Darren got killed and asked if you could get him out of this business clean, without his daughter's name being disgraced. And he probably gave you something to seal the bargain. Am I right?"

He didn't answer, and I thought for a moment my car phone had conked out again. I said, "Victor?"

"I'm here."

"Am I right? He's giving you a new living room suite?"

"I can buy my own furniture, Milan. As a matter of fact, I did buy some from Maniscalco recently, a really exquisite dining room set. Cost me a fortune."

"So what do you get out of this, Victor?"

He was a long while answering. "Let's just say future considerations. You know, the proverbial player-to-be-named-later."

I thought about it for a while. To Victor Gaimari, future considerations might mean all sorts of things. I cleared my throat. "What if I tell you I can't back off?"

"I can't make you. Or let's say I'm not *going* to make you," he added with uncomfortable emphasis. "You're one stubborn Slovenian son of a bitch, and when you get something between your teeth you hang on like a snapping turtle."

I pulled into my office parking lot and sat there in the Sunbird with the motor still running while I finished the call.

"Think about this too," Victor said. "Several times over the last few years you've come to me when you ran into a wall and needed the kind of information I can get my hands on. I've never said no you to, have I?"

"You've been a prince."

"And yet you tell me no all the time. Why is that?"

"Because I'm one stubborn Slovenian son of a bitch."

I said good-bye, punched the hang-up button on the cellular and turned off the ignition, but I didn't get out of the car right away; it was as good a place to think as any. So Tom Maniscalco wanted his connection with Darren Anderson—or rather his daughter Bethany's—kept quiet, whether for the girl's sake or for the sake of his own image, and he was anxious enough about it to ask the boys on Murray Hill for a favor.

And Maniscalco had to know that with Victor and his uncle, a favor asked is a favor owed.

I got out of the car, went inside, and climbed the stairs to the office, mulling it over.

I'd try to keep a lid on Bethany's little tryst with Darren; she was, after all, hardly more than a child. But this was a murder case, and sometimes innocent people have to take their lumps too.

Of course, in this instance, innocence was a relative thing.

Once upstairs, I pulled out my telephone directory and looked up Alan Braxton. I was in luck. There was a listing, with an address on the west side's Gold Coast, in one of the glittering high-rise buildings that hug the shoreline and keep the rest of us from being able to see Lake Erie. He probably had a one-eighty-degree view of the water and the downtown skyline through wraparound glass doors and windows, a sound system that cost a week's salary, and a TV set the size of one of the screens at the Cedar Lee Theater. And I was willing to bet he drove either a late-model Beemer or a Porsche.

I dialed his number and got his machine.

"This is Alan Braxton," his recorded voice said. "I can't take your call right now." I tried to remember the voice I'd heard two weeks earlier at the White Magnolia, but he'd only said a few words that evening, and they'd been angry ones. At the time I hadn't known there would be a quiz.

"Please leave a message and I'll call you back," the canned voice continued. "During the day, I can be reached at my office," and he gave a number that I knew to have a west side exchange.

I dialed it. "Braxton Software Systems," a nasal female voice answered.

So he owns his own company, I thought. That's how he can afford to eat at the White Magnolia. "Is Mr. Braxton in?"

"Is that Mr. Nathan Braxton or Mr. Alan Braxton?"

I revised my estimate quickly; probably his father's company. Not many people Alan Braxton's age are named Nathan anymore.

"Alan."

"I'm sorry, he's out at a meeting this afternoon. Would you like his voice mail, or do you want to speak to his secretary?"

"His secretary, please."

She put me on hold. Annoying prepackaged music poured from the receiver, a lush orchestra playing a syrupy arrangement of retro rock: Devo With Strings, or some such.

After a minute the music mercifully stopped. "Alan Braxton's office," a different woman's voice said. "This is Dierdre. How may I help you?"

Dierdre.

At least now I knew I had the right Alan Braxton.

I hung up.

At about six o'clock I finally got through to Sidney Friedman. He informed me that he didn't have time to talk to me because it was still midafternoon in Los Angeles and he "had calls in" to four different agents and needed to keep the line clear. Besides, he was sore at me. I know that because he told me so.

"Nobody walks off one of my pictures," he told me severely. "It's unprofessional."

I didn't bother reminding him that I wasn't an actor, and that I hadn't really been "on" the picture, because he was right—I had indeed behaved in an unprofessional manner, letting my emotions override both my business ethics and my sense of responsibility. I didn't tell him that either, though, nor of the guilt that nagged at my conscience.

I just apologized several times and offered to buy him a drink at the Velvet Tango Room later in the evening. He was thrilled to death; after all, he was the producer, and usually he bought the drinks.

I went home, watched the news, thawed some pork chops in the microwave and baked them in the oven with a sage and bread crumb coating, ate, and read awhile. I then put on my most expensive Ralph Lauren sweater and headed downtown again.

The Velvet Tango Room is as elegant as its name. It glitters like a diamond in a dumpster on the west side of the river, two blocks from the West Side Market in a dusty working-class neighborhood, its purplish neon sign cutting through the darkness, making the battered street look like an Edward Hopper painting. Inside it's long and narrow, the backbar is polished walnut, the lighting is subtle and indirect, and over the sound system came tangos from the forties and fifties and tunes like Gogi Grant's "The Wayward Wind." Order and a vibrant redheaded bartender named Melanie will never again forget what you drink. Up three steps in the cozy back room a sign on a gleaming black grand piano reads PLEASE ASK THE BARTENDER BEFORE PLAYING THE PIANO. NEVER PLAY ANYTHING FROM *CATS*. NEVER EVER.

My kind of joint.

Paulius, the owner, runs the place just the way he wants to, which gives it its unique character. On baseball nights, he tunes the TV above the bar to the ball game in black and white and pretends it's 1948, the Indians' world championship year. It's one of Cleveland's great bars.

Sidney Friedman and I sat at a table halfway toward the back. I asked for a beer and he ordered a pepper Absolut on the rocks. The things people will actually drink.

Sidney was still smarting over my defection, and he took every opportunity to remind me. "I don't know why I'm even talking to you," he said after our drinks arrived. "I've got enough to think about, what with having to find an actor to replace Darren Anderson and get him here by Monday or Tuesday. I don't have time for traitors."

In my mind, quitting my job on his movie didn't exactly make me Winthrop Ames, but Sidney was prone to hyperbole. "I'm trying to make amends, Sidney," I said. "Help me out."

"How?"

"By telling me everything you can remember about what happened when Darren Anderson was on the set. Who he interacted with, who he didn't. Every argument he had with anyone, anything that wasn't strictly ordinary."

Sidney Friedman looked tired, beaten down. "There's no such thing as ordinary on a shoot. Everything is larger than life."

"Including the egos?"

He regarded me narrowly. "If you don't have an ego, you don't belong in the picture business."

"I'm beginning to realize that," I said. "Look, I know you're mad at me. You have a right, I guess—but I had a right to walk out, too, because you didn't exactly level with me. If I'd known what I was dealing with, if you'd told me about Darren's penchant for adolescent girls, maybe I would have seen this thing with Bethany Maniscalco coming. And then I would have been there when Darren needed me."

He stretched his neck, "Do I hear the sound of mea culpa across the land?" he asked with obvious satisfaction. I itched to slap the smug smile off his face.

"How many times do you want me to apologize?"

"Frankly, I don't give a shit one way or the other," he said, suddenly weary again. "I've got more on my mind right now than your guilt, okay?"

"So help me out," I said.

A silver-haired man in a Coogi sweater and a young woman in a black and red minidress got up from the bar and went into the back room. The man sat down at the piano and started to play Rodgers and Hammerstein's "It Might as Well Be Spring" easily and fluidly.

"What's in it for me?" Sidney said. "In my business, the question you always have to ask is what's in it for me? Besides this drink, I mean? The way I see it, you're nothing to me but more aggravation."

"How do you figure?"

"If I help you—if I tell you about everyone on the shoot who had a beef with Darren, and it turns out one of them actually killed him—I'm screwed, blewed and tattooed. The investors will pull out, the distributor will tear up the contracts, this picture will fall through the cracks, and I might never work again, because everyone in the business will know that I hired a murderer. I can't risk that." He shook his head sorrowfully. "If I don't produce pictures, what the hell am I going to do? I don't know how to do anything else."

At least someone else was having a career crisis too. "What if you give me some cooperation and I prove that it wasn't somebody working on the picture? Wouldn't that be a good thing?"

He wrestled with that one for a while. "Bottom line," he demanded.

"If I can put the whole crew in the clear, you'll be in a good bargaining position with your investors."

He stroked his chin thoughtfully, grooming a nonexistent beard, the way a bad actor does when he wants to indicate that the character is thinking. "What's this going to cost me?"

"Cost you?"

"Yeah. What do *you* get out of this? Back on the payroll? I don't have anything in the budget for you anymore, and I'm losing money every day we're not rolling. As it is, we'll have to reshoot about eight days' worth with the new actor."

"One dollar," I said. "Will that break your budget? Give me a dollar, and then I'm officially working for you again."

"You're kidding, right?" he said. "A dollar?" He couldn't have looked more surprised and pleased if he'd discovered a fragment of the true cross on the bargain table at K Mart.

"I'll expect you to cover my expenses, though," I added.

He hesitated for a moment, then put out his hand. "Deal," he said. "If you keep the expenses down."

"Deal."

"You're a schmuck," he said, releasing my hand with a nasty laugh. "I would've put you back on salary if you'd pushed."

"It isn't about money with me, Sidney. I feel pretty bad about what happened to the kid."

"It's about money with everybody."

"Not with me."

"Whatever floats your boat." The ice cubes in his glass clinked as he swirled his drink around. He sipped at the pepper vodka, then gasping, he set the glass down and wiped his mouth. "That stuff packs a wallop."

I took out my notebook. "Did you know someone tried to burn his house down in Los Angeles?"

He nodded. "Sure. It made the L.A. *Times*. Don't even bother worrying about that. Almost every big star has had some sort of problem with stalkers and obsessed fans. The bigger the name, the more fruitcakes they attract. It didn't used to be that way, but the world has changed. Everybody's just that far away from the rubber room. The fire business was a while ago. When Darren was working on somebody else's picture."

"You might have told me about it."

"Why? You think the guy was going to come all the way to Cleveland and try it again?"

"Stranger things have happened. Did Darren have an agent?" I asked, shifting gears. "A publicist? A manager?"

"All of the above," he said. "And a private secretary, an assistant, and a housekeeper. And a personal trainer too. But they were all more than two thousand miles from here when he got shot. Besides, what would they want to kill him for? He paid their salaries. He was their cash cow. His agent stood to make eight hundred grand on this picture alone."

"Then that leaves us with the people who were here in Cleveland working with him."

"If you say so." He looked at his wristwatch. "So talk to me."

"You're the one that needs to do the talking."

"Right, right. Okay, let me think." He ran his finger around the rim of his glass. "I don't think Darren had any real enemies on the set, but he didn't have any friends, either, if you know what I'm saying. He was the star, he didn't bother being nice to the crew. He hit on almost every woman on the shoot, but I don't think his heart was in it. It was just the thrill of the chase." He caressed his glass with the ends of his fingers. "He wasn't pleasant to work with, because he knew that he held all the cards, that we were only making the picture because of him. A lot of big stars are like that. Hungry for power."

A thought struck him and he chuckled. "Like when you eat German food, half an hour later you're hungry for power."

I smiled politely.

He looked affronted. "When you eat French food, half an hour later you're rude."

I changed the subject to avert any more attempts at ethnic food humor. "What about Boyce Cort?"

"Ah," Sidney said. "Our resident genius. Boyce fancies himself an auteur, you know. And I don't think Darren was giving him the kind of performance he wanted. It wasn't the kid's fault. He doesn't—didn't—have the tools to be a really good actor. Boyce was pretty cutting sometimes." He inclined his head toward me, as if imparting a confidence. "PMS, you know." He raised a hand. "He wasn't *too* cutting. He knew that one word from Darren and he'd be out on his ass, back doing independent features with a Kodak Instamatic. But he's the kind of director who thinks that if he gives an actor a lot of shit he can get more out of him than might actually be there. The Otto Preminger syndrome."

"Is that the only reason Cort was in his face?"

His grin was smarmy. "You mean because he's a fag? Sure,

Boyce was hot for him. At first. Straight women weren't the only ones that thought Darren was a sex symbol. But Boyce wasn't in love with him or anything. It was just lust, and like most lust, it finally went away. Especially after Boyce got to know him. It's tough to sustain an erection for somebody you can't stand."

"Boyce couldn't stand him?"

"Boyce can't stand me, either. He's a cranky old queen, he can't stand a lot of people. That doesn't mean he killed him."

"All right," I said. "Who else couldn't stand Darren? In particular?"

He threw up his hands. "Jesus, I don't know. I wasn't on the set that much. And when I was I had other things to worry about."

"You don't care whether your crew is happy?"

"They're happy when they cash my checks," he said. "That's all I care about." He nipped at the vodka again, and coughed. "Maybe you ought to talk to Suzi Flores."

"Who's she?"

"The love interest. In the picture, I mean. Well, kind of the love interest. This is a guy picture—lots of action. But you gotta have good-looking broads around, too."

"What about Suzi Flores?"

He did something funny with one corner of his mouth. "She got pissed at him because when they shot their love scene he kept feeling her up out of camera range. Slipping her the tongue."

The piano player in the back room segued into a Cole Porter medley. The woman with him looked bored but was smiling gamely. At her age, she probably thought the Beatles were prehistoric, never mind Cole Porter.

"That's illegal these days, Sidney. It's called sexual harassment."

"Yeah, right. Tell it to the marines. Some spic cunt nobody's ever heard of like Suzi Flores finally gets a big break playing opposite Darren Anderson, she's not going to make a stink just because he gooses her a few times. See if she ever get cast again if she does."

Spic cunt. Fag. Broad. Sidney Friedman was nothing if not a marvel of consistency.

"It blows, but it's reality," he went on. "You gotta operate within reality or you're gonna get eaten alive."

"From what I've seen, you Hollywood people wouldn't recognize reality if it jumped up and bit you in the ass."

Sidney Friedman looked hurt. "Don't give me attitude about Hollywood, all right? I hate that. We're all just working stiffs, trying to make a living."

I clicked out the point of my pen. "Where can I find Suzi Flores?"

He put his fingertips to his forehead. "Let me see—not the Renaissance, not the Ritz Carlton . . . " He tiddled his fingers. "The Marriott. I think. Yeah, that's where we put her, the Marriott. Downtown."

"Tell her I'm going to call her, all right?" I said, writing it down. "Now, who else?"

He waved his hands, drawing them toward himself as though trying to sniff the aroma from a big pot of pasta sauce. "I don't know. You kind of took me by surprise here. Call me tomorrow afternoon, okay? After I've had some time to think." He belted down the rest of his drink, which made his eyes water.

"Okay, Sidney." I shut my notebook and put it in my breast pocket. "It's your dollar."

"Yeah, right. We should take care of that now, shouldn't we? Make it official." He dug into his pocket and came out with a roll of cash. Thumbing through it quickly, he looked up at me.

"Have you got change for a five?" he asked.

CHAPTER TEN

The next morning was jump-started by a phone call from a woman named Sherry Lipton, who informed me with her first breath that she was Darren Anderson's press agent.

"I got into town late last night," she said. "This whole thing is a fucking mess."

"It's tragic," I said.

"Look, I talked with Sidney this morning, and he said you were still on the payroll, investigating. I'm buried alive with all this crap, so I can't take a meeting with you, but I thought we should touch base so we can get the rules straight." She spoke loudly and rapidly, as if the meter was running.

"Rules?"

"First thing is, nobody talks to the media but me. Any reporters try getting in touch with you, refer them to me. I'm at the Ritz-Carlton."

"Why would the press want to talk to me?"

"Because this is the hottest story going," she said. "And you're involved."

"Just around the edges."

"It doesn't matter. I know these people. They're bottom feeders. And it's important we're all on the same page."

"What page is that, Ms. Lipton?"

"Sherry."

Ah yes, I forgot. First names only. "Sherry," I said dutifully.

"The sex thing," she rapped out. "With the kid. Nobody needs to know about that, all right? Not your wife, not your mother, not your best friend. And certainly not the press. Not a fucking whisper. Are we clear on that?" She rushed on, not waiting for an answer. "And not the marijuana stuff, either. In fact, don't even tell anyone that he drank. At all. Okay?"

"Okay," I said.

"It's important we protect Darren's name, all right?"

"Fine," I said. "Except I can't see what you're worried about. The kid is dead, after all."

"Are you serious? Darren Anderson is a multimillion dollar property, dead or alive. Posters, T-shirts, buttons, the whole enchilada. There's a fortune to be made here."

"Excuse me, but you don't have a client anymore, do you?"

"Hell yes, I do. I still represent his estate."

"He left a will?"

There was a brief pause. "I don't know. But until I hear different, I'm still Darren's publicist."

Of course, I thought. One of "Darren Anderson's people."

"So we understand each other?" she said. "No talking to the media, and no telling tales out of school. And if one of the tabloids offers you money to spill your guts to them, check with me first. Maybe we can match their offer—or better it. Okay?"

I was going to tell her okay again, but she didn't give me the chance. "Don't forget, I'm at the Ritz-Carlton if you need me. Gotta run. Toodles."

By the time I realized she wasn't on the line anymore, she was probably dialing someone else's number.

Toodles.

Braxton Software Systems occupied the standard industrial cube, an ugly, flat-roofed one-story building of sand-colored brick on Detroit Road in Westlake, the next suburb in from Bay Village, where Darren Anderson was killed. Probably built in the early eighties, the structure was strictly utilitarian; there were no windows in front, and on the roof an air-conditioning unit groaned noisily. The place had all the charm of a dead squirrel in the road.

I had called early that morning to find out whether Alan Braxton would be in. At first I'd been disappointed to hear he'd be out of town for the rest of the week, but when the receptionist once more asked me if I'd like to speak with his secretary, I decided that might be a better way to go anyway.

When I told Dierdre who I was and what I wanted, naturally she was not anxious to see me. As a matter of fact, she'd refused at first, but I bullied her into it.

"If I can't talk to you," I'd said to her, "I'll have to discuss it with Mr. Braxton when he gets back. I don't think either of us wants that, do we?"

There was such a long silence on the line that I thought she'd hung up on me. Finally she sighed heavily. "That's lousy."

"I'm sorry. But I really do need a few minutes of your time."

"All right, then. When do you want to come out?" she asked, reluctance dripping from every syllable.

She was right, it was lousy. Everything about this Darren Anderson business was lousy. But the death of a young man—even a young man who wasn't exactly a saint—was the lousiest thing of all.

I pulled my car into a visitor's space in the lot and went inside. It was a stuffy scorcher of a morning, and I'd dressed in a lightweight beige suit for my visit to the wonderful world of software. My dark brown tie—one of my collection of too-wide neckwear that every woman I've ever gone out with deplored as being out of fashion—felt constrictive in the heat. I ran a finger under my collar. It was going to be a long day; I had a dinner appointment for the evening, and lots of things to do in between.

The receptionist let Dierdre know I'd arrived, and she met me in the waiting room.

Dierdre O'Malley was wearing a short beige skirt and a chocolate-colored blouse with a tan scarf around her neck, and wire-rimmed glasses with small lenses that unfortunately emphasized a wide, flat face. She wasn't wearing much makeup; she looked even younger and not nearly as attractive as she had that night at the White Magnolia. She constantly licked her lips, but whether it was habitual or caused by my unexpected and unwelcome presence in her life I didn't know. Behind the glasses her green eyes were bloodshot and haunted-looking. She stared hard at my business card, then tucked it into her skirt pocket.

"We can use Alan's office," she said with a nervous look at the openly curious receptionist, and led me back through a long, undecorated corridor, her practical one-inch heels tapping noisily on the polished linoleum floor.

Alan Braxton's office was curiously lacking in personality, considering that the name of its occupant was on the front door of the business. The walls were bare save for a color photograph of the Flats taken during the Bicentennial festivities, with the bridges lit up, and a diploma from Baldwin-Wallace College. A cluster of racquetball trophies sat on a shelf behind the executive desk. But the office was in the rear of the building and at least had a window, which looked out on a stand of trees and a sprawl of undistinguished tract homes beyond.

Dierdre O'Malley didn't sit down in either of the two chairs that faced each other obliquely in front of the desk, and she didn't invite me to. She closed the door behind her and turned to face me, her arms crossed defensively over her breasts. "So what is this, a shakedown? You picked the wrong cookie—I'm a clerical worker. I don't have four figures in my bank account."

"A shakedown? Where'd you hear that expression?"

"I'm an Irish kid from the west side," she said. "I've heard almost everything. How did you find me?"

"It's my business to find people."

She hunched her shoulders. "I wish you hadn't."

"I'm sorry I sounded threatening over the phone, Dierdre. It's the only way I could get you to talk to me. All I want from you is a little information. I'm a licensed investigator, not a blackmailer."

"This is an invasion of my privacy."

"I apologize for it," I said. "But I'm sure you know that Darren Anderson was murdered a few days ago."

She just shuddered.

"You were seeing him over the past two weeks?"

"No!" The denial was loud and sharp, like a pistol shot.

"But you did spend some time with him, later that night we saw you in the White Magnolia?"

"You knew that or you wouldn't have called me." She quivered with humiliation. "This is so embarrassing."

"You only saw him that one time?"

She nodded, unshed tears waiting behind her eyes. She uncrossed her arms and clasped her hands together in front of her, almost wringing them. "I called him twice after that, but he wasn't—he couldn't see me. He said he was too busy." Her mouth twisted bitterly.

"You're Alan Braxton's secretary?"

She dipped her head, which I took for a yes.

"And you're also dating him?"

She blinked rapidly. "That's none of your business."

"Sure it is."

"Why?"

"Because if you are, Alan Braxton would certainly have a motive to kill Darren Anderson, wouldn't he?"

Her lips whitened around the edges. "That's ridiculous!"

"As far as that goes, you had a pretty good motive yourself."

Her eyes opened wide and she staggered backward a few steps.

"He slept with you and then dumped you," I continued. "A woman scorned and all that . . . "

"No! It wasn't like that!"

"Tell me what it *was* like, then."

She began pacing in front of me, her arms crossed in front of her again, the necessity of telling me warring with her shame. "It was—a one-night stand. I didn't expect anything else, really. I had no illusions. I mean, how could it come to anything? Look who he was, look who I am. Besides . . . "

She sank into one of the chairs.

"Besides?" I prompted.

After a moment she said, "Alan and I are—we're supposed to get married at Christmas."

"Oh."

Neither of us spoke for almost a minute. She was ashamed and I was embarrassed for her. She slumped in the chair, her eyes half-closed. "You probably think I'm a slut."

"No I don't," I assured her. "We all make mistakes. Sometimes things work out okay, sometimes they don't."

"This sure didn't," she said bitterly.

"Mind if I ask you a personal question?"

"Don't bother. I've asked it of myself a hundred times. Why did I call Darren Anderson? Why did I go out there and spend the night with him?"

I nodded.

"Because I'm only twenty-three years old," she rasped, "and dumb enough to think that going to bed with a movie star would be a big deal. Something I'd remember for the rest of my life." Her stifled sob turned into a hiccup. "I'll remember it, all right. I've already been to confession, but the penance didn't make me feel any better about myself."

I put my hands in my pockets. I didn't know what else to do with them. "Does Alan know?" I asked her.

"God, I hope not." She sat up a little straighter and shook her head. "We had a fight that night—about my flirting with Darren in the restaurant. He gets furious if I even look at another man.

I think he'd be a lot happier if I walked around in a veil, like women do in Iran." She lowered her eyes. "But he doesn't know—the rest of it."

"Are you sure?"

"As sure as I can be."

"What does that mean?"

She examined a red fingernail. "Alan is very jealous. Possessive. He's almost irrational sometimes. Once, about six months ago . . . " She put her fist to her mouth. "He actually had me followed," she said against her knuckles; I could hardly hear her.

"Followed? Who by?"

Her eyes narrowed in disgust, and she brought her hand down. "Somebody like you. A private investigator," she said, making it sound obscene. She took my card out of her pocket and threw it on the desk.

"Did he have a reason?"

She turned her face away from me.

I sat down in one of the other chairs, tired of waiting to be asked. "Are you sure you're ready to get married, Dierdre?"

"Is anybody ever really sure?" She swiveled the chair around and stared out the window, at the tract homes she probably thought were part of her destiny. "My father worked on the railroad for thirty years," she said. "I went to secretarial school right out of high school, and my parents had to scrape for *that*. Guys I dated took me to the movies, took me bowling, took me for dinner in cheap taverns on the west side where the house specialty was hot wings, and the Irish Rovers were always on the jukebox and pro wrestling was on the TV. When I started working here and Alan asked me out, it was like a dream coming true or something." She turned back to look at me. "I'll never have a better chance than Alan."

I waited while she dug a tissue out of the pocket of her skirt and blew her nose. "He's a good guy, basically," she went on. "Just not very exciting. I sometimes feel, I don't know. Stifled, when

I'm with him. And when I'm not, when he leaves or when I leave, it's almost like—freedom." Her sigh was ragged. "So when one of the biggest movie stars in the world slipped me his phone number, it was . . . "

"Last chance for a little excitement?" I suggested.

"Something like that." Her eyes met mine, pleading. "You're not going to tell Alan, are you?"

"No, I won't tell him," I said. "But the police are going to have to know eventually, and he might find out."

"No!" she said, her face contorted with real panic. "It could ruin everything for me."

"This has gone beyond you and Alan, Dierdre."

She clenched her fists and pounded them on her thighs. "How was I supposed to know Darren was going to get himself killed?" She hugged herself. "God, that's so horrible just to think that a man I actually made love with . . . "

The door to the office opened and a tall, gray-haired man came into the room and then stopped, frowning. "Dierdre?" he said severely.

Nathan Braxton's resemblance to his son was unmistakable— the same lean frame, the same high forehead, even the same outmoded glasses—but Nathan seemed somehow more vital. His aggressive floral tie was loosely knotted beneath the collar of a white shirt, the sleeves of which were rolled up to display his tanned, hairy arms. He was one of those people you'd somehow know was a boss even if you ran into him on the golf course or in the supermarket or draped in a towel in the health club sauna.

Dierdre stiffened, her eyes darting from him to me. Once more she licked her lips. "Oh, Mr. Braxton," she said. "This is . . . "

"Milan Jacovich." I stood up to shake hands.

"How do you do?" he said. He barely moved his mouth when he spoke. His grip was tentative, noncommittal. He looked a question at Dierdre, and her eyes met mine imploringly.

"I'm an old friend of the family," I told him. "I live on the east side, so I rarely get over here to Westlake, and since I was passing right by, I just dropped in to say hello."

"He and my dad have bowled together for years," Dierdre added quickly, and her glance at me was full of gratitude. I was less grateful to be relegated to her father's crowd.

"I see," Nathan Braxton said, as if he didn't. "Well, Dierdre, I need you to make some calls for me."

"I was just leaving anyway," I said, going to the door. "Say hi to your dad for me, Dierdre. Nice meeting you, Mr. Braxton."

He gave me a pompous nod and I went out, closing the door behind me.

As I crossed the lot to my car, I thought long and hard about Alan Braxton. A jealous, controlling man who constantly suspected his fiancée of cheating—for good reason, admittedly, but a little paranoid just the same. I'd seen his temper flare at the White Magnolia; maybe it had smoldered for a couple of weeks, finally catching fire again. Dierdre had said he didn't know of her fling with Darren Anderson, but a man who had employed private detectives before might even have followed her himself.

As for Dierdre O'Malley—if anyone found out about her one wild night with Darren, it would certainly threaten her plans to become Mrs. Alan Braxton, with the attendant lovely home, elegant dinners out, and social standing, heady wine for a working-class vocational school graduate. She had to be a little relieved that Darren was no longer around to tell anyone about it.

I wasn't crossing her off my list, either.

I headed back east on I-90, but just before it reached downtown I turned south on I-71, bound for Strongsville.

Where Tom and Alison and Bethany Maniscalco lived.

Strongsville is on the mostly white, mostly upper-middle-class south side, full of new housing tracts and condos, with well-tended lawns in front and above-ground swimming pools in the back yards of the recent escapees from the city and its near suburbs.

It was just past two o'clock when I pulled into the driveway of the Maniscalco's Greek revival house in an expensive tract just off Albion Road. The front walk was flanked by perfectly trimmed box hedges, and on either side of it a flowering dogwood neatly encircled by bricks stood precisely in the center of its respective half of the lawn. Two rows of hosta flourished in front of the house. The driveway curved around the back, so I couldn't see whether there were any cars in the garage, but I assumed Tom was not home, this being a workday, and that Bethany was at school.

I rang the doorbell; I could hear it bonging inside like Big Ben, low, rich, powerful tones. I waited thirty seconds or so, then rang it again.

The look Alison Maniscalco gave me when she finally opened the door was one of distinct displeasure. I think she'd been expecting someone else. I'd caught her on the way to or from a tennis game; my money was on the former, because there wasn't a wrinkle or a drop of sweat on her tennis outfit. She was decked out in a white Izod tennis shirt and a short white pleated skirt, and there were little puffy pink balls on the toes of her shoes, which matched the ones on her socks. A green sun visor completed the ensemble.

Her face grew stiff and rigid. "You're that bodyguard," she said, and the curl of her lip left no doubt as to what she thought of bodyguards in general and of me in particular.

"Actually, I'm a private investigator, Mrs. Maniscalco." I gave her a business card, which she took but did not deign to look at. "I wonder if you could spare a few minutes?"

"No, I don't think so. My husband would be very angry if he knew you were here."

"I'm sure he would be—but the anger would be misplaced. I know how upset you both are about what happened, and that you're anxious that it doesn't become public knowledge. If I have enough facts in my pocket, I might be able to make sure it doesn't. Just give me ten minutes."

She consulted her watch. The band was heavy roped gold. "Not a second more," she said. "I have a court reserved in half an hour."

I followed her inside. The furniture was all obviously pricey—undoubtedly from Home Works—and so new it gave the impression that this was a model home, nobody really lived here. The gleaming, deep red mahogany dining room table and chairs, and the matching breakfront and highboy, belonged in a stately mansion more than an expensive tract home.

My hostess led me into the two-story living room, and we sat across from each other at a large game table by the window, looking out at a broad expanse of back yard of a chemically enhanced green. A stone fish pond with a noisily burbling fountain broke the symmetry of the lawn; I figured it was occupied by koi carp or some other exotic fish that probably wouldn't survive an Ohio winter, but from where I sat I couldn't tell.

"You worked for that degenerate," she said accusingly.

"No, I worked for the degenerate's boss. It was my job to try and keep Darren Anderson out of trouble."

This time her lip curled into a bona fide sneer. "You mustn't be very good at your job, then, or you would have kept him from . . . from raping my little girl."

Although Alison Maniscalco was an attractive woman about my age, she hadn't much appealed to me in her little black velvet number at the benefit dinner, and less so now that she was snarling at me across the table like a captive wolverine.

She did, however, have a point. "I'm terribly sorry that he took advantage of Bethany that way, Mrs. Maniscalco. The moment I found out about it, I quit my job."

"Noble, huh?"

At least not cynical, I thought. "I just draw a personal line for myself between what's acceptable and what isn't."

"Then what are you doing here now?"

I wanted a cigarette badly, but didn't see an ashtray in sight; the Maniscalcos were probably the kind of people who treated cigarette smokers like hardened criminals. "The parameters have changed since Darren's death."

"Parameters . . . " Her hands were flat on the tabletop, fingers splayed. The diamond on her combination wedding-engagement ring was half the size of a golf ball.

"Have the police talked to you and your husband?"

"Yes. And I'll tell you exactly what we told them. Tom was at a Rotary meeting Monday night."

"Where?"

"Excuse me?"

"Where was the meeting?"

Her eyelids fluttered. "Right here in Strongsville."

"What time did he get home?"

"I don't know."

"You don't?"

She looked away, her face losing a little of its summer color. "I wasn't here when he got back. I was out for dinner with a friend."

"Did anyone at the restaurant see you? Can they corroborate your story?"

She closed her splayed fingers into fists, and a crimson flush rose beneath her tan. "I have no idea."

Unlikely, I thought, that anyone on the wait staff of a restaurant would forget someone who looked like Alison Maniscalco. I'd have bet the dollar Sidney Friedman gave me for a retainer that she hadn't been out to dinner at all. I remembered Victor Gaimari's attentions to her at the benefit on Friday night and wondered whether he moved as fast as Darren Anderson had moved on Bethany.

"And where was Bethany?"

Her eyes widened, showing white all around the pupils. "Here," she said. "She was grounded."

"And the first night of her grounding you both went off and left her?"

"We have lives, too, Mr. Jacovich. Surely you don't suspect I had anything to do with what happened to the actor? Or that Tom did?"

I remembered Peter Sellers as Inspector Clouseau saying, with great comic effect, "I suspect everyone. And I suspect no one." Actually that line was said first by Dana Andrews as the cop in the classic mystery film *Laura,* but nobody laughed at it then.

"I'm just trying to get everything straight in my mind," I told her.

"Why? You have no official status, do you?" She finally looked at my card. "Security. Private Investigations." She flicked it across the table toward me. "You're not with the police. I don't have to talk to you at all."

"No," I admitted. "You don't. But Darren Anderson is dead. And both you and your husband have a pretty good motive for wanting him that way."

Her features, not soft at the best of times, hardened into a plaster life mask. "You'll hear from our attorney about that."

"Don't kid yourself, Mrs. Maniscalco. On Monday morning you went to the police and accused Darren Anderson of statutory rape. On Monday night someone shot him. Do you think the police are too stupid to put those two things together and start wondering?"

The next ten seconds of silence were a little eternity, one of those empty moments in your life you realize with sadness that you can never get back.

"Your husband's Rotary meeting couldn't have gone on past eleven o'clock," I continued. "It probably broke up earlier than that, the next day being a workday. Since you weren't here when he got home, you have no idea whether he had the time to drive up to Bay Village."

"He wouldn't . . . "

"He might. Hell, if it was my daughter, I might think about it myself. And as for you, I presume your friend can vouch for your whereabouts?"

A little gasp escaped from her throat.

"Or maybe you don't want anyone to know who that friend was?"

It took a conscious act of will for her to unknot her fists. She began massaging her hands as if she was rubbing in moisturizing lotion. "You're putting me in a very awkward position, Mr. Jacovich." She pronounced my name with a hard *J*. I didn't correct her.

"Maybe we can keep this between the two of us." I took out my notebook and pen. "Maybe if you tell me exactly what happened when Bethany came home Sunday evening . . . "

"Are you threatening me?" she hissed.

"Not at all," I said, aware that I was doing just that.

"I don't respond well to threats, and neither does my husband."

"I don't want money. I want information."

She stood up, still rubbing her hands, and walked across the room to the empty fireplace. "Frankly, I don't see the necessity."

"The necessity is that even though Darren Anderson's behavior toward your daughter was unconscionable, immoral, illegal, and just plain lousy, he didn't deserve to be murdered. When I found out what happened between him and Bethany, I told him what I thought of him and walked out. If I hadn't, he might still be alive. I think I owe it to his memory to help."

"You may owe it to him," she said, "but Tom and I don't owe him a goddamn thing except our contempt."

"Fine," I said. "And the police know that too, which is what's putting you both in a very bright spotlight right now. Maybe I can get you out of it. But you've got to talk to me."

She sat down in a leather club chair near the fireplace and crossed her legs, the pink balls on her shoe and sock bobbing.

"What do you want to know?" she said.

"First, tell me about Sunday."

"The police know all of this."

The balls bobbed some more as she swung her tanned leg. They were mesmerizing; it took a conscious act of will to look anywhere else. "Tell me," I said, "and then I'll know too."

She blinked away her irritation. "It was fairly simple. Bethany lied to us. She told us she was going to spend Sunday with a girlfriend and have dinner at her house. She left here just before ten."

"How?"

"What do you mean, how?"

"On foot, by car, by taxi?"

"Oh. She was walking. Lavonna only lives about three blocks away."

"What did she say they were going to do?"

"She didn't. Girls Bethany's age don't like being questioned."

I nodded.

"At about seven I called there to talk to her. Mrs. Kinsley, Lavonna's mother, told me they hadn't been together all day." The legs were uncrossed and recrossed, and Alison Maniscalco drummed a tattoo on her bare knee, the pressure from her fingers leaving temporary little white spots in the tan. Her voice got tight and strained. "Bethany didn't come home until ten o'clock that night, and when she did there were grass stains on her shorts and all over the back of her blouse. Tom and I asked her where she'd been and why she'd lied about being with Lavonna, and she got angry and ran upstairs and slammed into her room."

"Teenagers," I said sympathetically, trying to ease the moment.

She ducked her head in agreement. "My husband is Italian," she said, "with all the temper and volatility that goes with it. He doesn't take slammed doors lightly. We went up after her. It took us about twenty minutes to get her to admit she'd been with— that actor." She blinked her eyes again, as if trying to blink away the dirty pictures inside her head. "Apparently they'd set up the date at the benefit two nights before. The actor picked her up in his car a few blocks away."

It occurred to me that not once had Mrs. Maniscalco used Darren Anderson's name. "How can you be sure they were intimate?"

Her fingers ceased their drumming. She raised her eyes to mine, looking suddenly much older. Older than God, as a matter of fact. "Bethany has been sexually active for more than a year," she said.

I suppose I looked shocked. I shouldn't have been. Kids today grow up a lot faster than we did. Still, fifteen years old— fourteen, when she started. Jesus.

"I know, I know," Alison Maniscalco said, even though I hadn't offered any comment or criticism. "But what can a parent do? We can't just keep her chained to the wall until she's eighteen."

It didn't sound like such a bad idea to me. "But you don't have any proof that they actually did anything?"

"She told us they did. After we questioned her about it. She threw it in our faces. Like she was proud of it. Rutting on the grass in broad daylight like a couple of animals . . . "

I scribbled in my notebook. "What happened then?"

"When?"

"When Bethany admitted she and Darren Anderson had made love?"

"Made love? Is that what you call it?"

"Call it what you like," I said.

She shook herself like a Labrador retriever that had just

come out of the water. "We told Bethany she was grounded until further notice." She gazed at the cathedral ceiling. "I may never let her out of the house again."

"And after that?"

She closed her eyes, remembering. "That's when Tom called Emmett Swindell."

"The lawyer?"

"Yes."

"Sunday night?"

"Yes?"

"It must have been after eleven."

"That's why you pay your lawyer a retainer."

"Were you going to sue Friedman and Monarch Pictures?"

She studied her bare knee as if the Dead Sea Scrolls were written on it. "I don't think that was discussed."

Curious, I thought. "What did Swindell suggest?"

"He said we should call the police first thing in the morning. So we did."

"And then?"

"Tom told Sidney Friedman he was going to pull his investment out of the movie unless that actor was fired."

I hadn't known that, but it made ultimate sense. "And what was Sidney's reaction to that?"

"He said he'd have to talk to his people."

"What people?"

"I don't know," she said.

That made sense, too. Hollywood types always have "people," as in "He's one of Bobby De Niro's people," or "She's with Demi Moore's people."

"Of course, then he got killed," she continued, "so it was a moot point."

"Not so moot," I said. "Darren Anderson's name above the title on a movie almost guaranteed its success. Now . . . " I shrugged, leaving the speculation unspoken.

She lowered her eyes. "Well, I'm—I was supposed to play a small role in the picture, too."

I couldn't keep my mouth from dropping open in astonishment.

"I did some acting in college and in community theater around here before I got married. It's not like they're doing me a favor or anything. I mean, it's just a five-line part." She inhaled, forcing her breasts against the fabric of her tennis shirt. "I can handle it."

Now it all started coming together for me. Wealthy Tom Maniscalco was spending four million dollars to buy his wife a little excitement. "You're still going to do that? Even after what happened with Bethany?"

She pointed her chin at me like the barrel of a howitzer. "What's the difference? What's done is done."

She was some piece of work, Alison. "All right, Mrs. Maniscalco," I said, standing up. "I won't take up any more of your time. I'd like to leave you with a word of caution, however."

She rose. "What's that?"

"It might come down to it that the police will want to know who you were with Monday night. I'm telling you so you and whatever friend you were with will be ready for it."

Her chin quivered. "Is there any way of avoiding that?"

"I'll do what I can," I said, and started for the door.

"This has been horrible," she said, following me out to the vestibule.

I turned to face her. "Just between us chickens," I said, "was the friend you were with Monday night Victor Gaimari?"

She gasped, putting one hand to her throat. All the muscles in her face quit working; her mouth and cheeks sagged, and all of a sudden she looked every minute of her age.

"Lucky guess," I told her, and let myself out.

CHAPTER ELEVEN

Before I went back to my office, I dropped in on Bob Matusen at Third District Headquarters, the fortresslike police station on Payne Avenue where I once worked. Where Marko Meglich had worked.

I had to avert my eyes from the door of Marko's old office; I'd spent too many hours sitting across his battered desk from him, laughing and arguing and drinking bad station-house coffee, and the memories were still too vivid, the nerves still too raw and exposed.

Matusen was at his desk near the window of the medium-size room on the second floor that was home to the cadre of homicide detectives. Since he hadn't yet earned his lieutenant's bars, he was only the acting head of the division, and the brass had thought it prudent to keep him at his desk instead of moving him into Marko's office. I was grateful for that; I don't think I could have sat across Marko's desk from him.

Neither of us made any move to shake hands. I sat down in a hard wooden chair that had bruised the behinds of hundreds of witnesses, complainants, and assorted skels and perps. The muffled voices of cops on the telephone was a not unpleasant buzz in the room, and the air smelled of stale cigarette smoke. I lit up in self-defense.

"You look like the overseer on a rubber plantation," he said, taking in my light summer suit, white shirt, and dark brown tie. "Just passing by? Or did you want something?"

"Since I'm a murder suspect, I just wanted to show my face so you wouldn't think I'd skipped to the Cayman Islands."

He interlaced his fingers behind his close-cropped, bullet-shaped head and leaned back in his swivel chair. Half moons of sweat darkened his shirt under his arms. "You're still on the list. But to tell you the truth, you're pretty far down. For what it's worth, I personally don't think you did Darren Anderson."

"Thanks."

His eyes got a fraction of an inch smaller. "If I did, I'd have been riding you like Bill Shoemaker on Man o' War."

"Shoemaker and Man o' War were about forty years apart."

"You must have me mixed up with some guy who gives a shit. Want some coffee?"

"Pretty late in the day for me to be drinking cop-shop coffee, Bob. Thanks, anyway." I flicked my cigarette into his already brimming ashtray. "So if not me, who did kill Anderson?"

"That's the big question. One thing, though. He wasn't exactly a choirboy." He brought his arms down and folded his hands in front of him on the desk like a little kid. "There were lots of people didn't like him."

"And millions who did."

He sat frowning at me for a few seconds. "Oh. Yeah," he said when he caught up with it. "Well, we went out to the house in Bay Village and gathered up all his personal stuff and brought it down here. Nothing there worth talking about, though, except maybe a dime bag's worth of boo and enough condoms to keep all those bad boys on the Dallas Cowboys in safe sex for a month."

"Can I assume forensics didn't find any prints of anything at the crime scene?"

"Assume what you want. There were prints, hair samples, fibers, stuff like that. Probably some of them are yours."

"You know I was there. Several times, as a matter of fact."

"Right. The house is a rental property—corporations take it short-term for their visiting executives or consultants." He glowered. "And movie companies. Nine different occupants have been in and out of there in the past two years."

"But how many people who were connected to Darren Anderson?"

"How do you suggest we find out? Round up everybody who ever met him and run their prints to see if we can get a match?"

"They found him in the kitchen, didn't they?"

"That was on the news, yeah."

"Was there any sign of a struggle? Or forced entry?"

"No. Whoever was in there with him came through the front door. Why do you want to know?"

"If I'm a murder suspect," I said, "even one who's way down on the list, I'd say my curiosity was natural, wouldn't you?"

"No, I wouldn't say that." He picked up a yellow pencil, rose, and went to the electric sharpener atop the file cabinet. "I think we need to set a few ground rules before we go much further on this," he said, and inserted the pencil. The sharpener whirred for a second or two. "You used to wear the same badge I do, and I respect that. I also respect the fact that you and Meglich were best friends your whole life." He inspected the point of the pencil and stuck it in the sharpener again. "I'm even willing to extend you certain departmental courtesies because of that. If he trusted you, then I trust you."

Again he examined the pencil; satisfied, he turned to face me. He was not smiling. "But that's as far as it goes. Sometimes Meglich would look the other way when you dealt yourself into an ongoing investigation. I know that. Sometimes he even helped you. Well, I won't help and I won't look the other way. You start sticking your nose into an open murder case in this town and I'm going to land on you with both feet.

"I don't want you to get your license pulled," he said, coming back to the desk. "And I sure as hell don't want to lock you up for obstruction of justice. But I'll do it in a New York minute if I think you're fucking around with me. Are we real clear on that?"

"Clear as a bell," I said, biting back my irritation.

He sat down. "I don't suppose there's anything you want to tell me?"

I thought about Alan Braxton and Dierdre O'Malley. No, there was nothing I *wanted* to tell him. "Not a thing," I said, grinding out my cigarette butt. "You know I wouldn't stick my nose into an open murder case in this town."

Regarding me narrowly, he pulled a folder on his desk toward him, opened it, and began making notes. "See that you don't," he said without looking up.

I hadn't been back in the office long enough to smoke a cigarette before I heard the unmistakable sound of high heels coming up the stairs. That was all right, I thought, high heels were always nice. I had no idea how nice until the door opened and Rebekka Sommars walked into my office.

It was a surreal moment, because I recognized her immediately, having seen her in my living room or bedroom on hundreds of occasions. At one time a reporter for one of the major networks, she'd been highly touted as the surest bet to be the next anchor of the evening newscast, one of the three most coveted berths in broadcast journalism. It hadn't happened; for perhaps the only time in television history, a woman's exceptional beauty had worked against her.

But here she was, standing in my office doorway, and despite my recent elbow-rubbing with Hollywood royalty, she impressed me more. Maybe it was because I'd never seen a Darren Anderson film and I'd seen Rebekka Sommars on TV five hundred times, on *American Tab,* the nightly tabloid show she hosted.

Or maybe it was because she was so very, very beautiful.

In any case, I was too stunned even to stand up. My mother

would have made a sad, clicking noise with her tongue and scolded me, my father would have slapped me in the head for failing to rise when she entered the room. I'd been brought up with better manners.

"Are you Milan Jacovich?" she said. She pronounced both of my names correctly. "I'm Rebekka Sommars."

"Yes, I know," I said.

She smiled as if my recognition of her had suddenly brought meaning and value to her very existence. The room temperature rose—or was it just my temperature? "Good. I wonder if we could talk for a few minutes?"

Finally the rudiments of common courtesy kicked in and I scrambled to my feet and escorted her to one of my client chairs.

"May I get you anything?" I said. "Coffee, a soda?"

She shook her head. "Don't go to any trouble."

I sat down in the other chair, trying not to look at her legs, her piercing blue eyes, her sultry mouth. She was wearing a severely tailored ecru linen suit, the skirt two inches above her knee, but she might as well have been in a teddy. Sex appeal radiated from her like a force field, making me fail to realize that her being in my office could mean nothing to me but trouble.

"I'm not the person you should be talking to," I said. "Sherry Lipton is handling the media. You can reach her at the Ritz-Carlton."

Rebekka Sommars laughed. "Oh, Sherry," she said. "Yeah. I've dealt with her before. But I'd rather talk to you. After all, you were here when it all went down." She took a tiny tape recorder from her purse and set it on the edge of the desk. "You don't mind if I tape this, do you? It's a lot easier than taking notes."

I minded a lot. When I moved into the office I'd been talked into buying an electronic gizmo that lets me activate my own tape recorder by means of a button beneath my desk, which I can hit with my foot. But since I wasn't behind the desk I couldn't get to it.

"I'm sure you know why I'm here," she said, futzing with the little gray plastic box.

"I imagine you want to ask me about—"

"This is Milan Jacovich," she said loudly in the direction of the recorder and gave the time and date. Then she turned back to me and flashed that meltdown smile. "This isn't for broadcast. Let's just talk, okay? You mind if I call you Milan?"

I started to tell her that I'd like nothing better, but she rushed right ahead.

"You were one of the last ones to see Darren Anderson alive, weren't you?"

"No."

"No?"

"I saw him at around noon. At least a hundred people saw him after that." I shifted my weight around; I don't often sit in the chairs on the other side of my desk, and I'd no idea they were so uncomfortable. "Could you turn that thing off for a minute?"

The smile went from seductive to brave and troubled. She reached over and pushed a button on the recorder. "Is there a problem?"

"We're just moving a little too fast here," I said.

"Okay." She waited, recrossing her legs more slowly than she might have needed to. She was good, all right.

"How did you find me, Ms. Sommars?"

"Rebekka, please. You're in the telephone directory."

"So is Jack's Deli on Green Road, but you're not over there interviewing them."

Now the smile became oblique, mysterious. "A good reporter never reveals her sources."

"Why am I doing this?" I said.

"Oh come on, Milan, one of the most famous movie stars in the world has just been murdered. Personal feelings and all aside, you have to admit that that's big-time news. This is not about some washed-up football player who took his wife out, it's not the *son* of some celebrity who's been killed, this is Darren Anderson."

"You don't understand," I said. "Why am *I* doing this? I mean, why should I talk to you?"

"Because the public has a right to know?" she offered.

"Try again."

She laughed. "I didn't think that was going to work. Okay, how's this: we'll talk for a little while, and if I think there's enough here, I'll come back in the morning with a camera crew and we'll talk some more, and tomorrow night it'll be on *American Tab* and you'll be the most famous private detective in the world."

"Sherlock Holmes is the most famous private detective in the world."

"But he's fictional. You're real. And having your face on national television could mean a fortune to you. Literally millions of dollars in new business."

"Look around you," I said. "Does it look like I'm equipped to handle millions of dollars in new business? I'm a one-man band."

"You don't have to be." She treated me to a conspiratorial wink.

"Anonymity is more important in my business than publicity."

She leaned forward, putting a hand lightly on my knee. Her fingernails were red and shiny. Everything about her was shiny— her eyes, her hair, her teeth, her lipstick, even her pantyhose, which looked as if they'd been brushed with silver. "With all that new business, you can hire a staff to be anonymous for you."

I laughed. "You're not very persuasive."

She froze for a second. Then she relaxed against the back of her chair, most of the smile disappearing to the fake-smile grave-yard. "Look. Just talk to me. If you tell me something I can use, I'll let you know and we can come back tomorrow and put it on tape or not—whatever you want. I can't use an audiotape, and I can't use your picture without your permission, so why don't you just stop being a tight-ass and play a little catch with me? It's not going to kill you."

"I think I like you better without all the phony bullshit."

This time her smile was genuine. "Without the phony bullshit I'd be back doing stand-ups at the garden show for *Good Morning, Omaha*."

I'd seen *American Tab* once or twice; *Good Morning, Omaha* wouldn't have been so bad.

"Go ahead and turn on your tape," I said. "But we're not in court and I'm only going to answer the questions I like."

"Fair enough." She switched on the tape recorder again. "What were Darren Anderson's last days like?"

"Mostly work. Making a movie is lots of hard work, lots of waiting around on the set, which can be more tiring than actual physical labor."

"Surely he had time to relax?"

"Not much," I said.

"What about his last weekend?"

"Let's see," I said. "That last Friday night he went to a party. On Saturday he and I had dinner. Monday he was back at work."

"What about Sunday?"

The skin on the back of my neck tingled. "Sunday was his day off. He kept to himself."

"As I understand it, you were hired to stay with him when he wasn't working."

"Not every minute," I said. "I took him places, showed him the city, took him to dinner. Things like that. I slept at home, he slept at his house. We weren't joined at the hip."

"But all day Sunday . . . ?"

"He wanted a day to himself."

She shifted in her chair. I could sense the tension in her shoulders, the way her breath quickened just a little. "What did he do?"

"I wasn't with him," I said.

"Was he with some local woman?"

"As I said, I wasn't there."

"Darren Anderson's reputation with women was well known," Rebekka Sommars said, and now I could see the tough, relentless reporter behind the dazzling surface. "Are you trying to tell me he didn't date anyone in the entire two weeks he was here in Cleveland?"

"I'm not trying to tell you anything."

"I interviewed him once, about a year ago, and he started coming on to me, right on camera."

"I don't blame him," I said, trying to take the sting out of it.

"Don't try to charm me, Milan. That's my game, and I'm better at it than you are. Darren Anderson was a relentless pussy hound. So I can't believe that just because he was here in Cleveland he was celibate for two whole weeks. I doubt if the public will, either."

"I can't imagine why the public would care. Could you turn that thing off, please?"

She raised her perfect eyebrows. "Why?"

"I'm finished talking."

"We're just getting to the good stuff."

I reached over and pushed the stop button on the tape recorder. "No, we aren't. Look, Miss Sommars, you'd be wasting your time coming back here with a camera crew tomorrow. I really have nothing that'll shed any light on this story for you. There is no good stuff."

She doubled both hands into little fists on her thighs, clearly annoyed that I'd defiled her tape recorder with my thick, clumsy finger. "Are you kidding? You were Darren Anderson's bodyguard the last two weeks of his life. My God, you just might *be* the story."

I shook my head. "I don't think so."

"You mean you won't talk to me on camera?"

"Sorry. It's just not my thing."

She put the tape recorder back into her purse. "You'll be a happier camper if you do."

"I'm pretty happy already."

"Yeah, right." She stood up, and this time I remembered my etiquette and rose too. "I'm at the Wyndham if you change your mind."

"I won't."

She shook her head as we went to the door, so efficient and capable I forgot how beautiful she was. Then she paused, her hand on the knob. "You'd better, Milan. You have until ten o'clock tomorrow morning."

"And then what?"

"You'll see." She smiled flirtatiously and waggled her fingers in an arch bye-bye wave before going through the door and down the stairs.

Her expensive perfume stayed in the office for days.

By prearrangement, Suzi Flores was waiting for me in the lobby of the Marriott. I'd never seen her before, but there was no mistaking her; she stood out like a beautiful, sensuous painting. She and I evidently hadn't been on the film set at the same times—I never could have forgotten her.

It wasn't her beauty alone that made her a magnet for every eye in the place. She had presence to spare.

If she'd been a movie actress back in the less sensitive days of the forties and fifties, she would probably have been characterized by the Hollywood flacks as a Latin Bombshell. She was about five foot four, her jet black hair was long and curly, with a few red highlights when the light hit it just right, her figure was more than lush, and most men would easily read promise in her dark eyes. She had a nice smile, I found out later, but she didn't display it very often. On this particular evening she was wearing a tight blue satin minidress and Joan Crawford fuck-me pumps. Everyone within hailing distance watched as we moved across the lobby and out the front door.

Despite her startling good looks, there was a brittleness about Suzi Flores, a hard shell that she wore like a suit of armor. As we went through the revolving door and emerged onto the sidewalk on St. Clair Avenue, she took care to keep at least two feet between us, and the defensive forward thrust of her chin negated the allure of her dancer's body and walk.

"I appreciate your taking the time to see me, Suzi."

She shrugged. When she did, all of her shrugged. "I'm just sitting around waiting for something to happen on this picture," she said. "I didn't have anything else to do, so I'm happy just to have some company. Besides, Sidney said it was important."

"It might be."

We walked down Ontario through Public Square. The night was warm and clear, the kind of weather that encourages slow and easy strolling, and the lights of the city were jewellike. Cars whizzed by us, their headlights making her dress glisten and shine.

"It's pretty here," she noticed. "Pretty buildings, all lit up like that. You hear bad things about Cleveland, but it's really nice."

"Thanks. We think so."

"I was born in Mexico City. Parts of it are pretty too. Parts of it aren't."

We cut over to East Ninth Street and headed toward Jacobs Field, where the field lights were blazing brightly, even though the Indians were out of town that week. She stopped and looked at it admiringly.

"Nice ballpark," she said almost wistfully. "Both my brothers played pro ball in Mexico. They never made it to the bigs, though."

We turned in at the Taverne of Richfield, Cleveland Style, which is directly across the street from the plaza where the bronze statue of Indians pitching legend Bob Feller stands. The marble benches, when viewed from above, spell out WHO'S ON

FIRST? and the paving stones are engraved with the names of loyal fans who paid fifty bucks a pop for the privilege when the ballpark first opened.

The Taverne used to be in the city of Richfield, down in Summit County, a few blocks away from the Richfield Coliseum. Popular as a before-and-after basketball haunt, the restaurant foundered and finally closed when the Cavaliers deserted the Coliseum and began playing in Gund Arena. The downtown version is similar to the original, casually elegant with rich, dark woods and hearty dining.

We got a table by the window. The slats of the wooden shutters were open a little so we could see across the street to the ballpark. Suzi Flores ordered a vodka tonic and I opted for a beer.

"Sidney said you wanted to ask me some questions," she said.

"I do. We want to find out who killed Darren."

She gave me a sullen pout. "You thinking I did it?"

"No," I said. "But eventually the police are going to get around to talking to you. Sidney says you and Darren didn't get along."

"You can say that again," she muttered. "He was a son of a bitch."

"You're a very beautiful woman, Suzi. You must be used to men coming on to you."

"Coming on is one thing," she said. She sipped at her drink, looking at me over the rim of the glass.

"Maybe he just liked you, wanted to date you."

"Is that what you call it, dating? He wanted to jump every woman he saw, so I wasn't interested. Or flattered, either." Her dark brown eyes turned cold as stones. "He said if I didn't put out for him, he'd have me fired off the picture. That's not dating."

"Why didn't you complain?"

"I did. I told Sidney."

"And?"

"He promised to take care of it, to talk to Darren and make him stop, but I don't think he did."

"You could have filed a formal complaint with the Screen Actors Guild, couldn't you?"

Her laugh was harsh. "Sure. And then I'd never work again."

I saw her point. Like the Italian mob, Hollywood prefers to handle their problems in-house.

"Do you really think he would have had you fired?"

"I don't know. I couldn't make a big stink about it, though. I just couldn't. There's few enough parts for Latinas as it is." She picked up the menu and studied it. "This is my fifth picture, but I never had such a good part before."

There was certainly motive here, I thought. *Street Games* was to be Suzi Flores's big break in the movies. Given the difficulty of the business, she might have been willing to kill to keep it.

We ordered dinner—fish for her, an end cut of prime rib for me. All on Sidney Friedman's tab.

"I don't blame Sidney," she said when the salads arrived. "He's been decent to me, giving me this chance and all. But Darren Anderson was a big star. If it came to making him happy or making me happy, Sidney would have dumped me without a second thought. That's how the business works." She sighed, with her whole body. "At least I didn't have any illusions. So I just kept quiet about it and hoped I wouldn't lose the job anyway."

"I guess you won't, now."

"*If* they finish the picture."

"You think they might not?"

"I don't know," she said, picking at her salad. "Monarch is supposed to release it, but it was financed independently, and most of the investors were putting their money into Darren Anderson. Now that he's gone . . . " She let the thought hang like the blade of a guillotine. "I guess it all depends on who they can get to replace him."

"Who else did he butt heads with?"

"Almost everybody," she said. "It wasn't that he was really mean to anyone. But if you weren't important, if you couldn't do anything for him, he'd look right through you, as if you didn't exist. He was a big star, and he was spoiled, like most of them are. Twenty-four years old and he's got it in his contract what kind of mineral water he has to have in his dressing room, what kind of snacks. M-and-M's, for God's sake, written right into his contract. He was Hollywood's golden boy of the year, though, and he thought he could get away with anything—and he was right. He could."

"Not quite," I said. "Otherwise, he'd still be alive."

She shuddered.

Our entrées arrived. I dug into my prime rib with gusto, but Suzi Flores didn't seem particularly hungry.

"Were there any other women in the cast or crew who were having the same trouble with him?"

"Probably most of them," she said. "He was one of those men who'd rather sleep with a hundred different women than with one woman a hundred times. Everybody in the picture business is like that—they love power, and they equate that with sex. Maybe it's something in the water."

"That must get old for you."

"It does. The trouble is, the rewards of becoming well known are so great, people are willing to put up with anything for the chance. Darren got away with a lot. There were probably a few women working on this picture who gave in. To keep their jobs. Or because he was a good-looking guy, and could be charming if he wanted to. Or maybe just because he was *the* Darren Anderson, and women wanted him on their résumés."

"Do you know that for a fact?"

"What?"

"That some of the other women working on the picture went to bed with him?"

"I can't give you names, if that's what you mean."

I sat back, disappointed.

"But I'd bet anything that it happened," she said. "It always does."

"Does it?"

She began squeezing a lemon wedge over her fish, not looking at me. "I'm not a bimbo," she said. "I'm a good actress, with a degree in theater. But five years ago, when I first got to Los Angeles, I had to give a casting director head to get my first small part in a TV movie." She tossed the lemon angrily onto her plate. "I swore I'd never do that again. And I haven't."

I didn't say anything. I just drank my beer and considered how tough it must be to be a show-business hopeful.

It made my job seem downright sunny.

CHAPTER TWELVE

I had several more beers and a cognac before delivering Suzi Flores safely back to her hotel at ten o'clock. The poisonous looks of envy I got from all the men on the street and in the Marriott lobby didn't mean much when I knew I was just going to shake her hand and go home alone. I didn't need anyone in my life who was more full of regretful angst than I was, much less one who was going to disappear after another two weeks.

Guys like Darren Anderson and that long-ago casting director made me mad. Made me sick. Guys like Alan Braxton. Guys like Victor Gaimari.

Selfish people, the exploiters and abusers, leave everybody marked and diminished. Suzi Flores was a beautiful, vibrant woman with what I imagined was more than her share of talent. But she was a sad and bruised one, too, full of regrets about the past and uncertainties over the future. It's a hell of a way to live.

Then again, we're all a little bruised, I guess.

I sure was when I stopped off at Vuk's for a beer or two on the way home, and the sad memories came shouldering their way up into my consciousness. Marko Meglich and I had drunk at this bar together for more than twenty years, watching baseball and football games and shooting the breeze with Vuk and his customers, people we'd grown up with in the old neighborhood.

And while it still felt like a cocoon of warmth and comfort, sorrow and regret knifed through my heart as soon as I walked in the door.

"Whattaya say, Milan?" Vuk almost always greets me that way, whether I've been in the day before or not for six months. He also knows what I want to drink—a Stroh's, which he dug out of the cooler the moment I appeared and set in front of me as I sat down at the bar. No glass, ever. He'd taught me on my twenty-first birthday when I'd ordered my first legal drink that it always tastes better right out of the bottle.

I lit a cigarette before taking the first sip. That made the beer taste better too.

Vuk rinsed out some glasses in the sink behind the bar. "That guy you were in here with the other night? He the movie star that got himself dead?"

"Yeah," I said.

"Rough deal. He seemed like kind of a jerk, though."

"He was a jerk. But he didn't need killing."

"Nobody needs killing," Vuk said. "But it happens, don't it? It's a violent world out there, just look at the papers. They oughta throw you a parade just for getting through the day without getting mugged or shot or robbed or thumped on."

I began scratching the label from the beer bottle with my fingernail. "That's what Marko was there for," I said. "To make sure you were still around to enjoy your parade."

He brushed at his bushy walrus mustache with the back of a thick wrist. "Ah, jeez, you still beatin' yourself up over that?"

I didn't answer him. The condensation on the bottle had softened the label, and I concentrated on its removal like a surgeon taking out a gallbladder.

"Listen, Milan. Nobody liked that boy more'n me. I knew him an' you since you was too little to see over the bar here, and I miss him as much as you, even though he didn't much come in here no more. But he was a cop. That's what made him tick. An' cops put their asses on the line every day. They know that goin' in, don'tcha see?"

"He was putting his ass on the line for me that night, Vuk."

"For you, for me, for some old colored woman up on East Seventy-ninth Street. What's the difference? It's what cops do."

I slugged down almost half the beer in one prodigious swallow, gasping as I came up for air.

"Sure the world kinda stinks," he observed. "But you don't just stick your head under the covers and hope the stink goes away—that's no answer. You get out there and fight, like you always done."

"I'm fighting," I protested. "Right now I'm working for a dollar trying to find out what really happened to that kid. But Jesus, I get tired sometimes."

He crossed his arms across his chest; his forearms were as big around as Popeye's. "You got the creepies tonight for some reason. But you don't really get tired. You're hooked."

"On what?"

"On the excitement. Bein' on the edge. Back when you was a kid, when you an' Marko was playin' football, I remember you wanted in on every play. You even got pissed when the offense was on the field an' you hadda sit. Then you went into the army. You didn't hafta go to Nam, you had a low draft number. People down there at Kent were protesting the war, marching, having rallies. A couple of kids even got 'emselves killed over it. But you, you *wanted* to go. And then after you come home you joined the cops because you wanted more excitement, but there was too much paperwork and salutin' for you to do. So now this, what you do right now, gettin' mixed up with murderers and gangsters and all that." He stroked his big mustache. "You're hooked on the rush, Milan."

I didn't feel much of a rush while driving back to Cleveland Heights three beers later, which was one or two too many. I was navigating the streets slowly and painstakingly, the way most people do when they know they've had too much to drink; it wouldn't do to get stopped for DWI.

I thought about it, what Vuk had said, and had to admit there was a little truth there. I'd invited myself into the investigation of the Darren Anderson killing because I'd wanted to. I felt responsible and guilty, sure, but Cleveland cops are good at what they do. The Dr. Sam Sheppard case might have taken them more than forty years, but they solved it. I could have left Darren Anderson's killing to them, relatively secure that they'd eventually get their perp.

But something in me wanted to do it myself, wanted to be in on the hunt.

I'd originally set up my owned-and-operated firm to handle matters of industrial security, but I find myself getting involved in the more dangerous end of the profession more often than I should. In the past few years I've been shot twice, knifed, run down a couple of times with a car, and pounded on more often than I care to remember. And now I'd dealt myself into finding a killer, and I wasn't even getting paid for it.

Except for the dollar. Let's not forget Sidney Friedman's dollar, which made the whole thing legitimate.

Maybe Vuk, a barroom philosopher who'd known me most of my life, was right. Despite my penchant for smoking and drinking and eating, and my endless and so far futile search for the right woman, maybe my main addiction is the rush, and I was hooked on adrenaline.

Just like Darren had been hooked on his own fame.

When I got home I kicked off my shoes, took off my jacket and tie, and fell asleep in my clothes again, just so I wouldn't have to think about it anymore.

In my office the next morning I was going over a list I'd obtained from Sidney Friedman of all the personnel who'd worked on the

Cleveland shoot of *Street Games*—actors, grips, technicians, administrative support, public relations people, security, even the caterers. Everyone.

There were one hundred twenty-seven names. Most of them were Clevelanders hired just for the shoot. They'd only had a couple of weeks to get to know Darren Anderson—which was more than enough time to work up a real hate for somebody, I knew. Still, it seemed unlikely.

The cast and the rest of the crew, the makeup and wardrobe people, production managers, assistant directors, camera people and so on, had been imported from Los Angeles. Some of them probably had past dealings with Darren, and some not. It's a big city and a big industry, but still a lot of movie people seem to know one another.

Odds were that not all of them had reason to dislike him personally, but some did. Maybe one of them had reason to kill him.

It was the process of elimination that was daunting.

Bob Matusen had the same list, I was sure. I decided to leave the cast and assorted crew of *Street Games* to him. I was more concerned with the Maniscalcos and Alan Braxton.

Braxton was a hot-tempered guy who was pathologically jealous of his fiancée; if he'd somehow learned she'd spent the night with Darren Anderson, he might have done something about it.

Except Dierdre and Darren had only spent one night together, if she was to be believed, and that had been two weeks before his death. So if Alan Braxton was the killer, he'd either found out about it long after the fact or had taken his sweet time planning his revenge. From his impetuous behavior at the White Magnolia, I'd say the latter was something of a long shot.

But if I braced him and he hadn't even known about Dierdre and Darren, I might be ruining the young woman's chances of marrying him, and I didn't think I had quite enough to go on to take that risk. She seemed like a nice kid who'd made a dumb mistake. Everybody makes them.

Me too.

Tom Maniscalco had the best motive: volcanic rage that his daughter had been dishonored. But if he was going to kill Darren Anderson, it was unlikely he'd have called the police and turned the spotlight on himself as a suspect. And I was pretty sure that Alison had been with Victor when the murder was committed.

For whatever reason, that family seemed like a dead end.

Unless of course they'd hired someone to do it.

If that were the case, I was fairly certain Victor Gaimari would have heard about it. And for all his admitted faults, I didn't think Victor was the kind of guy who would condone a murder.

I tried to get Sidney Friedman on the phone, but his line was constantly busy. I left a message with the hotel operator, asking him to call me back, but I supposed that getting his movie up and running again was more important to him than my problems.

The business of someone trying to burn down Darren Anderson's house was troubling me, and I wanted the name of his agent in California so I could learn a little more about that. It was a long shot, I knew, but I figured I'd have it pretty much to myself; Bob Matusen would put the California connections on the back burner until he'd exhausted all his leads here in Cleveland.

That's what I would have done if I was still a cop.

I took out a packet of three-by-five index cards and made one out for each of the players so far: Sidney Friedman, Boyce Cort, Suzi Flores, Alan Braxton, Dierdre O'Malley, and one for each of the Maniscalcos. I shuffled them around into different configurations on the top of my desk; I do that when I have a complicated situation to unravel, because I find I can make connections better when I have everyone's name spread out in front of me.

Nothing was making much sense, however.

At about eleven o'clock I heard footsteps on the stairs. It could have been someone heading for the surgical supply firm that shared the second floor with me, but I didn't think so. People just don't walk in off the street to buy scalpels and catheters and bone saws.

I wrapped a rubber band around the index cards, stuck them into my top drawer, and waited to see who my visitors were.

The two people who entered my office, hesitating at the door as if they weren't quite sure whether or not they wanted to come in, were unknown to me. The man was in his middle fifties, lean, with Brillo-pad hair and the sallow complexion of a heavy drinker. He was wearing a lightweight sports jacket over tan slacks and a nondescript tie. I probably wouldn't have remembered him if I'd had lunch with him the day before; his was the kind of undistinguished face you instantly forget. He would fade into a crowd if he was all by himself.

The woman with him might have been eight or ten years younger. She was dressed in severe dark blue and cute-pretty in a faded, dispirited way, although she wore too much makeup, and her lipstick looked as though it got onto her mouth by accident. Her dark blond hair was shoulder length and frilly, too self-consciously girlish. She was about five foot seven, with a figure that might once have been lush until she'd allowed time and dissipation to run away with it. She carried herself apologetically, in the way of a woman who knows she was once beautiful and feels guilty and diminished because she is no longer.

What was most striking about her was her eyes: they were haunted, hollow, the lids puffy, as if she'd recently cried a lot, and the color of irises in the spring.

"Are you Mr. Jacovich?" the man said.

I stood up. "That's right."

"My name is Ray Dinsmoor. This is my wife, Betty."

I nodded a hello.

"I'm Darren Anderson's mother," Betty Dinsmoor said.

The resemblance was unmistakable, once I thought about it. The eyes, of course, and a certain delicacy about the bones of her face. I came around to their side of the desk and took both her hands; they felt rough and dry. She wore a plain gold wedding band, and no other jewelry except inexpensive-looking gold earrings.

"I'm so sorry about your son," I said.

She murmured a thank-you and allowed me to guide her into a chair. Her husband took the other one.

"May I offer you some coffee? Or a soft drink?"

She shook her head. Ray Dinsmoor didn't answer one way or another, which I took to mean no. I went back around the desk and sat in my chair, leaning forward. "How can I be of assistance?" I said.

"We live in Los Angeles," Betty Dinsmoor said. "We don't know anyone here. We don't know what to do."

"We're in Sierra Madre, really," her husband said. "That's in the San Gabriel Valley. I was in Detroit when they called Betty about what happened to Ralphie. On a sales trip. I travel a lot. I sell hardware."

"Computer hardware?"

"Regular hardware. Nuts, bolts, screws, things like that." There was an anxious kind of desperation in his eyes and in the stiff way he held his head on his skinny stalk of a neck, as though he knew instinctively that when he talked, no one ever listened. I couldn't imagine the social pack in which Ray Dinsmoor would have been considered the alpha animal.

"Betty called to tell me. It was a shocker, I'll tell you. So she flew in to Detroit to join me and then we come down here together in the rental car."

"We're here to bring Ralph back home—" Betty's breath caught in her throat, and she had to wait a few seconds before she could finish. "Where he belongs."

"They say we need a permit," Ray grumbled. "We got to wait for the damn permit now."

"They call it a burial transfer permit," Betty explained. "To take the . . . " Her nostrils flared, then crimped almost shut. "To take him out of the state. The policeman—Mr. Matusek, is it?"

"Matusen," I said.

"Matusen. Well, he gave us the name of this funeral home we could contact here. They'll get the permit for us and, you know. Make all the arrangements."

"And how can I help you?"

"You can't!" Ray said. "It was Betty's idea to come talk to you, not mine!"

"Ray . . . " Betty's front teeth were pink from chewing off her lipstick; she'd obviously applied some just before coming upstairs. "We want to know what happened. How such a terrible thing could happen."

"The police are trying their best to find out," I told her. "You've talked to them, haven't you?"

"That Friedman guy said you were trying to find out, too," Ray said.

"I am. But the police have more resources, and—"

"They won't tell us anything."

"I don't think they have anything to tell, or they would."

"What the hell kind of a city is this where something like this can happen?" Ray raged.

"Bad things happen everywhere, Mr. Dinsmoor."

"Yeah, but wasn't it your job to take care of him? Weren't you like his bodyguard or something?"

"Something like that," I said. "But I quit the job."

"Yes, the day he got killed," Betty said softly, and with unbearable sadness.

"You quit your job lookin' out for Ralphie, and the next thing you know, someone shoots him!" her husband said. "A pretty funny coincidence, if you ask me."

Angry tingles ran across the skin on the back of my neck, and only the presence of a bereaved mother saved him from a wrathful answer. "One thing had nothing to do with the other," I said evenly. "I had no idea Darren was in any danger. If I had, I certainly would have stayed. That's why I want to find out what really happened almost as much as you do. I feel a responsibility."

He snorted unpleasantly.

"It shouldn't have happened," I said. "It's tragic. For someone that young to die like that."

"It don't surprise me at all," Ray said. "He was a little shit!"

His wife's eyes widened in shock; I had a suspicion mine did too. "Ray, you—"

"No, damn it, Betty, I say it like it is! I raised that kid since he was nine years old, like he was my own. God knows his real father didn't have nothing to do with him. But he never wanted for a goddamn thing! He had a roof over his head, three meals a day, I sent him to school . . . " He shook his head.

That seemed to me the least a parent owed a kid. But Ray Dinsmoor was nowhere near finished.

"And then when he makes it big, makes it in the millions, he's like we don't even exist anymore."

"Ray, Ralphie sent us money every month. He even bought us a house," Betty Dinsmoor protested.

"Sure. In Sierra Madre." Bile flavored his words. "He got a three-million-dollar estate up in the hills, he's driving a Mercedes, and we're living next door to beaners and rednecks in fucking Sierra Madre! Even here! He's only here in Cleveland for a month, and he had to have that fancy house with the big glass windows out on the lake there. God forbid he should live in an apartment or something like a regular person.

"The boy had no humility! He got to be a big, rich, famous movie star and forgot where he come from. That's what got him into trouble."

Ray Dinsmoor was starting to sound very much like someone who had accomplished little in his life and resented those who had done more. "Your wife has lost her son, Mr. Dinsmoor. Let's have a little respect, okay?"

Betty Dinsmoor looked at me with gratitude, but her husband scowled. "That boy didn't even know the meaning of respect," he said. "Just like his father!"

"Ray, please!"

He sniffed, rubbing a hand over his face, but he subsided a little, and the angry flush on his cheeks faded from purple to reddish pink.

"When Mr. Friedman told us you were investigating what happened to Ralphie on your own," Betty Dinsmoor said, "we came here hoping you could tell us something. Losing a child—it's the most terrible thing in the world, Mr. Jacovich. But not to know why . . . " She pressed a fist to her mouth; when she lowered it, most of her remaining lipstick was on her knuckles.

"I don't know anything yet," I said.

"Surely you must have some idea."

"I have lots of them. But I can't just accuse someone of murder, I have to have some sort of proof," I said as gently as I could. "And I'm nowhere near that now."

She seemed to deflate in her chair.

"But I happen to know the police are working very hard on this," I continued. "And so am I. I'm committed to finding out who killed your son."

"You're one to talk!" Ray Dinsmoor said, his anger returning in a rush. "You were the one that run out on him, and now he's dead!" And suddenly he was out of his chair and leaning across the desk, pointing a shaking finger in my face. There were white dots of spittle at the corners of his mouth, and the loose skin under his chin jiggled like the wattles of an angry rooster. "Well, you can just tell it to our lawyer! Because we're suing Monarch Pictures and we're suing that Jew Friedman. And we're going to sue your ass off too, for dereliction of duty!"

"Ray . . . " his wife said again, right on cue.

"No!" he said, swept along by his anger and bitterness. "People got to be made responsible! This man was supposed to take care of Ralphie and he didn't. That's grounds for a lawsuit right there."

I wasn't going to argue with him. But his truculence was irritating me, and I was damned if I'd let him point his finger in my face in my own office. I stood up, and my size backed him up a step or two. "This isn't getting us anywhere. Sit down, Mr. Dinsmoor."

Intimidated, he groped blindly behind him, then eased himself down into his chair.

I sat down again too. "If you want to sue me, that's certainly up to you. But it would be a lot more productive if you tried to help me."

"How?" Betty Dinsmoor said.

"For one thing—what do you know about someone setting fire to Darren's house a few months ago?"

"How would we know anything about that?" Ray Dinsmoor said, his hands closing into fists.

"That was probably some fan who was jealous of him," Betty Dinsmoor said.

"The police never found out who it was?"

She shook her head wearily. "It's so hard to prove anything like that."

"They didn't even have an idea?"

"That was six months ago and two thousand miles away!" Ray Dinsmoor barked. Maybe I'd managed to sit him down, but his truculence was still working just fine, thank you. "What are you wasting your time with that for? This is where you oughta be using your concentration, right here in Cleveland."

I pulled a yellow pad toward me. "Where are you staying here in town, Mrs. Dinsmoor?"

She gave me the name of a chain motel out near Hopkins International Airport.

"Do you know how long you'll be staying?"

She shook her head. "They want us to come down to the police station tomorrow and go through Ralphie's things. And with the weekend coming and all, we probably won't be able to get that permit until Monday at the earliest."

I stood up, hoping to end the interview. "I'll keep in close touch with you," I said. "If I find out anything, I'll be sure to let you know."

Ray Dinsmoor got uncertainly to his feet. "That don't mean we're not suing you," he said.

I was glad when they were gone. Their presence had been like a dark cloud in my office, Betty Dinsmoor with her quiet grief and her husband with his sullen resentment and anger.

As it turned out, they were just the beginning of a very lousy Friday.

CHAPTER THIRTEEN

❋ ❋ ❋ ❋ ❋ ❋ ❋ ❋ ❋ ❋

I drove up the hill out of the Flats to the Cleveland Public Library on Superior, its new Louis B. Stokes wing, named after the long-time congressman, all gleaming glass beside the stone facade of the original building. I parked in a garage across the street and grabbed a couple of Polish boys, which are spicy sausages, a bag of chips, and a soda from one of the rolling carts on Public Square. Not much of a lunch, but it was the best I could do. I ate it sitting on a bench beneath the statue of former Cleveland mayor Tom L. Johnson, then walked down to the library to pore over microfilm of the Los Angeles *Times* from the previous February.

I found the report of the fire at Darren Anderson's house fairly easily—it was on the front page of the February 24 edition. The *Times* reports the doings of its hometown movie stars as diligently and prominently as it does those of Congress and the president.

LOS ANGELES—Actor Darren Anderson returned to his Coldwater Canyon home late last night to find the sundeck and one side of the house smoldering from a fire arson investigators believe was deliberately set.

LAFD Battalion Chief Jamie Iniquez told reporters that traces of kerosene had been found in the scorched vegetation around the perimeter of the house. "The rains we had in December and January left the brush pretty damp," he said, "or the whole house and the entire hillside might have been involved, and we would have had a major problem with the entire canyon. We were very lucky."

The Anderson home is quite near estates owned by film actors Marlon Brando and Jack Nicholson, both of whom are out of town and could not be reached for comment.

No one was in Anderson's house at the time the fire was reported by a neighbor at approximately eleven thirty P.M. The fire department arrived on the scene within ten minutes and was able to contain the blaze quickly.

Anderson, whose film career has skyrocketed in the past few years, had been visiting several clubs on the Sunset Strip last night with friends and was visibly shaken when he talked to reporters.

"My bedroom opens out onto that deck," he said. "If I'd been in there asleep, the smoke might have finished me off."

The young actor said he had no idea who might have set the blaze. "When you're in the public eye you sometimes attract the attention of unbalanced people," he observed.

Los Angeles police are in possession of several unusual fan letters written to the actor in the past six months, some of which Lieutenant Cletus Bice characterized as threatening. He speculated that Anderson may have been the victim of a stalker, a phenomenon plaguing the celebrity community all too often in recent years.

The arson squad is investigating.

The incident was off the front page in a couple of days, and the latest mention of it was two weeks later, when police and fire inspectors admitted they had no leads as to the identity of the arsonist.

I'd just about finished making notes on the fire when my beeper chirred, and I discovered Victor Gaimari was trying to contact me again.

I left the library, ransomed my car from the garage across the street, and drove down Eagle Avenue to my office, where I called him back. I could have called from the car, but there had recently been reports in the papers about how drivers who use car phones are much more accident prone, and I didn't want to turn into a statistic.

"Milan, you've become a burden to me in my dotage," Victor said when I got him on the line.

"You're two years younger than I am, Victor."

"All the more reason you should mellow out and act your age. I'm beginning to think 'stubborn Slovenian son of a bitch' is an understatement."

"What did I do now?"

"You went to Tom Maniscalco's home and bothered his wife. He called me up and screamed for an hour. I'm not used to being screamed at. I don't like it."

"Gee, the rest of us think it's a day at the beach."

"The bottom line is, he's about ready to have you boiled in oil."

"I tried to do it the right way," I said, "but he wouldn't talk to me."

"He's nobody to mess with. I understand he's got a bad temper."

"So do I."

"I remember," he said. "To my sorrow. Sometimes in cold, wet weather I still have trouble breathing through my nose."

"Those must be the same days when my shoulder aches where your guys pounded it with a sap."

"That's all water under the bridge now, isn't it?"

"It was a long time ago."

"A long time. Milan, Tom Maniscalco would be a happy man

if he never heard your name again. He's trying to protect his daughter's reputation."

"That's a load of crap," I said. "Even if the story got out, there's no way in hell the papers would publish the name of an underage girl who had sex with a movie star."

"They might. Maniscalco is prominent."

"So is Michael Jackson—a hell of a lot more so than Tom Maniscalco. And no one knows the name of the kid he paid off. So what exactly is Maniscalco afraid of? I don't want to butt heads with you, Victor. So I hope this phone call doesn't mean you're leaning on me to back off."

"I only lean when I have something at stake," he said. "I'm calling you as a small favor to a friend of my uncle's. As I've already told you, Tom Maniscalco is nothing more than an acquaintance."

"What about Alison Maniscalco? Is she just an acquaintance too?"

Victor didn't say anything for a moment. Then, "Be careful," he told me. "You're getting into personal areas."

"I'd say you were the one getting into personal areas."

"Don't be crude."

"Some pieces are falling together here, that's all. You were with Alison Maniscalco the night Anderson was killed, and if the police zero in on Maniscalco, you're afraid it's all going to come out."

"I wouldn't say afraid," he said cautiously. "Let's just say it would be awkward for me. And extremely awkward for Alison."

"What happened to Darren Anderson was pretty awkward for him."

Now he sounded exasperated. "Look, I'm sorry the boy got killed, but I don't know anything about it. I'm sure you know me well enough to believe me."

"I do," I said. "And I believe you were with Mrs. Maniscalco when it happened, so that takes her off the hook. I'm still not so sure about her husband, and I'm not going to walk away from it until I find out. If that puts your nuts in a wringer, I apologize."

"You're a difficult man, Milan."

"Is that anything like a stubborn Slovenian son of a bitch?"

There was only the sound of his breathing for about ten seconds—thoughtful, measured. Then he said, "All stubborn Slovenian sons of bitches are difficult men. But not all difficult men are stubborn Slovenian sons of bitches."

I reflected this Lincolnesque assertion after we broke the connection, aware, as I was sure Victor wanted me to be, that it was a veiled warning. All right, I thought. That explains why Victor Gaimari wanted me to keep away from Maniscalco. Now why wouldn't Maniscalco give me the time of day?

The phone rang at my elbow, and I picked it up quickly. "Milan Security."

There was silence for a moment, and then a click. I waited a few more seconds and got a dial tone.

It could have been a wrong number—I get a lot of them. My name is similar to that of a dentist in Parma, and his patients occasionally call me by mistake. I suppose his office gets inquiries about security service and discreet investigations as well. Or it could have been one of those ubiquitous telemarketers. Or perhaps someone was simply trying to ascertain whether or not I was in my office.

I decided to find out. I hung up and punched *69 on the keypad, a handy little feature the phone company has come up with that allows you to immediately ring back the party who just called you. I waited through eight rings without getting an answer and then hung up.

I didn't have much time to think about it, though. I stood up, my intent being to make half a pot of coffee, to get me through the rest of the afternoon. But before I made it to the coffeemaker, Nathan Braxton walked in, closing the door behind him.

"I'm Nathan Braxton, Mr. Jacovich. We met at my office yesterday."

"I remember," I said. I went and shook his hand, then pulled out a client chair for him, into which he lowered himself carefully. His blue suit showed not a wrinkle, and his crisp blue and white striped shirt might have come from the laundry five minutes before. He had on another aggressive tie.

"I happened to find your card on my son's desk yesterday," he said, and produced it from his pocket. "Where Dierdre left it."

"Are you looking for a security system for the office?" I knew damn well he wasn't. People just don't walk in off the street for something like that, they invariably call first.

"I might be," he lied. "You never know. Is that what you do? Security systems?"

"Among other things."

"Other things, that's good. It's good to diversify a little bit. You learn that in the computer business pretty damn fast." He leaned back and put his right foot on his left knee, looking up at me pleasantly. "So you and John O'Malley are on the same bowling team? Isn't that what Dierdre said?"

"That's right."

"For years, I think she said."

I nodded.

"Then how is it, Mr. Jacovich, that you don't know Dierdre's father is named Patrick and not John?"

Suddenly I would have given half my kingdom for a nap. I went behind my desk and sat down, wishing I'd had time to make the coffee. "Just what can I do for you, Mr. Braxton?"

"You can answer a few questions."

"I usually ask them," I said.

"Humor me."

I fumbled a Winston out of my pack and lit it.

"You shouldn't smoke in the same room with your computer," he said. "It doesn't do your hardware any good."

"It doesn't do my lungs any good either," I said, but I waved the smoke away from the computer terminal at my elbow. "Why are you here?"

"To find out," he said, "if you're sleeping with Dierdre O'Malley."

The question took me so much by surprise that I was rendered speechless for a second. "I don't think that's any of your business," I told him.

"Oh, it's very much my business. She's engaged to marry my son."

"Then shouldn't he be the one to ask me?"

He put his right foot on the floor beside his left. "Count your blessings. He wouldn't ask you nearly as politely as I am."

"Is that supposed to scare me?"

"It's supposed to appeal to your compassion."

"How's that?"

He allowed himself the smallest of frowns. "Alan is my only son, Mr. Jacovich. He heads up our R and D section right now, but I spent a fortune sending him to Stanford, so he could take over Braxton Software when I retire in a year or two. I spent twenty-eight years building up that business. Think back to the early seventies, when the idea of a personal computer in every home was a vague dream, and you'll realize how far we've come for a small mom-and-pop firm. We were pioneers, and we made good even though we weren't in Silicon Valley or any of the other electronic-age hot spots. I don't want to see it all fall through the cracks."

I didn't see what that had to do with me, so I waited.

"Alan has seen fit to choose this woman, Dierdre O'Malley, to be his life partner. All well and good, I suppose, although I'd hoped he would marry someone a little more—suitable."

"How is Ms. O'Malley unsuitable?"

"The girl has no college," he said. "She went to secretarial school."

And, I thought, she's a west side Irish Catholic who'll muddy the waters of the Braxton gene pool.

"Alan doesn't always keep his mind strictly on business," Braxton continued. "And he's not so terrific at judging people. He's a good engineer, mind you, but sometimes he loses his focus. He's young yet, and I'm hoping he'll grow out of it. But I don't want him to be distracted by anything when he moves into my chair. I want him to have a happy and peaceful marriage."

"We all want that for our children," I said.

"Alan in particular needs a supportive marriage that will enhance his life and career. If his wife is going to cause him problems, he'll not only suffer, but the company will as well. So I want to know if she's going to play around on him. If she does it during their engagement, there's no reason to believe she won't after they're married."

He took a deep breath. "And so I ask you again if you're involved with her in an intimate way."

"Mr. Braxton, you can go straight to hell," I said. "And the first step is out the door."

"I thought you'd say something like that." He dipped into the inside pocket of his suit jacket and brought forth a white envelope with the flap tucked in but not sealed. "There are ten one-hundred-dollar bills in there. They're yours. It's worth it to me for a little peace of mind. And the truth. Are you in a relationship with her or not? All you have to do is say one word: yes, or no." He touched the knot in his tie. "Only the best-selling authors earn a thousand dollars per word."

He tossed the envelope onto the desk in front of me. I let it lie there as if it carried the Ebola virus.

"Count it," he said.

I ignored him. "What is it you really want here, Braxton?"

"I told you, I—"

"That peace-of-mind fairy tale doesn't wash."

"It's not a fairy tale, I assure you."

"All that's missing is a wicked witch. You want something else, don't you? Something that's worth a thousand dollars to you."

He bristled. "What do you mean by that?"

I leaned back in my chair and looked at him from under heavy eyelids. "You tell me, Mr. Braxton."

He glared at me. "Why did you lie about knowing Deirdre's father?"

"I didn't. She did. Probably because you and your son are the way you are, suspicious and controlling, and you'd think the worst of a strange man visiting her in the office unless she made up a plausible excuse."

"Why did you come to see her yesterday?"

"That's my business. But I've got a good mind to tell you I am sleeping with her if it'll keep her from marrying into your family."

His features solidified into granite. "If you aren't, that thousand dollars is yours if you'll find out who is."

"Get out of my office. I'm busy."

"Perhaps you'd get unbusy for two thousand."

"Not for ten thousand."

"Why not?" He leaned forward and pushed the envelope closer to me. "That sort of thing is what you do, isn't it?"

"You're an entrepreneur, you run your own business. That gives you a certain freedom to do the things you want to do and skip the ones you don't." I pushed the money back at him. "Me, too."

Braxton looked at the envelope for a moment as if it were something that had once been alive. Then he picked it up and put it in his pocket. "Someone else will do it for half as much."

"Good for them," I said.

He looked at the gilt-framed photos of my two boys on my desk. "Your children, Mr. Jacovich?"

I nodded

"Someday you'll want to do something like this for one of them—you'll possibly want to do anything within your power, to save him heartache. And then you'll remember."

"If I did something like this, my boys would probably take a swing at me for treating them like babies. For meddling in their lives."

He stood up. "I hope I don't find out you're involved with Dierdre O'Malley—and that Alan doesn't find out. For your sake."

"That sounds very much like a threat, Mr. Braxton."

"Rather think of it as a word to the wise," he said.

As his footsteps receded down the stairs, I wondered if he had discovered that his son was a murderer and had come to me with his envelope full of money to make me stop trying to find out.

Or if he'd killed Darren Anderson himself.

It was possible, of course, that he was telling the truth. What he'd said about my being willing to do anything to keep my sons from heartache had struck home.

I remembered a day, shortly after my divorce when my younger boy, Stephen, was little more than a toddler. It was one of my court-mandated Sundays with my children, and I watched Stephen laugh and run and play in Euclid Beach Park, a lakefront recreation area on the site of what was once Cleveland's most famous amusement park. The joy on his little flower face was so beautiful it hurt my heart, and I never wanted it to go away. I wished that there was something I could do to save him from all the disappointment, hurt, fear, and frustration he would undoubtedly face in his lifetime, to make sure he never cried himself to sleep at night, to somehow preserve in amber this innocent, ebullient moment when he laughed and played.

But we can't do that for our kids. The kindness is in letting them go, in trusting them to make their own way.

I found myself hurting for Alan Braxton, and for Dierdre

O'Malley too. Their inappropriate match and Nathan Braxton's resistance to it would bring problems down the line, but if they were lucky, very lucky, they would weather them. Once they married, with Nathan's reluctant blessing, Patrick O'Malley would claim boasting rights on his bowling team, and Dierdre would ease into her place as the boss's wife, give elegant dinner parties, and go to expensive restaurants like the White Magnolia every week. Braxton Software would prosper as Alan matured and rediscovered what his father called his "focus." After a while some of the rough edges of Dierdre's blue-collar upbringing would probably be smoothed away, and they'd have children, and Dierdre would, like Alison Maniscalco, take up tennis and volunteerism, and each would probably have an affair.

And at the end of their lives they'd each look back, if not with happiness, then with a certain soft satisfaction, that they had persevered and survived.

I hoped like hell that neither Alan nor Dierdre had any hand in Darren Anderson's killing. And I hoped that I wouldn't have to be the one that betrayed Dierdre's secret.

All at once I felt very alone.

I pulled out my wallet and searched for Connie Haley's business card.

It might have been the young guy behind the bar who answered the phone. I asked to speak to Connie, and he put me on hold. No music, which was a plus.

"This is Connie."

"Hi. It's Milan Jacovich."

"Well, hi!" she said with a warmth that left no doubt that that she was pleased to hear from me, a warmth I could feel inside. "What's up?"

Marko Meglich's ring pulsed on my finger. "I'm hungry," I said.

CHAPTER FOURTEEN

Leave it to me to pick a Friday, one of the White Magnolia's busiest nights of the week, to ask Connie for a date.

She told me that if I wanted dinner, it would have to be at ten o'clock. "We couldn't squeeze in the mayor any earlier than that tonight. Have a couple of crackers to tide you over." She chuckled. "It'll be worth the wait."

I was sure it would. Quick, funny, perceptive Connie Haley, there was something very vibrant and alive about her, something that announced to one and all that she knew life was there to be lived.

I could use a little of that, I thought. A little change of perspective.

I straightened up the office, washing out the coffeepot and dusting a little. I even vacuumed. I don't know why I got so industrious all of a sudden; maybe the thought of my impending dinner with an attractive woman energized me. It had been a while since I'd even thought about having a good time.

But, I was thinking about Darren Anderson, too, about who would walk into his home and fire three bullets into his body at close range. And about the Maniscalcos and Dierdre and the Braxtons, and Sidney Friedman, Boyce Cort, and Suzi Flores. There was a plethora of suspects, but none seemed to be emerging as paramount. I had nothing really substantial to go on, and there didn't seem to be any way of speeding things up. I found myself hoping that Bob Matusen would crack the case over the weekend, leaving me to get on with my life.

At about four thirty I'd done all the damage I could in my office, so I figured I'd go home, watch the news, and take it easy until it was time to shower and change and head back to the west side and the White Magnolia.

But not even that simple plan would go off without a hitch—when I got to the parking lot I found a scowling Tom Maniscalco waiting beside his car, looking ready to rend raw meat with his teeth.

He wasn't alone, either. The man who accompanied him—dwarfed him, actually—was two inches taller than I am, with an oversize head and a prognathous jaw that was several teeth short of a full set, as I could easily see, because he was breathing noisily through his mouth. He was probably in his forties; his hair was cut very short to disguise the fact he was losing most of it, and he sported a little toothbrush mustache that looked silly on someone of his bulk. He had a thin gold ring through his left eyebrow, and in a leather scabbard at his belt a hunting knife the size of a Scottish broadsword. His sleeveless khaki undershirt revealed the tattoos all over his arms and shoulders, colorful dragons and serpents and skulls and bloody daggers. My particular favorite, on his right bicep, featured two pigs copulating. The guy was a real class act.

Maniscalco said my last name and moved toward me, the set of his neck stiff and aggressive. Tattoos followed him, sleepy-eyed, loose-jointed, moving as if his spine was made of rubber. He reminded me of a dog that had been overbred.

"Mr. Maniscalco—"

"Shut up!" Maniscalco barked. He doubled up his fist and shook it under my chin. "You came to my home, Jacovich," he roared, like Al Pacino in one of his less effective performances, "*when I wasn't there.* How *dare* you come to my home uninvited when I'm not there?" he demanded. "How fucking *dare* you?"

"I tried to do it the right way. I asked Victor Gaimari to set up a meeting between us, and you said no."

"So you took it upon yourself to *come to my home*?"

"I have my job to do, Mr. Maniscalco. A man has been killed."

"He won't be the only one," Maniscalco said darkly, "if you bother my family again."

Tattoos gave me a menacing look and moved his arms and shoulders around as if getting the kinks out preparatory to doing something physical. The pigs on his bicep seemed to enjoy the activity.

"If you'd give me five minutes," I said, "we can straighten this out."

"I won't give you five seconds, except fair warning," Maniscalco snarled. "Keep your nose out of my business."

I glanced at Tattoos. To a casual observer he might have seemed almost relaxed, but I knew that inside he was tightly coiled like the mainspring of a ten-dollar watch. It was his eyes that gave him away, small and mean and bright. Feral, predatory eyes.

"Who's this?" I asked. "Your business manager?"

Tattoos straightened his backbone a little, bringing his height to about six foot five. "Smart guy, huh?" he mumbled with an accent I couldn't place, hitting the *t* in *smart* very hard.

"Nice eyebrow ring," I said. "I admire a guy who knows how to accesorize."

Tattoos grinned like a wolf who's just spotted a baby deer and moved forward a little. Maniscalco backed up a step and put an arm out across Tattoos' midsection, the way you do when you brake your car quickly and try to keep your passenger from flying through the windshield. "Take it easy, Albert."

"Albert?" I said.

The big man glowered so much his eyebrow ring almost got in his eye. He licked his lips and cracked the knuckles of his right hand, making the sound bubble-wrap makes when it's popped.

"I'm not going to tell you twice, Jacovich," Maniscalco said. "You stay the hell away from me and from my family. I don't want to hear your name ever again."

He spun around and walked back to his car, a Volvo that had been painted a sickly yellow. Albert imitated a statue for a moment, staring me down boldly, his eyes dark and flat, like the eyes of one of the stuffed animals in the Museum of Natural History.

"I'm gonna be seeing you again," he said; he pronounced it "seeink." He snorted deeply, hawked up a lunger and spat it deliberately toward my shoe.

I never knew I could move my feet so fast.

Albert didn't move very fast at all. He walked back to the Volvo slowly, giving me another hungry, lupine look before he got in—I think he'd seen Jack Palance in *Shane* a few times too many—and Maniscalco drove off with a backward shower of gravel and tore across the Eagle Avenue Bridge and up the incline out of sight.

I went back into the building and trudged up the stairs to my office. The finger on which I wore Marko's ring felt tingly, as though it was falling asleep.

Calling Victor Gaimari this late on a Friday afternoon was iffy at best. He frequently took off on weekends, for New York or Chicago, or Naples, near the southern end of Florida's Gulf Coast. Of course in mid August, chances were he hadn't gone south—it was hot enough in Cleveland.

But this time I was in luck.

"You caught me just as I was leaving," he said. "What can I do for you?"

I told him about my recent visitors.

"I warned you Maniscalco had a temper," Victor said sadly. "You should listen to me more often, Milan."

I ignored him; I don't care for being lectured. "Who was the guy with him?" I said. "Maniscalco called him Albert. Big tall ugly guy with close-cropped hair, little eyes, only about half his teeth. Speaks with some kind of accent. And he's got tattoos all over his body."

"Tattoos?"

"Lots of them. Including two pigs fucking."

"Tasteful," Victor said.

"He's a professional hitter. I can spot one a mile away. Is he on Maniscalco's payroll?"

"Maniscalco is a furniture importer. Why would he have full-time muscle?"

"An importer? I thought he was a manufacturer."

"He is, but he imports too. I can't think why he'd need a bodyguard or an enforcer."

"The tattoo guy isn't one of yours, then?"

"The only one of our people who comes illustrated, as far as I know, is John Terranova, my uncle's driver. He got his from a prison tattoo artist while he was doing two years in Mansfield. It's on his ankle. The Virgin Mary. He pulled down his sock and showed it to me once." He sighed. "One of life's unforgettable moments."

"So Maniscalco brought this guy along to make me nervous."

"Did he make a move?"

"Not if you don't count spitting on my shoe."

"Then maybe he was there just to get your attention."

"He got it, all right."

"Good. You'd better watch your back."

"I don't scare easily."

"I know. It's one of your major failings."

"Can you ask around?"

"About the tattoo man?"

"Yeah. I'd like to know who he is and where he came from."

"Albert, hmm?" There was a beat. "I'm feeling a little conflicted here, Milan."

"Why? Because of Maniscalco's friendship with your uncle?"

"Well . . ."

"Or because of you and Alison?"

He exhaled noisily through his nose. "I'd hate to see you get hurt."

"Me too."

He took a moment to think it over. "Are you asking me for our protection?"

I'd known Victor long enough to understand that in his world formal protection came with a price that had nothing to do with money, and I didn't want to be obligated. Besides, I didn't think I needed protection. I like to think I can take care of myself. Silly me.

"No," I said. "I just want to know everyone's name and number."

"I can't pull someone off you if he doesn't work for me."

"I understand that."

"I guess I can make a few phone calls and see what I can find out." And then he added meaningfully, "Information doesn't cost anything."

Translated from the Wise-Guy-ese, that meant it was a favor for which Victor and his uncle would not expect repayment. I'd repaid one of Victor's favors once and almost gotten myself killed for my troubles. "I'd take it kindly, Victor."

After I broke the connection I locked up the office again, went downstairs, and drove home in what Cleveland calls a rush hour, which in a lot of other, more populous towns like Chicago or Boston would be gratefully termed light traffic.

I parked in my appointed space when I got back up to my place in Cleveland Heights, but I looked around carefully before getting out of the car. Then I walked up the stairs casting glances above and behind me, unlocked my apartment door, and opened it with a lot more care than usual.

I *don't* scare easily, and I don't like having to look over my shoulder all the time. But after Tom Maniscalco's overt threat, and with someone like Tattooed Albert looking at me as though I were his lunch, I'd be a damn fool not to be on my guard.

I couldn't help wondering why, though. Maniscalco knew that I was aware of what had transpired between Bethany and Darren Anderson already, so there had to be something else. A furniture importer with a clean reputation and a charitable bent who suddenly shows up with a tag-along leg-breaker must have a lot more than a promiscuous daughter to hide.

Maybe he'd hired Tattoos to wreak revenge on Darren, although from the look of him, Albert wouldn't have had to waste bullets on a lightweight like Darren Anderson. He could have dismembered him with one hand.

Or maybe there was something else, in which case it was none of my business.

But I don't like being physically threatened; I like even less being spat upon. I was going to make it my business. I was going to find out why, and having made the decision, I felt a frisson of excitement run up my back.

There it was; the familiar adrenaline rush that was my own particular addiction. Old Vuk, as usual, was right.

I'd left the apartment air conditioner on low all day, but the weather was too hot and muggy for it to do much good. I cranked it up to high, took off my jacket, loosened my tie, and got a beer out of the refrigerator, which I took into my den and set down next to the phone.

I dialed Ed Stahl's number, certain that he'd be home, even on a Friday evening. I think the last time Ed actually had a date with a woman, they'd gone to see *Love Is a Many Splendored Thing*.

"This house feels like a pizza oven," he said. "I'm thinking of going to a restaurant just to get out of the heat. Want to come?"

"I can't, I'm happy to say."

"That must mean there's a woman involved."

"I don't know how involved, Ed. But I do have a dinner date."

"Good for you," he said. "And you're calling me up to gloat?"

"I'm calling to pick your brain."

"As usual. What do you need?"

"Ever hear of a guy named Tom Maniscalco? He owns Home Works Furniture in Middleburgh Heights."

"Heard of him, yeah. Catholic charities and the Republican Party. Nothing hinky, though. Why?"

"He's not one of my many fans," I said. "Came to visit me this afternoon with a hired goon on a leash."

"My God. Why?"

I hesitated. Ed is first and last a newspaperman. "It's not for publication, Ed."

"Does this have anything to do with the Anderson kid?"

"You're the one that got me into that," I reminded him.

"I know, but I already did my ten seconds of guilt for it. What's this business about Maniscalco?"

"It has to be off the record."

"Don't talk to me off the record," he said. "This is what I do for a living, Milan. I get fascinating stories about what's going on in this town, stories that no other journalist can come up with, and I verify them and then I write them and the paper prints them. We've done this dance before. Come on, give."

"There are other people to be considered," I said. "Innocent people, more or less. So I can't tell you."

I heard him puffing at his pipe. "Suit yourself, then," he said, sounding dyspeptic, and for a while after we said good-bye I worried that I had burned some valuable goodwill. I hoped not.

Ed and I often use one another professionally. He was my unofficial source for who-does-what-to-whom in Greater Cleveland, because what he doesn't know about something or someone is probably not worth knowing. And I'd never unraveled a case, especially one involving anyone prominent in the city, without giving the story to him before all the other reporters in town got hold of it.

But paramount was our friendship.

And I'd threatened it by asking him for something while refusing to offer a quid pro quo.

I'd done the same thing with Victor Gaimari.

Maybe I was turning into what I hated most—a user.

I'd mend those fences later, I thought. After Darren Anderson's killer was caught.

There wasn't much I could do about it now, though. The weekend was coming up, and nothing ever happens on weekends, especially in the summertime. Offices are closed, people are either day-tripping or else outside doing all the things they can't do during Cleveland's long, dreary, pewter gray winters, and those of us who are not nine-to-fivers and try to accomplish something on a Saturday or Sunday are stymied at every turn.

Even poor Ray and Betty Dinsmoor had to sit around all weekend cooling their heels in a motel near the airport, until the bureaucracy could arrange a burial transfer permit so they could take their fallen son home.

I checked my watch; it was twenty minutes after six. Maybe I could catch one more person before the indolent weekend kicked in.

Sidney Friedman sounded ecstatic. "Milan. Hey, hey. Guess what?"

"What?"

"We got Eric Winslow."

"Excuse me?"

"Eric Winslow. He's going to replace Darren in the picture—and I got him for four million. Not only that, Boyce figured we'd only have to shoot an additional six days to replace the footage we already had with Darren. Oh God, this is great. I'm kvelling!"

Five years earlier, Eric Winslow had been as hot a Hollywood property as Darren Anderson was at the time of his death, another James Dean wanna-be with sulky eyes, bad diction, bad manners, and what the moviegoing public perceived as sex appeal to spare. When his starlet wife walked out on him for another man, triggering a messy divorce that even bumped O.J. Simpson onto the third page of the tabloids temporarily, the luster of his star dimmed a bit, apparently because in the public perception, beautiful blondes just didn't walk out on sex symbols. His ten-million-dollars-per-picture price had plummeted, and his blockbuster box-office days seemed to be over, but he was still a viable commodity, and he would probably be a credible replacement for Darren Anderson.

"He's arriving tomorrow night," Sidney burbled, "and we start shooting Monday."

"That's great." My enthusiasm sounded tepid even to me.

"So you're back on the payroll, starting Monday. Same old same old. You'll come to the set late afternoon, you'll pick up Eric, you'll show him around just like you did Darren, take him to dinner, introduce him to important people in town."

"Sidney," I said.

"Of course, we're not going to put him in that house out in Bay Village—that'd be ghoulish."

"Sidney."

"Maybe you could talk your reporter friend, whatsisname, Ed Stahl, into doing a piece on him. You know, what it's like to step into a role after someone—"

"Sidney," I said again.

"What?"

"Get yourself another guy."

"What do you mean?"

"I'm not baby-sitting actors anymore. I don't want the job."

"What do you mean you don't want the job?"

"Which part don't you understand?"

"What are you, independently wealthy?" he sputtered. "All of a sudden, you don't need a job?"

"I still have your dollar," I said. "That'll tide me over."

"But I need you, kid."

If he thought I found being called "kid" by someone at least ten years my junior flattering, he was seriously mistaken. "Sorry, Sidney. I can't do it. Besides, I'm already working for you on another matter. I don't have time to do both."

"That other matter doesn't really count anymore, Milan. I've got the picture up and running again, and I'm behind schedule because of what happened to Darren. I don't want to take the time."

"So it doesn't matter anymore who killed Darren."

"Sure it does," he said. "To the police. But I'm a businessman. This is business. I've got a picture to get in the can. I need your help."

"Sidney," I said. "I'm not interested. But I do need *your* help."

"What?" he grumbled, sounding sullen, wounded. Sidney still had problems with no.

"Tom Maniscalco."

I heard him suck in his breath. "What about him?"

"Is he pulling out his investment in the picture the way he threatened to?"

"No, thank God. For a while I was scared he would, but now that Darren's not a factor anymore, he's okay with it."

"Now that Darren's not a factor," I repeated, hardly believing he'd talk that way about a young man who'd been shot to death.

"Right. And he and the other investors are thrilled we were able to get Eric. They're all staying in." He sounded inordinately pleased with himself again. "I had to do some pretty fancy talking, but they're sticking with us."

"And is Tom's wife still going to do a small part?"

"Sure. Hey, she's only got a couple of lines, how bad could she be? And he's paying about a million bucks for each one of them."

"Uh-huh."

"What difference does it make to you, anyway?"

"Just asking," I said.

"Well, look, Milan." He cleared his throat. "Now that we have Eric Winslow, now that the investors are back on board and the picture is going to go ahead . . ."

I waited.

"I'd just as soon you backed off this investigation thing. Darren has been replaced, the project's got a green light, and there just isn't any point anymore, you know what I'm saying?"

"Yes, I do; I speak English. Do you want your dollar back?"

"Why dig up a lot of crap on people when you don't have to, right?"

"Was this your idea, or did it come from Tom Maniscalco?"

"Come on, Milan. You know me better than that."

"I don't know you at all, Sidney. But I know Maniscalco wants me to quit digging around, and since he's one of your big investors, I thought he might have mentioned it to you."

"I'm offended," Sidney said. "I'm really offended that you'd think that of me."

"Does that mean Maniscalco didn't ask you to call me off?"

"It means that I'm offended. You keep walking out on me."

"I'm not walking out, I'm just turning down a new job. There's a difference."

"There is, huh? Not from where I'm sitting. Deserter! Weenie traitor! Listen, I don't want to talk to you, got it? Ever. You're not working for me anymore."

He banged the phone down, making my ear ring. I hung my own receiver up more gently.

Whether it offended Sidney Friedman or not, I thought it was entirely possible that Tom Maniscalco had applied some gentle pressure to make Sidney make me back off. He'd tried to offer me my job as wet nurse back, to a Darren Anderson clone this time, so I'd be too busy to do anything else. And when that hadn't worked, he'd simply told me to go away.

But if it hadn't come from Maniscalco, then maybe Sidney had his own reasons for jerking my leash.

I stripped off my clothes and spent ten minutes under a hot shower, feeling cooler when I stepped out, and managed to gash myself on the chin shaving. Then I switched on the TV in my bedroom and began dressing for my dinner date with Connie Haley.

Just as *American Tab* came on.

Rebekka Sommars looked beautiful in a silk pantsuit the color of chardonnay and a blue scarf that matched her eyes. She was reporting on the murder of Darren Anderson, which was no surprise. The murder had been the lead story on every local and national newscast for several days.

Hearing my name on national television, however—*that* was a surprise.

"*American Tab* has discovered that the producers hired a bodyguard for Darren Anderson while he was in Cleveland shooting the film," Rebekka Sommars was saying. "A local private investigator named Milan Jacovich. This is not Mr. Jacovich's first encounter with violent death; several of his earlier cases have involved some of Cleveland's most talked-about murders."

My limbs turned to lead; I sat down heavily on the edge of the bed, mesmerized by her lovely, animated face on the tube.

"Mr. Jacovich refused to talk to us on camera and was unable or unwilling to discuss Darren Anderson's whereabouts last Sunday, the day before he was killed. Given Anderson's reputation as a playboy, could there be a mystery woman involved in the murder of one of the world's most popular movie stars? Jacovich would neither confirm nor deny, which makes this reporter wonder if he himself has something to hide."

The program went on to show clips from Darren's movies, and candid shots of him with various women with whom he'd been linked in the past, including several well-known young actresses and an anorexic-looking supermodel. I'm not really sure what else she said. I just sat there on the edge of the bed in my underwear, a pair of socks dangling from my limp grasp.

Now I knew what Sommars' cryptic "You'll see" had meant. She'd made me famous, all right. Now people in Boise, Idaho, and Biloxi, Mississippi, and Scottsdale, Arizona, knew my name, knew who I was, and thought I had something to hide.

Big blue eyes, stunning figure, and starlet good looks and all, Rebekka Sommars was one tough reporter. She played hardball, all right.

The phone jolted me out of my stupor. It was my younger son, Stephen, and he could barely contain his excitement.

"Dad! Dad!" he burbled. "They were just talking about you on TV!" He stopped to take a breath. "Radical!" he said.

Now I belonged to the ages.

I was still brooding about it three hours later as I drove westward to the White Magnolia, my chin stinging where I'd applied a styptic pencil to stanch the bleeding. I always seem to cut myself shaving when I want to look particularly good. All sorts of disastrous scenarios were playing themselves out in my head, the foremost of which was that no one would ever trust me again and my career as an investigator and security specialist was over. In my imagination, everyone in the free world had seen the telecast.

Maybe this dinner date with Connie hadn't been such a good idea, I thought, since my mind was not only on my own problems and what *American Tab*'s report might do to my professional standing, but on Darren Anderson, and on whether Tom Maniscalco's hired Neanderthal was just there to get on my nerves or really meant business.

I hoped Connie Haley was well up to the task of diversion.

CHAPTER FIFTEEN

I handed my car over to the valet in front of the White Magnolia and walked inside. This time there wasn't anyone waiting for a table at the bar. It was, after all, ten o'clock in the evening, and Clevelanders generally go to bed early. Even on Friday night.

But the dining room was still buzzing. I spotted the CEO of a Fortune 500 company playing host to a party of six, and a well-known east side attorney who had traversed the Cuyahoga to hold hands across the snowy tablecloth with a pretty woman who was not his wife. I supposed he would pay the bill in cash.

Leo Haley was down at the curve at the end of the bar, wearing a white linen jacket over a lavender shirt and flowered tie that didn't quite fit with the iron gray crew cut. He came around and shook my hand as if he was genuinely glad to see me.

"It's the gumshoe," he said without rancor.

"Hello, Mr. Haley."

"Leo. Everybody calls me Leo. Maybe because Leo's not a real common name, and so everyone likes to say it. If my name was Jim or Bob or Joe I probably wouldn't hear it that much. But people like to say Leo." He cocked his head at me. "You must have the same thing with a name like Milan, huh?"

"I never thought about it," I said. "But I guess you're right. People do say my name a lot when they talk to me."

"That what's-her-name, she said your name on television plenty tonight."

I winced. "Rebekka Sommars. I was hoping nobody in the world was watching that."

"Don't let it bother you. By Monday morning everyone will have forgotten about it except you." He stuck his chin out at me. "And me, maybe. I hear you're having dinner with my daughter."

I nodded, half expecting to get an argument about it. "Is that okay with you?"

"You asking my permission?"

"No."

He relaxed a little, smiling. "Good. If you were the kind of guy who had to ask, I wouldn't give it to you. Connie wouldn't be going out with you if you had to ask her old man's permission. Since you didn't, I think it's great."

I smiled back. "Don't you want to ask what my intentions are?"

"I know damn well what your intentions are," he said darkly. "I didn't just fall off the turnip truck."

I felt myself blushing and was glad for the dim lighting in the bar.

"Connie's quite a woman," he said.

"That's why I'm here."

He turned and waved at the bartender, the young man in the Browns T-shirt I'd seen on my last visit. Tonight he wore a white shirt with a black tie and a black vest. "Kevin, this gentleman's drinking on the house tab," he announced. Then gave me a sly grin. "For tonight."

Beer seemed awfully inelegant for the occasion, so I started with a Black Jack. I'd barely tasted it when Connie came out of the office.

No one could possibly look better in a little black dress. Tonight her long blond braid was fastened with a tasty black bow that matched the dress. She looked at once young and terribly wicked, summer-fresh and slinky, solid and seductive. Her eyes sparkled and flirted and promised and smiled, and when her mouth smiled too it made her dimple deepen.

I tried to remember the last time I'd felt the way I did at that instant and either couldn't or wouldn't; I didn't want to put even a tiny smudge of old memory on the moment, because it was making new memories of its own before she even sat down. I slid off the stool to greet her.

"Hi, hungry man," she said, and stood on tiptoe to kiss my cheek. It was nice that she'd kissed me in front of her father and the bartender. She hoisted herself onto the adjoining stool; it was a warm night and she hadn't bothered with stockings. Her legs were tan.

"I hope you didn't have your face set for the shark with pesto," she said. "Because we're sold out of it."

"Well, that's it, I'm going home then."

"You have shark at home?"

"Almost as good—peanut butter and jelly."

"Smooth or crunchy?"

"Extra crunchy."

"A man after my own heart. So far. What kind of jelly?"

"Grape."

"Good boy. I was afraid you were going to be a blueberry guy."

"Do I look like a blueberry guy?"

"No, but a girl can't be too careful."

"Most people ask you your astrological sign, not what kind of jelly you like."

"You'll find," she said, "that I'm not most people."

"I know that already. That's why I drove all the way out here from Cleveland Heights."

"A geographical snob, huh? One of those east siders who never cross the river unless it's to go to the airport?"

"I only cross the river for 'not most' people," I told her. "What is your sign, anyway?"

She pulled my drink over toward her, raised it to her lips, and took a sip. "Slippery When Wet," she said.

"My sign used to be Dangerous Children Crossing."

"Used to be?"

"Before the vasectomy."

She threw back her head and laughed. "That's good. I've always wondered, just who are those dangerous children that are crossing anyway?"

"They're the ones who grew up and went into politics."

She pushed my drink back at me, the barest trace of lipstick on the rim of the glass. "Ah, it's hell to grow up, isn't it?"

"When I do, I'll let you know," I said. I was nearly breathless.

Leo came and told us he had a table and led us back through the dining room. Several patrons greeted Connie by name.

"No menus," Leo said gruffly when we'd been seated. "You'll eat whatever we fix for you."

"Milan likes chunky peanut butter, Leo," Connie told him.

"Sorry, but we're out of it," he said. "Since about twenty years before we opened."

"My second choice is shark with pesto."

He folded his arms and riveted me with a stern gaze. "This guy's gonna give us trouble, Connie, right?"

"I hope so," Connie Haley said.

The first course was calamari. I'm not a big fan—I think a squid is one of God's ugliest creatures, one I'm not fond of putting in my mouth, but I had to admit it was very tasty as prepared by the White Magnolia, gently sauteed and served in a spicy marinara sauce. I told Connie so.

"My father thanks you, my brother thanks you, and I thank you," she said. I was pleased to find that young as she was, she could paraphrase Jimmy Cagney in *Yankee Doodle Dandy*. I generally prefer vintage movies to today's brand of Hollywood special-effects schlock.

"Your brother?"

"Sean. He's the chef. The bartender is my other brother, Kevin."

"The White Magnolia is a family affair, huh?"

"Leo thinks it keeps the payroll down. And since we're all partners and all family, nobody skims from the cash drawer." She licked a speck of marinara sauce off her lower lip. "You ought to see this place on Saint Patrick's Day. It gets kind of insane."

"Does your mother work here too?"

She shook her head. "She died right after Kevin was born. I'm the oldest, so I practically raised my brothers while Dad was off being a marine."

"So I was right," I said. "I thought he was an ex-marine. He's got Semper Fi written all over him."

She laughed. "He's got that way about him, doesn't he?"

"Drill sergeant?"

"Oh my, no. A major. He was born in Cleveland, on West Seventy-eighth Street, but we lived all over the world. I was born in Bangkok, Sean in Virginia, and Kevin in California. After he had twenty-five years in, Dad took his pension and bought this restaurant. Both Sean and Kevin did four-year hitches, too."

"How come you didn't?"

"I didn't want to be a big-assed marine," she said. "It's my job to take care of the girl stuff in the family."

"You do the girl stuff very well."

She tasted the white wine that had arrived at the table with the calamari and nodded to herself. "I think that was a compliment, wasn't it?"

"I hope it was," I said. "Never been married?"

She hunched her shoulders. "Relationships yes, wedding bells no. I guess I just never had the inclination."

She finished up her share of the calamari with relish. "How

about you now, Milan?" she asked when the plate was clean. "Do I get a life story?"

"Only the Cliff Notes. My parents came from Slovenia," I said, "but I was born on East Sixty-seventh and St. Clair. A B.A. in business and a masters in psychology from Kent State. Vietnam— the army, sorry about that. I was an MP. Enlisted."

"Leo will forgive you," she assured me. "You were young."

"I got married when I came back from Southeast Asia. I spent a couple of years with the Cleveland PD. Since then I've been private. Divorced for a long time now. Two boys—Milan, seventeen, and Stephen, who's eleven."

She seemed to be waiting for something else. I turned my hands palms upward.

"No more?" she asked.

"Not much. I live a boring kind of life."

"Why don't I believe that?" she said.

The soup arrived, thick and brown and creamy. I inhaled its aroma.

"Garlic soup?"

"You don't like garlic soup?"

"I love it. But I may want to get kissed tonight."

"It'll be okay if we both eat it," she said, her blue eyes big and ingenuous.

It was a lot better than okay. It was wonderful.

So was the main course, filet mignon with a cognac and peppercorn sauce. It was accompanied by a rich merlot, which complemented the strong flavors of the steak but didn't clash with them.

"Fabulous," I said. "My compliments to the chef."

"You can give them to him yourself," she said, pointing with her chin at the dining room entrance. "Here comes Sean now."

The young man who came walking toward us, dressed all in chef's white and wearing his toque, was even bigger and more fit-looking than his brother. Connie introduced us. His handshake was bone-crushing, his eyes as big and blue as his sister's, and just as full of merriment.

"My father said I should stop by the table and check you out," he said good-naturedly.

"You always do that with Connie's dates?"

"Better believe it."

"Do I pass?"

"I haven't decided yet," he said. "I like your jacket, if that helps."

"And I like your cooking. The dinner is really spectacular."

He grinned. "*Now* you pass."

"Care to join us?" I asked.

"Thanks, but I've got to get back to the kitchen. Besides, you really don't want Connie's big brother hanging around on your first date."

"I thought she was the oldest."

"I said big brother, not older brother. I'll have a drink with you guys after dinner, though." He looked at Connie. "Unless you have other plans."

"If we do," Connie said, "they'll wait until after the drink."

I watched him weaving his way between the crowded tables. He moved with the grace of a puma.

"I like your family," I said.

"Okay, but you can't move in with us—we'd have to put in another bathroom."

"Not on my account. I can go outside in the bushes."

"Don't think you'd be the first."

She dug into her steak with evident joy. "Now wait a second," she said when she came up for air. "You say your life is boring, but I met you when you came into my restaurant looking for a killer. Two weeks before that you were in here with a movie star. And that Twinkie on TV said you'd been involved in several murders. That doesn't sound boring to me."

"I don't like to talk about murder on the first date," I said.

"Force yourself."

"Why?"

"Because *I've* never been involved with a murder before."

"You're not involved with one now."

"Well, you are. And I'm involved with you."

"Not yet," I said.

"Remember you said that." She picked at the new potatoes. "Okay, Milan, we'll play it your way. One step at a time. But when you came in here and asked for information, I gave it to you, no questions asked."

"So?"

"So," she said playfully, "now I'm asking a question."

I looked into the steady, bright gaze of those impossible eyes, not wanting to discuss anything as morbid as the Darren Anderson business with her, but not wanting to say no to her either.

This woman was getting to me. I tried to shake it off, to rationalize it. I hadn't been in a relationship for almost a year. I hadn't dated, had hardly spoken to a woman or anyone else since Marko died. I was lonely, I was vulnerable, she was pretty and sharp and smart and I liked her family, and she'd flirted with me shamelessly from the moment I first laid eyes on her. Was that all there was to this dizzying, spiraling flutter I was feeling in the hollow of my chest?

What the hell?

The shelves of bookstores are bursting at the seams with learned or not-so-learned tomes on how to find the mate of your dreams, how to trap a man, how to attract women, allusions to Mars and Venus, etc. But for me, I realized as I looked across the table at Connie Haley, it was simple. I am always most interested in the woman who seems most interested in me.

So I told her about Darren Anderson. I didn't name names, other than Darren's and Sidney's, and I didn't tell her about my visit from Tattoos that afternoon, but the rest of it was there, and she listened attentively, nodding occasionally, her brows knit in concentration, her blue eyes intent.

When I finished, she exhaled audibly, as though she'd been holding her breath.

"So," I said.

"So."

"You think you have it solved for me?"

"Not yet," she said, "but give me a few minutes."

"Everybody's got a motive."

"Uh-huh. But they all seem pretty lame to me."

"Lame?"

"Everybody can get angry. Really angry. Angry enough to fantasize about killing somebody. But to really do it? In a planned, premeditated way?" She shook her head.

"What then?"

"One simple question."

"And that is?"

"Who profits?" she said. "With Darren Anderson dead, who's the one who profits?"

❊ ❊ ❊ ❊ ❊ ❊ ❊ ❊ ❊

CHAPTER SIXTEEN

❊ ❊ ❊ ❊ ❊ ❊ ❊ ❊ ❊

It was a few minutes past midnight, and the White Magnolia was closed for the evening. The waitstaff and kitchen crew had gone home. Without the low conversational murmur of a hundred customers to drown it out, the traditional Irish music playing on the sound system seemed unnaturally loud. It was sometimes mournful, sometimes angry, sometimes full of Celtic exuberance; it didn't sound anything like the soothing show-tunes-with-strings that were usually piped in during dinner hour.

There's something wonderfully intimate about a busy restaurant after it's closed for the night. All the White Mag's dirty dishes had been cleared away and washed, and most of the lights in the dining room were turned off; the only illumination came from the discreet ceiling lights in the lounge area and the subdued fluorescents behind the bar. The air still hummed with the energy of all the people who had wined and dined there that night, but there was a peaceful feeling too.

Connie and I were sitting at the bar with the rest of the Haleys; Kevin, tie now removed and collar unbuttoned for comfort, was still at his post behind the stick, Connie sat between Sean and me, and Leo was around the curve at the end, in what I would discover to be his usual place, from where he could keep watch on the dining room and the lounge at the same time and still see who came in the front door. Leo was drinking Bushmills neat, Connie had a glass of red wine, and the rest of us had chosen Armagnac.

It all seemed very casual, except I understood—and the Haleys knew I did—that this was a sort of interview, an initiation ceremony I was sure most of Connie's gentleman friends went through. I figured she would date whomever she chose, whether her family approved or not, but that the ritual vetting of her beaux, the familial punching of the guy's ticket, had to go on anyway.

"So you're a divorced man, Milan?" Leo Haley said, smacking his lips over his Irish whiskey. "A little unusual, isn't it, for a Slovenian and a Catholic?"

"It wasn't my idea."

"Uh-oh. Still pining away?"

"Hardly. It was another lifetime ago."

"You have an interesting job, Milan," young Kevin said. "Being a private detective and all. You must meet all kinds of people."

"It generally holds my attention."

"And you get talked about on television," Sean put in.

"You saw that, huh?"

"Does it ever get dangerous?" Kevin asked. "Your job, I mean?"

I chose my next words as carefully as an elderly babushka selects tomatoes at the West Side Market. I'd had more than one woman walk out of my life because they were unable to accept or deal with the occasional danger that often attended my work.

"Driving over the Valley View Bridge on I–480 gets dangerous sometimes," I said. "So does standing behind a bar and serving alcohol to someone who looks just fine but is only half a drink away from becoming a serial killer. Danger comes with living in this century, in this time. I've gotten so I don't even think about it."

"But you have to watch your ass nonetheless," Leo said.

"You have to watch your ass to avoid getting mugged on a lonely street. And sometimes you do anyway."

"Hasn't stopped you from getting shot a couple times."

I turned on the stool to look at Leo Haley.

"I have some friends in the department," he continued. "You took a bullet in the ass about a year ago or so. They told me all about you."

"You mean you asked them."

He nodded easily. "I've only got one daughter."

"Maybe I should have had dinner with Kevin, then."

"I'd have something to say about that," Connie protested, and linked her arm in mine, pulling me closer to her.

"I survived Vietnam," I said, "and managed to get through two tours in-country without getting shot. It's just that the bullet with my name on it was in Cleveland, not Cam Ranh Bay."

"I don't want there to be any bullet with Connie's name on it. If she's running around with you . . ."

"Not likely, Leo."

"Not impossible, either."

"It's not impossible we'll get hit by a semi on the way to the movies," Connie said. "Come on, lighten up. When did you ever teach us to play it safe?"

"That's right, Leo," Sean put in. "All those years in the marine corps, any of us could've bought the farm."

"Dad's going to say that we're guys," Kevin observed. "Connie's a girl."

"I can assure all of you that Connie's safety will be my number-one priority." I glanced over at her. "If she ever wants to see me again."

She hugged my arm even tighter. "That depends, Milan."

"On?"

"On whether you let these big bullies intimidate you."

I looked levelly at Leo Haley. "I've been *un*intimidated by experts."

He returned my stare for a moment or two, then threw back his head and roared with laughter. "All right, then, we'll just have to get another drink or two into you. To soften you up."

"Perish the thought," Connie said.

We had a final drink. It was about one o'clock in the morning by the time I walked Connie out to her car.

She opened the passenger door of the white Ford Taurus with her key. "Sit a while and talk," she said. "I've hardly had a minute alone with you."

I slid in and reached over to unlock her door. When she got in, she put the key in the ignition, turned it far enough to activate the electrical system, and rolled down the windows. After a hot, muggy day the night had turned cool and pleasant, and the gentle breeze from the mile-distant lake blew through the car like a kiss.

"Sorry about all that in there," she said. "Leo and the boys mean well."

"I know they do. It didn't bother me. I like them a lot. You seem like a happy family."

"I don't know about happy," she said. "We fight like hell most of the time. And being the only female in a pretty macho crowd, sometimes I have to fight harder than anyone. But we're close."

"I can see that. Well?"

"Well what?" She put the steering wheel into its highest position and turned in the driver's seat to face me.

"Did I pass the test?"

"I'd say you aced it. Otherwise they would have all walked out here with us." She put out a hand and ran it over the side of my face and my ear, then around to the back of my neck. "To prevent us from making out in the car."

"But they didn't," I said. "So we can."

"Right," she said.

We moved toward each other with the eagerness of puppies, but our first real kiss wasn't in the least puppyish. Her tongue tasted like fine Merlot and her lips held a hint of strawberries, which I assumed came from the lipstick.

We hardly disengaged for about five minutes.

Finally she broke away, catching her breath and straightening her clothes. She didn't have much lipstick left.

"I'm not going to sleep with you tonight," she said.

"I haven't asked you to."

"I noticed."

"It doesn't mean I don't want to, though."

"I want to, too. But—there's no rush. I would like to see you again."

"That's good to know," I said.

"I get so tired of women whining about not having any dates, when all they'd have to do is be honest and let a guy know they're interested. Playing hard to get is just that—playing. And I don't like games." She brushed at a wisp of hair that had come loose from the braid. "I don't do casual very well. Not that I haven't been across the street a few times, but when I go, it's never casual."

"I guess that's why I had to take my orals with your menfolk in there."

Her laugh was hearty. "Orals," she said.

"That's not dirty."

"I know, Jacovich, I went to college, too. Baldwin-Wallace. I majored in accounting."

"Handy when you own a restaurant."

"Usually I just work days. In case you're worried we're only going to see each other in the middle of the night."

"I'm not worried about anything," I said. "Should I be?"

By way of an answer, she moved close to me again. "Don't you hate cars that have consoles in the middle like this? Life was so much easier when all cars had bench seats."

"Adjust," I said, and reached for her.

✳   ✳   ✳

Unless you're in the Flats or the Warehouse District, Cleveland is pretty quiet after one A.M., even on weekends. I made it home in about twenty-five minutes, pretty good time considering I live clear on the other side of town. If I'd been walking, my feet would never have touched the sidewalk.

I hadn't taken my beeper with me to dinner, and when I got in the light on my answering machine was flickering. There was a single message, from Victor Gaimari.

"Can we have breakfast tomorrow morning?" his recorded voice said. "I'll come by your way. The Stone Oven at nine o'clock. Call me early if that's not okay."

It was okay. On this particular evening, well wined and dined and very well kissed, just about everything was okay with me.

The Stone Oven is a coffee shop and bakery on Lee Road in what the locals like to call "downtown Cleveland Heights," on a stretch of street boasting several ethnic restaurants, Chuck's Diner, a place to buy and smoke fine cigars, the Cedar Lee, a movie house featuring art films, a health-food supermarket, and an old-fashioned hardware store like hardware stores used to be before they went corporate. The Stone Oven has great soup and sandwiches for lunch, too, but nine A.M. was a little early for roast beef and horseradish mayonnaise, even for me.

I parked behind the restaurant in the public lot off Meadowbrook Road a few minutes past nine on Saturday morning. As I came around to the front door, I noticed a long, black limousine at the curb windows. I nodded at it, figuring there might be a driver behind the wheel that I'd met before.

The car door opened and John Terranova slid out, a toothpick working at one corner of his mouth. He was usually Don Giancarlo D'Allessandro's driver, although he was occasionally called on to do some muscle work. Many years before he'd done some on me. My entire relationship with the D'Allessandro–Gaimari crime family was summed up by the fact that neither John nor I had taken it personally.

"How ya doin', Milan?"

He came around the gleaming hood of the car and we shook hands.

"How come you're not inside having coffee, John?"

"Doctor says I can't drink it no more," he said, tapping a fist on his breastbone. "No more booze either. I got an ulcer." Mob soldiers get ulcers now. It's not like the movies.

I went inside to find Victor at a table near the window, openly flirting with an attractive young woman in shorts and a T-shirt who was having breakfast with her husband and trying hard to ignore his attentions. He was a little too old for a GQ model, but just as well-turned-out in white canvas pants and deck shoes and a short-sleeved mock turtleneck shirt of an aggressive turquoise. Except that he was so handsome, he might have been any well-heeled youngish middle-aged man off to enjoy some outdoor adventure on that rare occasion when beautiful midwestern weather and a Saturday morning coincide.

I wondered what people would think if they knew this attractive, clean-cut man was the de facto head of a powerful crime family. Would they be frightened, thinking that, like Joe Pesci's character in *Casino,* he would suddenly snap and drive a ballpoint pen through someone's neck? Would they be dangerously fascinated by the idea of his power and influence? Would they envy him his relentless womanizing or recoil from it? Or have the American people become so comfortable with the mob through the gangster films of Coppola and Scorcese and Quentin Tarantino that they would accept him as if he sold term life insurance and regularly attended the church of his choice?

I waved at him, ordered my coffee at the counter, and brought it to his table. "Good morning, Victor," I said, sliding into my seat.

"I understand Rebekka Sommars did quite a number on you last night," he said. "You're nationally famous now."

"My God, is there anyone in the world who didn't see that?"

"I didn't see it. I was told about it." He smiled. "My uncle, as he's gotten older, is addicted to junk television. He even watches that Sally Jessie woman."

"Don Giancarlo watching talk shows? Please, Victor, leave me a few illusions."

He looked out the window. "Great day for a sail, isn't it?"

"Are you heading for the lake?"

"I have a friend with a boat over at the Edgewater Yacht Club," he said. "We're going out about ten thirty, probably run up to Put-In Bay. Want to come along?"

"I'm not exactly dressed for sailing," I said, acutely aware of my frayed jeans, worn leather sandals, and white polo shirt with Chief Wahoo, the politically incorrect mascot of the Cleveland Indians, grinning crazily from over the pocket. Next to Victor I looked like a moke.

"It'll just be four guys our age. There's no dress code."

"Thanks, Victor, but I'll pass."

"Suit yourself," he said. He took a little Spiral notebook with an electric blue cover out of his pocket and flipped it open. "I made a few phone calls regarding your friend with the tattoos."

"Oh?"

"He's not a very nice man."

"Gee, and he looks like such a sweetheart."

"Some of the people I know around town know him. His name is Albert Wysocki." He glanced up from the pad and smiled. "He is of the Polish persuasion. Born in Slavic Village—Fleet Avenue, as a matter of fact—forty-four years ago. Caught the tail end of Vietnam when he was a kid, and he seemed to like it."

"Nobody liked it."

"Apparently he likes the concept of war. Because if you want his phone number, you can look it up in the classified section of *Soldier of Fortune*."

Soldier of Fortune is a magazine in which professional mercenaries shop their wares to the highest bidder. "A killer for hire."

"Not officially. His police sheet only lists carrying concealed, three assaults, and an attempted rape, but that's just in the Cleveland area. As for what he did in Rwanda and some of those other African countries he spent time in during the late eighties, use your imagination. Now he freelances. I certainly wouldn't ever hire him; he's a loose cannon."

"What's a gunslinger doing with Tom Maniscalco?"

"If there doesn't happen to be a war on anyplace convenient, he does roughly some of the same things you do locally. Personal security."

"I doubt that very much. I know a leg-breaker when I see one."

"Not in any organized way," Victor said cautiously.

"And he's ugly, too."

He put down the notebook and closed the cover. "You can have the best muscle money can buy, but it doesn't mean a damn thing if you can't control it."

"And Albert is out of control?"

Victor preened his mustache. "The guy is a bug."

"A bug?"

"Buggy. Nutso. Or let's just say he's been known to bring a great deal of unbridled enthusiasm to his commissions."

"Victor," I said, "you're a rare rascal. Commissions?"

"Let's not talk semantics, it's too nice a morning."

"Let's talk Tom Maniscalco, then. Why does a furniture dealer go out and find a lunatic like Albert Winsocki—"

"*Wy* socki," Victor corrected. "*Win* socki is that school that's supposed to buckle down. In the song."

"One of my favorites. Why is Wysocki working for Maniscalco?"

"You'd have to ask Tom that."

"Trouble is, I can't get close enough to ask him because Albert wouldn't like it."

"I daresay he wouldn't."

"What's Maniscalco into, Victor? Besides manufacturing and importing furniture? Gambling? Drugs? What?"

"He's not into gambling, Milan, because if he was, we'd know about it. And we wouldn't like it."

"Drugs, then? Maybe he's smuggling heroin in sofa pillows."

"We wouldn't like that either. You know we're very antidrug."

"Just say no. Is Wysocki on Maniscalco's regular payroll?"

He opened the notebook again. "I wouldn't think so, since he was out of town for a month—Texas and Louisiana, I believe, teaching war games to some of those crazed idiots who run around in wheat fields shooting paper wads at each other and call it combat training."

"Then Maniscalco went out and got him especially for me?"

He shrugged. "Again, that's information I don't have."

"This couldn't be about his daughter's reputation," I said. "I mean, a guy like Wysocki—that's a little extreme."

"A lot extreme, yes."

"So Maniscalco has something else going on he doesn't want anyone poking into."

"You didn't hear that from me." Victor closed the notebook again, took the last bite of his healthful blueberry muffin, and washed it down with the remainder of his coffee. "I think you'd better tread very carefully, Milan. This Albert Wysocki is a mean man. He enjoys hurting people. I wouldn't like it if he got any of that enjoyment at your expense."

"I wouldn't either," I said.

"But we can't help you on this. We can't protect you, because he's not one of our people."

"I can protect myself, if it comes to that."

"Let's hope it doesn't," he said, rising. "You can ensure it won't by staying out of Tom Maniscalco's way." He looked at his watch; only Victor would wear a Patek Phillipe to go out in the middle of Lake Erie on a boat. "I have to get moving, I'm afraid."

I stood up as well and we shook hands.

"Happy sailing, Victor. Enjoy your day."

I watched through the window as John Terranova opened the car door for him. After the limo pulled away, I got a refill on my coffee and sat back down to read the *Plain Dealer*, comfortable in the coolness of the Stone Oven. I thought about Albert Wysocki. There just didn't seem to be any reason for him to be hulking behind Tom Maniscalco, at least none that had to do with Darren Anderson. Maniscalco wasn't a made guy, and if he had been with Gaimari's outfit, his rent-a-brute would have mob connections. He was no hot-blooded Sicilian, no old-world Mustache Pete; as angry as he'd been about Darren's thing with Bethany, surely he hadn't hired Wysocki to kill him. You don't call the police and send in your lawyer when you're planning to enlist a professional hit man.

My thoughts drifted to Connie, who was much more pleasing to daydream about than Albert Wysocki. But the warm rush of pleasure it gave me to think about her was slightly diluted by what she had said at dinner the night before, which was still thrumming around between my ears.

Who profited from Darren Anderson death?

Sidney Friedman had gotten lucky, finding another hunk like Eric Winslow to replace Darren, and saving a couple of million dollars in the process. But he hadn't known he could get Winslow, and he'd had every reason to think that with Darren gone, the investors who'd bought into a virtual sure thing would bail out, leaving Sidney with the broken pieces of a career and two weeks' worth of film he could cut up into mandolin picks.

Or had he known he could get Winslow? If so, there was a profit motive. If not, I was back stuck on the free-parking square, with no monopolies and no hotels and very little expectation of rolling doubles.

I didn't have my notebook with me, so I took a green Bic pen out of my pocket and scrawled a few notes on a napkin. It's always easier for me to make sense of things when I can look at them in black and white, or in this case, green and buff.

Suzi Flores was certainly better off now than when Darren had been alive and pressuring her for sex in return for her job. But again, the demise of *Street Games* had been a very real possibility after Darren Anderson's death, so for all she knew her job would still have been in jeopardy. And I didn't believe that a few unwanted gropes, no matter how unpleasant and unwelcome, made much of a motive for murder.

If she was telling me the truth and there'd been nothing more than that.

Boyce Cort might have been unhappy with Darren's performance, and even more unhappy that he was unable to get the young man into bed. Again, not grounds for murder, not logically.

But then when had murder ever been logical?

Tom Maniscalco was looking good for it, especially towing a supergoon like Albert Wysocki in his wake. But his motive—revenge for Darren's seduction of his daughter—sounded almost too archaic to be credible.

And if Tom hadn't killed Darren, why bring Wysocki around to scare me off? We all have dirty little secrets, but it seemed that Tom Maniscalco's were ripe enough to warrant hiring a persuader who thought hurting and killing people was a perfectly acceptable way to make a living.

❀ ❀ ❀ ❀ ❀ ❀ ❀ ❀ ❀ ❀

CHAPTER SEVENTEEN

❀ ❀ ❀ ❀ ❀ ❀ ❀ ❀ ❀ ❀

I went back home and put on gym socks and sneakers. Then I searched through a drawer looking for sunglasses; I rarely wear them unless I know I'm going to be driving into the sun, but today I thought they might serve as an effective disguise. I finally found a pair, blue blockers, which made the whole world look orange. I topped it all off with an Indians baseball cap, thus rendering myself indistinguishable from at least half a million other men in Cleveland, and went down to my car and headed south, with the warm air blowing through the open windows. Except on the hottest and muggiest days of summer, I prefer fresh air to the artificially cooled kind when I'm driving.

The Home Works factory and warehouse was located on about twenty acres; the offices and showroom in the front looked as if they had been recently added on to the older and larger building in the rear. The area was largely industrial, so there were few of the handsome trees that provide beauty and shade to most of northeastern Ohio; the midday sunshine was relentless in the cloudless bright of the sky.

I cruised by the front of the building, thinking perhaps that the boss might be working on a Saturday. If so, I hoped he'd be willing to talk to me more reasonably in his office than he had when he'd visited mine, and that Albert Wysocki wouldn't be hanging around a furniture company on a Saturday afternoon.

But the executive parking spaces nearest the door, six of which were reserved, were all vacant. A khaki-clad security guard lounged against the fender of one of the parked cars, smoking a cigarette and drinking a can of soda; his electric golf cart stood at the curb.

The warehouse and the factory seemed to be operating at a midweek pace, though. I drove around the corner and turned down what was little more than a utility road, which led me past the back of the complex and the shipping area. The gate was securely padlocked, but I could see through the chain-link fence that the employee parking lot was more than half full, and there were two more security men in the loading area. They might have been guarding the eight huge six-wheelers with the Home Works logo on their sides that were parked in the lot, but I didn't think so.

There was plenty of activity on the loading dock too. More than a dozen men wearing Home Works coveralls were in the process of accepting and warehousing some sort of large shipment. Through the open windows of my car I could hear machinery whirring and grinding from inside the building.

I drove down to the end of the road, hung an awkward U-turn, and drove back up to the fence again. Shifting into park, I opened the compartment on the console and took out a small pair of binoculars I always keep in the car. I was looking directly into the sun, and I had to shade the lenses with my hand to see ten husky men wrestling a few dozen enormous cardboard cartons up onto the loading dock with forklifts, then taking them inside one of the bays on rolling hand trucks. From the struggles of the warehousemen, whatever was in the boxes weighed a lot. Peering through the binoculars at the lettering on them, I was able to make out the word *Brazil.*

I dug into the console compartment again and pulled out a small camera; in my business it often comes in handy. Raising it to my eye, I squinted through the viewfinder to focus and began taking shots of the activity on the loading dock, first wide-angle and then using the zoom option for close-ups.

"Hey!" The voice sounded close in my ear.

I took the camera away from my face. A security guard was approaching the car; I'd been too intent on my photography to notice him. It wasn't the guard who'd been smoking in the front, nor one of the two that had been standing sentinel in the loading area. This one was older, probably retired from some other profession and working this job part time, and sported a mustache that looked like he'd inherited it from Groucho Marx. He wasn't wearing a cap, and his dark hair was combed over his balding scalp. The top of his head was pink from exposure to the sun. His shoulder patch bore the name and logo of a security company that is one of my more prosperous competitors, I'm sorry to say, and his gold badge identified him as P. Kristosek. Parked some twenty feet behind me was a Home Works golf cart that hadn't been there before.

"What's goin' on here?" he said in a tone that tried unsuccessfully to convey authority and sternness.

"Just taking a few snapshots."

"What for?"

"I'm a student of the industrial architecture of the Midwest, and this building is a fine example of the midcentury Bauhaus school." It was nothing of the sort, but I was gambling he wouldn't know that.

He didn't. "You can't take any pictures back here. This is private proppity."

"I don't think so. It's a public road. There were no gates, and no signs to indicate otherwise."

P. Kristosek hitched his thumbs into his Sam Browne belt. A walkie-talkie hung from his left hip, on the other was a leather-covered notebook, the kind cops frequently carry, a can of hot pepper spray, clearly labeled, and a short, thick billy club. But he wasn't wearing a gun, at least not one that was visible. "Let's see some ID," he demanded.

"I don't think that's necessary. I wasn't doing anything wrong."

He fingered the walkie-talkie at his belt. I tensed. I wasn't looking for trouble, but if he put his hand anywhere near the pepper spray I was going to have to hurt him. Instead he just kind of touched the walkie-talkie, maybe to reassure himself it was still there. Then he held out a hand. "I'll have to take that film."

"That's right, you will have to take it, because I'm not going to give it to you."

Kristosek frowned; this wasn't going the way it was supposed to, and he didn't know what to do. I could see him running through his options, deciding whether to call for backup, get tough, or turn tail and run.

"Well, you'd better," he warned, deciding to go with school-boy bravado.

"I'm not trespassing and I'm not breaking any laws, and even if I were, that little gold badge you're wearing carries about as much clout as if you'd bought it at Toys R Us."

Under his pink flush his face turned ashen. I felt kind of sorry for him, an older man who'd been given a postage-stamp piece of authority and suddenly thinks he's Dirty Harry. I didn't like the idea of bullying him, but I wasn't going to let him bully me, either.

"If I were you," I said, "I'd put some sunscreen on the top of my head. That sunburn is going to hurt tonight."

I put the car into gear and pulled slowly away from him, watching him in the rearview mirror as he whipped out his notebook and a pen. I figured he was taking down my license number.

Okay, I thought, if you give a guy with nothing better to do a useless badge and tell him to keep his eyes open, maybe he gets a little overzealous. I understand that. I also understand a company like Home Works needing industrial security; it is, after all, how I make my living.

And because it is, I knew that having four guards on duty at a furniture factory on a Saturday afternoon when there were nearly a dozen burly workmen on the premises was overkill, and that assigning one of them to patrol a public road so no stranger would get too close was that much more.

Thinking about Albert Wysocki, it occurred to me that overkill might be Tom Maniscalco's middle name. It was certainly enough to make me wonder.

As I got onto the freeway heading back north toward Cleveland, my beeper interrupted my enjoyment of Michael Feldman's *Whattaya Know?* on WCPN. I clawed it off my belt and looked at the readout; the number wasn't familiar to me, but the first three digits indicated a west side exchange.

I dialed up my own office number on the car phone and listened to my voice mail. My caller had been Dierdre O'Malley, evidently phoning from her home.

"Please call me as soon as you can, Mr. Jacovich," she'd said after identifying herself. "It's very important."

I wondered what it was all about but decided to swing by my office before I returned the call.

I stopped off on Lorain Avenue at a little hot-dog place about the size of a closet and had two chili dogs and a Coke, and then headed down into the Flats.

The Cuyahoga was supporting some heavy water traffic by the time I got back to my office, par for the course on a glorious sunny Saturday. Sailboats and stinkpots alike crowded the river navigating the hairpin turn of Collision Bend on their way out to Lake Erie, on the deck of almost every one an attractive swimsuit-clad woman. Happy summer fun for everyone except the attendants who raise and lower the many bridges that span the river—they must have been working their butts off.

The sun and sky were so bright, I didn't need to turn on any of the office lights. I opened the windows, took a Stroh's from the refrigerator, and sat down behind my desk to return Dierdre O'Malley's call.

A man with a coarse cigarette voice answered the phone, sounding irritable. When I asked for Dierdre, he put the phone down without comment and called, "Dierdre! It's some guy. *Not* Alan."

I figured it was probably her father. I should have said hello, old bowling buddies that we were.

After a moment Dierdre picked up the phone.

"Dierdre, it's Milan Jacovich."

"Oh," she said, nearly whispering. "Yes. Thanks for calling me back."

"What can I do for you?"

"It's Alan," she said. Her voice was flat, mechanical, like the electronic operator's when you call information. "His father told him about you."

Meddling old bastard, I thought. "Told him what about me?"

"About your coming to the office. About my lying and telling him you were friends with my father. Mr. Braxton has the idea that you and I are . . ."

"Oh, shit," I said. "And he told Alan that?"

"Yeah. We had a terrible fight about it this morning," she said. "Well, not a fight, really, because I never got a chance to open my mouth. Alan got back from his business trip last night and had dinner with his parents. Then he called this morning and asked me to come right over." She sniffed; I couldn't tell whether she was crying. "He sounded really funny on the phone, all mad like, so I thought I'd better do what he said. When I got to his apartment, he wanted to know who you were. He actually accused me of having an affair with you. I've never been so surprised in my life."

"I'm sorry." I wondered now if I should have called and told her about Nathan Braxton's visit to my office but disabused myself of the notion quickly. I had enough to deal with without involving myself in other people's family problems.

"He was like a madman, screaming and yelling and throwing me around—"

"He hit you?"

"Just once. Slapped me, really. He's never punched me."

"He's hit you before?"

She caught her breath; it's always difficult for someone to admit the person they love is abusing them, as if they secretly thought the abuse was really their fault. Finally she said, "Not that often."

"Once is too often."

"He's got a bad temper," she went on, ignoring me, "but he can usually control himself. This morning, though, he was grabbing me and throwing me down on the couch, squeezing my arms, things like that." She made a little whimpering sound in the back of her throat. "I've already got bruises."

"Can I do anything to help?"

"Well . . ."

I listened to her breathe. I took a sip of my beer. "Dierdre?"

"Um. I'd really appreciate it if you wouldn't tell Alan about me and Darren Anderson."

"Tell him? Of course I won't tell him. Why would I?"

"Because," she said, "he may be coming to talk to you."

I felt my shoulders slump. Alan Braxton was hysterical with jealousy and was coming to talk to me. About my sleeping with his fiancée. I'd seen her twice in my life, both times fully clothed and vertical, and now her jealous boyfriend was coming to talk to me.

This happy life.

I said, "If you don't want me to tell him about Darren, that must mean you're going to stay with him."

"Stay with him?"

"How can you even think about marrying a man who beats you?"

She didn't say anything for almost thirty seconds. Then, "He doesn't beat me. He just . . ."

"He just hits you," I finished for her.

"Not that often. He really has a good heart. I mean, what would you do if you were engaged to somebody and you thought she was sleeping with another man?"

"I wouldn't knock her around," I said.

"He doesn't mean it."

"Look at your bruises and tell me that."

"I know, but . . ."

"But what?"

Another pause while she gathered strength from somewhere I didn't know about. "It's what I want," she said.

"Jesus, Dierdre . . ."

"I told you before, Mr. Jacovich," she said, and all at once there was steel in the youthful voice. "I'll never have a better chance."

I brought the bottle to my lips. The icy beer I was so fond of tasted strangely bitter—or maybe it was just the flavor of my words. "It's your life, I suppose."

"That's right, it is."

"So why are you calling me?"

"To tell you that he's—well, he may be coming to see you."

"When?"

"I don't know," she said.

Through the receiver my own sigh sounded like a night wind blowing a discarded newspaper down a deserted street. "If he does, he does."

"Just please—don't say anything about Darren Anderson. It'll spoil everything for me."

"All right," I said.

"I'm really grateful." She gulped a couple of times. "So, uh, what *are* you going to tell him?"

"The truth. That we're not having an affair, and that I came

to see you about a case I'm working on. Why would I tell him anything else?"

"Well, the thing is . . ."

"What?"

"The thing is, Alan owns a gun."

So there I was, while a beautiful Saturday sifted through the
cracks of time like fine white sand, sitting at my desk twiddling
my thumbs and waiting for an insanely jealous, armed young man
to show up and see if he could win a kewpie doll for marksman-
ship. I felt pretty vulnerable, despite the .357 Magnum I keep in
my desk drawer.

But not much. One of the first rules of gun ownership is, if
you don't want to use it, don't even take it out of its holster, and
I certainly didn't want to shoot Alan Braxton. The thought of the
two of us blazing away at one another like the end of a bad cowboy movie was ludicrous.

Bouncing him off the walls until he learned not to beat up
women was another proposition altogether.

I finished my beer and resisted the urge to open another
one; if I was going to have company with an attitude, I wanted to
be sharp. Sitting here waiting for Alan Braxton to walk in and
shove a gun up my nose was, I supposed, better than walking
outside and letting him pick me off from afar. If Alan was that
wacko.

Maybe he just wanted to talk. Dierdre had said only that he
owned a gun, not that he was running around waving it. Maybe
he wouldn't bring it with him, when and if he came calling.

And maybe someday elephants will fly.

I'd give him until the end of the afternoon, and then I'd go
on about my life. If a guy's coming over to shoot me, he can damn
well conform to my schedule.

Since I was there anyway, I figured I might as well get some
work done, so I booted up my computer and began working on

my accounts. It's the part of the job I hate the most; maybe now that I was back in the saddle and would be taking on more work, I'd have to hire someone to come in part time and do it for me.

The telephone rang, making me jump. There seemed to be a lot going on, for a Saturday; I'd have to start coming in on weekends more often.

"Mr. . . . Mr. Jacovich?" The voice was small, female, hesitant. "This is Betty Dinsmoor. Ralphie's—Darren's mother?" She made it a question.

"Oh yes, Mrs. Dinsmoor. How are you?"

"I'm glad I caught you in on a Saturday. I didn't know how else to reach you."

I heard background noises from her end, traffic sounds. She was probably calling from a pay phone somewhere. "Well, it's lucky for both of us I decided to work today, then."

"I wonder if I could come and see you."

"Sure," I said, talking over the warning bells that started clanging in my head. "When?"

"Well, now, actually." Her giggle was flutey, almost desperate. "Ray is taking a nap, and I told him I just wanted to get out of the room for a while. I'm very close to your office, I think."

"Where are you?"

"Near . . . wait a minute," she said. There was a pause; a horn honked. After about twenty seconds she came back on the line. "I'm right across the street from the West Side Market. Do you know where that is?"

Everybody in Cleveland knows where the West Side Market is, but I guess not too many people from Sierra Madre do. "You're not far," I said, and gave her directions.

After I hung up, I went over to the windows and took a hefty sniff of river air, wondering whether I'd done the right thing. I certainly didn't want her running into a crazed Alan Braxton.

Betty Dinsmoor's husband had, after all, threatened to sue me. And that made me a little nervous, because after working all my adult life, I now actually owned something worth protecting—my building. So I just might be lying down with the enemy.

Then again, I have to live with myself. She was a mother whose only son had just been brutally killed, and chances are that if I turned down her request, one of these mornings I'd go into the bathroom to shave and there would be no one in the mirror.

I made a pot of coffee and checked the refrigerator, just in case she wanted anything. I was acutely aware that in my ragged jeans and polo shirt I looked like anything but the proper detective, but since it was a weekend I figured Betty Dinsmoor would forgive me.

It took her twenty minutes to get there, about ten minutes longer than it should have. She'd probably gotten lost. Cleveland is a fairly easy city to find your way around in, but only if you're hip to which streets are one-way and which ones happen to be under construction and rendered practically impassable.

As I heard her coming up the stairs I suddenly remembered that Alan Braxton might be on his way over too. I'd just have to pray he wouldn't charge in spraying lead while she was sitting in my office.

"Thank you for seeing me, Mr. Jacovich," she said when I opened the door for her. She was wearing a dark gray, long-sleeved jersey dress, entirely too hot for Cleveland in the summertime. Her frilly hair was held back behind her ears with two plastic barrettes, and her makeup looked hastily applied. In her hand was a white handkerchief, which she'd twisted into a point.

"There's fresh-made coffee, Mrs. Dinsmoor," I said. "And soda. Whatever you'd like."

"No, nothing, thanks." She sat down tentatively. "I don't have much time. My husband doesn't know I'm here." She glanced away. "He'd be angry."

I didn't want the broad expanse of my desk to be between us, so I took the chair next to her. "What can I do to help?"

She patted at a stray tendril of hair at her temple. "I don't know, really. I guess I was hoping you could . . . comfort me a little."

"If I can."

She unfurled the handkerchief over her knee, carefully smoothing out all the wrinkles before she spoke. "Ralphie didn't spend much time with us the past four years," she said. "He was almost like a stranger."

"That happens," I said as gently as I could. "A young man just starting his career, and finding so much success so quickly, he'd naturally build himself a new life, find new friends."

"Oh, I understand that. I did it to my parents when I was young. I thought that I knew everything and they knew nothing." She shook her head sadly. "It's just, now that he's gone, I realize I hardly knew him." She began folding the handkerchief into a square. "As an adult, I mean. Of course I remember him when he was little." She smiled to herself. "So handsome, so rugged. He was a very proud little boy. I always knew he'd be an actor, he so loved being the center of attention." A frown passed across her face like a cloud over the sun. "Other people's attention. He never much cared about ours. About mine, I mean. It seemed like everything he wanted, everything he valued in life, was . . ." She raised her head, pointing out the window with her chin. "Out there, somewhere. Not in his home, or with his family. It was all going to come from strangers."

I didn't say anything.

"And women. He always loved the girls." She smiled again in fond reminiscence. "The little girls he played with. When he was in first grade I got called to school because Ralphie was kissing all the girls. It's a good thing it happened so long ago, or he would've been in real trouble. Imagine charging a child with sexual harassment the way they do these days. A six-year-old doesn't even know what that means."

"Mrs. Dinsmoor," I said again, "what is it I can do for you?"

Now that the handkerchief was folded into about a two-inch square, she unfolded it again and began twisting it. "Nobody spent more time with Ralphie than you did those last two weeks," she said.

"No, probably not."

"Then tell me. What was his life like? At the end. Was he . . . you know. Happy?"

I swallowed hard, my stomach roiling, although I didn't think it was the two chili dogs I'd had for lunch. Happiness is such a vague, elusive concept, so hard to define. I don't know if anyone as driven, as compulsive as Darren Anderson could ever be characterized as happy. But I didn't want to tell his mother that; I didn't think it's what she wanted to hear.

"Darren was enjoying himself," I said finally. "He enjoyed his life, he enjoyed being a movie star. He liked what he was doing. Not many of us get to have our dreams come true. He told me once that he was living everyone else's fantasy. So I guess he considered himself a very lucky man."

"Lucky . . ." she murmured, staring at the floor.

I winced inwardly. It hadn't been the best choice of words.

"And he was rich, wasn't he?"

"Yes, he was rich."

"I suppose I'd be happy if I was rich," she said wistfully.

"I don't know about that, Mrs. Dinsmoor. You'd be free from money worries, but that's about it."

"That would be something, anyway. I'm glad Ralphie was rich. He didn't have a very nice childhood."

"Because of his father leaving? He told me a little something about that."

"Ralphie was only six. It hurt him a lot, but he tried not to show it. I think he mostly blamed me for his dad leaving." She colored slightly and put a hand to her cheek. "I don't think my husband ever really believed that Ralphie was his child. He was, though, I swear to you. But the two of them were never close. And then, afterwards, when I married Ray, well, he and Ralphie didn't get along very well, either."

"That isn't unusual," I said.

"It wasn't anybody's fault, not really. Ralphie resented Ray because he wasn't his father, and Ray resented having to support another man's child." She smiled wanly. "It's funny, really."

"What is?"

"I married Ray for Ralphie. So I could bring him up decently, with a father. So there would always be a roof over his head, and he wouldn't have to wear hand-me-downs all the time." She stared out the window at the bright blue sky, biting her lip.

"Things don't always work out the way we think they will," I said.

Her sigh came shuddering through her nose. "Ralphie left home as soon as he could, right after high school. And then all these wonderful things started happening to him. His acting career. I'd been in a few movies myself, but I knew I'd never make it big. I was so proud of him, so thrilled for him. But I couldn't really show it, because Ray was very resentful. Almost envious."

"But you said that Darren—Ralphie—sent you money. And bought you a house."

"Oh, he did. He was a good boy! But Ray thought he should have moved us to Beverly Hills or Brentwood or someplace fancy like that, instead of buying us a house out in Sierra Madre. Ray said he just wanted to keep us as far away from him as he could." She shook her head. "I suppose that's true. We wouldn't have fit in with all Ralphie's Hollywood friends," she said, sniffing into the handkerchief, even though I could see no tears. "It wasn't easy." She looked up at me with empty eyes. "But I couldn't desert Ralphie. Not after his father had walked out on him. I just couldn't do that."

"Where is his father now?" I said.

"I don't know for sure. The last I heard of him he was in Chicago."

"He didn't stay in touch? He didn't ever make any attempt to contact your son?"

"I guess when Ralphie got to be a big star, Nor tried to get in touch with him. Norbert Anderson, my first husband. But Ralphie didn't want anything to do with him. You can imagine."

"Yes," I said, "I can."

"I guess all he wanted from Ralphie was money."

"Ralphie worried that everyone wanted something from him," I said. "I think that's why he made such a point of keeping people away."

The sorrow that realigned her mouth and eyes made her look like a pre-Raphaelite madonna. "Even his own mother?"

"Everyone. I don't want you to feel bad, Mrs. Dinsmoor. Your son didn't have anything against you."

"Did he talk about me?" she asked, ever hopeful.

I'm a bad liar, but I tried to extract what little truth might bring her comfort. "He—mentioned you. But you know, he and I weren't all that close. We were of different generations. And I basically just spent evenings with him. At dinners and parties and things. We weren't really friends."

She looked sad again. "He didn't have many friends, did he?"

"Well, not in Cleveland. At last not that I was aware of. He was pretty busy working. I don't know about Los Angeles."

"And he had no male role model growing up, and he didn't have me because I was too busy trying to keep my marriage with Ray together. There were times I thought about just leaving both of them, frankly." She gave a single, staccato sob. She wasn't crying; I had yet to see her cry. "That's why I was wondering about his last weeks. If he'd found even a little happiness."

The gang of hairy-chested stokers in charge of keeping my heartburn aflame were pouring on the coals by the shovelful. "From what I could see," I told Betty Dinsmoor, because it wasn't exactly a lie, "the two weeks before he died, Ralphie was having a really good time."

CHAPTER EIGHTEEN

A depressing afternoon all in all, I thought after Betty Dinsmoor had said good-bye and headed back to the motel near the airport, presumably where her husband still napped unawares. But I was still chewing over the delightful Connie Haley's question. "Who profits?"

Mrs. Dinsmoor had talked wistfully about being rich; I had to wonder whether Darren Anderson had left any sort of will. What with all his employees and hangers-on—his "people"—taking care of his every need in Los Angeles, I supposed he had. Then again, twenty-four-year-olds whose only physical ailments are hangovers and sports injuries tend to believe they are invincible, immortal. If he had died intestate, the chances were that the bulk of his estate, which had to be substantial, would go to his mother, as his nearest relative.

And by extension, his stepfather.

Ray Dinsmoor hadn't been very fond of his stepson, had resented his success and envied the hell out of his wealth. Whether that envy and dislike had translated into murder was something I needed to look at quietly.

But I was not to do it on this particular Saturday afternoon. Not long after Betty Dinsmoor's departure, Alan Braxton burst into my office as if jet propelled, wild-eyed and unkempt, red-faced and red-eared, hyperventilating. His Guess jeans were starched and sharply creased; I never trust a man who has his jeans pressed. Over them he was wearing a lightweight green windbreaker, zipped halfway up his chest. It was too baggy for me to be able to tell whether he'd brought along his gun.

He froze when he saw me, and although it took some time, recognition finally kicked in.

"*You*," he breathed.

"Come in, Alan."

"*You're* Milan Jacovich."

"I know." I got to my feet and came around the desk. "Why don't you sit down?"

"I don't want to sit down," he said, his voice coarse with rage. His teeth were showing like those of a truculent Rottweiler, but I could tell that underneath he was all overbred Chihuahua, nervous and fragile and emotionally on the edge.

"Suit yourself," I said.

"I want to know what's going on between you and Dierdre."

"Nothing's going on."

"Then why did you come to my office to see her?"

"You think that everyone who comes to that office is having an affair with your secretary?"

"Why are you hanging around her all the time?"

"I'm not hanging around her. I've only seen her twice in my life—once at the White Magnolia and once at Braxton Software, which hardly qualifies as all the time."

"You're lying!"

I didn't like that much, but I let it go. "If I was sleeping with her, you think I'd walk into your office like that? I came to see Dierdre on business."

"What kind of business?" he demanded.

"My business."

"She's my fiancée! And I know she's fooling around with somebody!" He seemed on the edge of crying. I could have felt sorry for him if I hadn't known he was the kind of whiny coward who hits women.

"I think you should sit down and relax, Alan. You want something to drink? A beer?"

He sneered. "I'm fussy who I drink with." He'd probably heard that line in an old western. He didn't say it with nearly the conviction that Randolph Scott would have, though.

"Come on, Alan. You've got no quarrel with me."

He paced, breathing hard, his Doc Martens clunking on the newly finished hardwood floor. If he'd had a long tail like a tiger, he would undoubtedly have been lashing it. "I didn't think it was you. I thought it was that actor you were with that night. The one who got killed."

"You didn't by any chance go ask him if *he* was seeing Dierdre, did you?"

He stopped in his tracks, whipping his head around to look at me.

"The police don't know anything about you yet," I went on. "But they might be interested in what went down between you and Darren Anderson that night in the restaurant. They might be especially interested in that temper of yours."

"Are you crazy?" he squeaked.

"You're the crazy one, Alan, thinking your fiancée is sleeping with everybody who even talks to her. You and your father both."

The blood fled from his face into his already flaming ears, which turned as scarlet as the jerseys of the Ohio State football team. "My father?"

"He came here the other day asking the same questions you are."

His whole body jerked, and he stutter-stepped backward as if he'd been slapped. "He came here?"

I nodded. "And he's the one who told you I came to your office to see Dierdre. Isn't that why you're here?"

Alan hunched his shoulders and ducked his head.

"Your father doesn't want you to marry Dierdre, and this is

his way of sabotaging it. Get out from under his shadow and start pulling your own strings, Alan. He's screwing up your life."

"No, *you're* screwing up my life!" he shot back, suddenly straightening. "I want you to stay the fuck away from Dierdre."

His hand went to his jacket and he pulled out a silver-plated pistol, a .22. It was the kind of weapon people buy when they don't know the first thing about handguns. It didn't have much stopping power, but at close range it would get the job done. The way he was waving it around, though, he wasn't going to hit anything but an unlucky gull flying by outside the window—and only by sheer accident.

Nevertheless, any loaded gun makes me very nervous unless I happen to be holding it, and I could feel the hair at the back of my neck stand up. "You know you're not going to use that, Alan," I said. "Why don't you just put it away?"

"I will use it," he said, taking a few steps toward me, which brought him close enough to do real damage. "I goddamn well will use it, to protect what's mine."

"Dierdre isn't yours." I took a couple of answering steps toward him. "Lincoln freed the slaves. And if you're so anxious to keep her, maybe you ought to start treating her better."

His eyes went blank. "Huh?"

"Stop hitting her," I said, taking another step. I was now only a few feet away, where even the puny little .22 would blow a hole right through me. "Real men don't beat up women, Alan. So I guess you know what that makes you."

The gun wavered. "How did you—"

I brought the edge of my hand down on his wrist, knocking the .22 to the floor. Then I backhanded him across the mouth and brought my open hand back against the side of his face, putting some weight behind the blows, which landed with a sound like a whip cracking, and he reeled backward, hit one of the chairs, and went down in a tangle of arms and legs.

I kicked the gun out of his reach, sending it skittering across the room. Alan watched it hit the far wall and then looked up at me, his eyes as big as salad plates. I could tell he was getting ready to blubber.

I bent down and grabbed the front of his windbreaker, hauling him to his feet. I was going to hit him again, but the abject terror all over his face stopped me.

"How do you like it?" I said, my nose about an inch from his. "How do you like getting knocked around by somebody bigger than you?" I shook him hard, and his head bobbed so violently I was afraid his neck was going to break. Shaken-baby syndrome with a thirty-year-old man.

I pushed him away from me, and he tripped over his own feet and went down on one knee.

"Get out of my office, Alan," I said. "And don't come back."

Painfully, he got to his feet. His ears were still bright red, and my finger marks glowed hotly on his cheeks where I'd slapped him. He straightened his jacket, looked around, and made a move to go pick up the gun. I stepped in front of him and pushed him in the other direction.

"Uh-uh," I said.

"That's my property!" he complained.

"Not anymore. I'm kind of a gun collector—and I've just collected yours."

His nose was red too now, and a rivulet of clear snot was creeping down his upper lip.

"And anyway, if I ever hear of you hitting Dierdre again," I said, "you're going to need a bazooka. Don't," I warned when he started to answer. "Just keep your mouth shut. It won't take much to make me hurt you some more."

He stood blinking at me for almost a minute; then he seemed to shrink right in front of my eyes. Head bowed, shoulders slumped, he shuffled across the hardwood toward the door.

With his hand on the doorknob, he turned and looked back at me, a study in insecurity and misery. "Just tell me," he pleaded. "Are you fucking her? Can't you just tell me?"

I filled my lungs with air, feeling the oxygen energize my blood. It felt good, physically. "Beat it, Alan," I said.

So now I had three guns: the .357 Magnum I keep in my desk drawer, the .38 police special on the top shelf of my front closet in my apartment, and Alan Braxton's little popgun. I didn't want to keep it, but I couldn't very well turn it in to the police department, and I certainly wouldn't toss it in a Dumpster so some kid could get hold of it.

I held it in the palm of my hand and looked out the window, figuring the safest thing would be simply to throw it in the Cuyahoga, where it would join what must surely be hundreds of other discarded weapons rusting on the muddy river bottom.

I took the bullets out of it, put bullets and gun in a plastic sandwich bag, and stuck it on a shelf in my storage room with a Post-it reminding me where it had come from. Then I stood by the window, smoking a cigarette and watching the gulls quarreling in midflight outside.

Alan Braxton was a hothead; he'd come to me that afternoon, hot and bothered. If he'd found out about Dierdre and Darren and had wanted to do something about it, he'd have arrived at Darren's house that way, too, enraged and red-eared and waving his little gun.

But Darren had been killed with a .38.

Maybe Alan had more than one gun, but I didn't think so. If he owned a .38, he would have known enough about weaponry to know he didn't need a .22.

Besides, he'd shown me he didn't have the guts to actually pull the trigger.

So while I wasn't exactly crossing him off as a suspect, I was moving his name way down to the bottom of the list.

Closing up the office, I went downstairs and got into my car, drove over the Eagle Avenue Bridge and up the incline past Jacobs Field, and jumped onto I-71 heading west. The motel the Dinsmoors were staying at was one of those prepackaged chain establishments found within a few miles of every airport in the country, in which every room looks the same whether in Cleveland, Phoenix, or Missoula, Montana.

I was able to spot their rental car pretty quickly, a tan Mercury Capri, the only one there with a Michigan license plate. The frame around the plate read NOR'EASTER AUTO RENTAL. Obviously one of the discount places who barely hang on by their fingernails competing against the biggies like Hertz and National.

I looked around to see whether anyone was watching, or whether one of the Dinsmoors happened to be looking out the window, although why anyone would want to admire the view of the motel parking lot was beyond me. I peered in through the driver's side window and wrote down the mileage on the speedometer: 7,924 miles.

Then I went home.

I scrubbed a potato and put it in the oven to bake, took a package of pork chops from the freezer and stuck them in the microwave to defrost, and I opened a Stroh's. Sitting down at the kitchen table with the telephone, I rang up Detroit information and asked for the number for Nor'easter Auto Rental. "It's near the airport," I told the operator when he asked what city. When I finally got the manager on the phone, I told him I was calling from Cleveland about one of their customers, one Raymond Dinsmoor, and I wanted to know when he had rented the car and what the mileage had been when he drove it off the lot.

"We can't give out information like that," he protested, which didn't surprise me. From his voice, I took him to be somewhere in his early twenties.

"I understand," I said, trying to sound gruff and official. "But

I'm investigating a homicide here in the Cleveland area, and this could be key."

I heard him catch his breath. You tend to get people's attention when you mention homicide, even if they live in Detroit.

"Was it the customer . . ."

"No," I assured him. "But it's important, or I wouldn't be calling. You realize that it will be costly and time consuming if I have to subpoena that information. I was hoping we could count on you to cooperate."

"Oh," he said. "Oh, well, yeah. Sure. We want to cooperate with the authorities."

I had the feeling that the young man was no Rhodes scholar. But I hadn't lied to him, I hadn't told him I was a cop, only that I was investigating a murder. I couldn't help it he jumped to his own conclusions. It was weasely, but legal and effective, so I didn't even feel guilty when he put me on hold, so I could listen to bad orchestral versions of Andrew Lloyd Webber while I waited, and came back with what I'd asked for.

The tan Mercury Capri had been rented by Ray Dinsmoor from the Nor'easter office several blocks from DIA, the Detroit airport, six days before Darren Anderson had been murdered. The car had had 6,701 miles on it when Dinsmoor had taken possession of it. He'd secured it with a corporate Visa card in the name of San Gabriel Hardware; the clerk even gave me the number and the expiration date.

Now that's what I call cooperation.

I did some quick subtraction in the margin of that morning's *Plain Dealer.* Ray Dinsmoor had put 1,223 miles on the car since renting it almost two weeks earlier.

Detroit is a little less than three hours from Cleveland by car, I calculated. There were enough miles on the odometer for Dinsmoor to have driven down, killed Darren, driven back, and then made the trip again when Betty arrived in Detroit by plane.

Dipping the defrosted pork chops in beaten egg, I coated

them with bread crumbs and sage and put them in a frying pan. While they sizzled slowly I called Bob Matusen at police headquarters, but the desk sergeant told me he'd gone for the day, he'd be in first thing in the morning. From experience I knew that Matusen was pulling some heavy overtime, probably because of the Darren Anderson killing. A high-profile crime, with the entire world hanging on every tiny development, played hell with a high-ranking homicide cop's forty-hour work week.

I heated some frozen peas in the microwave, opened another beer, and ate my dinner quietly at the kitchen table, the radio tuned to classical music, WCLV. It was Saturday evening, and I had nothing to do and nowhere to go. I didn't feel like spending several hours in a bar, nor watching the Tribe game, which would be over by ten o'clock anyway unless it went into extra innings. I didn't want to think about Darren Anderson or anyone involved with him, and I didn't want to brood about Marko anymore.

I didn't want to do much of anything.

Every once in a while the lonelies get me.

I wanted more than anything to call Connie Haley, but I had to give it some serious thought first. If she wasn't home on a Saturday night, my imagination would go into high gear and I'd wonder if she was wrestling with someone else in the front seat of a car, her tongue tasting of strawberries and merlot. After one date I didn't have any sort of claim, but I didn't feel like getting hurt this particular evening.

Maybe Ed Stahl was right, maybe I was getting scared.

Screw it, I thought, take a chance. I dialed Connie's home number. When she answered after three rings, something inside my stomach fluttered; it wasn't the pork chops.

"I was hoping you'd call," she said.

"Isn't that what a gentleman does? Calls to thank the lady the day after the first date?"

"If I ever go out with a gentleman I'll let you know."

"I thought I was very gentlemanly last night."

She chuckled. "Too damn much so. But it's nothing that can't be fixed, is it?" I heard her take a swallow of something; I pictured her delicately holding a glass of wine, her hair in its braid, her dimple flashing an invitation. "Want to hang out tomorrow?"

"I can't," I said. "It's my Sunday with my boys."

"Oh. Sure," she said quickly, but she sounded disappointed, I was happy to note. "I know how important that is."

"Yeah. They usually stay over on Sunday night, but tomorrow they won't. Milan has a date and Stephen has two buddies coming over to his house to play video games, so they're both leaving after dinner."

"And what are *you* doing after dinner?" she said.

"I was thinking of straightening out my sock drawer."

"Oh, come on! A man can't do that alone. You're all color-blind. You can't tell the black ones from the blue ones."

"I wonder who I might get to help me, then."

"I'd volunteer, but I have to paint my toenails tomorrow night."

"Darn."

There was a short silence. "I suppose I could come over to your place and paint them, and we could do your socks while they dry. Especially if you have a good bottle of merlot around."

"It so happens I do. Was eleven o'clock this morning a good year?"

That got a hearty laugh out of her, a sound that warmed my innards. I'm not the kind of guy who dazzles friends at parties with bon mots and witty jokes; I'm perceived by almost everyone as a very serious person, and I think of myself that way too most of the time. So whenever I can make somebody laugh, it gives me a special, private pleasure. Especially when that someone is blue-eyed and dimpled and turns me on the way Connie Haley did.

"I'll make you a deal," I said. "You fix up my sock drawer for me, and I'll paint your toenails."

"Socks and toenails. You don't have a thing about feet, do you, Milan?"

"That would be my second choice."

We decided she'd come over at eight o'clock, which not only made me happy and abuzz with anticipation but gave me something to do with my Saturday evening—clean my apartment from top to bottom.

Listening to the Indians game on the radio, I did the dirty dishes that had piled up in the sink, picked the dirty clothes up off the floor, Comet-cleaned every surface in the kitchen and bathroom, Lemon-Pledged the coffee table and the end tables, dusted and vacuumed the living room, and Windexed all the mirrors. When I was finished, I hardly recognized the place; it looked like the apartment of an anal retentive. I was well pleased.

And in the morning I'd put clean sheets on the bed.

CHAPTER NINETEEN

I woke up early, feeling better than I had in months. I had every reason to look forward to the day. First I'd spend some time with my sons on my court-mandated every-other-Sunday; I miss them sorely when I don't see them for a while, and now that they're growing up and have their own agendas and responsibilities they have less time for me than when they were smaller. Then the evening with Connie Haley.

But there was something I had to take care of first, and while I was sitting at the kitchen table in gym shorts, a T-shirt, and stocking feet, I called my ex-wife Lila to tell her I'd be by for the boys at about noon.

"You're supposed to come at ten," she said irritably. "Can't you come a little earlier? Joe and I wanted to go to church and then to brunch."

The Joe in question was one Joe Bradac, who had worshiped Lila from afar ever since high school and had moved in on her, literally and figuratively, within two months of my moving out.

It doesn't really bother me anymore; Lila and I have been divorced for so long that whatever residual feeling remains between us is more habit than genuine emotion. The marriage was a stormy one. Lila is Serbian, with a dark and volatile temperament, while like most Slovenians I'm more easygoing. After I'd tried marital bliss for a long while, I'd decided I was happier being single anyway. It's not being able to see my kids every day that gnaws at me.

But I never understood what Lila saw in Joe Bradac. He looks like a geek and acts like a wimp; whenever I come over to the house to pick up my sons—the house that used to be mine— he runs upstairs and hides in the bedroom so he doesn't have to see me.

I find it very telling that after all these years he's never asked Lila to marry him.

"Go ahead to church," I said. "The boys don't need a baby-sitter."

"I know. But I hate it when you change things," she said. "It throws everything off kilter."

That was Lila; she can find a negative in a pot of gold if she's so inclined. And she usually is.

"I have to stop by police headquarters first. I'm in the middle of this Darren Anderson business."

"I know. Stephen heard that woman talking about you on national TV. It was humiliating—everyone in the neighborhood knows about it. I went to the market yesterday and people were looking at me and whispering. I almost died of embarrassment."

I checked the kitchen wall clock; it was twenty past nine. "Can we talk about this later, Lila?"

"That's the trouble with you, Milan. You never want to talk about things."

"The quicker we get off the phone, the sooner I'll be by to pick up the boys."

I knew the exasperated sigh was coming—God knows I'd heard it often enough before.

It's too bad Lila and I can't be better friends. The divorce wasn't acrimonious, exactly, but the friction between us has never gone away. I guess she gets along better with Joe Bradac because she can push him around.

I finished my coffee and toast, put on slacks and a polo shirt, laced on a pair of Nikes, and went downstairs to my car. It was a bright morning, and warm enough to bode high temperatures later in the afternoon.

I was inserting the key in the lock when something crashed onto the back of my neck like a grand piano dropped from the twentieth floor. At first it didn't even hurt, but the impact knocked my vision cockeyed, and the world tilted and swam. My chin bounced off the roof of the car, and I went down on both knees. The toe of a work boot caught me a glancing kick in the stomach, just missing my ribs, and I rolled over onto my back, fighting the nausea that came rushing up into my throat. My heart was beating in my head, and now little jolts of pain pulsated behind my eyes.

The morning sun created a nimbus around Albert Wysocki, who was standing over me wearing tattered Lee jeans. His T-shirt was long overdue at the laundry, but at least it covered up the fornicating pigs. He was smiling, the gaps in his teeth on full display. He looked like a happy guy.

"You just don't fuckin' listen, do you?" he said.

I was blinking my eyes rapidly, trying to chase the dizziness away. The muscles in the back of my neck felt like I'd barely survived a beheading.

"Mr. Maniscalco told you stay away, and whattaya do? You come around his plant, snooping around." He unbuckled his thick tooled-leather belt, pulling it slowly, almost sensuously from the loops of his jeans, and wrapped it around his right fist. He was evidently used to street brawling; the belt would be as effective as a set of brass knuckles.

"So maybe you didn't understand him so good," Wysocki said. "Maybe you're gonna understand this better."

He took a couple of running steps toward me like a field goal kicker, swung his right foot back, and his boot came hurtling toward my face. If it had connected, I would have spent the rest of my life looking out of the back of my head—if indeed I was to *have* a rest of my life.

Rolling over toward him, I caught his oncoming foot in my hands; the impact numbed both my arms up to the shoulders. I twisted his foot, putting all my weight against his standing leg, and he lost his balance and came down next to me like a fallen oak tree. The resultant tremor was somewhere around a 3.5 on the Richter scale.

He was in better shape than I was, and a whole lot meaner, but I outweighed him by about thirty pounds. Using what little advantage I had, I rolled over on top of him, immobilizing him somewhat, and drove a fist into his nose. Marko Meglich's ring crunched against the cartilage, and hot blood spilled onto my knuckles, but the punch didn't get much more than a groan out of him.

He pistoned his knees under me, bruising my thighs but not hitting me where he would have liked to. Blood gushed from his right nostril, splashing wildly as he thrashed his head from side to side. Then he growled low in his throat and bit me on the shoulder.

Except for a minor experience with a neighbor's dog when I was about seven, I'd never been bitten before. It hurt like hell.

With an angry yell I jerked away reflexively, which freed up his right hand—the one with the leather belt wrapped around it. He smashed it against the side of my face, hitting me high on the cheekbone just in front of my ear. It felt like I'd been hit with a brick. A little lower and it would have broken my jaw; a little further back and it would have blown out my eardrum. As it was, it set off a concerto of wind chimes inside my head.

I tried to pin his hand down with the side of my arm. He wrenched his other hand from beneath me and put it over my nose and mouth, his fingernails biting into my face. I fought for air, but he had a grip like a gila monster.

Managing to pry three of his fingers away from my face so I

could catch my breath, I bounced all my weight on his chest and stomach, knocking the breath out of him.

And then I deliberately broke his fingers.

He roared like a rogue elephant and rolled out from under me, the blood from his nose splashing onto my arm and shirt, and scrambled away on his knees.

"Fuckin' shit!" he screamed, shaking off the belt and clutching his left hand with his right. "You broke my hand! Fuckin' shit!" He'd probably suffered a broken nose before, but the carnage to his fingers must have been new to him.

Down on his knees that way, he was very vulnerable, and everything in me wanted to go after him and finish him off. But I just couldn't bring myself to continue a fight with a guy whose hand was broken. I got to my feet and stood over him—not too close, though.

"Tell Mr. Maniscalco that if I ever see you again, I'm going to break *his* fingers," I said. I was breathing heavily, and the side of my face felt about the size of a basketball.

Wysocki called me several foul names, but he was still down, writhing in pain, and the fire seemed to have gone out of him.

"Take a walk now, Albert. Before I break something else."

He got to his feet unsteadily and squeezed his injured hand between his thighs. The look he shot my way was so venomous it would have killed a small mammal at thirty paces.

"You and me, we ain't finished yet, Jacovich." His damaged nose made it sound as if he was suffering from a bad head cold. He pronounced my name with a hard *J*, but I didn't bother mentioning it to him. It was probably one of the only three-syllable words he knew.

I watched him lurch off down the street toward the big parking lot behind Nighttown, the Irish pub-restaurant at the crest of Cedar Hill, slowing down a little to shoot me another murderous glare. It gave me a chuckle to think he'd probably parked in a public lot and had to feed the meter.

A sudden wave of vertigo made me lean heavily against my car. The back of my neck hurt. The side of my face hurt. My head hurt. My hands and arms hurt. My stomach hurt, and I could feel my breakfast roiling around inside me, threatening to make a reappearance. My shoulder hurt where he'd bitten me. Somewhere along the line I'd lost control of the day.

After a few minutes, when the dizziness receded and I thought I'd be able to walk, I began moving slowly toward my building. My foot hit something, and I looked down to see Albert's leather belt lying on the pavement. I picked it up and slung it into the nearby Dumpster.

I hoped like hell the bastard's pants fell down right there on Cedar Road.

When I'd gotten myself back up to my apartment, I headed for the bathroom and stripped off my shirt and slacks, which were covered with blood. To my relief, it all proved to be Albert Wysocki's. The side of my face where he'd punched me was an angry red and badly swollen. His boot had raised a crimson welt on my stomach, and on my shoulder was a perfect impression of his teeth. But he had bitten me through my shirt and hadn't broken the skin, which saved me the trouble of getting a tetanus shot. Or maybe, considering the source, a rabies shot.

I took my second shower of the morning, as hot as I could stand it; there are few things more disgusting than someone else's blood all over you, especially in this age of AIDS.

Especially when it was Albert Wysocki's.

I stepped out onto the bath mat and put my bloody clothes in the tub, letting the cold shower run on them. The shirt was salvageable, but the slacks, I feared, were history.

Slipping on a terry cloth bathrobe, I padded into the kitchen, where I wrapped up an entire tray of ice in two kitchen towels, one for my throbbing face and the other for the back of my neck. Then I sat there at the kitchen table until it had almost melted, drinking a beer; it was pretty early in the morning for that sort of thing, but I figure I'd earned it.

I got dressed again. Taking my .38 police special down from the top shelf of the closet, I loaded it and, eschewing the holster, slipped it into my waistband at the small of my back. Then I put on my Indians jacket to cover it.

I don't like wearing a gun when I'm spending time with my sons, but I wanted to be ready in case there was another sneak attack, my own personal Pearl Harbor on this quiet Sunday morning.

Not that I thought my tattooed friend would be back today; he was probably in the emergency room getting his nose and his fingers set. But I knew in my gut that there would be another day, and only a damn fool wouldn't be prepared.

I drove down Cedar Hill toward police headquarters, the gun digging uncomfortably into the small of my back. When I got there I put it in the glove compartment—the police don't take it kindly when civilians march in armed.

The desk sergeant was an old friend from my uniform days; since he'd gotten older and put on a little more weight, he'd been assigned to what amounted to receptionist duties. He waved me up the stairs to the homicide division, as he always had whenever I popped in to see Marko.

In the bullpen, Bob Matusen was talking to a skinny, weasely-looking man of about fifty-five with grease-slicked brown hair and the unhealthy pallor of a heavy drinker. They were both smoking cigarettes; the area around the desk looked like London in a dense fog. Matusen looked up as I approached him.

"Well, don't you look lovely," he said. "Somebody slam a door on your face?"

"Something like that. Got a second?"

"Sure." He squibbed out his cigarette and made his excuses to his visitor and we walked out into the hall together. As usual, the station house smelled of stale tobacco, burnt coffee, fear, perspiration, and old sins.

"What brings you down to the precinct on the Lord's day?"

"A couple of things," I said. And I proceeded to tell him about Alan Braxton and Dierdre O'Malley.

His frown was like a thunderhead in a summer blue sky. "God damn it, why didn't you tell me about this before?"

"I don't like siccing the law on private citizens unless I have a good reason. But for what it's worth, I don't think either one of them did Darren Anderson."

"I'll be the judge of that," he said darkly.

"You have to walk softly, Bob."

"Why?"

"Because if Braxton finds out his girlfriend put out for Darren Anderson, it could throw a monkey wrench into her marriage plans. You don't want to do that if you can avoid it."

"Tell me why I should give a shit."

"Call it compassion," I said. "A little humanity."

"I see humanity in here all day every day. I'm not impressed."

"Then go on my gut instinct." It sounded lame even as I said it.

"I've spent fourteen years on the job going on *my* gut instincts. Now's a hell of a time to start trusting somebody else's." He took a pack of Camels from his shirt pocket and shook one out; he smokes the ones without filters. "You have any idea the kind of pressure cooker I'm sitting in? The guy was a movie star, for chrissake! Now I talk to the mayor's press aide more than I talk to my wife. The safety director calls me every hour on the hour for updates. And just in case I had any little snippet of time left to do my job, I've got NBC, CBS, and fucking *Hard Copy* sitting downstairs in the community relations office waiting for me to fall on my ass so they can tell America about it!" He struck a match—it took him two tries—and sucked the smoke down to his toes. "*Hard Copy.* And you want me to tiptoe through the tulips with a couple of yuppies from the west side!"

I hadn't paid much attention to Bob Matusen when he'd been Marko Meglich's shadow. He wasn't a big man, and he had usually deferred to Marko's rank. I'd always tended to ignore him unless he came right up front and said something to me. Now, working with him directly on a case for the first time, I was beginning to like him more every time I talked to him. He had a sense of humor, and a certain easy grace that is rare in veteran cops.

"I've got something better for you," I said. "Tom Maniscalco."

He stuck the cigarette in the corner of his mouth, where it waggled when he spoke. "Don't tell me any Tom Maniscalco. Tom Maniscalco is alibied for Anderson's death up the rootie kazootie."

"Yeah, but Albert Wysocki isn't."

"Who in hell is Albert Wysocki?"

I told him. All of it, Wysocki's visit to my office with Maniscalco, my recon of the Home Works factory and warehouse, the attack this morning outside my home. He nodded, listening quietly, squinting as the smoke from his cigarette drifted up into his eyes. When I was done, he said, "That's where you got the face? From Wysocki?"

I nodded.

"What'd you do to him?"

"I broke his fingers," I said. "I think I broke his nose too."

"Good for you." Matusen looked almost impressed. "Tough guy, huh?"

"I'd like to think so."

He wandered a few steps away from me, smoking and thinking. He held the cigarette strangely, resting it on the knuckle of his middle finger with his index finger bent around it like a shepherd's crook.

"Even if Maniscalco could hire a goon like Wysocki to bounce me around," I said, "he wouldn't have sent him after Darren Anderson for screwing his daughter. You don't make a formal statutory rape complaint to the police and then go out and rent a hit man to avenge it afterwards."

"Besides, from what you tell me about this Wysocki," Matusen said, "he wouldn't have used a gun, at least not right away. He would've made the kid suffer some first."

I nodded. "But then why me? Just because I went to Maniscalco's house and talked to his wife? That doesn't compute."

"No. There's got to be some other reason. You said you went to his factory yesterday and it was crawling with rent-a-cops, right? And one of 'em makes you, and now this morning this pain-giver shows up at your house to teach you a lesson?"

"Right, that makes more sense. It's something at the factory that Maniscalco wants to keep me away from." I took out a cigarette of my own and fired it up. "They were warehousing some great big cartons from Brazil. You think he's smuggling?"

"Could be," Matusen said. "Narcotics?"

"Not likely. The cartons were too big. And you know how the D'Allessandros feel about drugs. They'd have his ass."

"So what else do you smuggle from South America? Maracas?"

"If I find out I'll let you know."

"You'd better," he said. "And get that face X-rayed; something might be broken."

I gingerly touched the sore place; the flesh was pulpy under my fingers. "It doesn't feel like it."

"Small favors." He regarded his cigarette; he'd smoked it down to a half-inch-long butt. "Since you're here anyway, come on back in with me. Somebody you ought to meet."

I followed him back into the bullpen. He snagged a chair from someone else's desk and indicated I should sit in it, next to the weasely-looking man he'd kept waiting.

"Milan Jacovich, say hello to Norbert Anderson," Bob Matusen said. "Darren's father."

CHAPTER TWENTY

Norbert Anderson was like his son, a few inches under six feet tall. The resemblance ended there. Darren Anderson had fortunately inherited his mother's good looks. His reed-thin, wiry father was sallow of complexion, low of forehead, and had watery blue eyes that moved around a lot like a silver ball in a pinball machine, racketing off walls and ceilings and windows, as if he suspected that the enemy was lurking somewhere in a corner of the room. Shifty-looking.

His handshake wasn't exactly weak, but it was indifferent. His fingers were deeply stained with nicotine.

"I'm sorry about Darren, Mr. Anderson," I said.

He shook his head, bitterness pulling at the corners of his mouth. "You never think a thing like this is going to happen to your own kid," he said, his voice a metallic, smoker's rasp.

"Mr. Anderson is in from Chicago. He's very anxious to find out who shot his son," Matusen said, but I could tell from the look on his face and the way he said it that he didn't like Norbert Anderson at all.

"Well, wouldn't you if it was your kid?" Anderson complained. His suit was discount-store shiny and too tight, his shirt an ugly beige that his sickly green polyester tie did nothing but clash with. He was wiggling around in his chair, crossing and uncrossing his skinny legs, exposing a couple of inches of hairy calf between his light tan socks and his pant cuffs. It occurred to me that a police station might not be among his top ten favorite places in which to spend time.

"When did you get into town?" I asked.

"Yestiddy," he said.

Curious. Darren had been killed on Monday night, and the reports were all over the news by Tuesday morning. If it *had* been my kid, the unthinkable suggestion Norbert Anderson had made, I wouldn't have waited five or six days.

"Mr. Jacovich was your son's security guard while he was here in Cleveland," Matusen explained, and Anderson gave me a hard look.

"Not the day he died, though," I added quickly. "I no longer had the job."

"I'll tell you this much," Anderson said. "Somebody's gonna pay. That movie company, whoever rented him that house . . ." He squinted up at me. "Maybe you," he said. "I'm not some dumb jag-off from out in the boonies, y'know. I already got my lawyer working on this in Chicago."

Norbert Anderson didn't look like the kind of man who'd have a lawyer, unless it was a defense attorney. He looked like he'd have a bookie.

"I understand how upset you must be, Mr. Anderson. We're all trying very hard to find out what happened to Darren." I flicked a glance over at Bob. "Detective Matusen is very good at his job."

"Where do they got the body? I wanta see my kid."

"The Cuyahoga County Coroner's Office," Matusen said. "It's in University Circle, not far from here."

"The morgue," Anderson mumbled.

"Have you seen your ex-wife yet?" I said. "She and her husband are in town, naturally."

Anderson jumped about six inches off his chair. "She is, huh?"

He squirmed. "Sure, that figures. Vultures circling in the sky. Nah, why should I wanta see her? After all these years, what's the point?"

Matusen and I exchanged looks, and he moved his head slightly to indicate he wanted to see me out in the hall. I gave Anderson one of my business cards. "I spent a lot of time with Darren—with Ralph, I mean—in the two weeks before he died. If you need to talk to me, please don't hesitate to call."

"Private security?" he said, reading the card. He had to hold it at arm's length. "What's that mean?"

"Just what it says. Industrial security, private investigations. Things like that."

He put the card in his shirt pocket. "Yeah, all right," he said. "I might do that. I'm grieving here, man."

We didn't shake hands again. Matusen followed me out into the hallway.

"Creepy little man, isn't he?" I said.

"Grieving, my ass!" Matusen growled. "Fucking phony! First question he asked me was about the kid's will."

My skin crawled, and I had to clear my throat to get rid of the giant frog that croaked in it. "What?"

"He wanted to know who Darren's attorney is, whether there was a will. Scumbag! The kid isn't even in the ground yet."

"Bob," I said, "if Darren didn't leave a will, the estate goes to his next of kin. That's his mother and his father. Norbert Anderson stands to be a very rich man."

"He left a will. I talked to his attorney in California. He'll fax me a copy in a day or two—after he's notified the beneficiaries." Matusen puckered up his mouth as if sucking on a sour ball. "I just can't feature a guy killing his own son for money."

"I had a long talk with his mother yesterday."

"Why?" he asked, regarding me with suspicion.

"She called me. She wanted a little comfort, I think. A little closure. It turned out she did most of the talking."

"About what?"

"The past, mostly. The old man walked out on them years ago. Didn't even keep in touch, for more than twenty years. Darren told me the only time his father tried to contact him was after he became a star—and that his old man wanted money."

"Did he give him any?"

"He said no."

"Even so . . ."

"One of the reasons he abandoned them was that he thought his wife had been fooling around on him. He wasn't even sure the kid was his."

Matusen looked over his shoulder into the bullpen, where Norbert Anderson still sat and fidgeted. "If the kid wasn't his, he doesn't get the money," he said thoughtfully.

"Yes, but legally, Norbert is listed on the birth certificate as the father. It'd take DNA testing to prove otherwise, and I don't think Mrs. Dinsmoor would want to go through that. And if Anderson thinks he's not Darren's real father, if as far as he's concerned the kid was a virtual stranger, it might not have been so tough to murder him."

He scratched his chin; he needed a shave, and his fingernails rasped on the stubble. "Maybe I'd better give Norbert Anderson a closer look, then."

"You might want to give the stepfather a look, too."

"Why?"

"Look, Bob, it's the same damn motive. The mother stands to inherit; that means the stepfather too."

"I don't know . . ."

"Dinsmoor didn't like the boy anyway. And he was bitter about not getting a bigger piece of Darren's money after he got rich and famous."

"Jesus!" he said, shaking his head. "Talk about your lousy childhoods. Two fathers, and neither one of them wanted him."

"It's probably why he wanted to be an actor. He needed love;

everybody does. He didn't get any at home so he got it from a bunch of faceless strangers sitting in the dark."

"And from a bunch of different women. Also probably in the dark."

"Yeah," I said, "but if you're going to check out every woman Darren fucked and forsook, you'll be an old man before you finish. The two fathers are looking good to me right now. Dinsmoor could've driven down from Detroit, Anderson could have driven in from Chicago. No big deal either way."

Matusen took his notebook from his hip pocket and made a few scribbles.

"As far as that goes, Sidney Friedman came up roses too. He's got a new star for a lot less money than Darren was costing him. He's a pretty happy guy right now."

"Okay," Matusen said.

"And Maniscalco is still bothering me. Or rather, Albert Wysocki is."

"Jesus, you're giving me everybody in *Who's Who!* Anybody else? Like Lee Harvey Oswald?"

"Oswald is dead," I reminded him.

When I arrived at my house to pick up my sons, Lila and Joe were gone. To church, Milan told me. She'd made a big deal out of my arrival time for nothing, just to bust my chops. Sometimes it seems as if that's Lila's hobby, like bridge or gardening or needlepoint.

"Hey, Dad!" Stephen said, opening the door for me with a big grin on his broad, open face, his blond hair tousled and falling into his blue eyes. "What happened to your face?" he asked when he saw my bruise, suddenly grave and serious.

"Little accident," I said.

"Jeez." Accepting it with equanimity, as he did most things, Stephen sat down on the bottom step to put on his shoes. He wasn't much for wearing shoes unless it was absolutely necessary.

Sadly for me, Stephen has reached the age where hugging his father was unthinkable. Milan hasn't done it for years. I missed it, but it didn't surprise me. Boys don't hug their fathers again until they're well into their twenties.

Poor Darren Anderson had never had a father to hug.

I waited in the living room for a while. I'd long ago stopped looking at the furniture and the decorations and knickknacks and remembering when Lila and I had bought them or recalling some funny or telling incident about them. Lately they'd begun to look only vaguely familiar to me, as if I'd seen them among the furnishings of some sitcom character's television home.

Milan Jr. came down the stairs slowly. Nearly as tall as I am, my broad-shouldered older son looks very much like his mother, with her Serbian dark hair and dark eyes. He'd be on his way to Kent State in the fall to pursue a degree in business administration, and he'd already made the freshman football team, and I was bursting with pride and gratitude that he was following in my footsteps. He didn't have the bulk to be a defensive tackle like his father; he'd played wide receiver in high school, but the Kent coaches hadn't yet decided what to do with him.

"Hey," he said. Then he took a look at my face. "That looks like it hurts."

"Not so much."

He tried not to let me see the concern in his eyes. "Are you going to tell us what happened?"

"I got punched."

"Again?" He shook his head. "Ever think about going into another business?"

"All the time. But whenever I check the classifieds I can't find any listing for Emperor Wanted, so I guess I'm stuck."

Stephen came running in, the laces of his left shoe flapping. "Let's blow this soda pop stand," he sang.

"Tie that," I told him, pointing at the errant laces, "before you fall on your face."

He bent down. "Then I'll look like you," he said.

We stopped at Skinny's, a restaurant-bar on East 222d Street, and picked up some bratwurst sandwiches and chips, then made our way to Euclid Creek Reservation where we got into a pickup softball game. While I never had the bat speed to play hardball, I have enough upper body strength to give a softball a pretty good ride. I went two for four, one of them a double, even though running it out made my bruises throb. Milan, who was shaping up into a better all-around athlete than I'd ever been, got three hits, and Stephen got a single and a walk. Afterwards we went to a pizzeria on Mayfield Road where the boys argued over the toppings; Milan loves green peppers and Stephen hates them. We solved the problem by getting Milan a pie of his own while Stephen and I shared one, sans peppers.

When I brought them back to their house at six o'clock, Joe Bradac's car was in the driveway. No reason it shouldn't be; he lives there.

"You want to come in for a while?" Stephen said.

I thought about it. For one reason or another I hadn't seen Lila in about six weeks. But after all these years I was getting tired of Joe's scurrying up the stairs to his hiding place in the bedroom whenever I entered the house.

"Not tonight," I said. "Are you guys up for a Tribe game next time if I can get tickets?" They were. They got out of the car, Stephen scrambling awkwardly from the back seat.

"Hey," I said through the open window. "I really love you guys."

Milan looked uncomfortable and kind of nodded his head abruptly.

"We love you too, Dad," Stephen said with a kind of wonder, as if he held some truths to be self-evident.

Connie Haley was right on time. She was wearing a muted yellow print dress that came almost to her ankles, and this time there was a gold felt bow at the end of her French braid. I welcomed her with a kiss that ended up being longer and deeper than I'd planned. Not that I'm complaining, mind you.

When she broke away, she regarded the side of my face narrowly. "That looks painful."

"It needs to be kissed well," I said.

She didn't kiss it well, but she put gentle fingers on the swelling and it did suddenly feel better. "A couple more of those," she said, "and you won't be cute anymore. I only hang out with you because you're cute. What happened?"

"Occupational hazard," I said, setting a couple of wineglasses on the coffee table. I picked up the corkscrew and twisted it into a bottle of merlot.

"That's it? That's all you're going to tell me?"

"That's all you want to know. Trust me." I wrestled the cork out and set the bottle on the table so the wine could breathe.

"Maybe it's you who ought to trust me, Milan. No fair keeping secrets." She cocked her head a little, the better to see the extent of the trauma to my face. "You were in a fight."

"Sort of."

"I didn't figure you for the macho type who starts fights."

"I didn't start it. And I'm not the type. It wasn't a bar brawl."

"What then?"

My heart began beating hard, which made my cheek start throbbing again. I didn't want to get into this with Connie. I'd lost a marriage and several other relationships because the women involved couldn't come to terms with what I do for a living and the fact that it often involves dangerous situations and violence. They also couldn't live with my dedication to my work. Maybe I was forever picking the wrong women, but more likely it was my fault too. Victor Gaimari was right when he said I grabbed hold and hung on like a snapping turtle.

So I didn't want what had happened with Albert Wysocki to blight whatever it was Connie and I had between us, didn't want it to spoil everything so soon. Like the red wine, a relationship needs time to breathe.

"I don't want this to be a thing, Connie," I said.

"What?"

"My business. My work. Most of the time it's routine; sometimes it isn't. Sometimes it can get hairy. I don't want it to scare you off."

The windows were open to admit the gentle summer breezes, and I could hear the traffic outside on Cedar Hill. In the brief silence that followed it sounded like a roar.

"Give me a little credit, okay, Milan? I grew up in a marine corps family; it takes a hell of a lot to scare me. I understand about having a job to do—and the guts it sometimes takes to do it. And don't forget, I already know you got shot in the ass last year, and I'm still here." She sat down on the sofa. "So pour that wine before it turns to vinegar and tell me the whole story."

I poured us each some merlot and sat down next to her, we clinked glasses, and I told her everything, the whole case. She took it all in calmly, sipping her wine, nodding occasionally, her eyes glittering with interest. She didn't even flinch when I told her about breaking Albert Wysocki's fingers.

When I finished, she took a deep breath and held out her now empty glass. I refilled it, and mine.

"This guy with the tattoos, you think he'll come back for you?"

"I don't know. Probably. I think it's personal with him now."

"He might even try to kill you."

"He might. It's been tried before. But I'm like that Jason guy in *Friday the 13th,* Connie. It's hard to kill me."

"But not impossible."

I shrugged.

"I suppose it's a waste of time telling you to be careful."

"I'm always careful."

"Good," she said. "Now that I know what's going on I can

relax." She put down her glass and slid over closer to me. "Does your face hurt too much to kiss?"

"Let's try."

We tried; we succeeded. After about fifteen minutes we broke apart and looked at each other and there was a tacit agreement; it's always nicer when you don't have to discuss it. I stood up, took her hand, and led her into the bedroom.

Striking a match, I lit the fat bayberry candle on the nightstand; it hadn't been burned for a long time, and I guess it was kind of dusty because it sputtered a little. But it cast warm, jumpy shadows on the wall and created instant intimacy. I didn't turn on the radio; they don't play romantic music on the radio anymore, and I didn't want to make love to Connie for the first time with Nine Inch Nails in the background.

I started to unbutton my shirt, but she gently took my hand away and began to do it herself. "It's like Christmas morning when you were a kid," she said. "Half the fun is unwrapping."

The unwrapping took a while, mostly because Connie's yellow dress had about a million buttons down the back. It was fun—but not *nearly* half the fun.

About ninety minutes later she said, "You can smoke the postcoital cigarette if you want to. It doesn't bother me."

"That's all right," I said. "I don't like to smoke in the bedroom."

She rolled over on her side to face me. The gold bow from the end of her pigtail was lost somewhere in the tangled sheets, and her braid had come loose; her hair was falling around her shoulders. "You had condoms."

"Yep. It's the turn of the twenty-first century, and I'm a man of my time."

Her dimple deepened with her smile. "Pretty sure of yourself, weren't you?"

"It's a no-win situation," I sighed. "If a guy has a condom, he's too sure of himself; if he doesn't, he's a pig."

"I didn't say there was anything wrong with it. I was just making an observation." She reached over and touched the bruise on my face. "Is this okay?"

"It's fine. I think it feels better."

Her fingers traced other old wounds—the scar on my arm from a knife slash in an alley on an obscure Caribbean island, the bullet scar from a drug dealer's gun in a ghetto on Cleveland's east side and its corresponding exit wound.

"You must be a good healer," she said.

"In some ways."

Her hand traveled up into my hair, and she pulled my head to her, nibbling gently on my lips. "Is this a regular thing with you?"

"What?"

"This," she said. "You have lots of women friends?"

"Hardly. It's been a while."

"You can't even remember the last time, huh?"

"Oh, I remember it vividly. It was just quite a while ago."

She propped her chin in her cupped hand. "How come? A good-looking guy like you, single in a very married town, I'd think you'd have women banging the door down."

I reached out and touched the ends of her hair. "I was in a relationship that broke up last year. By the time I was ready for another one, my best friend got killed. That was in the spring, and since then I haven't been much interested."

"What got you interested again?"

"You."

"Good answer." She reached out and pulled me toward her, cradling my head against her breasts. It felt good. Warm. Safe.

"I'm sorry about your friend," she said.

"This was his ring." I showed it to her.

"And since then, all you've been doing is chasing bad guys?"

"No. I wasn't doing much of anything, not until this Darren Anderson business."

She sighed deeply; from where I was, it was a delight. "Poor kid. He got a double whammy—two jerks for fathers. You suppose either one of them killed him?"

"I don't know what to think anymore."

"All that money is a lot of motive."

"Not to kill your kid."

"He wasn't his stepfather's kid, and his own father didn't think he was his."

"Could we not talk about Darren Anderson for a while?"

"What do you want to talk about, then?"

It didn't take much thought. I cupped her buttock with my hand. "Could we just not talk?"

"Slut," she said, her dimple appearing.

CHAPTER TWENTY-ONE

It was six o'clock in the morning. The sun was over the horizon and casting a cool orange glow over everything, but I wasn't fooled; it was going to be hotter than hell later in the day.

Connie came out of the bathroom looking young and fresh, flushed with warmth and damp from the shower. She was wearing my terrycloth bathrobe and had a towel wrapped around her hair.

"What's your father going to say when you walk in at such a disgraceful hour?" I said.

"He might ask me if I had a good time, but I think he'll take one look at my face and know." She unwrapped the towel and began rubbing her hair vigorously. Without makeup and with her hair all tangled, she appeared to be about eight years old—from the neck up. "You're not going to send me home without any coffee, are you?"

"I'm not going to send you home at all. If you go, you go on your own."

She disappeared into the bathroom again and I heard the whir of my blow-dryer. I went into the kitchen and fixed the coffee. While I waited for it to drip I checked the refrigerator; I was woefully unprepared for a breakfast guest. Toast and Cheerios was about all I had to offer. I set two mugs on the table, filled a pitcher with half-and-half, and took down the sugar bowl. I don't take cream or sugar myself, but I couldn't remember whether Connie did or not. I guess when we'd had dinner at the White Magnolia Friday night my mind had been on other things.

She reappeared, barefoot and wearing the yellow dress with the buttons open, her hair dry and combed and loose around her shoulders. She'd applied some lipstick but no other cosmetics I could discern. "Make yourself useful," she said. "Do my buttons."

She turned her back and I buttoned all the buttons I had unbuttoned the night before. In the cool light of morning I could see there were not a million, as I'd thought, but only twelve.

"Thanks," she said, turning around and kissing me on the lips. "You're handy to have around."

"What do you do about that dress when I'm not?"

"That's what brothers are for."

"You want some toast with your coffee? I'm afraid that's all I have."

"With grape jelly?"

"Naturally. You don't think I'd try to foist blueberry off on you, do you?"

She put a hand to her chest. "I should hope not. But I'll pass this time, Milan. I'm not a breakfast eater." She winked playfully. "You might keep that in mind."

"Shame on you. The most important meal of the day."

"*You're* the most important meal of the day," she said, and kissed me again, this time with a little more feeling behind it.

She sat down at the table and I poured us both some coffee, pleased that she took it black the way I do. Pleased too that someone vital and beautiful was in my kitchen to watch the sun come up with me. We drank in silence for a few minutes.

"I want to see you again," I said finally.

"You will. That was never in doubt, or I wouldn't be here. I told you, I don't do casual very well."

"Me neither."

"Besides, you make damn good coffee."

"You make damn good love."

"We're a team then." She finished her coffee and held out her cup like Oliver Twist. "Please sir, I want some more."

"More?" I rumbled in mock outrage. "You want more?"

She nodded. "And not just coffee, either."

It went on that way until the pot was nearly empty; easy, comfortable bantering. I hated like hell to see her leave.

But it was Monday morning; she had a job to go to. And so did I.

I kissed her good-bye at the door, I made some more coffee, half a pot being insufficient to jump-start my day. I showered while it was brewing, put on dress slacks, a white shirt, and a tie, and drank it while I read the paper and listened to a psychologist who had written a book on relationships get put through her paces on the Lanigan show.

When I'd worked up enough of a caffeine buzz, I went to the closet, got down my .38, and strapped the holster under my left arm. Then I went into the bedroom for my jacket. The sheets were a tousled wreck, and I didn't want to come home to them that way, so I began making the bed, aware of the absurdity of doing such a mundane domestic chore while packing a firearm. The scent of Connie's perfume rose up to stimulate my short-term memory, and I finished the job smiling.

I found her gold hair bow down near the foot of the bed.

I thought about calling Matusen and telling him about Ray Dinsmoor's rental car mileage, but I'd already turned him loose on Alan Braxton and Dierdre O'Malley, and God knew what trouble that would cause in their lives, even if they had nothing to do with Darren Anderson's murder. Out of respect for Mrs. Dinsmoor's feelings, I decided to go to the source first.

When I got to the motel out near the airport, I used the courtesy phone in the lobby to call the Dinsmoor's room. Mrs. Dinsmoor answered.

"Mr. Jacovich," she said, sounding out of breath. "Have you found out anything?"

"Not much, ma'am," I said. "How are you this morning?"

"Oh . . ." She sighed shakily. "We have to go down to the county coroner's and sign the final papers," she said. "They're going to let us take Ralphie home tomorrow."

"That's good," I said. "Uh, Mrs. Dinsmoor, I'm really calling to talk to your husband. Is he up yet?"

"Oh, yes. We're early risers. Just a moment."

She put the phone down, and I heard her talking to her husband. Then he got on the line.

"What the hell do you want?" he said.

"I'm downstairs in the lobby, Mr. Dinsmoor. I want to talk to you."

"I already told you I'm suing you. If you came here to talk me out of it you're wasting your breath."

"I want to talk to you about something else," I said. "Can you come downstairs for a few minutes?"

"What's in it for me?"

It seemed everyone even remotely connected with the late Darren Anderson had the same question.

"A get-out-of-jail-free card, maybe."

There was a long silence. "I don't know what you're talking about," he finally said.

"Come downstairs," I said, "and I'll explain it to you. Come alone, Mr. Dinsmoor."

"Why?"

"Because I don't think you want your wife to hear what I have to say."

Another silence. "All right, then."

I went over to the modest buffet the motel had set out, poured myself a cup of coffee, and selected a glazed doughnut. It took Dinsmoor about ten minutes to come downstairs.

"Let's go outside by the pool," I said.

We went through the glass doors to the small swimming pool, which was separated from the parking lot by a chain-link fence. Two small children, a boy and a girl, were splashing around in the shallow end under the watchful eye of their mother, who wore a sundress, oversize sunglasses, a smear of zinc oxide on her nose, and sneakers with lime green socks.

"What's this all about?" Dinsmoor demanded.

"You own a gun, Mr. Dinsmoor?"

"What's the difference?"

"Just tell me."

He shoved his hands into the pockets of his tan slacks. "Sure I do. You live out there where I do with a bunch of greaseballs and spooks, you damn well better have a gun."

"You bring it with you?"

He looked at me as if I were insane, "Course not! I never take it on the road with me. Too much trouble to get it on the airplane. Besides, when I'm not home Betty needs it more than ever."

"You know how to use it?"

"Sure. Betty too."

I nodded.

"What's all this shit about?"

"You didn't like your stepson very much, did you?"

The corners of his mouth turned down. "He was all right. We didn't get along very good, but lots of people don't get along with their spouse's kids. He could've done better by his mother— by both of us. But he didn't." He heaved a sigh. "That's the way it goes sometimes. There are people who do what's right and people who don't. You can't change human nature." All of a sudden his eyes narrowed to suspicious slits and his back stiffened. "Hey, I hope you're not thinking *I* shot Ralphie."

"Your wife stands to inherit a lot of money, Mr. Dinsmoor. That means you do, too."

His expression wavered between anger and fright. "Christ

sake, I wouldn't do that to Betty, not for all the money in the world. This has almost killed her, y'know."

I pulled out my notebook. "As of yesterday, you'd put over twelve hundred miles on a car you'd rented two weeks ago in Detroit."

First he looked startled, then furious. "Howd'you know that?"

"I know it, let's leave it at that."

"So what's the difference?"

"The difference is that Detroit is only three hours away from here. You could have driven down to Cleveland, shot Darren, and driven back in time for your wife to call you and tell you he was dead. There are enough miles on the rental car."

"I was all over the place," he protested. "Seven calls in Detroit, then Lansing, Ann Arbor, Grand Rapids. Toledo, Dayton. This was my first trip to this part of the country in eight months, I had a lot of ground to cover."

"Can you prove it?"

He thought for a minute. "Wait here," he said, and hurried back into the motel. I went into the lobby and snagged a coffee refill and another doughnut. I wasn't really hungry, but I guess there's enough cop left in me to make free doughnuts irresistible.

By the time I got back to the pool the kids had come out of the water and their mother was toweling them down vigorously, scolding the little boy about something. She gave me a dirty look I hadn't done anything to deserve.

I sat down at a metal table by the deep end and waited for Dinsmoor to return. He could have flown down from Detroit to do the deed, I suppose, but he would've had to rent a car here in Cleveland to get out to Darren's house in Bay Village. You just don't take a taxi to commit a murder. In any case, Matusen's people could check it. If Ray Dinsmoor could justify that mileage, it would make me feel better, anyway. I had no wish to bring any more misery down on the head of Darren Anderson's mother.

Dinsmoor came out of the motel carrying a faux leather briefcase. He sat down opposite me, opened the briefcase, and brought out a sheaf of papers.

"Here," he said, spreading them out on the table. "Here's the orders. Look here, now. Dayton. I had two calls in Dayton, here are the orders. Two in Toledo. See, they're signed by the buyers, that means I didn't do them over the phone. Here, look at this, Grand Rapids. . . ."

I calculated rapidly in my head as he paged through sheet after sheet. He had done pretty well saleswise; the orders amounted to about forty thousand dollars. And the mileage added up correctly. He couldn't possibly have made all these sales calls plus a trip to Cleveland. In all probability, he was telling the truth.

Nevertheless, I jotted down the places and dates of his sales calls in my notebook.

He clenched his bony fists, his mouth a single, thin slash. "You satisfied now?"

"I am for the moment," I said. "I didn't say anything to the police about the mileage."

He snatched the papers up from the table and began stuffing them back into the briefcase. An errant few were caught and taken by the breeze, and he had to chase them down.

"You better not," he shouted, glaring at me and shaking his fist as he returned. "Or I'll sue you for *twice* as much, you son of a bitch!"

He stomped across the concrete deck of the pool and back inside the motel. The mother of the two swimmers shouted out, "What kind of language is that? There are children here!"

She was yelling at me, even though I hadn't said anything.

I guess it was my week to get blamed for things. But it served to remind me how very much I dislike being threatened.

* * *

I didn't stop off at my office but went right to Matusen's. He wasn't happy to see me. He didn't even offer me coffee. He sat at his desk, hunched over reports, wearing a shockingly plum-colored sports shirt that had not been designed to accommodate the black knit tie he'd knotted under the collar.

"You should have told me about the mileage in the first place," he grumbled. "It could have been important." He ran both hands through his kinky hair. "How'd you get that information anyway?"

"I asked for it, Bob."

"And the rental company gave it to you just like that?"

"I asked nicely."

He looked up at me quickly. "You didn't pass yourself off as a police officer over the phone, did you?"

"I never told him I was."

"But you never told him you weren't."

"He didn't ask."

"You're skating on pretty thin ice, Milan."

"Yeah, but I haven't gotten my socks wet yet."

He looked at me closely. "Do I gather, since you have no new cuts or bruises, that you haven't had a return visit from Maniscalco's goon?"

"Not yet." I knocked twice on the edge of his desk, and a mist of cigarette ashes rose into a beam of sunlight fighting its way through the dirty window. "You get anything on Norbert Anderson?"

He shuffled through some papers. "I checked with Chicago PD. *Lots* on Norbert Anderson."

"Is it a secret?"

"Give me one good reason why I should tell you."

"Give me one good reason why you shouldn't."

He didn't say anything.

"I was the one who suggested you run a check on him," I said. "Don't I get points for that?"

"Sure," he said. "How many points before you win a prize?"

"They're Brownie points, Bob, they don't work that way."

He pulled a few sheets of paper from the middle of the stack. One of them was a faxed mug shot, taken when Norbert Anderson's sideburns were a little longer and he needed a shave. "Norbert stinks to high heaven," he said. "The past seven or eight years he's been a low-level errand boy in Chicago, for some not very nice people on the West Side."

"Not nice how?"

"Drugs, that's how. They popped him for possession with intent to sell a couple of years ago, but they couldn't make it stand up in court. Picked him up a couple more times for various petty bullshit, including carrying concealed, but had to release him. The guy's Teflon; nothing sticks. Probably had a mob lawyer helping him out."

"He's been in Chicago ever since he left Los Angeles?"

He ran his finger down the sheet. "His record there goes back seven years, that's all I know. Lived in a residential hotel on Lincoln Park West up until three weeks ago."

"And then what?"

"Then he checked out."

"And came here?"

"I guess so. He gave his current address as a third-rate motel in Elyria."

Elyria. Just over the Lorain County line from Bay Village.

"Elyria's right next door to where Darren Anderson lived, Bob."

"This may come as a shock to you," he said heavily, "but I know that."

I reached over and pulled the mug shot toward me. Norbert Anderson's rat face looked drawn and frightened, though he affected a tough-guy snarl. "Mind if I make a copy of this?"

"What for?"

"To put on my bathroom wall. My *Playboy* subscription expired and I'm tired of looking at last year's Miss November."

He considered it. "I don't suppose it'd hurt anything," he said, taking the paper from my hand. "But I'll do it. That's all I need, for somebody to see me letting a civilian use the copy machine."

He rose and went to the copier and set it whirring. "You *are* a civilian, you know," he said, coming back to the desk with both photos. "Used to be is yesterday's news."

"I appreciate your help."

"Well, you've been helpful to me." He looked at the copy. "Came out pretty dark."

"That's okay."

He handed it to me. "Just don't step over the line," he warned. "Keep acting like a civilian. You make a monkey out of me and the only way you'll get back in here is if you murder your dry cleaner."

"Gotcha," I said. "Thanks." I stood up.

"Listen, this other thing."

"What?"

"The guy who gave you the fat face."

"Yeah."

"He may try again."

"I imagine he will," I said.

"You carrying?"

"I know better than to walk into a precinct house packing heat."

"That's not what I asked you."

I thought it over. "I left it in the car."

He nodded. "Watch your ass. You got it shot once; don't make the same mistake again."

"I never do," I said, folding Norbert's mug shot and putting it in my jacket pocket. "Not when there are so many new ones out there just waiting for me to make them."

The sergeant at the front desk waved to me as I was on my way out.

"Hey, Jacovich," he said. "How about those Indians, huh? Sandy Alomar and Jim Thome. Boom-boom! I don't even miss Albert Belle anymore."

"I didn't miss Albert Belle five minutes after he left," I said.

CHAPTER TWENTY-TWO

It was a fairly simple matter to find out where *Street Games* was shooting on location that Monday; I just called the police public relations officer at the Justice Center downtown and asked her.

It wasn't that far from my office. I had only to drive past the back end of the Nautica Entertainment Complex on the west bank of the Flats, with its trendy restaurants and dance clubs, go over a small bridge, and hang a hard left and I was there. Looming against the bright summer sky were several gigantic white mountains, some perhaps a hundred feet tall.

Salt.

Millions of years ago what was to be Ohio lay under a vast salt sea; today Lake Erie boasts one of the country's most productive salt mines. The mined salt is stored along the bank of the old Cuyahoga riverbed until it's processed and distributed. It's a creepy place, especially at night, when it's very quiet. Turn your head one way and you see nothing but the ghostly white mountains; it's almost as if you were on a distant planet. Turn slightly to your left and there about a mile away is the glittering modern skyline of downtown Cleveland.

It didn't look very ghostly in the bright sunlight, especially with the Winnebagos and equipment trucks, the generators and lights and cables and camera booms, and more than a hundred members of the film crew running all over the place with their ubiquitous clipboards. From a distance, they looked like worker ants, crawling around and over the white hills. A movie company with all the attendent visual pollution can render the most romantic or unique location about as exotic as the boiler room in a junior high school.

I parked as close as I could to what seemed to be the center of things and took the long walk toward the cluster of Winnebagos, my shoes quickly turning white from the salt dust. It was eleven thirty, and the sun blazed almost directly overhead. I pulled off my jacket and carried it over my arm; a wet puddle formed at the small of my back.

It took me three different queries to find Sidney Friedman. He was sitting in a canvas chair under a large umbrella, conferring with one of the people he'd first introduced me to in that trailer weeks before; I think it was the production manager.

"Hello, Sidney," I said.

He looked up, startled to see me. His brow furrowed, but then he almost instantly relaxed. In fact, although from what I'd seen he was congenitally incapable of being low-key, he seemed entirely more at ease than at any time since I'd known him.

"Milan," he said mildly. "I didn't expect you to turn up. But I'm glad to see you, even if you are a rat who deserted a sinking ship. Even if you do look like someone slammed a manhole cover on your face. I'm glad to see everybody today—because we're a day ahead of schedule."

"I'm glad things are going well," I said.

"Well? Eric Winslow is a pussycat. A fucking prince! We should have gone with him in the first place. He's not only cheaper, he's a better actor. Not to speak ill of the dead, of course," he added quickly, looking pious, no mean feat for a man who wore his cynicism like a coat of arms.

"I've got a couple questions, Sidney. If you have the time."

"As long as it's just a couple," he said. He turned to the production manager. "Give me a minute, Fritz."

Fritz nodded and went off, while Sidney waved me to a chair under the shade of his umbrella. From that vantage point we admired the salt mountains.

"Is this a gorgeous location or what?" he said. "Right in the middle of Cleveland! You couldn't get a look like this anywhere else in the country. In the world!" He considered this. "The Gobi Desert, maybe. Remember that movie with Richard Widmark? *Destination Gobi?*"

"Sure," I said. "I cried at the end."

"It was a piece of shit. But it's the look I'm talking about."

"Speaking of looks, Sidney . . ." I took the photocopy of Norbert Anderson's picture from my pocket, unfolded it, and handed it to him.

He glanced at it. "Too ugly. Maybe if I was making a prison picture."

"He's not an actor. Do you remember seeing him hanging around the shoot anytime while Darren Anderson was still on the picture?"

"Milan, give me a break. I don't recognize half the people who're working for me, much less the rubbernecks."

"Give it a closer look."

"I don't have to," he said. "I don't pay any attention to the lookie-loos. I don't have time. There might be anywhere up to a hundred of 'em a day, snooping around for a sniff of Hollywood glamor." He kept his face turned away from the photo, as if it were a dead cat.

I knew when I was licked. "Okay, Sidney. Then do you have any objection to my showing this around to other people?"

He waved a hand at me. "As long as you don't get in the way. I want to *stay* ahead of schedule."

"You won't even know I'm here," I said.

He gazed off over my left shoulder. "Eric!" he called as his new star walked by about ten feet away. He got up abruptly and pushed past me without so much as a beg-your-pardon.

Eric Winslow was probably ten years older than Darren Anderson, but had about the same build and the same sulky good looks. His normally dark hair had been dyed dirty-blond to match Darren's; obviously they were trying to save money and time, so to avoid reshooting everything, they would use as many existing shots of the back of Darren's head as they could.

I circulated among the crew, showing them Norbert Anderson's picture. Some of them recognized me, but most didn't, and nobody remembered seeing Norbert hanging around.

Boyce Cort didn't want to tell me anything. "Those hyenas who hang around on the edge of a shoot don't even register with me," he said. "What I do when I'm directing is very . . . private. I have a very private talent. With all those people gawking behind the barricades, it's like going to the bathroom in front of an audience. So I just put them out of focus. In my mind."

"Could you just take two seconds and see if you recognize this man?" I said, holding the photo in front of his nose.

Two seconds was all he gave it. He looked at the picture and wrinkled his nose in distaste. "What a monumentally ugly man!" he said. "I don't look at pictures of ugly men." He walked away without bothering to find out why I was asking.

At one point I noticed Suzi Flores and Eric Winslow talking, their heads very close together. His hand rested easily on the hollow at the small of her back, just above where her hips swelled into lush sensuality.

Perhaps they were discussing the next scene.

I found the woman who'd been wearing the "Will-power" T-shirt my first day on the shoot; it appeared she'd washed her hair sometime since. Today her shirt read A WOMAN NEEDS A MAN LIKE A FISH NEEDS A BICYCLE. She looked at the picture for a long while. "He looks like Harry Dean Stanton," she finally decided. "In *Repo Man.*" She didn't recall seeing Norbert either.

Suzi Flores and Eric Winslow strolled past. His head was inclined toward hers, his arm encircled her waist. They looked like high school sweethearts three days before the senior prom. "Your two stars are working on their love scenes full time," I remarked to the T-shirt woman, trying to sound offhand.

"Christ, when they were introduced it was like a bad Calvin Klein commercial," she said. "Flores took one look and pounced like a cat on a baby robin. Like Yogi Berra said, it was déjà vu all over again."

"Déjà vu?"

"She did the same thing with Darren, except he didn't get all goony about her."

I tucked the photograph of Norbert Anderson back into my notebook. "You're saying that Suzi Flores was coming on to Darren? I thought it was the other way around."

She shook her head. "This is the second picture I worked on with Darren. She's not his type; he likes them younger and dewy-eyed. Suzi looks and dresses like a Tijuana hooker. That'd have to be a turnoff for Darren."

"Sounds as if you liked him."

"I did like him," she said. "He was funny and silly and just a kid. We could be friends because there was nothing sexual between us." She compressed her lips into a thin line. "What happened to him was shitty. I hope they find the bastard who did it and hang him up by the balls."

I jotted down the T-shirt woman's name—Brenda McKelvey—just in case I needed to talk to her again. My brain was clicking away like a high-speed printer. I quickly re-evaluated Suzi Flores and wondered why she'd lied to me.

I tracked the big guy with the yellow sunglasses and the Debbie Reynolds ponytail for about half an hour, having to stop every time Cort went for a take. I'd never found out his name or what his job was; I'd just seen him around.

"What's up?" he said when I finally caught up with him. "I thought you were outta here after what happened to Darren Anderson."

"I was. I'm back. Temporarily."

He shook his head. "Lousy break. A lot of the crew didn't like him much, but Darren wasn't a bad kid. That's all he was, a kid. Make a kid a star, you're gonna fuck up his head, no matter what." He stood lost in thought for a moment. "What brings you back here?" he asked.

"You got a second to take a look at a picture?"

"What kind of picture?"

I showed it to him.

"This is a mug shot," he said. "This guy a criminal?"

"Penny-ante stuff. Maybe worse. You recognize him?"

"He looks like Harry Dean Stanton on a bad day."

I had to laugh. "That seems to be the consensus. You didn't happen to see him hanging around during the shooting, did you? A few weeks back, before Darren Anderson got killed."

He studied Norbert's picture; then he took off his yellow glasses and studied it some more. His eyes were a watery blue, and he squinted against the glare. He probably hadn't been outside in daylight without shades in twenty years.

"Maybe," he said. He chewed on the earpiece of the sunglasses. "Yeah. I think maybe I did see him around. He'd shaved off the sideburns, though. And he looked older."

I could feel my heartrate increase, as if I'd just done thirty minutes on a treadmill. "Where did you see him? Do you remember?"

"Well, that's the thing. He was around a couple of days when we were shooting in that neighborhood on the other side of the bridge there."

"Tremont?"

"Is that what it is? Yeah. I didn't pay much attention to him. I thought he was one of the people from the block. But then I think I saw him again out at Squire's Castle. I thought it was funny, that he'd drive all the way out there from Tremont just to watch the picture being made. But that's about it."

"Did you ever see him anywhere near Darren? Did you see Darren talking to him?"

He shook his head. "I didn't pay any attention. We're pretty busy around here during the day."

"Listen, could I have your name?" I said, taking out my notebook.

"Sure. It's B.A. Stankaus."

"Rumanian?"

"Lithuanian. I'm originally from Pittsburgh, but I live out in Los Angeles now. So Cleveland is almost like home. We had some epic battles with you guys—the Browns and the Steelers."

"We sure did. And we will again, as soon as the NFL gives us a team. Where can I reach you, B.A.?"

"I'm at the Courtyard out near the airport."

I nodded as I wrote it down. No tony downtown luxury hotels for the little people; an airport motel would suit them just fine.

"You may hear from me. Or from a cop by the name of Matusen."

"You think this might be the guy who killed Darren?"

"Stranger things have happened," I said. "Tell me, what's your job on the movie?"

"I'm best boy," he said, and at that moment the assistant director yelled something through a bullhorn and B.A. Stankaus nodded and moved off into the crowd.

I put the photocopy back in my pocket and started the long walk back to my car. The inside of my nose felt dry from all the dust.

Someone could put Norbert Anderson in town and on the shoot before Darren's death; I could hardly wait to tell Matusen.

But I was a little disappointed too.

I'd seen it in a thousand movie credits: best boy. I never knew what it meant. And when I actually got to meet one face to face, I hadn't had the chance to ask.

I got back to my office at a few minutes past noon—there's little or no traffic on the industrial back roads of the Flats at that hour—and immediately put in a call to Bob Matusen to tell him that Norbert Anderson had been seen on the movie location, but Bob wasn't in. I wondered if he was out beating the bushes for Darren Anderson's killer, or if he had three other cases equally pressing.

No, I didn't think so. The death of a movie star was too high profile to get bumped back by some sordid drive-by shooting or a neighborhood love triangle that had turned deadly.

I considered what Matusen had told me about Anderson's Chicago rap sheet. He'd gotten my attention. Darren's estranged father was a mob soldier, and he'd been in town when Darren died. I wanted to know more. So I called the one guy in town who could educate me.

Victor Gaimari's secretary put me on hold for quite a while. She's never liked me. I held the phone away from my ear to lessen the effect of the treacly music.

"You want me to make a phone call to Chicago?" Victor said when I finally told him what I wanted. "To ask about someone who may be connected? Who is this guy, anyway?"

"He's Darren Anderson's father," I told him.

Victor drew in a sharp breath. "This is getting interesting. Still, my friends in Chicago don't like to talk about their people any more than we do. It will be an awkward phone call."

"Taking a couple of caps was awkward for the kid."

"I daresay." He took a long think-pause. "Anything from that Wysocki character?"

"All quiet on the western front."

"Don't get complacent, Milan. He might be back."

"I never get complacent, Victor. That's why I'm still alive."

"Mm-hm," he said. "All right, I'll see what I can do for you.

I'll make the Chicago call this afternoon. They may tell me to go to hell, you know."

He's a comedian, Victor. The Cleveland mob doesn't have the clout it once did, but I couldn't imagine anyone within the complicated infrastructure of organized crime in America telling the nephew of Giancarlo D'Allessandro to go to hell.

"Take the chance," I told him. "Live on the edge."

"Why don't you come out to the house this evening for cocktails, then? Around seven. There'll be a few other people there, but we can take a moment or two to talk."

I started to protest but thought better of it. Victor was doing me a small favor, too small for a make-good he could call in later. So he was summoning me out to his home just because he knew I didn't like to go there. It always gave him pleasure to watch me dance on the end of his string.

"All right, Victor," I said.

"And Milan . . ."

"Yes?"

"Why don't you bring a date? The rest of us will be couples."

I hung up angrily, but after a while I had to laugh. Victor knew that whatever our professional relationship, I disliked bringing anyone from my private life, my life away from my work, into the aura surrounding him. He was a manipulative bastard, and he was tweaking me, openly.

Well, he could have his fun this time. I needed him.

I drummed my fingers on the edge of my desk for a while, stewing. Then I dialed the White Magnolia. Sean answered the phone and chatted with me for a while in that innocuous but very careful way brothers have of talking to their sisters' boyfriends.

"Want to meet for a drink after work?" I asked Connie when Sean finally put her on the phone.

"Sure," she said. "Mondays are always hell. By tonight I'll probably be dying for one. Where?"

"Come over to my place at six thirty," I said.

"Are you trying to seduce me?"

"Of course. But I really do have another purpose. We'll go on from there. Drinks are at a friend's house."

"You're introducing me to your friends already? La, sir, I'm flattered."

"Well, he's not a friend, exactly."

"Then what, exactly?" She sounded the tiniest bit suspicious.

How does one explain Victor Gaimari? "I'll tell you when I see you."

"Private-eye stuff?"

"Sort of, sweetheart," I said.

"Are you going to get punched around again?"

"With any luck, no. But I can guarantee you an interesting evening."

"In that case," she said, her voice low and husky, "I'll guarantee you an interesting evening too."

Talk about offers you can't refuse.

I went out and had a sandwich at Shooter's, washing it down with a Stroh's. Then I drove back over the to salt yards at the far end of the Flats.

Lunch hour was evidently over, because almost everyone was back out in the sun, setting up the next shot. I saw Boyce Cort, Eric Winslow, and two other actors—at least, they were wearing heavy makeup—standing near the camera conferring. The makeup woman was patting away at Winslow's face with a powder puff, looking disapproving. Suzi Flores was nowhere in sight. I went to find Brenda McKelvey, who told me Flores wasn't going to be needed until later that afternoon and was probably in her Winnebago.

She was, and she didn't seem very happy to find me on the steps when she answered my knock. They had given Darren an entire Winnebago of his own; Suzi, not yet a big enough star, only occupied half of hers. Black hair in sultry disarray, she was wearing a silkily synthetic robe in an almost violent magenta hue, and my guess was that was all she was wearing. Despite the refrigerated air inside the motor home she looked flushed and sweaty, as if she'd been exercising. I could see over her shoulder that the plaid throw across the built-in sofa against the far wall of the Winnebago had fallen halfway to the floor.

Maybe she *had* been exercising.

"Hi, Suzi," I said. "Got a minute?"

She flushed even more deeply, crossing her arms defensively across her breasts. "As a matter of fact I don't."

"We really need to talk, I think."

"I can't see you right now," she said. "They're going to need me at about three o'clock, and I have to get some rest."

I went past her into the Winnebago. "Maybe you should have rested during your lunch hour."

She closed the door a little harder than was absolutely necessary. "What is it you want, Mr. Jacovich? I said everything I had to say to you at dinner the other night."

"It was a nice dinner," I said.

She nodded. "It was."

"It would have been better if you'd been straight with me."

Her nostrils flared, but she didn't try to deny it. "I could call security and have you thrown out of here," she warned. "I didn't invite you in."

"You won't call security, because you lied to me at dinner, and if it gets around, a lot of people—like the cops—are going to start asking why."

The sigh came up from her toes. "All right," she said wearily. "You're in here—take your best shot."

"You told me that Darren was harassing you," I said. "But actually it was you who were after him, wasn't it, Suzi?"

She sat down in the only chair that wasn't built into the wall or screwed into the floor, an easy chair covered with flowery chintz that could have come from the home of one of my mother's friends in the old neighborhood forty years ago. "I didn't see that it made any difference."

"It didn't. That's why I can't understand the lie."

"Maybe I wanted you to like me," she said softly, clutching the lapels of her robe together at the throat. "Maybe I didn't want you to think I was just a slut trying to sleep her way into a career."

I shook my head. "Sorry, but that won't fly. You're an about-to-be Hollywood movie star and I'm a private investigator from Cleveland. We'd never even met before. Why should you care what I thought of you one way or the other?"

She fluttered her eyelashes—if that was her idea of seductive, she probably wouldn't make it in the business after all. "Did it ever occur to you that I might be attracted to you?"

"No," I said. "I've been single a long time, and I don't miss signals like that very often. You hardly looked at me all evening."

She shrugged, and the rest of her body did remarkable things under the robe. "I didn't want you to think I was easy."

"You expected me to make a pass at you?"

"A lot of men do."

"I think there was another reason."

"Think your ass off," she said.

"You told me—and the police—that Darren was pressuring you for sex."

She crossed her legs angrily, without bothering to hold her robe closed. "So?"

"You and Darren were seen together on the set a lot, just like you and Eric Winslow are now, and someone was bound to say so. So maybe you thought a woman who was being sexually harassed—especially a beautiful woman like you, who as you just admitted gets hit on by a lot of men—would be less of a suspect than one who'd been scorned by the murder victim."

"Jesus Christ," she said, her lip curling. "Who writes your dialogue?"

"I don't have a committee like you do, Suzi. I make it all up myself."

"You'll never win an Oscar."

"I'll try to get through the rest of my life without one, then."

"All right," she said. "So I lied. Like you said, I'm right on the edge of what could be a pretty good career. It's bad enough to be on a shoot where the leading man gets killed—people could start thinking of you as some kind of bad luck charm. But if there was even a whisper that I was a suspect—even if they catch the real killer eventually—then maybe I watch my career go swirling down the toilet."

"I doubt that," I said.

"Look at me, Mr. Jacovich. I've got one thing going for me right now, my looks. I have the kind of body that's going to get chunky early, and if I don't capitalize on what I've got while I've still got it, ten or fifteen years from now I'll be playing chubby, middle-aged Mexican housekeepers whose dialogue runs to things like, 'Ay, madre de Dios!' " And she put both hands to her face as though in shocked surprise; it looked a lot like every Latina housekeeper I'd ever seen portrayed on the screen. "So yeah, I lied to you."

"About everything?"

"No," she said. "I do have two brothers who played baseball. And I did go down on a casting director to get my first job." She tossed her hair defiantly. "The difference was, it was my idea. This is a tough business, and you do what you have to do. I tried it with Darren, and I'm trying it again with Eric Winslow. With a hell of a lot more success, I might add."

"Good for you, Suzi. I hope you make it."

She rearranged her robe over her legs and pulled it together again at the neck. "So now when you see me on the screen, you'll think I'm just a spic whore, right?"

"No," I said. "I'll just think you're very, very sad."

I turned and went out into the heat of the afternoon.

CHAPTER TWENTY-THREE

Connie Haley arrived at my door promptly at six thirty. I was to find out that she was almost fanatically punctual; she later told me that if she was more than fifteen minutes late and hadn't called to say why, I was to check the hospitals and the highway patrol.

She was dressed for the heat in a sleeveless gray and white print shirtwaist shift, a style I usually don't care for. Her hair was down around her shoulders, the ends softly curled, and she was wearing three-inch heels with no stockings. I thought that night that she was the most sensual-looking woman I'd ever seen.

I greeted her at the door with a hello kiss that turned into something much more significant lasting several minutes.

"Jeez!" she said when we finally broke apart. "I thought you said we were going out tonight."

I nuzzled my nose in under her hair and gently took her earlobe between my lips. "I'm rethinking that," I replied around it.

She pushed me away. "Think again, Buster. I didn't get all dressed up just to take everything off. If I'd known we weren't going anywhere I'd have worn shorts and a halter top, in this heat. Besides"—she gave my tie a gentle tug—"you're looking pretty spiffy yourself. We're going out to show off tonight."

"You're the boss."

"I don't want to be the boss," she said, turning serious. "I'm much more into partnerships."

"Equal partners?"

She smiled with one corner of her mouth. "Maybe down the line. For right now, limited partners."

"I guess that means I should get my jacket."

"Among other things, that's what it means."

We headed east on Cedar Road, our eventual destination the village of Orange, where Victor Gaimari lives. The summer sun was still brilliant, but it was at our backs, so neither of us wore sunglasses. Unless you're driving directly into the glare, Cleveland is not much of a sunglass town. Wearing them in the gray of winter could even get you punched out.

"Tell me where we're going," Connie said, looking at me. "You were kind of mysterious on the phone."

"We're going to have cocktails at the home of a man named Victor Gaimari."

"And you said he's not exactly a friend."

"That's right."

"What is he?"

"A—stockbroker."

"Sounds dull."

"I guarantee you it won't be." And I told her what else Victor Gaimari was.

"Now I'm really impressed," she said when I was finished. "This should be fun."

"I wouldn't call it fun," I said. "And no horses-head jokes, no sleeping-with-the-fishes cracks either. These people are serious."

She fell silent for a while. "Are you mixed up with them, Milan?" she said at last.

"I'm not part of the mob, if that's what you mean. But Victor and I seem to cross paths a lot in the course of my business, and I've found out it's easier to be on good terms with him than to butt heads all the time. I'd be a happy man if I never had to deal with him again, but that's not how the cards fall."

"So why are we going for cocktails?"

I turned right on Brainard Road. The far eastern suburbs of Cleveland are heavily wooded; it's not unusual to see a deer bound across the road in front of you. More than one person has totaled his Lexus in a collision with one of Bambi's relatives. "He has some information I need," I said. "Making me come to his house for a drink is his way of exacting payment." I glanced over at her. "Compared to a lot of ways Victor and his friends have of getting a favor returned, this is pretty benign."

"You mean you could be flying home from Colombia with a condom full of cocaine up your ass?"

I laughed. "You see too many movies, Connie. Besides, the Cleveland mob is very antidrug."

"You're kidding!" she said.

"Not at all. Back in the seventies they tried very aggressively to keep drugs out of Cleveland, and for a long time they did. Victor's uncle was really the one behind it."

"What happened?"

"The bad guys from Detroit moved in, and the D'Allessandro family couldn't do much to stop them. Drugs are like the common cold in this country. You can't ever really get rid of them. You can only do what you can to control them."

We rode in silence for a bit. Then she said, "Is that where you got all those scars? That big long one on your arm, and the one on your side that looks like it could be a bullet wound. And the one over your eyebrow—did all those come from your mob pals?"

"None of them did. It's not that kind of relationship."

"Good," she said.

"Why?"

"Because if they did, I was going to walk in there tonight and kick your friend Victor right where his mother never kissed him."

"That's real loyalty, Connie."

She looked out the window at the lavish homes of Pepper Pike. "Damn right," she said.

Four large expensive cars were lined up in Victor's crescent-shaped driveway. There was no parking valet as there had been the last time I'd visited. Apparently tonight's gathering was small and intimate.

There was, however, someone to greet guests outside the door. In his dark suit, under which cultivated muscles bulged, and bad tie, he looked like a failed cruiserweight. He had a short list of names in his hand, and he squinted at them as if they'd been written in an arcane language.

"Mr. Jacovich?" he finally said through a nose broken too often to ever function properly again.

"Yes," I said. "And guest."

He opened the door and we stepped into Victor's elegant, modern home. The sound system, which seemed to be built into the wall, was playing opera. My guess was that it was Verdi or Puccini, and that the voice belonged to Pavarotti, but I'm not nearly well-versed enough in opera to know.

"I wasn't expecting this," Connie whispered.

"What were you expecting?"

"Remember Marlon Brando's house in—"

"We don't even mention that movie in this house," I warned her.

Victor came up the steps from the sunken living room into the foyer. He was dressed in dark gray and held the stem of a martini glass delicately in three fingers. "Milan," he said, "how delightful that you're here." He looked at Connie and seemed to expand a little. "And how delightful that you've brought this beautiful woman to my home."

I introduced them. Victor kissed her hand, like George Sanders in everything.

"Come in and meet everyone," he said. He took Connie's arm and guided her down the three steps into the living room, where seven people observed our entrance. Or they observed Connie's entrance; when she was around, no one seemed to notice anyone else. Even the black-vested waiter scurrying about with a tray of drinks slowed down to look at her.

Only two of the party weren't elegantly dressed for a night on the town and I knew them both. One of them very well, in fact. He was Don Giancarlo D'Allessandro, Victor's octogenarian uncle, the capo de tutti capi of the Cleveland mob. He was wiry to begin with, but he had suffered health problems for the past few years, and tonight he seemed more fragile and brittle-boned than when I'd last seen him several months earlier. His beige sports jacket, which looked as if it had come off the rack at Value City, hung loosely on his skinny frame, as did his plaid trousers. The tie he wore was probably as old as I am. With him was his longtime companion, Mrs. Regina Sordetto, wearing a severe black suit. She's the widow of one of Don Giancarlo's associates, Vincent Sordetto. Twenty years earlier Vinny Sword had turned the key in his car's ignition and died in an inferno in the parking lot of a *shvitz*, a steam bath, on Kinsman Avenue. Mrs. Sordetto— no one ever called her by her first name, not even Victor—had been the don's consort ever since. Now in her sixties, she was still possessed of a dark, hawklike beauty that made her more interesting to look at than many younger women. Tonight she wore a maroon dress with a southwestern cut and a huge necklace of silver and turquoise. She was stunning.

"Milan Jacovich," the don said, inclining his head in a kind of ritual bow. He had been born and raised in Sicily, and while he unfailingly pronounced my Slavic name correctly, he did so as if it were a particularly ruthless tongue twister. "Always good to see you." He took my face in his hands and kissed me loudly and wetly on the mouth. Then he turned to the other six guests. "This is Milan Jacovich. I love this man. This man is a real detective." He tapped his temple with an arthritic forefinger. "He got the smarts."

"Coming from you, that's quite a compliment, Don Giancarlo. Good evening, Mrs. Sordetto."

She nodded at me almost brusquely, but her big dark eyes were warm.

Victor kept his arm through Connie's while he introduced us to everyone else, including his date. Her name was Caroline Something, and she was very tanned and strikingly beautiful, except for the fact that there was a sleek health-club hardness about her that negated any sex appeal, at least for me. She looked a lot like Jimmy, whom he'd squired to the Maniscalco benefit.

"You can't stand around without a drink," Victor chided. "Let me get you something." He turned to Connie. "Angelo makes a great martini, if I might offer a suggestion."

Connie gave him her most radiant smile. "I'd be a fool not to try the *specialité de la maison,* Victor."

"Milan?"

"Sure, why not."

Victor signaled the waiter. "Angelo, two of our best martinis."

Angelo, who looked to be about twenty-two years old and fresh out of the juvenile house of correction, nodded and disappeared into the kitchen.

"It's my own recipe. He uses Bombay Sapphire gin," Victor confided to Connie in hushed tones. "And then he adds just the tiniest drop of Scotch. It's so smooth it's like drinking velvet."

"I can hardly wait," Connie told him.

They seemed to be enjoying each other's company, so as soon as Angelo reappeared from the kitchen with our drinks, I wandered over to Don Giancarlo. Everyone else had been arm-twisted into martinis, but he and Regina Sordetto were drinking red wine from exquisite Irish crystal goblets.

"I hope you've been well, Don Giancarlo."

He lifted his frail shoulders. "At my age, if you wake up in the morning you're well." He ran his fingers over the bruise on my face. "You, you don't look so good. You getting yourself in trouble again?"

"Nothing I can't handle," I assured him.

He shook his head. "You young guys, you think you walk on the water, that there's nothing you can't handle. You go along for years, and then one morning you wake up and you can't even pee no more, and they tell you got a swollen prostrate. Or you get a pain in your belly you think is from eating spicy foods, and the next thing you know they cut away part of your guts." He pinched my cheek. "So you go on, handle everything while you still can. Before the years catch up to you."

He raised the goblet and took a long pull, nearly emptying it.

Mrs. Sordetto took it from his hand gently and put it on an end table. "No more now, Gianni." It was the first time I could remember hearing her speak, and the first time I'd heard anyone call the don by his first name alone, much less its diminutive.

Don Giancarlo looked at me, this legendary crime boss, and turned up his hands. "See?" he said sadly.

I tasted my martini; it was as advertised. I took another sip.

A couple, whose last name I think was Balducci, came over to chat with the don. He was in his sixties and was a partner in a medical malpractice lawfirm that advertised aggressively on television; she was about fifteen years younger and sported on her finger a diamond big and heavy enough to cause carpal tunnel syndrome. She looked at me closely, as if she were considering buying me.

"Didn't I see you with that poor actor at the benefit a few weeks ago?" she asked.

I admitted she had.

"That's right. You were supposed to be his bodyguard or something." This from Mr. Balducci.

"No," I said. "I was more of a tour guide."

"What really happened there?" Balducci asked. "I mean, there's been a lot of speculation . . ."

"I know as much as you do," I said.

"Come on, now, Jacovich—you're on the inside. Don't you have any juicy gossip you can share with us?"

"If Milan says he don't know, he don't know," the don said with authority.

Balducci lost a little color. "Oh, sure," he said quickly. "I know that. I was just wondering—"

"I know Milan a lot of years now," D'Allessandro continued, "and while we don't always agree about things, he never lied to me once."

Victor, ever the gracious host, was instantly at his uncle's side. I looked around for Connie; she seemed to be deep in conversation with Caroline.

"Can I get anyone another drink?" Victor asked heartily. He looked at Don Giancarlo, then at the empty wine goblet on the table. Mrs. Sordetto shook her head almost imperceptibly.

"Milan and I have just a moment's worth of business to transact," he went on when everyone else demurred. "Will you all excuse us?"

He took my arm and guided me toward his den, although I knew the way—I'd been in there before. To my surprise, Don Giancarlo came with us.

The den was cozy, furnished in a more masculine fashion than the rest of the house, and built for work; a computer station, a fax machine, a high-tech phone console with speakers took up most of the surface space. On the wall was a small Modigliani nude I had no doubt was genuine.

Victor and I had taken our martinis with us. "Will it bother you if we drink in front of you, Don Giancarlo?" I asked.

He beamed, pleased at my show of respect. "Yes. Like it bothers me that you're young in front of me," he said, "but I learn to live with it."

"Then to your health," I said, raising my glass, and both Victor and I drank. "You were right about these, Victor. They're very good."

We sat down, Victor and I on a leather sofa and the old man in Victor's big thronelike executive chair.

"We talked to Chicago," the don said. "When you make an inquiry about one of their people in relation to a police matter, they don't like it. It gets . . ." He frowned, searching the ceiling for the right word. "It's—delicate. *Capisce?* You gotta walk on the eggs."

"I understand."

"Now this Anderson. What's his name? Norwood?"

"Norbert," I corrected gently. "Norbert Anderson."

"Jesus, and they think Italian names are funny!"

"And Slovenian names too," I said.

"So. This Norbert." Don Giancarlo looked at Victor.

"We got lucky, Milan," Victor said. "Anderson is obviously not part of the family." There was the slightest of pauses before *family.* "So they were more willing to talk about him."

"And?"

The old man's upper lip curled back over his yellowing teeth in disgust. "He's a junkie."

"That's right," Victor went on. "He uses horse. That's why he's not held in very high esteem in Chicago. He's untrustworthy."

"You can never trust a junkie," Don Giancarlo said.

"Most of what he does is errands. Low-level stuff, mule work, maybe once in a while a collection or two. Nothing important, nothing sensitive. And he's not always around when they might need him. It's strictly a contract situation. He's not on anyone's payroll."

"So he's a freelance hoodlum," I said. "What else?"

"What else do you need? I'm sure you've seen his police sheet."

I nodded. "I don't know. This just seems a little thin."

"He's a thief," the don rasped. I looked over at him. "Penny-ante shit."

"He's been fired from three legitimate jobs in the last four years for stealing," Victor said. "Warehouse work. And nobody was really sure, but they think he might roll an occasional drunk when he needs money for his habit."

"Does he steal from the outfit too?" I said.

Victor looked at me with something akin to pity. "Don't be silly, Milan."

"Anyone ever hear of him doing any wet work?"

The don coughed. I looked at him and he favored me with a glare like a thunderhead. Properly chastened, I played with the stem of my martini glass, taking a deep breath. "Well, I guess that's it, then."

"Milan Jacovich," the don said.

I waited.

"You know I'm fond of you."

"I'm fond of you too, Don Giancarlo."

He nodded. "But this here, this thing of asking about people might be connected to people we know . . ." He shook his head.

"It put us in an awkward position," Victor said.

D'Allessandro leaned forward, his elbows on his bony knees. "And it would put us in an awkward position to have to tell a friend no, too."

"I understand, sir. I won't ever jeopardize our friendship, which I value, by putting you in an awkward position again. And I thank you this time for your consideration."

There was a long moment during which no one moved. Then the don slapped his hands on his thighs and got shakily to his feet. "Well then," he said. "I think I'll go join the women. Prettier than you two by a lot."

I stood too and shook the don's hand. He put his other hand around the back of my neck and squeezed. "Good," he said, and went out.

I turned back to Victor, who was still sitting on the sofa. "I asked you to come here tonight so my uncle could be present," he said. "I don't want any misunderstandings between us ever again. That was a long time ago, and I do consider you a friend." He held up a hand to stave off my reply. "It doesn't matter how you feel about me. I'd like us to be closer, to be more social friends, but I know that you sometimes feel, well, conflicted about our relationship. But in the past few years I think there's been a mutual respect here. And you show respect to my uncle, which I like. He's an old man, and there's no question he's lost a step or two. But he's still operating on all cylinders, if a bit more slowly than he used to. And he's still the head of the family. I wanted you to know that. And I want you to know you're welcome in my home anytime."

I hated it that I was touched by what he said. "I appreciate that, Victor. And I do like you. It's hard not to. I certainly am very fond of Don Giancarlo. And I always hope that nothing I'm involved with ever conflicts with—with your interests."

"That's our hope too, Milan." He stood up. "I have to apologize, but all of us are invited for dinner elsewhere, or I'd ask you and your lady to join us." He smiled that pure white smile of his. "She's lovely. I'm glad you brought her."

"Thanks," I said. "I'd tell you to lay off, but she's not really your type."

"On the contrary, she's exactly my type," he said with a wink. "But don't be concerned. I always seem to wind up with women like Carolyn or Jimmy—bitter divorcées who like going to expensive restaurants and parties where everyone knocks themselves out trying to impress each other, and then wouldn't know a true feeling if it bit them on the ass." He sighed. "My uncle would have a fit if I ever married someone who wasn't Italian anyway."

"I guess so," I said.

"You know, there are lots of times when I'd just like to put on jeans and sneakers and go to a craft fair or a street festival, or sit in the bleachers at the Jake and just have fun. But the women I seem to attract would faint dead away if I didn't take them to the ballet or the theater or a benefit, or at least to Classics for dinner. It's my cross."

He threw an arm around my shoulder. "Anyway, Connie is very pretty, and charming and funny too. I envy the hell out of you. Is it serious with you two?"

"It's early days yet, Victor."

"Do you want it to *get* serious?"

"On one level, yes. Very much. But I've tried serious a couple of times in the past few years, and I've always crashed and burned. It scares me."

"I'm impressed. I didn't think anything scared you, Milan. Well, come out and have another drink; I hope to get you hooked on these things."

In your dreams, I thought. "They're good enough that it might happen," I said.

We went along the corridor toward the living room, but Victor tugged my arm gently and took me across the atrium entrance and into the dining room.

"I wanted you to see my new furniture," he said.

It was beautiful, I had to admit, gleaming from repeated waxing. There was something familiar about it, something I would have thought of even if he hadn't given me a hint.

"I got it from Home Works. Very rare wood. Maniscalco is one of the only dealers in the country to carry it. It's making him rich."

Our eyes locked. His gaze was level, impenetrable, but there was a sardonic little smile playing at the corners of his mouth.

"That's another reason I wanted you to come out here for a cocktail," he said. "I wanted to show it off."

I got it. Full bore. "Once more I owe you my thanks, Victor."

We went back into the living room to join the other guests,

and I took advantage of Angelo's mixological expertise and had a second martini. Connie was now in head-to-head conversation with Don Giancarlo, and they were laughing together. She was something, Connie.

And so was Victor. He'd given me an answer to a piece of the puzzle without really telling me a thing. I should have known when I visited the Maniscalco home and saw their dining room set, and then again when I watched the cartons from Brazil being unloaded at the Home Works factory, but I just hadn't been thinking along those lines.

Tom Maniscalco was importing endangered hardwoods like mahogany from the Brazilian rain forests, something strictly frowned upon by the U.S. government. Then he was making fine furniture out of them and selling it for perhaps twenty times the price of ordinary furniture. That's why there was such heavy security around his factory, and that's why he'd engaged Albert Wysocki—to keep me from poking around in his business. It doesn't do to get into a pissing contest with the feds.

And this cocktail invitation was Victor's way of letting me know why I had to watch out for Wysocki.

Connie and I said our good-byes, promising Don Giancarlo that we would be his guests for dinner very soon. Victor walked us to the door and came outside with us into the warm twilight. Cleveland being pretty far west in the eastern time zone, it stays light a long time in the summer. Then again, it stays dark well into the morning in the wintertime.

Victor gave Connie a full-fledged hug this time. He turned to me and squeezed my hand. "I meant it, Milan. You're always welcome here."

"Victor," I said, squeezing back, "you are full of surprises."

"That's what keeps everybody on their toes," he said. "*Ciao.*"

Connie and I got into my car. "Where do you feel like eating?" I said when we were underway.

"I don't care," she said, "but it'd better be damn quick or those martinis are going to catch up with me and make me do something crazy."

It was a playful comment that seemed to beg for a reply, but I didn't make one. I was brooding. I knew it, I recognize it in myself when it happens. But I felt a kind of paralysis overtaking my brain, and it had nothing to do with Angelo's martinis.

We rode on in silence until we reached the intersection of Richmond Road and Chagrin Boulevard, a five-minute trip.

"Something's wrong," Connie said.

"It'll go away."

"With proper diet and treatment, yes."

I attempted a chuckle, which died a-borning.

"You're not mad because Victor was flirting with me?"

"My God, no. I'm not all that insecure."

"Ten points for you. So what *is* wrong?"

"It's hard to explain . . ."

"Talk real slow, then."

I was a little at sea, driving down Chagrin Boulevard toward town and flailing around in a conversation I didn't know how to have.

I took a deep breath. "Connie, I'm kind of a black-and-white guy. I've always taken a certain pride in that."

"Black-and-white like Robert Mitchum in *Out of the Past*?"

I had to smile; I'd forgotten that she was an old-movie buff, like me. "No," I said. "Black-and-white like there's right and there's wrong and there's no such thing as a gray area."

She frowned a little but nodded.

"It's an attitude that's cost me a lot, but it's the way I am. The way I've always been."

"So you decided tonight you were going to get depressed about it?"

"No. Not exactly."

"What, exactly?"

I ran a hand over my face. "I spent part of my misguided youth as a cop. I guess in my heart of hearts I still am one. My best friend was a cop—he got killed a couple of months ago, covering my ass when he didn't have to. He was a black-and-white guy too. Always by the book. When he put the book down, he died."

She put a comforting hand on my thigh.

"So I've got a certain way of looking at the world. It's not always easy, but it's my way. That's something I guess you should know."

"I have a feeling I knew already," she said. "Don't get me wrong, I haven't got a father complex, but I see an awful lot of Leo Haley in you. And I admire it."

"But then there's Victor."

She nodded.

"Victor Gaimari and his uncle represent a lot of things I've fought against all my life. They're organized crime. They're amoral at best, evil at worst. They certainly don't fit with my vision of myself, of my world."

We drove on for another minute or so while I tried to marshal my thoughts into something that wasn't too weird for her to understand.

"And yet I find myself *in* their world, Connie. They even like me."

"I think the old man loves you," she said.

"And God help me, I find myself liking them back. Victor and I had our problems in the old days—we tore at each other like a couple of pit bulls. I broke his nose, he had his boys beat the crap out of me. But now it seems there are chummy phone calls, favors back and forth, invitations to dinner, and all of a sudden I feel like I'm crossing some dangerous line where there's no backtracking. I'm compromising the principles that have kept me standing up straight all these years, and it bothers the shit out of me."

"You can't accept even the possibility that there might be something between the black and white?"

"I never have," I said. I fumbled in my pocket for my cigarettes and lit one with the dashboard lighter, cracking the window slightly so the smoke would be sucked out into the slipstream.

Just shows you how bothered I was; I never smoke in the car when there's a nonsmoker with me.

Connie thought things over for a while. I was to find out that for all her shoot-from-the-hip humor, she was one of the most logical, judicious people I'd ever know.

"Did Victor ever murder anybody?" she asked.

"Not that I know of. I doubt it."

"And when's the last time there was a mob killing in this town?"

I remembered a mob boss named Danny Green who got blown all over a parking lot at a medical plaza in upscale and oh-so-proper Beachwood, and the legendary Shondor Birns, whose death by car bombing took out an entire corner on the near west side, just over the Detroit-Superior Bridge. But they were hazy memories, part of Cleveland's old legend. "A hell of a long time ago," I said.

"Exactly. The mob doesn't operate like a Martin Scorcese film anymore. The sugar wars were seventy years ago."

She was speaking of the mob war that went on during prohibition when whoever controlled the shipments of sugar in Cleveland controlled all the manufacture and distribution of bootleg whiskey. It was a wild, violent time, and to this day the intersection of 110th Street and Woodland Avenue is remembered as Bloody Corners.

"What's your point?" I said.

"Just that Victor and his uncle are businessmen. They probably take some short-cuts and do things that aren't exactly legal, but they aren't monsters. They certainly aren't anywhere near evil. And they're the ones that tried to keep hard drugs off the streets in Cleveland. So what's your problem?"

I chewed that over for a while. Victor had involved me in some election funny stuff a while back, and in an aborted search for a piece of priceless English porcelain, and both times he'd revealed a less than admirable side of himself. But was all that enough for me to make a sweeping judgment about them? Maybe she was right. In the last few years Victor and the don had shown me nothing but friendship, and they'd always been there when I needed them.

"It's just hard for me," I said.

"You really can't tolerate any gray areas between the black and white, Milan? You think that going to Victor's home for a drink or having dinner with a frail old man is going to strengthen the forces of evil and disorder, to give aid and comfort to the dark powers?"

She opened her own window, to let more of the smoke out and I realized I was being thoughtless. I stubbed my cigarette to death in the ashtray.

"Well," I said, "it's my problem and I'll deal with it."

"Hard-ass, huh?"

I felt my spine stiffen; I'd been called that before, and I didn't like it any better this time. "Call it what you want."

She snickered and began whistling the Village People's "Macho Man."

"All right, all right," I said. "Have you decided where you want to go for dinner?"

"I've decided I don't want to waste the buzz of Victor's martinis. I want to go back to your place." Her hand was still on my thigh, and now she ran it all the way up. "I want us to take off our clothes and do kinky, immoral things to each other, the kind you read about in dirty books. And we're not married, so that makes it a sin in a lot of people's eyes, which makes it even more interesting. And after we're all through, after you're so wiped out you can't even get your head up, much less anything else, I want you to tell me about black and white, and that there are no gray areas."

And she gave me a squeeze, taking my breath away.

"Or," she said, "we can go someplace and get a hamburger instead."

"What a ridiculous idea," I replied.

CHAPTER TWENTY-FOUR

Connie left me comfortably, deliciously sated at about ten thirty in the morning, after I'd made an early run to Bialy's in University Heights, where they sell the best bagels in town. I toasted them and spread indecently thick layers of cream cheese over them, and we each had two apiece, along with coffee and classical music on WCLV. When she finally went home, I finished up what was left of the coffee and reflected on all I'd come to understand in the past twelve hours about the various shades of gray.

It was making me nervous, making me want to dig in my heels and slow things down. Connie was getting to me in a major-league way, and it was scaring me. I didn't want to get hurt again.

But I had more on my mind than a wondrous, sensuous night of exploration and discovery. I called a contact I had at the FBI and blew the whistle on Tom Maniscalco and his illegal imports. They promised they'd look into it, and I had to be satisfied. With my face still tender from Albert Wysocki's ministrations, it was the least I could do to get even.

That left the more important stuff, like the fact that Darren Anderson's killer was still at large, and that what seemed to be inescapable logic to me was also unthinkable.

Norbert Anderson, the low-rent Chicago bagman. Norbert the junkie. Norbert who just might have motored over from

Chicago to kill his only begotten son. Just the thought made me sick.

The last of the coffee tasted suddenly bitter, and I poured it into the sink and went to stand under a hot shower for a long time. My elbows and knees were pleasantly and memorably raw from last night's exertions, and the hot water felt good on my facial bruises, too.

I dressed casually in a bright blue sports shirt and khakis, leaving the shirt hanging out of my pants so the .38 in my waistband wouldn't show. It had caused Connie some consternation last night when we undressed, but I explained that Albert Wysocki still roamed the land like a hungry T. rex, and I didn't want to be caught unprepared again.

Besides, I didn't know whether I'd need to be armed on my little foray this morning. I didn't want to be like the guy who shows up at a formal banquet wearing a brown suit, the only one at the party not carrying a weapon.

Driving west under the mid-day sun is always a bear in Cleveland, and I found myself squinting all the way as the urban landscape of Cuyahoga County became practically unbroken rural countryside between Avon Lake and Elyria. With traffic, the trip took about forty-five minutes.

It was another ten minutes before I found the sleazy motel where Norbert Anderson was staying. Back in the postwar era, when Americans had rediscovered the romance of the road, they would have called it a tourist court. It was L-shaped, with a second floor on the short end of the L but not the long one, as if they'd run out of money halfway through construction. A sign proclaimed SINGLES FROM $25.95 and WEEKLY RATES. Norbert Anderson had either never heard that living well was the best revenge, or he just plain didn't give a damn.

Motels of any kind generally refuse to give out information about their clientele, for obvious reasons, so instead of inquiring at the office, I searched the parking lot.

I found an ancient Chevrolet Monte Carlo with Illinois tags and a Chicago license-plate frame. Its red paint job had oxidized a long time ago, its ashtray was overflowing, its floor was littered with the greasy detritus of at least twenty fast-food meals. A horizontal rent in the driver's seat was hemorrhaging dirty gray stuffing and in the back was a half-empty carton of Marlboros, a road atlas, a crumpled *Chicago Sun-Times,* and a dirty T-shirt.

I figured it was unlikely someone had picked him up and taken him somewhere, and he didn't seem much like the type to take a brisk stroll, especially in noontime Ohio heat—from the look of him, his preferred form of exercise was twisting caps off beer bottles. So if his car was there, chances were he was too.

The Chevy was parked nose in, facing room 9, which luckily was on the single-story wing of the court, or I would have had to knock on several doors on both levels. I rapped firmly on the cracked and faded green paint. After thirty seconds I tried again, with again no success.

To the right of the door was a window, but the blackout drapes were drawn, so I couldn't peek in. The old air conditioning unit grumbled its basso lament beneath it. It would take a heavy sleeper to snooze through the night with that incessant noise hard by his ear.

I tapped on the glass with Marko's ring, hoping that if Anderson was indeed asleep the sound would cut through the air conditioner's drone and penetrate his consciousness.

I twisted the doorknob. The door didn't open, but I heard some clicks and rattles. I tried a little body English, first pulling up on the knob, then down, then out toward me, then leaning in. The door hadn't been hung very well; it would be a miracle if anything at that motel worked properly. Finally after about fifteen tries, the tumblers caught, the knob turned, and I swung open the door and walked in, ready to draw my .38 if I had to. Anderson ran round with some bad boys in Chicago, and it wouldn't surprise me if he was armed.

The noisy air conditioner couldn't dispel the smell of body odor, cigarette smoke, and decay. Norbert Anderson was lying on his back on the unmade bed, wearing a sleeveless undershirt and the kind of striped boxers I thought had gone out of style in the forties. He was asleep, all right—the kind of asleep you never wake up from. I could tell. His waxy pallor and the way his lips were drawn back into a rictus over uneven yellowed teeth left little doubt, but the bullet hole leaking blood and brain matter through his right sideburn was the clincher. I couldn't tell how long he'd been dead without touching him—and I didn't want to do that at all. From the smell, though, I figured he'd been there like that for at least twelve hours, maybe more.

Looking at dead bodies is always tough. If they've gotten dead through unnatural means, it's even worse. I shuddered and turned my head away.

Hanging on a clothes rack near the door was a plaid sports jacket I wouldn't have worn to a cockfight. Next to it were wash-and-wear slacks and a lightweight windbreaker with a cigarette burn on the front of it.

I began moving around the room, taking it all in, keeping my hands stuffed into my pockets so as not to disturb the integrity of the crime scene.

An open plastic suitcase on the floor at the foot of the bed further displayed Anderson's wardrobe: a few short-sleeved wash-and-wear shirts in various bilious colors, some undershirts and sorts, and several pairs of white socks rolled up into balls. Between the edge of the bed and the wall was a plastic supermarket bag stuffed with dirty laundry.

Nudging the bathroom door open with my shoulder, I went in. In the unzipped dopp kit I could see only a deodorant stick, shaving gear, and a couple of condoms. I was dying to see if he had his junkie works in there, his spoon and syringe, but I didn't want to touch anything before the police arrived. There was no telephone; this really was the Bare Bones Motel, or perhaps Notel would be more accurate. Taking one more quick look around, I went out through the open door, pulling it shut behind me, since my fingerprints were already on the doorknob.

The man behind the desk in the office was probably near sixty. Pear-shaped and jowly, he had the kind of lived-in face that has seen just about everything in the way of bottom feeders, bar pickups, roadrunners, and the permanently transient; clerks in low-rent motels get quite an education, but sometimes the tuition is dear. His short-sleeved white nylon shirt revealed a tattoo of the Statue of Liberty on his forearm. Everybody has tattoos but me.

The office smelled just like Anderson's room—a little BO, a lot of tobacco smoke, and the rotting smell of dreams that had died in the corner. The clerk, who turned out to be the owner, put his left hand flat on the chest-high counter, keeping his right one out of sight. He bristled with undisguised suspicion, and I had no doubt that his fingers were inches from a gun, a baseball bat, a can of pepper spray, or something else with which he could defend himself. His attitude was pretty defensive, too.

"I saw you poking around outside," he said. "You looking for something you can't find?" His voice issued from a throat that had processed fifteen thousand cigarettes.

"I need a telephone."

He nodded toward the door. "There's one outside, around the corner."

"What about that one right there on the desk?"

"People just can't come in here and use the phone. It's for official motel business only."

"Oh," I said.

"Now you know," he said.

"Well, this *is* kind of motel business. You've got a stiff in room nine, courtesy of a very big bullet hole in his head, and I'm afraid he's bled all over your pillows."

His gray face became grayer, and his pendulous jowls sagged even more. "Oh. Oh, for Christ's sake," he said.

"Now *you* know," I said, and went behind the counter to call the police.

A forensic team from the Elyria PD was busy in room 9. The coroner's wagon had arrived, flashbulbs were popping like outside a Hollywood premiere, and there was yellow crime-scene tape all around that wing of the motel, bright against the drab building. The owner was stalking around with his fists on his hips, looking very unhappy.

Just outside Anderson's room Detective Larry Ledbetter leaned against his unmarked Ford Taurus, chewing on a piece of shockingly pink bubble gum that clashed with his expensive tan suit and blue and yellow tie. Another man with his name surely would have earned the departmental sobriquet "Leadbelly," but his conservative style of dress, his less-than-medium-height, and whippet-thin physique, and his precise, almost elegant demeanor somehow made me doubt that anyone took such liberties with him. His hair was cropped short enough to reveal the scalp beneath, his skin was the color of rich Colombian coffee, and his gold-rimmed glasses only emphasized his quick, intelligent brown eyes. His manner was deceptively easy, and despite the heat of the afternoon, his suit showed nary a wrinkle.

"Let me understand this," he said. He had a very deep voice for such a small person, and his speech was like that of a TV anchorman, without any trace of regional accent. "You came out here to interview the deceased, Norbert Anderson, and when he didn't answer the door you broke into his room? Do I have it right?"

"Not exactly. I didn't really break in," I said.

"Not exactly? Was the door locked?"

"It was—kind of locked."

"Not exactly and kind of locked." He shot me a gimme-a-break look.

"I fiddled with it and then it opened."

"You picked the lock?"

"No. I just fiddled around with the doorknob."

"You always fiddle with locked doors?"

"I saw Anderson's car and I figured he was in. When he didn't answer I got worried. So I fiddled."

"And?"

"And that's it. I went in, he was dead, I called you."

"You didn't touch anything?"

"No." I said. "I used to be on the job."

"I know," Ledbetter said. "I know who you are. I read the papers. You get your name in the papers a lot."

"I'll have to remember to thank my press agent."

"You were also a friend of Mark Meglich, no?"

"That's right. You knew Marko?"

"A little bit, yeah. I remember seeing you at his funeral."

"You went to his funeral?"

"Every cop for miles around went to his funeral. When a cop goes down, especially a high-profile cop like Meglich, everybody turns out to show respect. Not many of them were crying, though. You were there when he got killed, too, weren't you?"

I made a concerted effort not to knot my hands into fists. "I was there for a lot of things. He and I were friends since fifth grade. What's this got to do with Norbert Anderson?"

"It's got to do with whether or not I arrest you for breaking and entering, of which you happen to be stone guilty. This is my ball game here." He blew a big pink bubble, sucking it back into his mouth before it popped. "So what do you know about the late great Norbert Anderson that made you want to talk to him bad enough to force your way into his motel room?"

"I know he's got a sheet. In Chicago."

Ledbetter looked bored—if you didn't notice his quick, inquisitive eyes. "His ID shows a Chicago address; we would've found that out anyway. What else?"

"He's a junkie. Somewhere in his belongings you're going to find works."

"I figured that when I saw the tracks on his arms. You're not telling me anything I don't know, Mr. Jacovich."

"Do you know he's Darren Anderson's father?"

Ledbetter straightened up off the fender of the car. "Darren Anderson?"

"The late movie star. I was hired to keep him out of trouble while he was in Cleveland," I said. "I quit. He was killed. I want to know why."

"You have a client who's involved in this?"

"Not really."

"Just a nosy Parker, huh?"

"More like an ethical obligation."

"Ethical. I like that. You're poking around in two open homicide cases because it's ethical. Wait till my lieutenant hears that one."

"Anything to make your lieutenant's day," I said.

"Yeah. So the kid got killed in Bay Village and the Cleveland cops are handling it. What was this Norbert Anderson doing in Elyria?"

"He drove in from Chicago. Maybe he just got tired before he hit Cleveland. That's a guess. He's been registered here for three weeks," I said, "which means he was here before Darren got shot. Why he was here I don't know. That's one of the things I wanted to ask him."

"One of the things. What was the other one?"

"Whether he killed his son."

Ledbetter took his gum out of his mouth, looked around for a trash receptacle, then shrugged and deposited the wad behind the scrub bushes that grew along the side of the motel wall. "That's pretty heavy," he said. "Killing your own kid."

"If it's true."

"What makes you think it might be?"

"Motive and opportunity—the gold-dust twins. Norbert would have come into a lot of money if his son died without making a will. And twenty-four-year-old kids aren't much for estate planning."

"Anything else you're not telling me, Mr. Jacovich?"

I thought about what I knew regarding Norbert Anderson's mob ties, but I wasn't giving that to Ledbetter under any circumstances. I knew damn well that was the price of Victor's help, and of his uncle's. The old Sicilian law of *omerta*, of silence, was not one to be broken lightly, even by a Slovenian.

"I think you've got all of it," I said.

He took another piece of bubble gum from his pocket, unwrapped it, and popped it into his mouth, crumpling up the wrapper and putting it back in his pocket. "I'm trying to quit smoking," he said. He waited until the wad was fully chewable before he spoke again. "Would it do me any good to take you in and sweat you all afternoon?"

"Probably not."

"How about booking you on B-and-E?"

"Go ahead, if it'll make you feel better."

"Seats right behind the third-base dugout at Jacobs Field and a nice cold beer would make me feel better. Or I could hold you for seventy-two hours on suspicion of murder. Of course, the motel owner says he saw you fooling around with the door here, and that you were only inside for a minute, and my guess is that Anderson's been dead a hell of a lot longer than since you first showed up. But I could still hold you. Three days of jail food and pretty unpleasant company might make you a little more friendly."

"You could also shoot me down right here and claim I pulled a piece on you first," I said. "I am carrying."

"I know." Ledbetter smiled. "I saw the bulge right off. Don't assume I'm some small-town black cop who got his job on an affirmative-action gimme, Mr. Jacovich. I'll tear you down and put you back together again wrong."

"I'm not assuming anything, Detective. And I think I've treated you with deference and respect, but if you think otherwise, I apologize. When I walked in on a dead body, I called the police; I didn't have to, I could have just taken off and waited for someone from the motel to find him when the wind shifted. You have the right to book me, you can even take me downtown and bounce me off the walls a few times, but it's not going to get you anything more than you've got right now, because I've told you everything I have. So I ask, respectfully, that you either arrest me or shake my hand and say good-bye."

Ledbetter blew a long, leisurely bubble. I watched it, fascinated, almost mesmerized; that's one of the things about bubble gum. This time it burst, so loudly that inside the motel room one of the forensics people kneeling beside the bed with rubber gloves and tweezers and plastic evidence bags took an anxious, startled look over his shoulder.

He sucked the gum back into his mouth; it really is a disgusting habit. "Elyria's very blue-collar, Mr. Jacovich. We're too far away from Cleveland to be rightfully considered a suburb, and too close to avoid the fallout of some of your big-city shit. There are nice decent people here, white and black, trying to make a living and raise their kids. Cutbacks at the Ford plant have hurt us a lot, but we'll bounce back, 'cause that's what the folks in the middle of America do. My feeling is, the Elyria taxpayers don't need to foot the bill for any high-profile homicide, and this one, seeing as he's a dead movie star's father, is going to be as high-profile as Madonna's pointy bra. So here's what I'm going to do."

Inside the room, the paparazzi of the homicide crime-scene team were immortalizing Norbert Anderson on film. The Lorain County medical examiner was doing her thing too. The room was as crowded as the hospitality suite at a Shriners convention.

"Cleveland PD has the Darren Anderson shooting," Ledbetter was explaining. "And I'll lay you eight to five that his father's getting shot is related. So what I'm going to do, I'm going to lateral this one to Cleveland and let them solve both of 'em together. That way I don't get my name in the paper, my wife doesn't have to answer a lot of embarrassing questions at work, and I get to go home at six o'clock every night and drink a beer in front of the TV."

"So?"

"So that means that you're Cleveland's problem. They can book you or not, and they can ask you all the hard questions. Until that time, you wouldn't even believe my lack of interest in whether you hang around Elyria or go home or keep on driving west until you hit South Bend and enroll at Notre Dame."

The sun glinted off his glasses for a second. He raised his chin a fraction; his dark brown eyes were fixed on me.

"Just stay the fuck out of my ball game," he said.

CHAPTER TWENTY-FIVE

I drove back home, more than a little put out. I'd thought I had it all figured out.

Norbert Anderson, tired of living on the edge and rolling drunks to feed his heroin habit, drives from Chicago to Cleveland to reestablish ties with his wealthy movie-star son, from whom he'd been estranged for years. He puts the bite on the kid for money, gets turned down, and either in a rage or ruthlessly carrying out what had been plan B all along, he kills Darren, assuming that some of the boy's millions will filter down to him.

But that theory wasn't looking so good right now, because someone had blown a substantial hole in Norbert's head.

He'd been a little rodent of a man who'd walked out on his wife and kid, gone to Chicago, and chosen to live on the dark edge, and to stick a needle full of heroin in his veins and doom himself to a life of addiction. With all the information available today it never ceases to amaze me that anyone even tries drugs, much less gets themselves hooked on them.

So I wasn't feeling sorry for Anderson, exactly—I don't have much sympathy for self-destructive junkies. But nobody deserves to die like that, and I couldn't help reflecting on the life he had wasted. Except for fathering a child, which is no great feat in and of itself, he'd lived fifty-some years on the earth and never left a footprint, and there would probably be no one to mourn him, no one even to claim him out of the morgue and bury his remains. That's a sad, empty, lonesome thing to be thinking.

It didn't figure now that Anderson had murdered his son. It was possible, and that someone else had shot him either in retribution or for another reason altogether—God knows Anderson had some hard-guy friends in Chicago. But it seemed to make ultimate sense to me, as it obviously had to Detective Ledbetter, that the same person was responsible for both killings and for me there was a kind of peace in that. There are things people do, while reprehensible, that are at least within the realm of understanding, and others that are not. I was glad Darren Anderson had not died by his own father's hand.

I got home pretty close to five o'clock. The gun in my waistband felt as though it had been in a toaster oven, and I pulled it out before stripping off my soaking-wet shirt.

There was no blinking light to indicate that anyone had called and left a message on the answering machine, and my beeper, which served my office phone, hadn't gone off all day. For the merest flicker of an instant I felt unloved and unwanted.

Then I remembered Connie.

She made me feel wanted, all right. But I couldn't tell whether she loved me or not, and I wasn't sure whether I loved her. All I knew was that I felt better when I was with her, and I thought about her—probably too much—when I wasn't. I had the urge to call her right then, but she would have asked how my day was, and I was hesitant to tarnish the glow of the previous evening by recounting to her my encounter with a corpse and with Detective Larry Ledbetter of the Elyria PD.

I called Bob Matusen, but either he was still out beating the bushes on the Anderson case or he'd taken the day off. It didn't matter; not in is not in. I left a message, putting a little urgency into it. Better he should hear about Norbert Anderson and my involvement from me before he got Ledbetter's version.

I took a shower, first hot and then cold, and changed into running shorts and a red and gray T-shirt that said REMEMBER THE NATIVE AMERICANS which I'd somehow acquired during Cleveland's bicentennial in 1996. Putting on fresh clothes in the summertime always makes me feel better.

That left me to think about dinner. I hadn't eaten since breakfast, and my stomach was beginning to gurgle raucously. I defrosted a link of Slovenian klobasa in the microwave and set it in boiling water for about five minutes, chopped up half an onion, and sautéed it in a frying pan along with the sausage and about a quarter of a stick of butter. While it all sizzled, I cut a loaf of dark rye in half, sliced one half lengthwise, and slathered it with Stadium mustard, the delicious dark brown kind that seems to taste of Eastern Europe and reminds me of my parents, who emigrated from Ljubljana to the Rust Belt fifty years ago. I shaved some thick hunks from a wedge of cheddar cheese, and when the sandwich was built I opened a beer and went into the den to watch the evening news.

The Norbert Anderson murder led off the telecast. It had only been a few days ago that his son's death had been the lead story, and now journalists were scenting a long-running O.J.–Tonya Harding kind of story, one with "legs," one that will run for a year. I had little doubt that they'd be coming after me again pretty soon, not just the tabloid TV shows but the more legitimate press as well. I considered seriously not answering my phone for the next month. But that wouldn't be any help; like *American Tab*, they'd simply show up.

The Channel Twelve field reporter stood outside the motel room door, right where I'd conferred with Ledbetter. His forehead was glistening with sweat, and he'd removed his jacket to do the standup in his shirtsleeves. He outlined the story in suitably solemn fashion, saying that the body had been discovered by "a visitor." I gave a little sigh of relief; I'd dodged the publicity bullet so far. I knew it wouldn't last, though.

The reporter also said that the Cleveland police department would be handling the investigation, because of the possibility that the two cases were connected. I had to smile—Ledbetter had completed a neat shovel pass and wouldn't have to get his jersey dirty.

I bit into my sandwich, and sausage juice squirted into my mouth. Maybe love of sausage and onions is in my Slovenian genes, but there is nothing else I eat that is quite so satisfying on a quiet night at home.

The scene on the TV shifted to the motel where Ray and Betty Dinsmoor were staying. Another reporter was following the couple across the parking lot. The Dinsmoors were moving quickly, and the reporter was having a tough time keeping up with them in her tight skirt and high heels. It didn't stop her from shoving a microphone into Mrs. Dinsmoor's face.

"Did your ex-husband make any effort to contact you while he was in the Cleveland area?" the reporter demanded.

Betty Dinsmoor was ashen—anyone would be. First her son, then his father. What a week. Her hands were shaking, and she was ducking her head in a touchingly futile effort to maintain some privacy. Her husband tried to insert himself between her and the TV reporter, making a heroic effort to look stoic.

"I knew he was here in town, but I've had no contact with him," Betty said. "Please. I have nothing more to say."

The pitiless camera followed them as they got in their car and drove away, spraying gravel behind them. Then it swung back to the reporter, coming in so tight that viewers could admire every detail of her elaborate makeup. "Betty Dinsmoor," she said, "mother of slain film star Darren Anderson and the ex-wife of Norbert Anderson, who was found dead earlier today in an Elyria motel. Back to you, Brad."

Slain film star. I tried to remember if I'd ever heard the word "slain" spoken aloud before, other than in an old biblical movie with Charlton Heston, and decided I had not. I suppose there are words like that, words that seem written and not spoken.

I was biting into the tail end of my sandwich when the lightning bolt hit me. I guzzled down the remainder of my beer, took the bottle and the plate with the sandwich remnants into the kitchen, and dug into my notebook. What I read there made the hair on the back of my neck prickle.

I called Bob Matusen again, even though I held out little hope of his being there at that hour. I thought about speaking to another cop, but that would require too much explaining. As acting head of homicide, Matusen didn't have a partner, and I couldn't be sure that any detective I might speak to would be up to speed on the two Anderson homicides.

After leaving yet another message with the cop who'd answered the phone, I stood there drumming my fingers on the kitchen counter, wondering what Marko would do in this situation. Marko, the by-the-book cop, who'd put the book face down once in his life and paid the ultimate price for it.

Then again, I wasn't a cop anymore. I didn't have a book to go by, only my own gut instinct. And that was telling me to get dressed again, put the pistol back in my waistband, and get busy doing what I do.

But I'll tell you one thing—I was getting damn tired of driving out to the west side.

When I got to the Dinsmoors' motel, there were vans or cars from each of our local TV stations parked in the lot, and I recognized a couple of print reporters from the *Plain Dealer* and the *Sun Press*. Like cats, they would wait quietly and patiently for hours until the mouse came out of its hole. Poor Betty Dinsmoor of Sierra Madre, California, had suddenly become hot news.

I pulled into one of the few available parking spaces at the far end of the lot. I knew Betty Dinsmoor probably wouldn't answer the door if I knocked, so I used my car phone to call the motel switchboard.

"Mr. and Mrs. Dinsmoor aren't accepting any calls," the operator told me.

"I think they'll accept mine," I said. "Tell Mrs. Dinsmoor that it's Milan Jacovich calling."

The operator gulped. "What was the name again?"

I pronounced both my names again, very slowly, and suggested she write them down phonetically, but she seemed to think it had something to do with telephones.

She put me on hold and I waited for about thirty seconds, sweating in the car despite the early evening cooldown. There wasn't any music playing in my ear, which was some sort of small blessing.

"Is that you, Mr. Jacovich?" Betty Dinsmoor said when she finally answered. She sounded tired.

"Didn't the operator tell you?"

"She said it was a Milo somebody."

"Close enough. Is your husband there?"

"No," she said. "He said he felt like a caged animal with all those reporters out there. He ducked out and went to get a drink somewhere. I don't know where—I don't think he knew where he was going. He was just going to drive until he saw a bar."

"That's all right," I said, something burning in the middle of my stomach that was not the klobasa with onions. "Can I come in and talk to you?"

"Well . . ."

"It's important, Mrs. Dinsmoor."

"Ray won't like it."

"We won't tell him then." I waited for almost a minute and then added, "It'll be our little secret."

"Well . . . all right. They moved us to another room—an inside room. Otherwise we wouldn't even be able to go to the candy machine without twenty reporters chasing after us. It's number two-three-seven. On the second floor."

"Okay," I said.

"Where are you now?"

"In the parking lot," I said. "On my car phone. Can I come up?"

"Come up in five minutes," she said.

After another steamy several minutes in the car, I got out and started across the asphalt toward the motel entrance. Halfway there I was stopped by an eager young woman with a notepad.

"Hi, who're you?" she said.

"Why, hello there, little lady," I said in my worst briarhopper accent. "What's a purty li'l thang lak you doin' runnin' round in thissere heat?" I fanned myself with my hand. "Hoo-ee! Ah reckoned it'd be lots cooler here up nawth."

Uncertainty flickered in her big brown eyes. "I'm with the *News-Herald*," she said. "You're from out of town?"

"Jes' here visitin' my momma. She's up in the Cleveland Clinic." I leaned closer to her, making my face look sad. "She got a cancer," I told her mournfully.

The young woman looked shocked. "Oh, I'm so sorry," she said, putting a hand on my arm.

"What's all thissere about that's got y'all hot 'n' bothered?" I asked her.

She backed away. "It's okay. I mean, it's no big deal. I hope your mother gets better." She turned and almost ran back to the knot of other journalists waiting near the motel office. Lucky she was so young and innocent, I thought, or she never would have bought my hayseed performance. I do a few things well, but acting isn't one of them.

Climbing the interior stairway to the second floor, I went down the hall until I found room 237. I rapped on the door three times. Nobody answered, but I sensed a presence behind the door. "It's Milan," I said softly.

Betty Dinsmoor opened the door wearing a frilly white

blouse and a dark skirt. From the look of her, she'd used the five minutes to put on fresh makeup. You could take the girl out of the movies. . . .

"Thanks for seeing me," I said.

"The press is hounding me," she said. "I can't stand it anymore." She closed the door behind me and shot the dead bolt. "What is it you want, Mr. Jacovich? You said it was important."

"It is. It might be." The king-size bed was made up and the TV turned on, but the volume was too low for the human ear. The curtains were drawn over the single window. I sat down in the chair in front of the built-in writing desk and took out my notebook.

"Where were you last night, Mrs. Dinsmoor?"

"Right here," she said.

"Was your husband with you?"

She hesitated one beat too long before nodding.

"All evening, and the whole night?"

She worried a fingernail with her teeth. "He went out for a drink," she said. "Just like tonight. It's hard being cooped up in this little room. Ray just got antsy."

"How long was he gone?"

She tossed her head in irritation. "I don't know. I didn't pay that much attention. Ever since we got here all I do is watch TV and sleep." She shuddered. "It's an escape for me. I sleep so I won't have to deal with my boy being dead."

"And what about your ex-husband?" I said. "Now he's dead too."

She went past me to the window and pulled the curtain aside to peek out. "I haven't seen Nor for fifteen years. I'm sorry what happened to him, but it really doesn't mean anything to me. Not anymore."

"He didn't try to contact you here in Cleveland?"

"No. I can't imagine why he'd want to," she said.

At my belt my beeper twittered. I glanced at the readout, but it was an unfamiliar number. "I saw you on TV tonight," I said. "On the news."

"Yes," she said absently, her hand going automatically to primp her hair.

"You said you knew Norbert Anderson was in town but that you hadn't seen him."

She nodded.

"How did you know he was here?"

She looked blank for a moment. "Why, that policeman told us."

"Detective Matusen?"

"That's right. He told us Nor was staying at that motel out in—I can't remember the name of the place."

"Elyria."

"Yes," she said. "He asked if I wanted to get in touch with him, since Nor was Ralphie's father. But I said no. I didn't want to see him at all. And Ray wouldn't have liked it much either."

"Ray knew Mr. Anderson was at that motel in Elyria?"

"He was there when the detective told me."

I flipped through the pages of my notebook, frowning. "You flew from Los Angeles to Detroit to join Mr. Dinsmoor when you heard about Ralph?"

She nodded.

"And that was on Wednesday? Two days after he died?"

"That's right. Why?"

"You still have your airline ticket?"

"Of course, it was round trip. Mr. Jacovich . . . ?"

I stood up and put my notebook back in my pocket. "I'm sorry I had to bother you, Mrs. Dinsmoor. Just a word of advice—don't talk to those reporters."

"I won't, believe me. But what was it that you wanted to ask me about that was so important?"

Full of rue, I said "I've already asked it."

CHAPTER TWENTY-SIX

When I got back to the car I used my cellular phone to call the number displayed on my beeper. Whatever did we do before the age of high technology?

It turned out to be Bob Matusen's home phone number.

"You've been calling me all day," he said accusingly.

"You didn't call back until now."

"I called your house first, but you weren't home. I left a message on your machine. Then I called your office."

"That's the one that got my beeper's attention."

"What's got your shorts in a twist?"

"You guys get the Norbert Anderson killing in Elyria?"

"Yeah. The Elyria PD doesn't want the best part of that one, and our brass figure it's connected with the kid getting killed, anyway. You were the one who found the body, huh?"

"I wanted to tell you that myself, Bob. That's why I was calling."

"Too late. You've got a bad habit of being in places where people get killed. You better come in tomorrow morning and we'll talk about it."

"I think we should talk tonight."

His sigh was exasperated. "I'm sitting here in shorts, drinking a beer and watching the ball game. I don't feel like getting dressed."

"Then don't. I can come there, or you can meet me at my office."

I heard him slurp and swallow, and then an exhalation that is best described as resounding. "Nothing personal," he said, "but I don't like doing police business in my home. You know what I mean?"

"I know."

"You want to come here for a beer, a barbecue, you're more than welcome. You want to talk homicide . . . well, just not in my home, okay?"

"I understand, but this is important. Real important, or I wouldn't bother you. I'm out on the west side now. My office in half an hour?"

"Make it forty-five minutes," he said.

Matusen was lousy at time management this evening; it was an hour and ten minutes later that I heard his footsteps on the wooden stairs.

"Hey," he said as he came in the door. He was still in shorts, nylon exercise shorts, but he'd put on shoes and socks and a black Baltimore Ravens T-shirt.

"I never thought I'd let anyone walk into this office wearing a shirt like that," I said. The Cleveland Browns drove a stake through this town's heart a few years back when they defected to Baltimore and took a new name. In northeast Ohio nearly every football fan's favorite team is whoever happens to be playing the Ravens.

"Some of the guys in the precinct gave this to me as a gag gift when I took over Meglich's spot," he said with some embarrassment. "They told me I could wear it to wash the car."

"You should *use* it to wash the car," I said.

"Yeah. Well, it's black, so the piece doesn't show through it." He hiked up the right side of the shirt to show me his 9-millimeter in a neat hip holster. On or off duty, policemen always go heeled.

"You're on your own time now, Bob. Want a beer?"

"I wouldn't say no."

I went to the little refrigerator against the window and pulled out two Stroh's. Built to look like a late nineteenth-century safe, it had nearly perished in the office fire I'd suffered a few months earlier, but I'd managed to get it repaired so it was almost as good as new, except for some blistered paint on the front that really makes it look like an antique.

"What's so important, Milan?"

"The killer of Darren and Norbert Anderson."

He crossed one hairy leg over the other. "You sound like it's the same perp for both."

"I think it is. And I imagine when ballistics gets through with the bullet they dug out of Norbert's head, they'll get a pretty good match with the ones they found in Darren." I came back to the desk and passed one of the beers across to him. "Norbert came here to Cleveland from Chicago when he read in the paper that Darren would be here shooting a movie. Two weeks before Darren died."

"He hadn't seen the kid in years."

"It wasn't fatherly love that brought him, it was money. Norbert had a drug habit, and he figured with a multimillionaire son he could make a much needed score. He hung around the movie location trying to get Darren to talk to him—he was seen by a member of the crew. Probably more than one, if you want to talk to all of them."

"So?"

"Darren didn't have much use for his father, so my guess is that Norbert's pitch was unsuccessful."

Matusen nodded.

"For a while I figured Norbert had found out where Darren was living and had gone out there to make one last plea. And that when that didn't work, he killed his own son for whatever inheritance he might get. It wasn't something I liked thinking about, but there you go."

"You changed your mind, though."

"Yes. After Norbert died. It got me to thinking."

"That's dangerous."

"You bet," I said. "Norbert would have no reason to believe that Darren had written him anywhere into his will; he knew Darren resented him for walking out all those years ago."

Matusen took a healthy quaff from his beer bottle. "But Darren was a kid, more into drugs and sex and making hay out of being a movie star than worrying about financial stuff like a will. What if he'd died intestate? Wouldn't Norbert stand to inherit something as next of kin?"

"Ordinarily, yes," I said. "But if Betty and Ray Dinsmoor wanted to fight that in court—a guy who walked out on his kid fifteen years ago, and not so much as a phone call since—I can't think of too many judges who wouldn't be sympathetic to them."

"Okay. So Norbert didn't kill his son, and he sure as hell didn't kill himself. Now what?"

"Now you have to start eliminating other people. Sidney Friedman, Boyce Cort, Suzi Flores—they all might have had more or less compelling reasons for killing Darren. But Norbert? What did he have to do with any of them? They probably didn't even know he existed."

"I'll give you that."

"Then who's left with a motive? The motive of a small fortune?"

"The mother?" Matusen shook his head. "I don't see that. I bet that woman don't use cockroach spray in the kitchen for fear of offending the roaches."

"I agree. But if she inherits ten, twenty million dollars, who else gets an automatic free ride on the gravy train?"

He put his beer down on my desk; it was going to leave a ring. "The stepfather? He's got an alibi. He was on a sales trip."

I took out my notebook and put it on the desk facing Matusen. "Look. This is a record of his sales calls while he was on that trip."

Matusen leaned forward. "Detroit. Pontiac. Southfield," he read aloud. "Ann Arbor. Grand Rapids. Lansing. Detroit. Toledo. Dayton. Detroit again, twice. So what?"

"He was basing his operations in Detroit, remember? That's where his hotel was. You notice that after his Toledo trip there's an open date where he made no sales calls."

"Right."

"Now if you were in Toledo and you were going to Dayton next, you wouldn't drive all the way back to Detroit, would you?"

"Maybe, maybe not. What's your point?"

"That in all probability he didn't go back to Detroit. And he didn't stay in Toledo, either. When he and his wife first came to see me, he made no bones about not liking the kid, about resenting the fact that Darren didn't give them more money. I think he used that spare day to drive to Cleveland and kill Darren Anderson."

Matusen ran a hand through his hair. "Possible."

"And then when you told them Norbert Anderson was in town, Dinsmoor got scared that someone was going to cut him out of half of that money. So he offed the father too. His wife told me he went out for a drink last night. He does that a lot, I guess— that's where he was tonight. He's probably still out. But they've gotten all the papers necessary to take Darren's body back to California, and they'll be out of here tomorrow on a plane. Unless you do something."

Matusen nodded. "We don't have enough for an arrest, here, Milan."

"Probably not. But you have more than enough to hold him for questioning."

"We do at that." He finished his beer in one long swallow and stood up. "Let me use your phone, huh?"

I locked up the office, and Matusen and I walked downstairs together. He had put out an APB on Ray Dinsmoor, and I was feeling pretty good about things.

"I don't know if the Dinsmoor beef is going to stand up, Milan," he said. "But that was damn good work anyway. I appreciate it."

I wasn't used to praise from the police department, and it took me aback. I just nodded.

"Meglich thought very highly of you," he went on. "Now I see why."

I shook my head. "It had nothing to do with police stuff, Bob. Marko and I grew up together. He was best man at my wedding, I was best man at his. When I came back from Vietnam, he was my guardian angel on the job. Outside of my father, he was the finest man I ever knew."

He put out his hand. "You're okay with me too," he said.

I watched him drive off. Things had wrapped up nicely, I thought as I climbed into my own car. *If* Ray Dinsmoor turned out to be the bad guy.

I didn't head across the Eagle Avenue Bridge toward Ontario Street but instead, turned right, planning to drop by the movie location where I thought they might still be shooting, and tell Sidney Friedman that he no longer had to worry that one of his cast or crew would get nailed for Darren's killing, or about the bad publicity that would bring. He wasn't a client anymore, but I thought it was the right thing to do.

Like Marko. The right thing to do for him, the last right thing, was to back up a friend in jeopardy, and he did it, against departmental regulations and his own common sense. Doing the right thing myself seemed the least I could do to honor his memory.

I drove into the salt yards and parked between two white mountains. Everything was deserted, as still and creepy as a lunar landscape; evidently *Street Games* was not shooting at this location tonight. Even the Winnebagos were gone.

I got out of the car, smelling the slow-moving water in the old riverbed alongside. The air was muggy and still, the lights of downtown sparkling in the distance. Somewhere in the night a train whistle sang a love song to the long-gone glory days of the railroads.

I went to the water's edge and lit a Winston and stood there smoking awhile, thinking about Marko and feeling sad. Then I thought about Darren Anderson, which made me even sadder. The kid never had a home, a place to go to and be accepted and be safe from the predators, from the thousand natural shocks and ten thousand unnatural ones that come along with celebrity. And in the end, it was someone from the home he never really had who snuffed out his life.

And Betty Anderson Dinsmoor was perhaps the saddest of all. Her son and her ex-husband killed by her current husband. She didn't have very much left in her life—besides several million dollars. I was pretty sure it wouldn't be worth it.

I shook my head. The press was going to be all over me now, not just Rebekka Sommars but all the networks and major metropolitan dailies and even Ed Stahl, my friend who had gotten me into this in the first place. Well, I'd talk to Ed, because I owed it to him. As for the rest of them—I thought seriously of leaving town for a few weeks so I wouldn't have to deal with them; as Detective Ledbetter had pointed out, I have a way of getting my name in the papers. Maybe I'd drive to New England, catch a Red Sox game in venerable Fenway Park, visit the great Boston restaurants and eat seafood that had been swimming in the bay that morning, and perhaps take a long, meandering tour of the countryside and stay at inns that were older than the republic. Someplace where nobody knew me.

I'd miss my boys if I did that. A lot.

I'd miss Connie too. Maybe I could talk her into coming with me, at least for part of the trip. Maybe I could talk Leo into letting her off work for a week; everybody needs a vacation, even when they work for a family business.

I tossed my cigarette into the river and lit another one. I knew I was smoking too much, but I always did when in the middle of a situation where people died. When I work my regular beat, industrial security, I go through between five and ten cigarettes a day. I chain-smoke when I'm dealing with murder.

"Jacovich!"

My skin prickled.

"Turn around. Slow."

I threw my second cigarette into the water and turned, my hands up at about chest level. It was too dark to make out his face, but even if I hadn't recognized his voice, I'd have known by his sheer size that the man who stood silhouetted not twenty feet from me was Albert Wysocki.

He held up his right hand so I could see the knife, huge and wicked-looking, and took a few steps forward. There was a big white plaster across his nose, and a metal splint on the fingers of his other hand.

"I know you're carrying," he said, "so take it out real slow, wit' two fingers." He gestured with the knife. "And don't get cute. I can throw this sucker way faster than you can draw."

I started to reach behind me for the gun in my waistband.

"Use your left hand," he ordered.

I did, taking my .38 out and holding it in front of me with two fingers, as he'd told me.

"Toss it away," he said. "Far."

Stupid, stupid, *stupid,* I called myself for letting him take me unawares. I should have been paying attention. But my thoughts had been on Ray Dinsmoor, not Tattoos. I threw the gun about twenty feet away from me; it landed with a soft *chunk* at the foot of a mountain of salt.

"I was at your office," he said. "But you were wit' the cop. He ain't here to save your ass no more."

The truth of that didn't make me feel any better. "Mr. Maniscalco must be really mad at me."

"Got nothin' to do wit' him. This is you an' me."

I kept my eye on the knife.

"You broke my nose," he said quietly, advancing toward me. "Now I'm gonna break your nose."

I could see his face clearly now. It was sheer savagery. Two black eyes formed parentheses around the nose plaster.

"You broke my fingers," he said. "I'm gonna cut yours off."

My head throbbed where he'd hit me the last time, but this time he obviously had more than a beating in mind. I wiped my palms on my pants. I've been shot before and I've been knifed before. The knife is worse, somehow. More elemental, more painful. Sweat was puddling in the small of my back, and it was cold.

Drifting slowly and cautiously to my left, I tried to get somewhere near the gun I'd just thrown away. But Wysocki was more experienced in hand-to-hand combat than I, and he was too canny for that; he moved to his right and cut me off. It was a deadly pavane in slow motion, set against the eerie backdrop of the salt mountains. A rare summer breeze kicked up for a few seconds from the lake, and I heard the river water plash gently behind me.

The distance between us closed slowly. He waved the knife in front of me, slashing the air near my face. It made a noise like an insect buzzing.

"C'mon," he said.

I had my hands out in front of me now, for all the good that would do me. The hunting knife was big enough to gut a moose.

"What'samatter wit' you? Scared?"

Wysocki wasn't all dumb. I was scared silly.

Nevertheless, I moved in on him. My only other option was running, and I wasn't about to do that.

He made another swipe with the knife, right to left and then back again. On the backswing I managed to grab his wrist. He chopped at my face with his free hand, and the metal splint opened a cut over my right eye, right where the old scar tissue had grown, but I hardly felt it, I was so astonished that he could hit me that hard with broken fingers and not scream in agony.

I decided to see just how tough he really was. I popped him in his broken nose with my fist. He howled with pain, his head jerking back, and blood dripped out from beneath the bandage and down his mustache. He spit a gobbet of blood and saliva at me, and it spattered on my shirt.

I gripped his right wrist with both hands, trying to twist the knife from his grasp. He flailed away at me with his left hand, grunting each time his damaged fingers came into contact with my head. I grunted too.

I kicked at his kneecap and missed, hitting him in the shin. I had no qualms about fighting dirty—this was a man who had bitten me and now was trying to cut off my fingers.

The battering on the side of my head became too much to bear, and I grabbed that wrist too. Now we were nose to bloody nose, two big men straining against one another like two bull elk with locked antlers. Our hands and wrists were slippery with sweat, and I didn't know how long I'd be able to hang on to him. He was terribly strong, and I had to dig my toes into the gravel to keep my balance.

He brought his knee up, and I turned my body slightly to take it on my thigh instead of between my legs, but that was enough for him to wrench his wrists out of my grip.

We broke apart and stood there panting, two white mountains of salt framing us like a proscenium. The blood from the cut above my eyebrow was trickling down into my eye, making it hard to see, and I tried to wipe it out with the heel of my hand.

He spit some more blood out and dragged the back of his hand across his mouth.

I stayed focused on the knife, which Wysocki was waving hypnotically in front of my face. We started our wary circling once more. My arms felt almost too heavy to raise.

We were starting to come together again when a bullet whistled between us; I heard the shot a millisecond later.

Both Wysocki and I froze, staring at each other, completely flummoxed. Then we dived for cover. Wysocki scrambled behind the nearest salt hill, and I fell flat on my face and crawled behind another.

"You got a lotta people don' like you," he gasped.

I nodded at him. I couldn't see anyone in the dark, and I only had a general idea of where the shot had come from. I had a more specific idea of who had fired it.

I was about fifteen feet away from the gun I had dropped. I tried to crawl toward it but another shot kicked up a spray of gravel that stung my cheeks and forehead. I slithered back behind the wall of salt.

I looked over at Wysocki. He had started climbing his hill, sending a small avalanche of salt down behind him.

At the far end of the yard a wiry figure emerged holding a gun. I didn't need any light to know that it was Ray Dinsmoor. Like Wysocki, he had probably been lurking somewhere around my office and had followed me here. I figured that his wife had told him about my visit and he'd decided to shut me up before I could tell anyone else.

"You might as well come out, Jacovich!" he shouted. "You can't hide forever!"

"Give it up, Dinsmoor!" I yelled back. "This is crazy!"

His gait was uncertain, and he stumbled over the uneven ground. "Why couldn't you just leave us alone?" he said plaintively. "It was none of your business."

He had me there; it was none of my business. It was just one of those things I couldn't let go of. The right thing to do.

And now I had two people trying to kill me—a greed-crazed hardware salesman with a gun and a professional killer with a knife. I looked longingly at my own weapon lying on the gravel only a few yards from me, for all intents and purposes a million miles away.

I wiped some more blood from my eye. The cut wasn't deep, but head wounds have a way of bleeding like hell.

Circling around the salt hill, I poked my head out on the other side. Dinsmoor was wandering around, squinting into the dark. He seemed almost disoriented. Another locomotive whistle hooted through the night, and I knew the train was crossing the Conral Bridge, the gateway to Lake Erie.

And then Albert Wysocki appeared at the top of his mountain, a colossus in combat camos, and Dinsmoor turned and snapped off a shot at him. I could hear the sickening thunk of the bullet, and Wysocki screamed "Shit!" and staggered backward, his leg crumpling under him. He slid halfway down the hill before he was able to stop himself. Then he started climbing up the ever shifting mound of salt again.

Albert Wysocki was far from my favorite guy, but I had to feel sorry for him. His broken fingers and nose must have been giving him excruciating pain, and now he was dealing with a bullet wound too. Sometimes it just isn't your day.

It sure wasn't mine. If Ray Dinsmoor was smart, he'd just keep coming after me until he found me, and there wasn't much I could do to stop him.

Wysocki was struggling up the mound again. I reached down and picked up a handful of rock salt. If Dinsmoor got close enough to me before he shot at me again, I could throw it in his face—assuming my aim was that good. Then I could try for the gun. I couldn't say I liked my odds very much.

Timidly peeking around the hill, I saw that Dinsmoor was indeed still coming, his gun held high. I didn't think he saw me, but I knew it was just a matter of time.

And then Wysocki was on top of his salt hill again, outlined against the dark sky, and as Dinsmoor whirled around to look at him, he brought his hand up and let the knife fly.

Ray Dinsmoor screamed as the blade sunk into the right side of his chest. He looked down at the protruding handle, dropped his gun, and fainted dead away.

I ran out from behind my salty barricade and scooped up Dinsmoor's gun. Then I raced over to my own gun before Wysocki could get to it.

But Albert wasn't moving very fast. He started down the front of the incline, slipped, and slid the rest of the way down on his ass. He sat there at the bottom, his face contorted with pain, trying to stanch the bleeding from his thigh with one hand and wiping the blood away from his mouth with the other, which can't be easy with three fingers in a metal splint.

I walked over to him and stood above him, a gun in each hand, feeling like Henry Fonda in *Warlock*.

A very wise Clevelander once told me that gratitude is not only the greatest of virtues but the parent of all the others. So I said, "Thanks, Albert. You saved my bacon."

He looked up at me, gasped for breath, and shook his head. "Forget it, Jacovich," he said. "I'm finished."

I regarded the bullet hole in his camouflage pants. "I don't think so. That doesn't look too bad."

"No. I mean I'm finished wit' you. No more."

I let the guns dangle at my sides. "That's good news. You probably would've killed me."

"I didn' wanta kill you. I wanted to hurt you—like you hurt me. Hurt you bad, so you'd always remember me."

"It's a pretty safe bet I'll always remember you, Albert." I glanced over at Dinsmoor. His chest was rising and falling, and he was moaning. "I'd better call for an ambulance. For both of you."

He wagged his head violently from side to side. "Fuck that," he said.

"You can't run around with a bullet in you. Don't be a damn fool."

He got slowly and painfully to his feet, the effort producing a gravelly hum in the back of his throat, and stood weaving for a moment. "I'll get it took care of. Don' worry. No hospitals. Too many questions."

"So you're going to just leave me here to answer them when the cops arrive."

He shrugged his massive shoulders, and gave me a gap-toothed grin. "Shit happens," he said.

He limped over to where Dinsmoor lay, reached down and yanked the knife out of his chest. Wiping the blade on his camos, he stuck it back into its leather sheath. Then, clutching his thigh with one hand, he raised the other in a small wave, and went limping away out of the salt yards into the sultry night.

I knelt down beside Ray Dinsmoor. He was still breathing. I hoped he'd stay that way—there were some questions I wanted him to answer.

Then I got to my feet and went to my car to call 911.

✤ ✤ ✤ ✤ ✤ ✤ ✤ ✤ ✤ ✤ ✤ ✤

CHAPTER TWENTY-SEVEN

✤ ✤ ✤ ✤ ✤ ✤ ✤ ✤ ✤ ✤ ✤ ✤

The insistent thump of polka music filled the warm night, as people of all ages circled the makeshift outdoor dance floor. The scents of pierogis and sausage and rigatoni warred in the air with those of cotton candy and elephant ears and Amish funnel cake. All up and down the makeshift midway, pitchmen entreated passersby to try and win a stuffed bear for their dates by throwing darts or baseballs or basketballs. A few blocks away a rock group was playing, but they didn't have a chance against the polka band.

It was the East 185th Street Festival, a twenty-year-old tradition for this enclave of Poles and Slovenians and Hungarians and Germans in Cleveland's northeastern corner, a few blocks from the lake. People from all over the area show up at the festival, but at its heart it's just a big neighborhood wingding.

Connie Haley and I sat together at a large table several yards off the dance floor. Sharing it with us was an elderly man wearing a T-shirt that said SLOVENIAN, only the letters *L-O-V-E* were enclosed in a heart. Connie was eating a roast pork sandwich with fries, and I had a combination plate of pierogi, noodles, cabbage, and potato pancake. We were both drinking Stroh's, and although I don't think it made her want to give up merlot, Connie seemed to be having a great time.

"You have to take me to the Irish Festival next month so I can get even," she said. "I'll get you eating soda bread and corned beef and cabbage, and washing it down with a Guinness."

"It's a deal," I told her.

"And there's always great Irish music too. Not 'Danny Boy,' the real stuff."

I toasted her with my plastic cup of Stroh's. "We have to keep things ethnically even, don't we?"

"Ethnically and everything else." She glanced at the polka dancers. Most of the couples were middle-aged or older. Sometimes two women would be dancing together. There was one teenage boy out there all alone having a high old time dancing by himself, and I admired his guts; fourteen-year-olds usually don't have such self-possession.

"You've got us on the dancing, though," Connie admitted.

"You mean all Irishmen don't dance like Michael Flatley?"

She smiled. "Only after a pint or two." She put her hand over mine on the table and tapped out the polka rhythm on my knuckles.

It felt good, relaxing, after a long ten days when the print and electronic journalists had hounded me like Inspector Javert going after Jean Valjean. I'd managed to ignore all of them, even Rebekka Sommars, who had evidently decided not to get even this time and had blessedly ignored me in her follow-up reports on the deaths of Darren Anderson and his father. I'd given my story to Ed Stahl, and after that I was as silent and inscrutable as an ancient statue of Buddha.

"They read Darren Anderson's will this afternoon," I said. "Or this morning I guess it was, in Los Angeles."

"My bet is he didn't leave you anything."

"Nope. My buying a new pair of Nikes will have to wait."

"And here I thought you were going to set me up in a big apartment on the Gold Coast and smother me with mink and diamonds."

"You'll have to settle for being smothered by me."

The elderly man across the table smiled paternally at us.

"Darren's mother, however, is a little bit better off. He left her a million and a half, his Ferrari, and his house and furnishings in Coldwater Canyon, which is probably worth another two mil."

"That's all?"

"That's all. There were smaller bequests for some of his people." I laughed at myself, at how easily I used the Hollywood term. "His agent and manager and secretary and public relations person. The rest all went to charity."

"How much was the rest?"

"Somewhere around twelve million."

She sipped at her beer. "So Ray Dinsmoor's payoff wouldn't have been as big as he thought."

"No. But big enough, I guess, to kill somebody for." I shook my head. "He's going to pull through from the knife wound, so they'll probably try him here for the two killings."

"Will the county prosecutor go for the death penalty?"

I shook my head. "He's cooperating. He confessed not only to killing Darren and Norbert and trying to kill me, but to setting the fire at Darren's house in California last spring. Even double murderers get points for that. He's probably looking at lots of time, though. At his age he might not outlive the sentence."

She finished the last bite of her sandwich. "At least he's off the street."

"Yeah, but there's a million more like him. Small, sour people who consider themselves failures and blame everyone else for it."

The polka band swung into a spirited rendition of "I Wish I Was Back in Slovenia." The crowd applauded.

"That's a big thing with you, isn't it, Milan?" Connie said. "Taking responsibility."

"It's what makes a successful human being, I think. We all have lousy things happen to us at one time or another. It's up to us to deal with it. How well we do that is a measure of our success in life. Otherwise we blame other people, or the government, or God, and that makes us victims. I refuse to look at myself that way."

"Darren Anderson was a victim."

"In the end, maybe. But for all his faults and his womanizing and his taking advantage of young girls, he fought his way out of lousy circumstances, a lousy childhood, and made his own luck. I admired him for that."

"You admire Victor Gaimari too."

"In a very real way, yes. Victor and I have different sets of ethics, but he could have grown up a punk, or a rich, pampered wimp. But he took the good cards he was dealt and raked in the whole pot."

She finished her beer. "Come on," she said. "Let's walk around and people-watch."

We strolled hand in hand through the crowd. Nice people, I thought. Real people, the kind of people that make Cleveland such a good place to live. Families, young couples in love or lust, grandparents, teenagers taking advantage of an opportunity to mingle with a big crowd and maybe connect with someone of the opposite gender. Sometimes when I find myself knee-deep in the dregs of humanity, it's easy to forget that most people in the world are good, or at least try to be.

And then there are those like Norbert Anderson. He lived small and he died small. There's more than a little truth in the observation that what goes around comes around.

"What about the furniture dealer? The one who was cutting down the rain forests to make a buck?"

"Tom Maniscalco? The federal government came down on him like an avenging angel. My guess, though, is that he won't do time, or at least not a lot. But he'll pay a big fine, seven figures at least, and his influence with the local politicians will dry up like the end of a summer cold. That'll hurt him more than eighteen months in a federal country-club lockup. He liked being a big shot in this town, he thrived on it, and so did his wife. That was their particular addiction."

"What's yours?" she said.

"Lately, you."

"Thanks, but I'm serious."

"So am I."

"Come on, Milan."

"I don't know, Connie. My sons. My friends. My work, I guess."

"Justice?"

I laughed. "That's an abstract concept. I don't like to see people get away with murder, if that's what you mean." I thought about what Vuk had said to me, that I was addicted to the rush. "I guess," I went on, "that I'm hooked on that—on trying in a very small way to make wrong things come out right."

"You're just one guy, though."

"I know. But one and one makes two, and so on. If everybody tried to do right, we'd all be better off."

"But you almost got killed, and you didn't even have a client."

"I had an obligation, though. To Darren, to his mother. To my pal Marko. I had to try. Michael Jordan says that you always miss the shot you don't take."

We walked by a booth where the local city councilman was taking the opportunity to press voter's flesh, and another booth where people were lined up for Belgian waffles. Next to that, a large busty woman in a tank top sat beneath a sign proclaiming her to be a psychic. For ten dollars she'd prove it to you.

"Do you want to get a psychic reading, Connie?"

"You just want to look at her cleavage."

"Not when I have you to look at."

She linked her arm in mine. "I know what the future holds," she said. "A big, stubborn Slovenian with a Superman complex and a black-and-white sense of what's right and wrong. I don't need any overstuffed gypsy woman to tell me that. I feel it in my bones."

"They're nice bones."

"Your opinion."

I took her arm, turned her around, and started walking back the way we came.

"Where are we going, Milan?"

"I'm going to teach you the polka," I said.